HOLY SISTER

Ace Books by Mark Lawrence

The Broken Empire

PRINCE OF THORNS
KING OF THORNS
EMPEROR OF THORNS

The Red Queen's War

PRINCE OF FOOLS
THE LIAR'S KEY
THE WHEEL OF OSHEIM

The Book of the Ancestor

RED SISTER
GREY SISTER
HOLY SISTER

HOLY
SISTER

Third Book of the Ancestor

MARK LAWRENCE

ACE
New York

ACE
Published by Berkley
An imprint of Penguin Random House LLC
1745 Broadway, New York, NY 10019

Copyright © 2019 by Bobalinga Ltd.

Library of Congress Cataloging-in-Publication Data

Names: Lawrence, Mark, 1966– author.
Title: Holy sister / Mark Lawrence.
Description: First Edition. | New York: Ace, 2019. | Series: Book of the ancestor; book 3
Identifiers: LCCN 2018042275 | ISBN 9781101988916 (hardback) | ISBN 9781101988923 (ebook)
Subjects: | BISAC: FICTION / Fantasy / Epic. | FICTION / Action & Adventure. | FICTION / Fantasy / General. | GSAFD: Fantasy fiction.
Classification: LCC PS3612.A9484 H65 2019 | DDC 813/.6—dc23
LC record available at https://lccn.loc.gov/2018042275

First Edition: April 2019

Printed in the United States of America
1 3 5 7 9 10 8 6 4 2

Cover art by Bastien Lecouffe Deharme
Cover design by Judith Lagerman

For my grandfather, "Bill" William George Cook, who lived most of his first decade under the reign of Queen Victoria and who with great patience helped me make my first treasure box

ACKNOWLEDGEMENTS

I'm enormously grateful to Agnes Meszaros, whose beta reading has seen Nona through the course of her convent education. It has been extremely helpful to have chapter-by-chapter feedback from someone who cares passionately about these books.

I should also thank, as always, my wonderful editor Jessica Wade for her support in bringing my third trilogy to its conclusion. And of course my agent, Ian Drury, and the team at Sheil Land.

THE STORY SO FAR

———— ✦ ————

F OR THOSE OF you who have had to wait a while for this book I provide brief catch-up notes so that your memories may be refreshed
and I can avoid the awkwardness of having to have characters tell
each other things they already know for your benefit.

Here I carry forward only what is of importance to the tale that follows.

The people and places in the brief summary I start with are expanded
on further down, so if it means nothing to you, skip the next paragraph
and then come back to it.

Grey Sister ended with Nona, around fifteen years old, escaping Sherzal's
palace with troops in pursuit. She had friends with her, including Zole,
Ara, Regol, Abbess Glass and Sister Kettle, and assorted other survivors.
Zole had the Noi-Guin's shipheart, stolen from the assassins' headquarters
beneath the palace. Clera helped Nona escape but went back to Sherzal's
service. Nona's enemy from the convent, the novice Joeli Namsis, is still in
the palace and her actions led to the death of Nona's friend Darla during
the escape. Nona and her companions are in the mountains on the border
with Scithrowl and a long way from the convent. The story does not begin
with this scene but will return to it presently.

Abeth is a planet orbiting a dying red sun. It is sheathed in ice and the vast majority of its people live in a fifty-mile-wide ice-walled corridor around the equator.

An artificial moon, a great orbiting mirror, keeps the Corridor free of ice by focusing the sun's rays into it each night.

When, thousands of years ago, the four original tribes of men came to Abeth from the stars they found the ruins of a vanished people they called the Missing.

The empire is bounded by the lands of the Scithrowl to the east and by the Sea of Marn to the west. Across the sea the Durns rule. At the end of *Grey Sister* Scithrowl hordes under their battle-queen, Adoma, were massing on their side of the mountain range that forms the border for an attack.

The emperor's sister, Sherzal, commands the defence against Scithrowl from her palace in the mountains. She was going to betray the empire and let Queen Adoma's forces through the Grand Pass. The deal included combining the shipheart held by the Noi-Guin assassins and the shipheart stolen from Sweet Mercy Convent by the ice-triber Yisht, with the two shiphearts Queen Adoma has, thereby making the quartet of shiphearts believed necessary to open the Ark. The Ark lies beneath the emperor's palace and was built either by the Missing or by the first humans and is said to allow control of the moon.

Shiphearts are objects of disputed origin that may have powered the ships that brought the tribes of man to Abeth. The closer a person gets to one, the more enhanced their natural talent for magic is. Get too close, though, and the shipheart's power begins to break your mind apart. Undesirable pieces of your personality like anger or greed or malice split into sentient fragments called devils and exert greater influence over you.

As the sun weakens, the ice continues a slow advance despite the warmth of the moon's nightly focus. As the Corridor is squeezed, nations look to their neighbours for new territory.

The empire's nobility are the Sis. The suffix is attached to the name of ennobled families (e.g. Tacsis, Jotsis, etc.).

The four original tribes that came to Abeth were the gerant, hunska, marjal, and quantal. Their blood sometimes shows in the current population, conferring unique powers. The gerant grow very large, the hunska are fantastically swift, and the marjal can manifest all manner of minor to medium magics, including shadow-weaving, sigil-writing, and mastery of elements. The quantal can access the raw power of the Path and manipulate the threads that are woven to create reality.

The Missing left behind structures called Arks. Three exist within the Corridor. The emperor's palace is built around one. There are no reliable records of anyone being able to open the Ark, but a faked prophecy predicts the coming of a Chosen One who will be able to. Others believe that four shiphearts used together can open an Ark.

Nona Grey was a peasant child from a nameless village. She was given to the child-taker Giljohn, who sold her to the Caltess where ring-fighters are trained and pitted against each other. She ended up at the Convent of Sweet Mercy, where novices are trained in service to the Ancestor. Novices take orders as one of four classes of nun: Holy Sister (entirely religious duties), Grey Sister/Sister of Discretion (trained in assassination and stealth), Red Sister/Martial Sister (trained in combat), and Holy Witch/Mystic Sister (trained to walk the Path).

Nona has proven to be a triple-blood, an incredibly rare occurrence. She has hunska, marjal, and quantal skills. Nona has wholly black eyes, a side effect of taking a dangerous antidote. She has no shadow, having cut it free whilst fighting Yisht.

Yisht is a woman of the ice-tribes and is in the employ of the emperor's sister, Sherzal. Yisht stole the Sweet Mercy shipheart and killed Nona's friend Hessa.

Nona is hated by Lano Tacsis because she killed his brother and also left his father, Lord Thuran Tacsis, bound to his own torture device.

Joeli Namsis is the daughter of a lord with close ties to the Tacsis family. She is skilled at quantal thread-work and poisoning. She became Nona's enemy at the convent.

During the theft of the shipheart, Nona was betrayed by her friend and fellow novice Clera Ghomal. Among Nona's remaining friends are novices Ara, Zole, Ruli, and Jula. Arabella Jotsis is from a powerful family and is a rare two-blood, having both hunska and quantal skills. Ruli has minor marjal skills. Jula is very studious and hopes to become a Holy Sister.

Zole is a significant novice. She is from the ice-tribes and came to the convent at Sherzal's insistence, used as an unwitting distraction to help in the theft of the shipheart. She is the only known four-blood with access to all the skills of the original tribes. Many consider her to be the Chosen One from prophecy. Under the prophecy Zole is the Argatha, and Nona is her Shield.

The Convent of Sweet Mercy has been led by Abbess Glass, a woman whose connections in the Church and beyond reach further than expected.

Most senior among the nuns are the Sisters Superior, Wheel and Rose. Sister Wheel teaches Spirit classes. Sister Rose runs the sanatorium. Other important figures are Sister Tallow, who teaches Blade; Sister Pan, who teaches Path; and Sister Apple, who teaches Shade. Sister Kettle is a Grey Sister based at the convent. She and Apple are lovers.

There are four classes/stages that novices move through as they train to take holy orders as nuns: Red Class, Grey Class, Mystic Class, and Holy Class. *Grey Sister* ended with Nona in Mystic Class.

Novices take new names when they become nuns. Nona will become Sister Cage. Ara will be Sister Thorn.

PROLOGUE

⸻ ✦ ⸻

THE ROAR OF a crowd invades you like a living thing, reverberating in your chest, taking its answer from your lips without permission. The press of bodies overwhelms barriers and unknowingly the many become something singular, the same emotion bleeding from the skins of different people, the same thought reverberating in a hundred skulls, or a thousand. For a marjal empath it can be a thing at once both terrifying and glorious, expanding their control, making it easier to reach into the minds around them, but also allowing the possibility that in such a storm of humanity they may lose themselves, may be lifted out of their flesh, never to find it again.

Markus watched the defeated fighter being helped from the ring beneath the jeers and complaint of the crowd. The victor still stalked the perimeter of his raised battleground, arms lifted, sweat running down his ribs. But already the crowd were losing interest in him, turning to their neighbours with speculation, observation, or jest, turning to the odds-mongers to lay new wagers, turning to the counter in the far corner to fill their cups with wine. And some, seeking new thrills, now faced the second ring at the far end of the hall.

The gerant fighter waiting behind the ropes threatened nine foot in height and Markus didn't believe that he had seen a larger man. The fighter was still young, in his early twenties perhaps, and his muscles crowded along his bones, the battle for space heaping them up in great, veined mounds. He watched the world from pale eyes beneath a thicket of short red hair.

At the Caltess the gerant contests were the most popular. The sight of enormous fighters pitting their strength against each other never failed to draw the masses, and on nights with an open ring the folk of Verity loved to see that strength turned upon hapless challengers. Bouts between hunska ring-fighters had a strong following among the more experienced watchers but the speed of the combatants often left the common crowd bewildered. Mixed matches were a rarity but the contest of speed against strength was always interesting.

From the baying press of humanity around the base of the giant's ring a challenger emerged: a powerfully built man who stood head and shoulders above those pressing him on all sides. In normal circumstances Markus would have been impressed by the fellow's physique and backed him against any three bar-room brawlers.

An undercurrent of whispers and speculation flowed around the hall. The man was a refugee from the port of Ren, which now lay within the Durnish incursion. He had some reputation from pit-fights in the frost towns along the north margins.

"Five says he doesn't last the round against Denam." Someone behind Markus seeking a private wager.

The roar as the newcomer climbed into the ring drowned out further conversation. Markus hadn't ever been inside the great hall of the Caltess, though years ago he had spent hours waiting in the compound with the other children from Giljohn's cage. The child-taker had never intended to sell Markus to Partnis Reeve, though. He'd suspected Markus of marjal blood and had taken him on to be offered where such talents would fetch a richer price. The great hall had stood silent and dark on that midnight long ago, and as the night had shaded into morning young Markus had shivered and clutched himself and never suspected that he would one day stand within, part of a sweating, heaving mass baying for blood.

Even though it was Markus's first time before the rings, he knew Denam's name. Despite his tender years the young man was the new champion among the gerant ring-fighters, famed for his brutality. For Denam open-ring night often proved to involve nothing more than glowering at the sea of resentful faces before him. Finding no one to answer his challenge, he would cede his place to another fighter and once more the crowd would discover its courage.

"Milos of Ren!" the fight-master called out.

Milos raised his arm in acknowledgement and walked to his corner to await the bell.

Markus didn't hear the chime above the roar but the two men closed, Milos dwarfed by Denam. The gerant full-blood kept his hands down and let Milos take a punch. It was as if he had swung at a tree. Denam's head moved slightly to the left with the blow. Milos clubbed him two-handed across the other side of his face and Denam's head lurched to the right. Denam returned his gaze to his opponent and grinned, his teeth bloody. Milos didn't appear to understand. He looked down at his fists as if there might be something wrong with them.

Denam slapped the man, brushing his arms away. Blood sprayed from Milos's mouth and he staggered as if drunk. Denam caught him in two great hands, one wrapped around his neck, the other encompassing his thigh, and lifted him four yards above the boards before slamming him down, full-bodied, face first.

Milos did not rise. An apprentice scrambled in to scatter sand across the crimson smear left behind when they dragged him out beneath the lowest rope.

Markus wasn't alone in thinking that Denam was finished for the night, but the flow of the crowd indicated another challenger coming to the fore. The newcomer appeared, climbing clear of the throng. From be-hind, Markus saw only a dark cloak and black hair. This challenger stood even shorter than Milos, little more than six foot and of considerably lighter build. The audience hushed in surprise.

"Hunska?" the whisper went round.

"Fool!" came the reply.

The challenger might not be a giant but even so hunskas were never this tall or broad-shouldered. Denam fixed the newcomer with a stare so mur-derous that Markus felt the need to run boiling up inside him. As an em-path he was used to swimming in the currents of others' emotions, but the ring-fighter's anger ran swifter and more deep than anything he'd felt be-fore and at each moment threatened to overwhelm his senses.

The challenger ducked beneath the top rope.

"Drunk," someone speculated.

Markus tried to imagine how drunk a person would have to be to think this a good idea. Too drunk to stand, probably. This one didn't move as if inebriated, though.

The hush fell to silence as the challenger's cloak fluttered from the ring. The woman wore the same as the ring-fighters, just a white loin-cloth and a white band of cloth bound tight around her chest, her pale skin accentu-ating the redness of Denam's complexion.

The fight-master didn't approach to learn the challenger's name. In-stead he raised his voice: "Nona of the convent."

Nona didn't lift her arm to acknowledge the crowd's roar but she did make a slow turn, and when the black orbs of her eyes swept across him Markus knew that he had been seen.

"Fight!"

Denam came slowly to meet the novice, fists raised to protect his throat and eyes, his stance closed to defend his groin. Markus watched Nona intently, trying to see anything of the girl he'd known over those weeks in Giljohn's cage. She was two years his junior so she would be around

seventeen, but she looked every inch a woman. Long-limbed, lean, an ath-
lete's body, each muscle chiselled in hard relief, flat belly above the jut of
her hip bones. Even frightened for her as he was, Markus couldn't deny she
drew his eye in ways unbecoming to a holy brother.

Nona stepped in with a swift confidence, striking Denam just below the
ribs on his left side, five or six blows with the rapidity of a woodpecker hammering at a tree. She punched with her whole body, swivelling at the waist.
Denam laughed the blows off and swept a hand at the novice. She evaded
him with ease, landing three or four more punches in the same spot. Hard
as she must be hitting the man, Markus couldn't see what hope Nona
had of victory. The muscle covering Denam's bones lay inches thick and
the bones beneath must be like those of a draught horse. She might as well
try to punch a bear into submission.

Denam squared up against Nona, his hatred for her obvious even as he
tried to laugh at her efforts. Nona stood her ground and the crowd drew
in its breath. Denam swung with an arm that looked as thick around as
Markus's chest. The fist he drove at Nona was the size of her skull.

She took the punch in the face, her head snapping to the right. The
follow-up came from the left, snapping her head back the other way. Markus
imagined those fists would shatter a skull, leave cheekbones in fragments,
break a neck . . .

Nona looked up at the fighter towering above her and smiled, her teeth
unbloodied. Denam seemed astonished; the crowd roared in wonder. Magic?
But Markus had sensed no enchantment, not the slightest crackle of it. He
could only imagine that she had moved her head at the same speed as the
fists seeking it, allowing only a gentle contact.

Again Nona peppered the same spot below Denam's ribs with half a
dozen blows in the space of a heartbeat or two. She leapt back, rolling under
a sweeping hand, rising in the same motion, kicking at her target, evading
a second questing hand and spinning to land another kick in the same spot.

Denam came towards her, his own roar louder than the mob. As he advanced he favoured his right side. A small thing that could easily pass unnoticed. Nona twisted clear, bounced off two sets of ropes, and landed a flying kick, just below his ribs.

For long minutes the fight continued, Denam's attacks almost brushing Nona's pale skin but never quite finding it, Nona landing a score of punches and kicks on her target, perhaps two score. Denam's rage grew, his face crimson, spitting and foaming, howling threats and promises. But he crouched over the injured side now, the bruised lower ribs, covering them with his elbow. He leaned against the corner post, hitching in a breath.

"Come on, big boy." Nona's first words in the fight.

They worked like a spark to flash-powder. Denam threw himself forward with a scream. Nona dived beneath his outstretched arms, rolled head over heels between his legs, through the opening left as fury overcame caution, and drove her heel into his groin with all the speed and strength she possessed.

Denam made it two more strides before he realised that Nona was no longer in front of him, and a further stride before the pain hit home. The gerant's legs forgot whatever orders they had and dropped him to the planks where he curled around his agony, blind to the world.

Nona sprang to her feet, the fight still in her face, teeth bared. With the awful gale of Denam's hatred subsumed into his wordless agony, Markus could now feel Nona's emotions and found himself rocked back upon his heels by the raw animal aggression bleeding off her. He had experienced something similar when a wrong turn had taken him to the dog-pits beyond the walls of Old Town. A bloodied mastiff with its jaws locked around the throat of another hound had given off the same explosive violence that the novice did. Markus fully expected Nona to fall upon her prey, gouging Denam's eyes from their sockets or stamping his face to pulp. But instead, in the space of five deep breaths, she drew it all back in, every piece, until there was nothing he could read above the mixed sea of emotion all around him. Of all that he'd seen that night it was this quenching of fury that was the most remarkable to him.

Ignoring the cheers, and the fight-master coming to question or reward her, Nona vaulted the ropes and dropped into the crowd. Within moments she was at Markus's side, vibrant, sweat-soaked, alive, the alien blackness of her eyes level with his.

"You came," she said.

Markus shrugged. "You asked me to."

1

HOLY CLASS

Present Day

MARKUS HAD GROWN beyond Nona's expectations. She remembered a fierce spiky-haired farm boy who had welcomed her to Giljohn's cage by demanding her age and had appeared to find comfort in establishing his seniority over her. A bad beginning, but his affection for the child-taker's mule had softened her opinion of him by the end of their journey. Now he stood a solid six foot two, handsome in a friendly way, a face that would laugh with you. The black hair had been tamed with oil and lay flat to his skull in the way of monks. The only sign of the boy from the cage was a sharpness to his features and a quickness in the dark eyes that studied her.

Nona had wrapped her cloak around her once more. Sweat stuck the material to her back, making her uncomfortable, or perhaps that was just the frankness of Markus's regard. She offered a smile in return for his and hugged her hands under her arms. Her knuckles ached from repeatedly punching Denam. Nona was sure she'd punched practice timbers that were softer than the gerant's side. She felt good, though, her body glowing, her step so light that with a little effort she might just shrug off gravity entirely.

She leaned in. "Let's talk outside."

Markus nodded. They pushed a path towards the main doors. Already the Caltess's patrons were flocking back to the other ring. A couple of hulking apprentices were helping Denam over the ropes of the first.

"I'm surprised the convent lets novices come down here to fight," Markus said behind her.

"They don't." Nona slipped between the doors as they opened to admit more thrill-seekers.

"Why did you—" Markus broke off to draw his robes around him, the black habit of a holy brother. He followed her out into rain-laced wind, a loud *brrr* escaping at the cold shock of it.

"An old dispute that needed settling," Nona said. It was partly true. Mostly she had wanted to hit someone, hard, again and again. Markus probably knew that already; classified church reports named him as one of the most effective marjal empaths currently in the Ancestor's service.

Nona led Markus around the corner of the great hall where they would be sheltered from the gale. The walls loomed dark above them, the sky crossed with tatters of cloud beneath the crimson spread of a thousand dying stars.

"Why did you want me? Send the message, I mean?" Markus seemed less sure of himself than she had expected. Someone who could read her like a book should be more confident. She certainly wished her own empath skills would tell her more of his mood than she could glean from the intensity of his stare or the tight line of his lips.

"That day at the Academy." The words blurted from her. "Did you make that girl attack me?" Nona forced her mouth closed. She had had it all planned out, what she would say, how, when. And now her idiot tongue had cut through all of it.

"She . . . she was already attacking you." Guilt came from him in waves.

"She was using the darkness to scare me. Or trying to. But then she went mad." Nona remembered how an animal fury had risen across the girl's face. "You did that!"

"I did." A frown now, his brow pale and beaded with rain.

"She tried to shadow-rend me. I could have been torn apart!"

Markus raised his hands. "I made her angry. I didn't know she could do that."

"Well, she could!" Nona felt her own anger rising from the well she'd thought emptied in the ring.

"I'm sorry." He looked down.

"Well . . ." It felt like honesty, but Nona supposed he could fake that better than anyone she'd ever known. "Why?"

"Abbot Jacob told me to."

"Jacob?" A chill ran through Nona. "High Priest Jacob? I mean the one who used to be?"

Markus nodded, still looking down.

"But . . . he's not . . . you don't have to . . ."

"He was appointed to St. Croyus as abbot a year after Abbess Glass had Nevis replace him as high priest."

"St. Croyus? But Jacob's a monster!" Nona couldn't see how the former high priest could have risen from disgrace so swiftly.

"A monster with friends in high places. Including the Tacsis." Markus shrugged. "And he's not a stupid man, just a cruel and greedy one."

"So he bought you from Giljohn, sent you to St. Croyus, and followed you there to take over?" Nona had seen the high priest beat Giljohn's mule to death and leave Markus broken. And that was just on the day he'd purchased him as a frightened boy of ten. How must it have been to grow up under that man's command?

"I'm sorry." Markus looked up and met her eyes. She gave him points for not using his power to try to influence her. She would know. At least she hoped she would know. He couldn't be *that* good, could he? Markus coughed. "So, did you ask me down here to beat me senseless? Kick me in the groin? Or is my apology enough?"

A man hurried around the corner before Nona could answer. He approached them, hunched against the rain.

"Regol?" Nona asked. She'd looked for the ring-fighter in the crowd before she took on Denam but not spotted him.

"At your service, my lady!" He made a sweeping bow, managing to keep both eyes on Markus.

Nona couldn't help but smile. "I'm not your lady, or anyone else's."

"A remarkable victory, novice." Regol straightened. "Our ginger friend can be a stubborn fellow." His eyes held a certain distance, a reassessment perhaps.

"You saw?" She had wanted him to.

"The whole thing. And did you hear the newest recruits cheering in the attic?"

Nona flexed her hands, grimacing. "I thought he wasn't ever going to go down."

Regol winced. "The real question is whether he's going to get up again, and what he'll sound like." He squeaked the last part, then turned his gaze on Markus as if noticing him for the first time. "I would ask if this monk is bothering you, but I guess if he was he'd be on the ground looking for his teeth." Again that look, as if he saw a different person before him tonight.

"I'm sure Nona can have a disagreement without punching anyone in the face." Markus returned Regol's stare. "Not everyone who climbs out of the ring just steps into a bigger one."

Regol shrugged, that mocking smile of his firmly in place. "The whole Corridor is a ring around Abeth, brother. And when the ice squeezes, everyone fights."

"Go away," Markus said.

Regol opened his mouth with some reply but a puzzled look overtook him. He turned to go, then spun back as if he had forgotten something.

"You would rather be watching the fights." Markus spoke without emphasis but the waves of power bleeding from him shocked Nona with their intensity. It was as if someone had opened a furnace door and an unexpected wall of heat had broken across her.

Regol turned back and walked off without comment.

"He won't be pleased when that wears off," Nona said.

"No." Markus nodded. "But it would have been worse if he'd stayed longer. He didn't like me at all, and we both know why."

"Oh." Nona laughed, though it came out wrong. "Regol's not like that. He flirts with all the girls. The ladies of the Sis practically worship—"

"It's you he wants, Nona. You don't have to be an empath to know that."

"No, he's just . . ." She trailed off as Markus shook his head, his smile half-sad. "Anyway, you got rid of him easily enough." A twinge of disappointment had run through her at that.

"Easily?" Markus leaned back against the wall. "He put up a hell of a fight. I would never have suspected it of a Caltess brawler." He put his fingers to his temples. "I'll probably have a headache all night . . ."

Nona said nothing, only glanced towards the corner. After Joeli had made Regol abandon Darla mid-fight at Sherzal's palace the ring-fighter had asked Nona to help him. He hadn't wanted to be manipulated like that ever again. Nona had spent hours training him to erect barriers against that kind of thread-work. He would take this defeat badly.

Nona defocused her vision and looked at Markus amid the glory of the threads, the Path's halo. Marjal empathy was essentially thread-work that concentrated only on living threads and manipulated them more intuitively, based around emotional clusters. It was, in many senses, a tool designed for a specific job; whereas a quantal thread-worker had ultimately more potential and flexibility, the task was always more fiddly and harder work. The threads around Markus formed a glowing aura, brighter and more dynamic than any she had seen before. The host of threads that joined him to her—some years old, some freshly formed—ran taut, shivering with possibility, unvoiced emotions vibrating along their length. Markus would read it better than she could, but he would feel the answer rather than seeing it before him in the complexity that filled the space between them.

In fact, Sister Pan had revealed that all marjal enchantment was simply the power of the Path and the control of thread-work, but collected together into useful tools in the same way that iron and wood may be turned into many different implements, and many of those are of more immediate use than a log and a bar of iron and the option to shape both.

"Nona?"

Nona realised that Markus had said something she missed. She looked back.

"You asked me here . . ."

"I did." She stepped closer and he pressed his shoulders to the wall, every thread he had bent towards her, like the reflex of a river-anemone to touch. "I need your help."

Markus frowned. "I can help you?"

"I need to do something dangerous and illegal."

Markus's frown deepened. "Why would you trust me? Because we rode together for a few weeks in a cage when I was ten and you were eight? I nearly got you killed two years later."

"I trust you because you didn't ask me why I thought you would help, just why I would trust that help. And also because you didn't lie about what happened at the Academy."

"All right." He met her eye. "Why *would* I help you? It's dangerous and against the law."

"You'll help me because when they put us in that cage we never really came out of it again. And because your Abbot Jacob is still tied to the Tacsis name and so are his plans for further advancement. Doing this will help make sure that never happens. Hessa told me what happened to Four-Foot when Giljohn took you to Jacob's house."

"I suppose you think me weak, serving a man who did something like that? I suppose you would have beaten him to death?" Markus didn't try to hide the mix of anger and shame bubbling through him.

"Maybe I would have killed him, but you're a better person than I am. I'm not proud of my temper."

Markus twisted his lips into half of a doubtful smile. "So, you need me, and you trust me. What is it that you need me for, and trust me not to betray you over?"

Nona glanced over her shoulder into the night. From inside the Caltess the crowd's roar swelled. Another bout coming to a bloody end, no doubt. "I have to break into the Cathedral of St. Allam and steal something from High Priest Nevis's vault of forbidden books."

2

THE ESCAPE

Three Years Earlier

IN THE DARK of the moon by the side of the Grand Pass two dozen citizens of the empire huddled away from the wind. Dawn would show them an unparalleled view of that empire, spread out before them to the west, marching between the ice towards the Sea of Marn.

Nona stood close to the rock wall, pressed between Ara and Kettle. Her leg ached where the stump of Yisht's sword had driven in, pain shooting up and down as she shifted her weight, the whole limb stiffening.

Abbess Glass had gathered the survivors in a bend where the folds of the cliff offered some shelter. There were among their number men and women who owned substantial swathes of the Corridor, who had been born to privilege and to command. But here in their bloodstained finery, with flames from the palace of the emperor's sister licking up into the night behind them, it was to Abbess Glass they turned for direction.

"It will take Sherzal's soldiers a while to navigate around Zole's landslide but they'll come. It won't take long then to alert the garrisons and send riders down the road to Verity. There's no chance of making the capital that way."

"We don't need to reach Verity." Lord Jotsis spoke up. "My estates are closer."

"Castle Jotsis is formidable," Ara said, looking between her uncle and the abbess.

Abbess Glass shook her head. "Sherzal will bottle us up anywhere but the capital. She might not be insane enough to lay siege to your castle, my lord, but she would likely encircle your holdings to prevent word reaching the emperor. And besides, I fear that closer is not close enough."

"So we've escaped only to be hunted down on the road?" One side of old Lord Glosis's face had swollen into a single bruise but she still had enough energy to be temperamental. "Unacceptable."

"It's the shipheart that Sherzal wants above anything else." The abbess nodded to where Zole waited, some thirty yards closer to the landslide, her hands dark around the glowing purple sphere she had recovered from the Tetragode. "If we give her good reason to think that it has gone in another direction she won't spare many soldiers for chasing us. Maybe none."

"And how," Lord Jotsis asked, "can we make her think we haven't taken the shipheart with us?"

Abbess Glass turned to stare at the darkness of the slopes rising above them. "By making them think it has gone south, towards the ice."

"How can we make them think it's been sent south?" Lord Glosis asked, leaning on the arm of a young relative.

"By actually sending it south, to the ice," the abbess said. "Zole will take it and let them see the glow upon the slopes."

"But that's madness." Lord Jotsis drew himself to his full height. "You can't entrust a treasure like that to a lone novice!"

"I can when it's the lone novice who somehow stole that treasure from the heart of the Noi-Guin's stronghold in the first place," Abbess Glass replied.

"She won't be alone." Nona limped forward.

Ara hobbled to stand beside Nona. Kettle put her hands on their shoulders. "In our state we're going to be slowing the abbess down on the road. None of us will be any use to Zole trying to outdistance soldiers across the mountains."

Kettle was right. Nona gritted her teeth against the pain in her thigh and refused to let the admission out.

The abbess advanced on them, wind-swept grey hair straggled across her face. "The Noi-Guin's shipheart is a marjal one. It's said that in the hands of a marjal healer it can mend any wound but that it can also bring harm."

"Well, I don't want to go near it." Nona shuddered. She knew what harm the shipheart could bring. It had even squeezed a devil out of Zole, the most tightly bound person she had ever met. "And we don't have a marjal healer."

"We have Zole," the abbess said, and raising her voice she called to the ice-triber. "Zole, time to show us what Sister Rose has been teaching you."

ZOLE BECKONED THEM rather than approach and bring with her the awful pressure of the shipheart's presence. Nona took a few uncertain steps towards the girl, Ara behind her, then Kettle, all of them limping, the novice because of the arrow wound in her calf, the nun because of a knife wound in her thigh.

"We shouldn't be doing this, abbess." Nona looked back. "The Sweet Mercy shipheart did terrible things to Yisht."

"And yet Zole is untouched." The abbess and the others were black shapes now, with just edges picked out here and there by the deep purple light of the shipheart.

But Zole was not untouched . . .

"Find your serenity." Zole's voice resonated through the night. "Serenity will preserve you."

Nona didn't feel serene. She felt scared and in pain, but she reached for her trance, running the lines of the old song through her head, imagining the slow descent of the moon and the children of her village chanting in a circle around the fire. And with the moon's fall a blanket of serenity settled upon her, setting the world apart, her pain not gone but no longer personal, more a curio, an object for study.

Zole held the shipheart out towards them, a sphere the size of a child's head, resting on both palms, dark purple, almost black, but somehow glowing with a violet light that seemed to shade beyond vision. Nona advanced. She felt the pressure of the thing, as if she had fallen into deep water. She had plunged into the black depths of the Glasswater sinkhole before, and this was no less terrifying. The need to breathe built in her and threatened her serenity, before, with a gasp, she remembered that there was no reason not to draw breath.

With just a yard between them Nona's skin began to prickle and then burn, as if the devils were there already just waiting for their true colours to be made known. Nona had shared her skin with a devil before, Keot, not one of her own making but one that had infected her when she killed Raymel Tacsis. The rocks around the man's corpse had been stained black beneath the crimson.

"Hold to yourself." Zole closed the remaining distance that Nona's feet proved unwilling to cross. Zole had seen Nona's old devil and kept the secret. Zole said they called them *klaulathu* on the ice. Things of the Missing.

Without preamble, Zole pressed the heart's orb to the wound above Nona's knee. Nona had expected her flesh to sizzle, the blood in her veins to boil like the water in Sweet Mercy's pipes, but instead icy fingers wrapped around her bones and a black-violet light stole her vision. For a moment she saw strange spires silhouetted against an indigo sky, swept away in the next beat of her heart as if by a great wind. The Path opened before her, not the narrow and treacherous line that had to be hunted, but broad, blazing, so wide that its direction became uncertain, a place one might wander, drunk on power until the end of days. Voices began to sound within Nona's head, all of them hers but speaking from different places, some raging, some jealous, some whispering secret fears or wants, a babble at first but each taking on a separate identity, becoming clearer, more distinct.

"Done." Zole pushed Nona back, the base of her palm against Nona's sternum.

Nona staggered and Ara kept her from falling with help from Kettle. The heart-light caught their faces, making something alien of them both.

"Are you all right?" Kettle asked.

"I . . ." Nona stood straight, stamped her leg. It still ached but the flesh had been made whole, a white line of scar tissue marking the passage of Yisht's blade. "Yes." The voices that had filled her mind became jumbled together once more, fading back into the shadows.

"Go on." Kettle sent Nona back towards the abbess and the rest of the group, giving her shoulder a small shove to get her going.

By the time Nona reached the ruins of the wagon that they had escaped the palace in she was calm again, her serenity intact.

"How do you feel?" The abbess watched Nona's eyes with an uncomfortable intensity.

"I don't know," Nona said. "Tired. But full of energy. If that makes sense." She looked back down at her leg, the scar visible through the tattered smock. The cold no longer touched her. "I don't know how Zole can stand it." Part of her wanted to tell the abbess about the devil she had seen at Zole's wrist when she first arrived with the shipheart. She bit down on the impulse. She had lived with Keot for years and Zole hadn't informed on her. Zole would have to deal with her own demons. The abbess probably couldn't help in any case. And the inquisitors with her would want to burn the devil out of Zole.

Abbess Glass took Nona's hand and led her back to the main group. "You're mended? You can walk the distance now?"

"I could run it!" Ara caught them up, her hair rising around her head as if backcombed, a blond confusion defying the wind. She had a wild look in her eye. Nona met her gaze and a grin broke across both their faces, a shared understanding, and something more complex that perhaps neither understood. Nona wanted to run with her, to chase her. Wanted her friend.

The three of them turned to see Kettle silhouetted against the shipheart's glow, Zole on one knee, applying the heart to the nun's inner thigh. Kettle broke away with a cry after just a moment's contact. She came hurrying down the road, not glancing back. She moved quickly, though still with a slight limp.

"Sister Kettle?" The abbess stepped forward to meet her.

"Mother . . ." Kettle's wide eyes sought the abbess as though she were night-blind.

"Here." Abbess Glass took the nun's hands. "You're safe."

Nona raised her brows at the enormity of that lie but said nothing.

"I can't go near it again. I can't." Kettle shot a glance over her shoulder as if Zole might be approaching with the shipheart even now.

"It's all right, sister." The abbess led them farther away. "I need you to protect us as we journey west. Even if all Sherzal's forces follow the shipheart towards the ice, the empire roads are no longer a safe place for the vulnerable. And unguarded Sis lords are likely to be a tempting prize to any bandits we might pass."

"But Zole . . ."

"Zole will have her Shield."

3

HOLY CLASS

Present Day

AFTER LEAVING MARKUS at the Caltess, Nona ran to the city gates. She covered the five miles from Verity's walls to the foot of the Rock of Faith at a near sprint. The burning of her muscles and the hot thrill of her blood battled the night wind's chill.

Doubt dogged her footsteps, each mile and each yard. The voices of her suspicion were almost as real, almost as disembodied as Keot's voice had been when he lived beneath her skin. *Will he be true? Can he be trusted?* Questions Nona had no answer for, just the feeling in her gut. *Clera betrayed you*, the voices whispered, *and she was a friend.*

"She saved me too." Panted out between breaths as Nona picked up her pace, trying to outrun her doubts.

Nona shook her head, sweat flying in the wind. She was to be a nun. She would choose from the disciplines offered to her. Just a handful of final tests stood between her and the vows. She was to stand her life upon a foundation of faith. Faith that the branches of the Ancestor's tree would hold her, and that those branches would carry all of humanity into a future less dark than they feared. If a nun could not have faith, then who could? The bonds of friendship had always borne her more firmly than those of blood. Markus had ridden with her in the cage and that bond would suffice. She had faith that it would. Also she had a backup plan. With a gasp of effort she ran faster still, until any that she might have passed on the road that night would have stood amazed and watched her fly.

At last she came to a halt, breathing heavily. The base of a great limestone cliff rose above her. From its heights the southern windows of Blade Hall offered a view of the city and, twenty miles beyond, the ice glimmering red beneath the moon. Those walls were closer now than they had been when Abbess Glass had first brought Nona to the convent. North and south the ice squeezed and all the nations of the Corridor bled.

The start of the Seren Way lay close at hand, just a few minutes' walk around the Rock, but Wheel had taken to watching it of late. The old woman spent whole nights seated at the narrowest part, wrapped in a great blanket and staring at the night with watery eyes, just waiting to catch any errant novice. Why she didn't just check the dormitories was unclear, but Ruli claimed Wheel had been made to vow never to enter the building under the tenure of the previous abbess following an unspecified "incident." Ruli claimed a novice had been killed, but when pressed she had to admit making that part up.

Nona craned her neck and looked up at the dark acreage of stone. Here and there moonlight picked out a line where it caught upon an edge of rock. She took a deep breath, swung her arms, and began to climb. She followed an old fault-line, digging her leather-clad toes into the crack, reaching up for fingerholds. Her flaw-blades would make a quicker, easier job of it but Nona had learned the danger in relying too much on something that might not always be there. Besides, the pattern of regular slots driven into the rock might be spotted one day, and it would be hard to deny her own signature.

As she gained height Nona's arms began to join her legs in complaint.

Her hands ached from punching Denam over and over. The thought of him falling gave her fresh energy, though. She had wanted to fight him for years. She could say it was to take him down a peg or three, punishment for being a bully, or that it was payment for his attempt to break her in the ring on the instructions of Raymel Tacsis. The truth though was something less laudable, and came in two parts, both now settling into her mind as truths often do when a head is empty of all things save the demands of hard labour.

Nona had fought Denam because even with Keot gone a hunger for violence burned in her and if left unfed too long it would break out in dangerous ways. Much of what she had blamed on Raymel's devil seemed instead to be some fundamental part of who she had grown into. Denam represented that rare someone, a person she could hit over and over without the danger of killing them, or any need for remorse over pain inflicted.

The other reasons for the contest had been Markus and Regol. She had asked Markus to break holy law. She owed it to him to show him who he was breaking those laws for. And Regol . . . Regol needed to see it too. Regol who spoke foolishness into the pillows when she joined him beneath the roof that Partnis Reeves put over his head. Regol who thought her something precious, as holy as the vows she broke. He needed to see what really lay behind the eyes he claimed to lose himself in. Something sharp-angled and vicious—not the princess he sometimes let himself pretend she was. Nona knew better than to allow him to build his hopes upon a lie. Regol fulfilled a need, as Denam had: one in the ring, one in the furs. She and Regol were friends whose bodies were pleasing to each other. She couldn't let a friend build their hopes upon such a flawed foundation as her. She hadn't saved Saida, or Hessa, or Darla. Even as an agent of vengeance she had failed. Sherzal, the architect behind so many deaths, still walked the world, as did others who had served her will.

Nona hauled herself over the edge of the cliff and lay on her back on the cold stone, just inches from the fall. Her arms trembled, her body knew the bone-deep exhaustion of prolonged mistreatment, but her mind still raced, images rising from the darkness, one after the next. Denam's anger, Regol's surprise, Markus's caution, a hundred other scenes, drawn by threads of memory.

In time she rolled onto her side and levered herself up. She passed around the far end of Blade Hall, slipping along the perimeter of the courtyard before Heart Hall. Moving between moonshadows she skirted the buildings, placing each foot with the caution of one born to the Grey.

"Novice Nona." A soft voice at her shoulder. "You smell of man-sweat."

Nona turned, unable to see anyone in the darkness behind her. "And you smell of apples, sister. One red Apple, to be more precise."

"Then our sins are evenly matched." The shadows melted from Sister Kettle and she stepped forward with a half-smile.

"Perhaps." Nona grinned. "But I earned mine in front of an audience—"

"Well, that's novel." Kettle widened both eyes and her smile.

"In a ring at the Caltess."

"No Regol tonight?" Kettle frowned.

"That's a habit I should discard," Nona said. "This one, I should keep on." She patted her garment. "I'll be taking a nun's vows soon. If they don't mean more to me than the promises novices make, then I shouldn't say them."

"There are other ways to serve." Kettle pursed her lips. "You don't have to stay. Nor do you have to be perfect. But . . . you do have to go to bed." She pointed.

Nona nodded. "Bed sounds good. A bath would be good too. But I would probably fall asleep and drown." She shrugged and turned to go.

"Watch out for Joeli." Hissed at her back.

NONA APPROACHED THE dormitories. She examined the main door before opening it and entering the hall beyond. A sleepy novice emerged from the Red dorm, lantern in hand, and passed her without looking up, bound for the Necessary. Nona moved on, climbing the stairs to the Holy floor at the top of the building.

She studied the door to her dorm more closely than she had the main one. Defocusing her sight, she picked out a glowing thread laid across the floor just in front of the door, another looping the handle, both veering off at strange angles to the world. They were trip-threads most likely, set to warn Joeli of her comings and goings, but there could be more to them. Some threads could cut you; others could just make it hurt as much as if they had cut you; others could wreak more complex damage, or adhere and trail out behind you, providing information to anyone holding them closer to where they joined the Path. How many of those tricks Joeli had mastered, Nona couldn't say, except that she had definitely used both trip-threads and pain-threads in the past. Nona's own talents still lagged behind, but not so far as they once had.

Nona removed the threads, pushing them temporarily out of alignment with the world. They would return shortly and appear untouched. She saw the third thread just as she reached for the door handle, gossamer thin, turning virulent green as she brought it into focus. Something new and unfriendly. Fortunately it too gave way when she worked to remove it from her path, though it scalded her fingertips before it vanished.

A moment later Nona entered the dorm. Almost half the top floor was given over to individual study rooms. The Holy Class novices slept in a long hall not much bigger than the one given over to the novices in Red Class. The girls were not yet trusted with the privacy of a nun's cell, but the class code was to overlook each other's indiscretions, and Wheel would undoubtedly have apoplexy were she to watch a typical evening unfold.

Nona moved silently down the row of beds, her eyes returning several times to the long curves beneath Joeli's blankets. The abbess had been forced to accept the girl's return a year earlier as part of the emperor's efforts at reconciliation and unity after the events at Sherzal's palace. Lord Namsis had secured his daughter's re-entry by having her submit to the

Inquisition. The interrogator had been armed with one of Sister Apple's bitter little truth pills. To the astonishment of everyone who knew her Joeli had affirmed her innocence with a black tongue. She had used her thread-work against Darla and Regol only with the intention of scaring them into retreat, hoping to end the bloodshed that way.

Nona slipped into her bed, still watching Joeli in the dim glow of the night-lantern. Her own thought was that Lord Namsis had paid an Academy man, a quantal thread-worker, to undertake the delicate task of altering Joeli's memories. The girl now believed her own story and hadn't lied, even though what she said was not true.

In the warmth of her blankets Nona released the breath she had been holding and surrendered to exhaustion. The next day would be a long one. Not only would she undergo her final Blade-test, she needed to steal the convent's seal of office from the abbess. Neither task would be easy.

4

---◆---

THE ESCAPE

Three Years Earlier

"Nona's not going alone!"

"Correct, she is not going alone. She's going with Zole." The abbess turned from dispensing brief advice to Nona and set a hand to Ara's shoulder. "We have a long road ahead of us, novice, charged with the protection of the emperor's subjects, including many of his most powerful supporters, your own uncle among them. Would you leave us with a lone Grey Sister and a single Inquisition guard for protection? We will likely need someone among our number who can call on the power of the Path . . ."

Nona saw the anguish in Ara's expression and tried to ease her mind. "We have to bring two things back to Sweet Mercy to make it right again. Zole and I will bring the shipheart. You'll bring the abbess."

"But . . ." Ara glanced up the curve of the road towards Zole, painted in violet light amid the darkness. "Sherzal will send an army after you!"

"When we make it to the ice, armies won't matter," Nona said.

"Because the ice will kill you!" Ara shook the abbess's hand from her shoulder, anguish on her face.

"Zole was raised on the ice." Nona smiled. "You'll be in more danger down on the plains than we will up there."

"Also," Abbess Glass interjected, "consider that if Sherzal doesn't get the shipheart back she will very definitely find her alliance with the Scithrowl in tatters. And likely the Noi-Guin turned against her. As soon as the odds shift against recovering the heart Sherzal would be sensible to recall her forces to defend the Grand Pass against the battle-queen's hordes. It's certainly what any sane person would do. My guess is that if you reach the ice she won't dare risk mounting further pursuit in any significant numbers."

THERE WERE NO preparations to be made, no rations to be apportioned, no equipment save clothing to be dispersed. Nona stood ready, wrapped in Kettle's coat. She was armed with a Noi-Guin sword, a knife, and eighteen throwing stars.

Kettle embraced Nona, her hunska quickness allowing no escape. "It's a hug, Nona, not spiders down your back. Relax."

Nona tried to unstiffen, and smiled. "Get the abbess home."

Ara hugged Nona next. "Come back to us," she breathed into Nona's ear. "To me." She pressed some coins into Nona's hand. "This may help."

Kettle and Ara retreated, leaving Regol standing before her, looking almost nervous.

"Careful on the ice." His old smile covered up any uncertainty.

"I should watch for hoolas and ice-bears?"

"If you like. I just meant that it's slippery." He turned to go. "You should visit us at the Caltess when you get back." And he walked off to rejoin the group. "I know Denam misses you."

Nona watched as Abbess Glass, flanked on the drop-side by the Inquisition guard, Melkir, led the way down towards the main road and the long descent from the mountains. Ara brought up the rear, Regol by her side. Nona knew a moment's jealousy. A day earlier she would have blamed it on Keot. She turned back towards Zole farther up the track. In the distance the flames from Sherzal's palace lit the slopes but seemed less vigorous than they had been.

"Time to go," she said to nobody in particular: now that she had lost her devil, she lacked both an audience for her passing thoughts and a scapegoat for unworthy emotions. The peaks loomed somewhere above her in the darkness, and an arduous journey lay ahead with only Zole for company.

"Do not fall behind." Zole led the way, her gaze fixed upon the fractured rock before her.

"I'll try to avoid falling in any direction." Nona snatched a cold breath and hauled herself up.

Kettle's coat blunted the wind's teeth. Other items of warm clothing had been recovered from two guests who made it into the carriage but thanks to arrows from Sherzal's soldiers did not make it out again. She wore a dead man's shoes, a poor fit but better than bare feet on icy rock. Back on the road Nona had considered herself well wrapped. On the slopes, despite the strenuous climb, she found herself shivering each time they rested.

Nona kept a distance of no less than two to three yards while following Zole. If she came closer the beat of the shipheart started to vibrate through her bones and each thought threatened to coalesce into its own creature that would then run roughshod through her mind. Any farther away and she lost the light.

The shipheart's glow served both to draw any pursuit and to illuminate the girls' progress across the mountains' slant. Nona quickly began to learn how to interpret the confusion of night-black shadows and dull violet surfaces revealed by Zole's strange lantern. Gravity and rocks provide a harsh but swift education.

Navigating the raw flanks of the Grampains proved a worryingly slow affair. Nona had no experience of mountains and Zole had little more. The ice was, as she said, mostly flat. The first shock had been in discovering how quickly a sharp incline could sap your strength. Nona knew herself to be fit, but within half an hour her breath came in ragged gasps and her newly healed leg ached almost as badly as it had when the wound lay open. The strength and coldness of the wind was an unwelcome revelation too. The Grampains forced the gale to climb just as the novices must, and the wind seemed displeased by the task, dumping any warmth it might have held back on the plains as if to lighten the load. Above them the rocks glistened with frost, and ice collected in every crevice.

"They're catching up." Nona's glance back showed a serpent of fireflies weaving its way along the ridge she'd toiled up not long before. Distance reduced each lantern in the pursuit to a glowing point. Slowly but surely Nona and Zole were losing ground. The soldiers giving chase knew these slopes and patrolled across them regularly. The advantage was theirs. "Close now."

Zole grunted.

"We're not going to be able to outrun them." Nona felt as if she were whining but the truth was that she was frozen and exhausted. Also terrified of the invisible drops beyond those jagged edges picked out in violet light on either side. The unseen falls held more fear than the empty yards below the blade-path ever had. "Zole!"

Zole paused, not looking back. "We are not trying to outrun them."

"What then?" Nona furrowed her brow.

"I am looking for the best place to kill them."

"Kill . . ." Nona turned to face the pursuit. "But there are hundreds . . ."

"Hundreds foolish enough to follow into the heights someone who has already shown them a landslide."

Nona watched the points of light twinkle, their advance almost imperceptible. A warm hand held each of those lanterns, and other soldiers clambered up between them.

"Can't we hide instead?" Killing came easy when an enemy raised their weapon against her, but to end so many lives, soldiers of the empire following the orders of their commander . . . it felt wrong. She pictured Zole's face when she had first hauled herself up onto the road, lit from beneath by the heart-light, something demonic in the play of shadows. Did devils own her now? Their claws around her heart?

Zole turned and the light flooded across Nona's shoulders, the pressure building, an almost physical push. "It is harder to hide ourselves in the rock than to bring it down upon them. And if we hid we would not be able to travel. They would surround us. There will be Noi-Guin among their number and some may be able to sense the proximity of the shipheart just as you and I can. We might not stay hidden long."

Nona hugged herself and said nothing. There seemed to be nothing to say. For once Zole had said it all.

Dawn broke over the peaks, a grey wave spilling pale light across the slopes. The black serpent, its head now only a few hundred yards behind them, began to resolve into individual figures.

Zole set to scaling a rock-face so close to vertical that "cliff" seemed a reasonable description. Nona, staring at the smooth stone, could see no way it could be climbed, and yet the Chosen One made relentless progress, the shipheart in her backpack now, its illumination no longer required.

"How . . . ?" Nona shrugged, gathered her strength, and started to follow, stabbing her flaw-blades into the rock.

Here and there as she climbed Nona spotted patches where the rock-face looked different, the stone somehow rippled, like butter melted and then returned to solid before it could flow away. Zole was digging herself handholds and allowing them to reseal as she moved on. It would buy them time. The soldiers would need to find a true mountaineer among their number to lay them a rope, or they would have to discover a longer path.

After sixty or seventy yards of climbing, Nona joined Zole on a ledge of fractured stone that led across the gradient, with another cliff rising above it. She hauled herself onto the flat space between the two rock-faces and lay bonelessly, drawing a deep lungful into her aching chest. Clera would have moaned, "Carry me." The thought made Nona cough out a painful laugh.

"Are you well?" Zole frowned at her from a perch several yards off.

Nona rolled to her front. "No."

Below them the first soldiers had arrived at the base of the cliff and were starting to puzzle over how their prey had scaled it.

"What now?" Nona asked.

"We wait."

Nona didn't argue. She lay as if dead until the coldness of the stone forced her to sit, huddled against the cliff for any shelter on offer. Seventy yards down, the soldiers gathered until they ran out of space. With a queue stretching behind them they began to argue, loud enough for the edges of their conversation to reach the novices.

"They can't fit any more down there," Nona said. "You should do whatever it is you're going to do."

"Wait."

"What for?"

"The leaders. And the Noi-Guin."

"How will you know when they're here?" Nona squinted at the helmed heads far below.

"Once they start climbing, that will be the Noi-Guin. To see the officers watch where the troops face."

"There!" Nona pointed to where one soldier, looking no different from the others, started to scale the unclimbable rock-face. "And there." Two more had started up a little farther along.

"We are never more vulnerable than when giving chase," Zole said.

"Is that what they say on the ice?" Nona snorted. "The wisdom of the tribes?" There might be half a thousand soldiers on the mountain and they looked far from vulnerable.

"Abbess Glass said it." Zole shrugged off her pack. She took the ship-heart out, holding it in one hand. It looked too big for her to grip securely. "Hold on." She voiced Nona's thought.

Zole brought her hand round in an overhead swing and smacked the shipheart into the top of the rock-face just below her. The impact was a strange one; no fragments of stone flew off, there was no great crash, just a deep pulse that seemed to spread out through the mountain. Nona felt it through her back where it pressed the stone. All three climbers froze. A moment passed. Another. Then a lurch that sent Nona flying towards the drop. It seemed the whole mountain twitched. Only hunska reflexes combined with stone-piercing flaw-blades saved her from falling.

Everything below the two novices, except for the top dozen feet of the cliff, broke away and began to fall, a descending curtain of rock, fracturing as it slid over the deeper parts of the mountain that remained fixed. The scene below them vanished beneath a rising cloud of dust.

Zole stood and returned the shipheart to her pack. "Follow me." She began to walk away along the ledge.

"If we keep climbing we could lose the survivors," Nona said, still staring at the dust in horrified fascination.

"We do not want them to lose us," Zole called back, not looking around. "Just that they not catch us."

Nona hesitated for one more moment, then hurried after the ice-triber before the wind-driven dust could take her from view. She didn't feel like a shield, or anything else useful. Spare baggage at best. Her head felt fuzzy from the shipheart's constant pressure, her thoughts unorganised and slow.

+   +   +

Zole led them back to the north for a way, then began to climb on a south-leading ridge. She called a halt where a spire of rock offered some shelter from the wind, and marvellously produced both food and water.

"How . . . ?" Nona accepted a strip of dried meat and a near-full water-skin.

"I prepared for my journey." Zole crammed a strip of the blackened trail-beef into her mouth and began to chew methodically.

"You came after me," Nona said. After so long surviving on cell slops the leathery meat seemed to explode with flavour, her mouth flooding.

"I followed Sister Kettle." Zole spoke around the rhythm of her jaws.

"But you knew she was looking for me."

"Yes."

"Why did you come?" Nona wanted to hear it from Zole's lips.

"You are the Shield. I need your protection." If the ice-triber was mocking her she let no sign of it show.

"You don't believe that stuff. It's all made-up." Nona forced herself not to drink too deeply from the skin.

"Everything ever said was made-up. The Ancestor, the Hope, all the small green gods of the Corridor who will die when the ice closes."

Nona wiped her mouth. "And on the ice. Don't you make gods of the wind?"

Zole shrugged. "Some do."

"And you tell stories about the future."

"Perhaps we have a prophecy about a black-eyed goddess who will save us all, and the four-blood child of the ice whose job it is to lead her home." The smallest smile quirked the corner of Zole's mouth. She stood and shouldered her pack. "Time to go."

"Up?" Nona's heart fell.

"Up." Zole nodded. "They will try to get ahead of us. The Noi-Guin will try to come at us from several different directions at once."

"Can't you just drop rocks on their heads?"

"It is . . . tiring." Zole rubbed at her wrist, where Nona had seen the devil. "It would be better if we do not find out whether I can or not."

It was true. For the first time ever Nona saw lines of exhaustion in Zole's face. The shock of it surprised her. Before she started to work wonders Zole had never seemed quite human.

5

———◆———

HOLY CLASS

Present Day

NONA ROSE WITH the bell, rolled from her bed, and hurried into her habit oblivious to the room around her. The rest of the novices were still dressing when she left, Ruli only just poking her head from beneath the blankets at Jula's urging, hair in a tangle of amazing proportions.

"Good luck today!" Alata, flashing a grin as she plaited Leeni's hair into a single red rope.

Nona paused only to check the doorway for malicious threads, then took the stairs four at a time. She was first into the refectory and was reaching for the bread as she slid her legs beneath Holy Class's table. By the time Ketti joined her Nona had heaped her plate for the second time and was attacking a pile of bacon with purpose.

"I wouldn't be able to eat. Not with the Blade final in front of me." Ketti started to help herself to eggs.

Nona grunted around a mouthful. Meals at Sweet Mercy were not as large or varied as they had been when she had arrived as a starveling child. The Durns held much of the Marn coast and the Scithrowl had crossed the Grampains. With both advances slow but seemingly as inexorable as the ice, good and plentiful food wasn't something that could be depended on, even within sight of the capital's wall. "Eat while you can." Nona reached for her water. It was a point of regret to her that she'd proved unable to pack on any reserves. She would be the first to go in any famine, where someone like Sister Rose could lose half her body weight and still survive. Even so, she didn't plan to give up on trying.

"Good luck today!" Jula sat herself opposite, eyes tracking across the various steaming bowls lined along the centre of the table. She always spent five minutes in careful consideration of her options. Then chose porridge.

"Here." Ketti leaned forward and pushed the porridge bowl towards Jula.

"I thought I might try something different today." Jula frowned at the mushrooms.

Ketti and Nona exchanged a quick "no you won't" glance.

Joeli seated herself at the far end of the table, hair gleaming as if the sun had found a way through the clouds just for her. Somehow her habit looked as if it had been tailored to her personal requirements, as flattering as any ballgown. "Blade final! Why, Nona, you're quite pink with excitement." She smiled brightly. "Pray Ancestor it will be a good one."

They all ignored her. Joeli had been relentlessly nice since her return, as if they were all best of friends. Nona could almost imagine that Lord Namsis's Academy man had rearranged Joeli's opinions where she was concerned in addition to her memories regarding the events at Sherzal's palace. The thread-traps scattered around the convent gave the lie to all those pretty smiles, though.

Ghena came to the table, raindrops beading the tight frizz of her hair. "Good lu—"

"It's not about luck!" Nona bit back a snarl and forced herself to lower her voice. "My thanks. I will try to acquit myself well." She regretted ever telling anyone that the test date had been set. She manufactured a smile, pushed her chair back from the table and stood to go, aware now of the tension in her limbs. Today she would face Mistress Blade, without armour, sword in hand, and her performance would decide whether she could take the Red.

A downpour greeted her exit from the refectory. She ran to Blade Hall, head bowed, crashing through the main entrance to stand dripping in the foyer. Ara waited in the shadows by the doors, a practice blade in each hand.

"Thought you might want some help warming up." She offered one sword, hilt first.

"Thanks." Nona smiled, slipped off her shoes, and moved across the sand towards the changing room, skirting the area marked off for the test to come.

She emerged a short while later, wearing a white exercise habit to match Ara's. The pair of them began the blade-kata side by side, the slow version first, stringing together all the core movements of the form in a way that gradually warmed and stretched the muscles. Nona watched Ara move as she made her own forms. Although Nona knew her own kata met Sister Tallow's exacting standards, somehow there was a beauty to Ara's that made her heart ache.

"You'll be fine." Ara grinned, her breath now quickened following the double kata.

They crossed blades. Normally they would both be wearing the heavy blade habit with a wire facemask. Today wasn't going to be normal. Nona hadn't any real concern that she would fail to meet the required performance. The question in significant doubt concerned her sword. She would receive her blade on taking orders, just like any other Red Sister. It should be an Ark-steel sword like Sister Tallow's, a weapon that in the right hands could shatter a lesser blade and cleave a block from a castle wall in two. But

Nona knew that none of the most recent novices to graduate to the Red had been given Ark-steel. Over the years swords had been lost and the Red Sisters' ranks had grown. These days sisters new to their names were most often given a fresh blade. The steel for these came from the forges of the Barrons witches. As fine a steel as could be made within the Corridor, but nothing compared to that of the ancients.

"Ready?" Nona asked. When the time came, she would miss sparring with her friend.

Ara attacked by way of answer and Nona barely turned the thrust from her face. She replied with an immediate counter-cut.

If Nona made a sufficiently good impression today she might have one of the few Ark-steel swords awarded to her on her first day in the Red rather than having to wait for an older sister to die or to set down her weapon and retire to prayer as a Holy Sister. New Reds without Ark-steel were known as "pinks" in certain quarters.

Ara's blade crashed against Nona's, flickered away, sliced in, parried, cut. A stillness always settled on much of Nona's mind when she sparred, and in that stillness a realisation reached her.

"Pink."

"What?" Ara paused, and Nona attacked with renewed vigour.

No matter how tightly she held herself against thread-work Joeli could still pull her strings, in the way that required no magic. Just dropping the word "pink" into the conversation around the breakfast table earlier had nearly made Nona bite Ghena's head off for daring to wish her good luck...

Nona rocked back to avoid Ara's slash and spun in behind the swing. She drew on her anger at the Namsis girl, feeding the fire that already burned there. Joeli thought to spoil her concentration, to put her out of the cold centre of her serenity where a Red Sister was supposed to dwell in the heat of battle. What Joeli failed to appreciate was that Nona had never followed that part of Mistress Blade's instructions. When she fought in earnest she fought angry, and her rage seldom wanted for fuel.

Nona kicked out at Ara's knee and leapt in as the girl jumped back. At the very limit of her speed Nona got her off hand to block Ara's wrist, deflecting the downward blow that should have felled her, and brought her own blade up, into Ara's side, managing to turn the iron flat just before it hammered into her ribs.

"Good . . . one." Ara stumbled back, clutching her side, sword dropped to indicate surrender. "Ah." She hugged her ribs. A black line would show there tomorrow. "Did anyone ever tell you you look scary as hell when you fight for real?"

"Never." Nona stuck her tongue out. "Are you all right?" She moved forward to check Ara's side, suddenly concerned. She set a gentle hand to Ara's ribs.

"Fine." Ara pushed her off. "I hope you don't make faces that scary in other kinds of . . . battles."

"What do you—"

"The late-night sort you might get into with Regol . . ." Their eyes met, and for a moment Nona wondered if she saw something hidden . . . something hurt? The look vanished as quickly as it showed, replaced with Ara's impression of Nona's expression.

Nona shoved Ara who fell, laughing, until she hit the sand and jolted her injured ribs. Nona was helping her up, still apologizing, when Sister Tallow entered the hall.

THE ABBESS AND sisters superior followed Sister Tallow out into the hall, turning to take their seats in the stands. Tallow approached Nona and Ara, her weathered face inscrutable. A nun Nona had never seen before dogged Mistress Blade's heels. She looked a good twenty years younger than Tallow, tall, slim, skin the colour of old leather though smooth save for the scars on both her cheeks. The twin wounds might be ritual markings or perhaps their curious symmetry had arisen by chance. The newcomer fixed Nona with a piercing gaze. She had a beauty to her, but there was nothing soft about it, her cheekbones almost sharp enough to cut you if you slapped her.

"Novice Arabella, you may leave." Sister Tallow nodded to the doors. The final Blade-test never had any audience but the abbess and her sisters superior. Novices who attempted to watch through the windows had been whipped in the past, even expelled from the convent. Ara gave up her practice blade and ran off with a last encouraging glance.

Tallow waited between Nona and the unknown nun until the doors closed. Nona stood a hand taller than both women and was of heavier build. Some said she had gerant in her but if so it wasn't more than a touch. There had been no blood-war as there had been when her marjal traits started to show.

Tallow lifted a hand to indicate the other nun. "This is Sister Iron, Nona. She is to be the new Mistress Blade. She takes over today."

"No—"

"I am getting old, child. We hunska do that fast too. I will join the Holy Sisters and give the Ancestor my full attention as the abbess instructs."

Nona shot a glance towards the stands. The sisters superior flanked the abbess. Sister Rose sat to Wheel's left. Wheel, the older looking of the two, though they were of an age, glared at Nona with those pale, watery eyes just as always.

"You will fight Sister Iron for the Red, novice." Tallow drew a sword from a second scabbard at her left hip. A Red Sister's blade, Barrons-forged. She handed it to Nona. "Control. Restraint. Respect." Tallow folded Nona's fingers around the hilt. "You'll be judged on these. But in the Corridor . . . winning is also quite important."

"I'll win then." Nona stepped back, circling away from Sister Iron. She didn't want a new Mistress Blade, though she couldn't quite suppress the relief that she wouldn't have to face Sister Tallow with sharp iron in hand in an earnest fight.

Sister Iron drew her blade, a sword identical to Nona's since pitting

Ark-steel against Barrons-steel would damage the latter and likely ruin it. The nun made no move, only cocked her head to the side and watched how Nona positioned her feet. Her gaze slid up the length of Nona's body, coming to rest on her wrist and the fingers around the sword hilt. Nona felt as if she was being judged and found wanting.

"You're ready?" Nona asked, unsettled by the woman's stillness.

Back against the wall Sister Tallow rolled her eyes.

Nona came forward, sword extended before her. She didn't reach for her speed but instead waited to react, a lesson she had learned from Zole. Sister Iron did nothing, only watched her move, her own blade loose in her hand, the point in the sand.

Nona came closer. Closer still. The point of her sword just two feet from the nun's chest. She could lunge and run the woman through. She glanced towards Sister Tallow, uncertain.

The moment Nona's eyes moved from her Sister Iron pushed Nona's sword away, the back of her hand flat against the side of the blade. The nun released her own sword and slapped Nona across the face, hard enough to rattle her teeth. Nona leapt away and by the time she was clear Sister Iron had kicked her falling sword back into the air and snatched hold of it once again.

"You think this one is ready?" Sister Iron asked Sister Tallow.

Nona spat blood into the sand. A dozen sentences wanted to escape her tongue, some bitter, some angry, but she swallowed them all. The fault was hers. There were no rules. "Try me again."

Sister Iron came forward, blade extended as Nona's had been. Nona let her get just as close. The nun's gaze never faltered. She lunged, showing no reservation about skewering a novice. Nona sank into the moment and made to push the sword away as Iron had, only to find the cutting edge angled towards her hand. She pushed it anyway, sparks flying as Barrons-steel scraped over flaw-blades. She made to slap the woman but Iron proved swift, Nona's fingertips missing her cheek by a hairsbreadth.

Nona kicked her falling blade back into the air and caught it as Iron had but with far less grace. The pair of them ended two yards apart, gazes locked, one on the other.

"No claws today, novice." The abbess's voice from the stands. "Just the blade you hope to earn."

Nona nodded her acknowledgement. She moved smoothly into attacking. No more playing, no more games. She told herself that Zole stood before her. With the exception of Yisht and Sister Tallow, Zole had been her most lethal opponent, faster than thinking, merciless, efficient.

Sister Iron replied with a storm of blows, feints, and counterattacks every bit as swift and ruthless as Zole's had ever been. She had more than that, though. Something in her touch, a kind of mastery that let her tame a blow on her blade, guide it, twist it. At every exchange Nona felt on the edge of having her sword torn from her grasp. Sister Iron used combinations that Nona hadn't seen before, series of moves that drove Nona step by inexorable step into the wrong place, her balance lost, her momentum stolen, sword unready.

Sister Iron ended a lengthy combination attack with a rising slice. An extravagance of speed saved Nona from being struck, though she would not have been surprised to find a thin line of blood across her front had she the time to look down. She spun away, sliding to a halt on one foot, spraying sand.

"Ah!" Nona staggered; her heel felt as if a hot wire had sliced part way through it.

Sister Iron came forward, pressing her attack. Nona defended with desperation, hobbling back before launching sideways on her good foot to win space. She rolled across the sand, biting down a scream as something cut into her just above the elbow. Coming to her feet she expected to find blood sheeting down her arm but the skin lay unmarked despite the agony.

Nona got to her feet, wincing, sword raised, injured arm held close to her body. As Iron came in Nona saw it. Where the sand had been scuffed away almost to the stone she glimpsed something, a nearly invisible distortion running over the slab beneath. If she had time to defocus she knew her Path-sight would show a thread, lurid green no doubt, as so many of Joeli's curse-threads were.

As Sister Iron drew close Nona swept away the sand in front of her with one foot. It proved a useless endeavour: pressed to defend, she had no time to clear more ground or study the area exposed. Their swords met and met again, beating out a high-tempo tattoo. Sweat flew from the ends of Nona's hair, sparkling droplets mired in the moment, unable to fall in the space between half a dozen strikes.

Another pain-thread caught Nona's foot and she fell backwards with a cry, turning a thrust and a swing as she dropped. Nona rolled through three more pain-threads, evading Sister Iron stamping at her. Finally the nun backed off, perhaps remembering that the exercise was a test rather than murder.

Nona stood slowly, meeting Sister Tallow's puzzled frown.

"It's only pain." She muttered the words, forcing her hunched body to straighten, relaxing the tight muscles of her arms and legs. She had suffered worse. Thuran Tacsis had pressed his sigil-marked toy called the Harm against her. It had hurt more than a thousand pain-threads. Later she had glued it to his flesh. He hadn't been found for over a day. They said he sat drooling upon his lord's chair now, ruler of the Tacsis in name only. Why his remaining son, Lano, didn't have him quietly killed nobody could say.

"Only pain." Spoken loud enough for Sister Iron to take note. Nona thought of Joeli creeping out in the dead of night to lay her threads in the Blade Hall sands, each full of malice and carefully attuned just to Nona. It was a work of art really. Nona doubted there were six thread-workers in all the empire who could match it. Maybe not so many. A red anger rose through her, its heat burning through the agony that lanced from her invisible wounds. Lips curled back from teeth, a savage grin.

Nona threw herself back across ground already trodden, the potency of the thread-traps there now spent. She attacked Sister Iron not with the calm efficiency Sister Tallow taught but with the honest and savage desire to do her opponent harm, acknowledging the beast that dwelt within her, the hot core of her that Tarkax the Ice-Spear had seen. Passion lent her a strength that Sister Iron had to grit her own teeth to turn. Rage put an edge on a quickness that was already blinding, and Sister Iron was forced back for the first time, weaving her defence within the depth of her own serenity.

Perhaps no battle so ugly had ever played out across the Blade Hall sands before. But the simple fact was that Sister Iron, the presumptive Mistress Blade, retreated before the sword of Nona Grey, her own hair wet with sweat now. Sister Iron's own swordwork was now stretched to extravagant lengths, all within a packed handful of seconds that few possessed the vision to follow.

Another thread snagged Nona's foot. She hardly winced but in the missed quarter-beat Sister Iron parried her wide, kicked the inside of her left knee, and punched her square in the face before following up with the hilt of her sword to the side of her neck. Nona fell hard, and trying to rise found the point of Sister Iron's sword inches from her face.

"Enough, novice." The woman stood, apparently calm but with her chest heaving.

Nona repressed a snarl and let her head fall back against the sand.

"Sister Tallow taught me to fight," Sister Iron said. "She did not teach me to fight like that." She stepped back, allowing Nona to sit.

Sister Tallow stepped forward, offering Nona her hand and then pulling her to her feet. "You seemed to be in pain while fighting, novice. Did you sustain some injury sparring with Arabella?"

"No, Mistress Blade. Just an old injury returned to haunt me." Nona sealed her lips. Joeli's reinstatement was a matter of palace politics. Even if the abbess could be convinced of her guilt, a Namsis would not be punished or sent from the convent. Not with the Scithrowl in the east advancing mile after mile and the Durns raiding from captured ports on the shores of the Marn.

Sister Iron studied Nona with evident displeasure. "The question is whether the Ancestor would be properly represented by such a warrior. Where was your serenity? You fight like a wild animal. I cannot recommend you be given an ancient blade. Would it even be proper for you to wear the Red?"

Nona ground her teeth. Revealing Joeli's tricks might change the judgment but she wanted nothing of the Namsis girl in her trial. Others would say Joeli's actions earned her the Red, then stand between her and her revenge.

"She is to be denied the Red then. Sister Iron has said so!" Wheel called down from the stands, her cracked voice reverberating with long-sought triumph.

"*When* we leave this hall Sister Iron will be Mistress Blade." Sister Tallow raised her voice, a thing Nona had heard on maybe three occasions in the half of her life spent at Sweet Mercy. "But she is not yet." Tallow set her hand on Nona's shoulder. She had to reach up. Once she had seemed so tall. She had no recollection of the woman touching anyone except to adjust a fighting stance or deliver a stinging reprimand. The hand remained on her shoulder. "Nona has passed the Blade-test. If she accepts ordination and takes on her new name, then when I take up the devotions of a Holy Sister she shall have my sword." Tallow turned towards Iron, her voice low now, conciliatory. "Many of the lessons I tried to teach this girl have not stuck. But the important ones have. And when the ice presses we need sisters in the Red who can win, however ugly that victory may be."

What followed passed in a blur. The bows given to, and reciprocated by, the sisters superior, the required formal embrace with the abbess, the long march from the hall. Before she knew it Nona found herself hurrying from the building, the Blade-test behind her. With her arms raised against the sharp burden of ice carried on the wind she set off to find her friends.

+ + +

NONA CAME DRIPPING and shivering to the well-head. It lay in a seldom-used back chamber to the rear of the laundry wing, a structure that formed one arm of the novice cloister. She defocused her sight to check for any traps Joeli might have placed. She didn't think the girl knew of the oubliette beneath the centre oak, but then again there were clues if one paid attention, and in past weeks she had seen Joeli gazing at the laundry wing, her brow furrowed.

Nona went down the rope hand over hand, not using her legs. The Blade-test had left her muscles tired and aching but not so weak she couldn't climb a rope. At the bottom she swung, released her hold, and landed on the rocky edge of the subterranean pool. Jula, Ruli, Ara, and Ketti waited to one side of the chamber, hunched around a single candle. Glimmers of their light picked out the descending, stone-clad forest of the centre oak's roots.

"Nona! Sister Tallow didn't cut your head off!" Ruli jumped to her feet as Nona approached.

"It was Sister Iron, our new Mistress Blade." Nona wasn't supposed to speak about the test but she felt she could share this much.

"New what?"

"But Sister Tallow—"

"Did you pass?" Ara cut across the others.

"Yes, I passed." Nona raised a hand to forestall Ara's next question. "And I got a sword."

"We're not to call you Nona Pink then?" Jula grinned.

"No." Nona sat down with Ruli. "If they let me take my orders I'll be a proper Red."

"So how did—"

"We're not here to talk about my Blade-test," Nona said. "We're here to talk about Jula's book."

"Hey, it's not *my* book," Jula protested.

"A pity. If it was your book we wouldn't have to go to all this trouble to steal it." Ketti frowned, then brightened as if finding new resolve.

"We've been talking through it again, Nona. We're agreed. We need two things to pull this off, and we're going to have to steal both of them, and I've no idea how." Ara held up two fingers to count them off.

"We have to steal before we can steal," Ruli interrupted, showing no sign of remorse at the proposed criminality. "And we're meeting underground with one candle. It's like we're Noi-Guin!"

Ara scowled at Ruli's enthusiasm. "One, we need the *Book of Lost Cities* from Sister Pan's secret stash. That's got to be in the Third Room. Unless we have a forbidden book to take back we're not going to have a reason to be anywhere near the high priest's vault." She pulled her second finger back. "Two, we need the abbess's seal of office. Without her seal on our message they'll never let us in."

Nona raised one of her fingers. "We also need the eye-drops the Poisoner was working on."

Jula looked shocked. "She stashed those away for good reason, Nona. They're dangerous. She said you could go blind using them."

"They're the only way I'll get in there unrecognised," Nona said.

"Plus they make you look good," Ketti added.

"It doesn't have to be you, Nona," Ara said. "Any of us could do it."

"It has to be me. And it doesn't matter about looking good, Ketti." Nona shot her a narrow glance. Though it was true that she had loved those few days when her eyes had looked like any other person's. Regol had said he liked her the way she was normally. Unique. But whatever he said he had spent a long time looking into her newly cleared eyes and part of her wanted that again. "Four!" Nona said before Ara and Jula could object. "We need a brilliant marjal empath or this just won't work."

"So, four impossible things then." Ara swirled darkness around the candle flame, making shadow birds take flight.

"No." Nona shook her head. "Just two. Like you said."

"But—"

"I found us an empath at the fight rings last night. The strongest I've ever met." Four mouths opened. Nona spoke first. "And I have this." She drew from her habit a disc of amber, carved in deep relief on one side, its edge guarded by a hoop of gold, the whole thing making slow revolutions on its golden chain.

"The abbess's seal . . ." Jula stared at it, wide-eyed. "How . . . ?"

"I stole it from her when she embraced me after the Blade-test."

6

———— ✦ ————

HOLY CLASS

Present Day

KETTLE MOVED THROUGH the town wrapped in a cocoon of shadow. In an hour the great red eye of the sun would see the carnage for itself but no other witness remained to watch it roll back the night. The fires had burned out, the smoke stripped away by the wind, but the stink of burning remained. The stink and the dead and the ruins of their homes.

The Scithrowl had spared none. They left the corpses of their own scattered infrequently here and there among the bodies of farmers, weavers, shepherds, and of children who might one day have taken up those trades. A small blond girl lay broken in the doorway to an unburned hut, her hair straw and mud. A woman nearby curled around the wound that had killed her. The mud showed how far she had dragged herself to reach her daughter, but she had died three yards short of touching her child that last time.

In the harbour a single boat still burned amid the blackened and half-sunken wrecks. From behind Kettle's eyes Nona wondered what its cargo was that it should sustain a flame when all else had long since guttered into darkness. She knew that Kettle had drawn her sleeping mind along their thread-bond to show her something. Too often lately Nona had rolled yawning from her bed after first waking in the small hours to find herself inhabiting Kettle as the Grey Sister stalked her prey. Last time it had been a Scithrowl commander amid his army of five hundred soldiers. Kettle had ghosted among the lesser tents and cut her way into the grand pavilion in which the officer slept beneath hoola furs. Nona could make no sense of it: signposting their leaders with such luxury. The empire generals slept in tents identical to those of the common soldiers to foil just such assassination attempts.

Kettle turned from the dark lake and moved on through the town towards its margins. She had something to show Nona. She rarely spoke on these tutorials, needing all her focus to keep herself alive. Even here Scithrowl softmen might be lurking, ready to kill or capture scouts, or Noi-Guin assassins, loyal to neither side, only to the coin that paid their fee.

Ahead of them loomed a larger building, no detail hidden from Kettle's darksight. A stone construction, the roof gone, presumably taken by flames, though the stink of burning hung less heavily here. Kettle closed the distance. Grave markers stood behind the building. Dozens of them. A church then. Kettle glanced skyward to where the Hope burned white amid the crimson-scattered heavens. A Hope church then, roofless by design so that the white light could reach in and wash away all sin.

And suddenly, as Kettle approached the shattered doors, Nona knew where she was. White Lake, not eighty miles from the walls of Verity. White Lake, where her mother lay beneath the ground and doubtless now Preacher Mickel lay sprawled upon it. Adoma had splinter armies pillaging just five days' march from the capital. Swift horses could bring them to the foot of the Rock of Faith in less than half that time.

Something caught Kettle's eye. Something Nona had missed. Kettle pressed herself to the church wall, pulling darkness to herself as if drawing a breath. The night entered her as ink soaks into blotting paper. There, out across the graveyard, a pale, questing tentacle, almost flat to the ground, insubstantial as mist. Another, yards long, snaking out between the graves. A pain spider, some creature of the softmen in service to the Scithrowl battle-queen Adoma. Rumour had it that they bred such monstrosities, releasing demons from the black ice into unholy alliance with flesh.

More tentacles insinuated themselves across the barren ground, one thin as leather and broad as a hand sliding noiselessly over the top of the church wall just yards from Kettle's head. Even at that distance her skin sang with echoes of the agony its touch would bring.

Nona woke sweat-soaked and alone, her body hunched, arms tight around her. She lay in the darkness of the Holy Class dormitory trying to still a racing heart. Kettle had kicked her out, requiring her whole concentration.

Sleep did not return that night. They were coming to the sharp end of things. The peace of the convent, seemingly eternal, would not last. Idle days, bickering among friends, the rivalries of children, all of it was passing into memory. A black tide was coming from the east and all the empire hadn't the strength to stand before it.

"WE DON'T EVEN know the book exists. It's not as if the high priest posts a list of forbidden books on his door." Ara stood with Jula and Nona in the lee of the Dome of the Ancestor, watching Path Tower, a dark finger of stone.

"The Inquisition burned my *History of Saint Devid*," Nona said.

"It wasn't yours, and Kettle shouldn't have allowed it in the scriptorium library," Jula said primly. "And that was a banned book, not a forbidden one. Banned books are burned, forbidden ones are just . . . forbidden."

"So how come Sister Pan has one, if it even exists?" Ara asked.

"We know it exists because there are references to it that they forgot to remove from other books by Aquinas. And we know that Sister Pan has a copy because she quotes from it when talking about the lost cities."

"You haven't read it! How do you know she's quoting from it?" Ara rolled her eyes.

"Aquinas has a very distinctive prose style." Jula folded her arms.

"That's it? We're breaking into Sister Pan's secret room based on *distinctive prose style*?" Ara asked.

"How do you know she hasn't memorized the quotes?" Nona demanded.

"She still calls you Nina sometimes." Jula grinned.

"Fair point." Nona nodded slowly. "So I just have to get into the Third Room . . ."

"Or I do," Ara said.

"Do you know how?" Nona asked.

"No, but you don't either."

Nona started towards the tower. "We'll both try, then."

NONA NARROWED HER eyes at Path Tower, black against the wash of the sky. Sister Rule taught that it was the oldest building on the Rock of Faith, predating the convent by centuries. Given that all save the top and bottom-most rooms lacked doors or windows, Nona supposed it had been built for a powerful Path-mage though no records remained to name the first occupant. She approached the east entrance, apprehension rising. It wasn't as if they were about to attempt the impossible. Every novice with ambitions to be a Mystic Sister had to enter the Third Room unaided. It was part of the Path-test. Maybe all of it. Nona would choose the red habit, not the sky colours of the Mystics, but she wanted to pass the Path-test even so.

Ruli followed Nona in through the east door; Ara entered by the north. They met at the bottom of the stairs in the room of portraits. Two dozen or more Mystic Sisters regarded them from wooden frames. Each woman was pictured amid abstract representations of her magic, the variety remarkable. Nona's favourite was a young redheaded Holy Witch whose hair became flames. When you looked closer at her you could see that in the darkness of each pupil a tiny star burned crimson.

"We know two things," Nona said as Ara joined them.

"What?"

"Firstly it's all about Path. Otherwise Joeli would have cracked it months ago." Ara and Nona had been waiting an age for the individual training Sister Pan gave candidates for the Path-test. The old woman liked to instruct one novice at a time and whatever lessons she had been trying to teach hadn't been getting through Joeli's skull. "Joeli Namsis couldn't take two steps on the Path if you threw her at it."

"True . . ." Ara nodded.

"And secondly we know that it must be different for each person, otherwise Pan would just have trained the three of us together."

Ara began to climb the stairs, Jula and Nona on her heels. They went up in silence, stopping just below the classroom.

"Should we really be doing this?" Jula asked for the tenth time that morning.

"No," said Ara.

"We're not doing this. At least you aren't, Jula. And it was your idea! Forget whether we should be doing it. Will the book get us into the high priest's library? Will the library have Aquinas's *Book of the Moon*? And will the moon save the empire?" Nona watched the girl's face, pale in the daylight that filtered down from the trapdoor to the classroom.

"The moon's the only hope," Jula said, her voice small.

Nona nodded. Jula had real faith in Aquinas and his book. Kettle had shown Nona the conflict's horrors through their thread-bond. The empire was losing on both fronts. It would not be long before those horrors arrived at Verity's walls, and if the emperor fell, then the empire was lost, the Ark taken. Kettle had said the end would come in months rather than years. The Grey Sister scouted for the emperor's armies both east and west. Adoma's hordes seemed to be endlessly replaced, ready to spend their lives for the battle-queen, and she ready to spend them. Sherzal had all but filled the Grand Pass with Scithrowl corpses and still they had flooded over the Grampains.

The ferocity of Sherzal's defence and the cleverness of her stepped retreat had been what forced the emperor to overlook reports of her planned treason. Sherzal had organised and directed the ongoing attacks in the mountains to continually disrupt Adoma's supply lines. That and a scorched-earth withdrawal had slowed Adoma's advance from a charge that would have reached Verity in weeks to a crawl that had taken almost two years to get just over halfway, but like with thin ice, a slow creaking could become a sudden plunge into freezing death, and the empire's defence had started to fracture weeks ago. Emperor Crucical needed his sister.

The Durns to the west were a different breed, not fanatics these, and given to quarrelling among themselves, but blood-hungry and backed by the magics of their priests. They had crossed the Marn Sea in their barges, coming in force once news of the Scithrowl victories reached them. Their holy men came to war wielding sickwood staves and wreaking havoc with both marjal fire-work and water-work. Nona had seen too many towns aflame, too many families strewn across the fields from which they tried to feed themselves.

The emperor kept the Red and the Grey close, and the Mystics as a last reserve, but soon he would unleash them all. Whether that would turn the tide of war, push the Scithrowl back beyond the mountains, drown the Durns in a red sea, Nona didn't know. She only knew that in the land left behind such a conflict, the dead would outnumber the living.

SISTER PAN ALWAYS led the way when she took novices to the sealed rooms. She had taken Nona and Ara to the first two rooms. The third they knew to exist only because the tower held space for it and because every novice knew that the Path-test required you to reach the Third Room unaided. Nona turned and walked down the spiral stair, squeezing past Ara and

Jula. She defocused her vision as she always did when she followed Sister Pan to the sealed rooms. Normally that gaze would be fixed between the ancient's shoulder blades. She focused her thoughts on the Third Room: the place where it should lie, the shape of it, the wall where a door would likely be set.

Nona was so deep in her search it was a shock to find someone on the stairs blocking her way as she followed the spiral down. "Abbess . . ." The abbess rarely came to Path Tower.

"Where's Pan?" the abbess snapped, eyeing the girl before her with evident distaste.

"Mistress Path is in the scriptorium, abbess." Nona met the hostility of the old woman's stare.

"Hmmph." The abbess turned away, evidently unable to find fault with Nona's reply, her bad temper further inflamed by this failure. She glanced over her shoulder, new suspicion in her pale eyes. "What are you doing here, girl? Stealing?"

"No, abbess." Nona had stolen from the abbess that morning, and she would be stealing from Path Tower this afternoon with any luck. But right now she wasn't stealing.

"Praying, in the Dome, that's where you should be." Shaking her head, the abbess stamped off back down the stairs, thumping her crozier on every step.

Ara came into view behind Nona, smoothing her palms over the stonework. "Was that Abbess Wheel?"

"Yes." Nona returned to her own search.

"Ancestor's blood!" From behind Ara. As close as Jula got to an oath. "We really shouldn't be doing this."

Nona searched more quickly than her friends, leaving them behind her. About halfway down, her vision shook for a moment. After that, nothing. Not even a tingle. She returned to the spot and studied it with threadsight. Nothing. She visualised the Path and tried to see past it into the wall.

Nothing. She placed both hands upon the stone and exerted her will, pressing as hard as she could. "Open, damn you!" At the same time she set one foot upon the glowing glory of Path, the river of power that joins and defines all things. Nona felt something give, a lurch within her as if she had fallen through thin ice. The cry of victory died on her lips, though. She was still standing on the stairs, her hands against the cold stone. Feeling foolish, she reached for her serenity and tried again. Nothing, not even a twinge. She wiped her palms on her habit and continued down the stairs, calling on her clarity trance to reveal any faint trace that might indicate a place to exert her magics.

One of the others stumbled behind her. "Keep it quiet," Nona hissed without looking back. "Abbess Wheel might still be lurking downstairs."

Nona reached the bottom step without finding any further hint of an entrance. The abbess seemed to have decided against waiting for Pan and to have taken her leave of the tower. Nona sighed and turned to climb the steps again. Something caught her eye. A new portrait hanging amid the others. Just to the right of the door that the abbess had left by. She walked across to the painting, marvelling that she had never seen it before. It seemed impossible that she had simply missed it in the past given that she had visited the tower almost every day for the best part of a decade. Perhaps Sister Pan had hung it recently. There was something familiar about the woman: her face pinched but friendly, high cheekbones, blue eyes. She had pale hair, curling close to her skull but with wisp after wisp trailing off into the air to create a faint haze of threads that filled the space all around her.

Nona cocked her head. The nun looked thirty at least. And yet . . .

"Hessa?" Nona's eyes blurred with tears. "How—" She bowed her head, wiping at her face. Hessa had died as a child and Nona had missed her friend every day since. Her death at Yisht's hands had taught Nona many of the bitter lessons that stand as milestones along the road between girl and woman. Her own fallibility wasn't the least of those lessons. How many times had a friend died because she lacked what had been necessary to save

them? How often had her own faults tripped her up? Her pride, her anger . . .
Losing Hessa taught her the hollow lie of vengeance, a conceit to distract
oneself with, an addiction that offered no cure.

"I miss you." But as she looked up again the world lurched, a new layer
of ice breaking, and somehow the room was a different room and she was
on her knees beside a bed.

"Nona?" Abbess Glass lay in the bed, grey-faced, the comfortable weight
wasted from her, leaving skin on bones. "Don't cry, child."

Nona snapped her head up, looking wildly around. The abbess's bed-
room in the big house. This was where she had died. This was how she
died. Taken by disease, something that ate her from within and that neither Sister Rose nor Sister Apple could touch with all their pills and po-
tions.

"I don't understand . . ."

"Meaning is overrated, Nona." A cough convulsed the abbess for a moment, rattling in her chest. She had said exactly that, *meaning is overrated*;
Nona remembered it, but not the question she had asked to prompt it.
"There might not be a meaning to the world, or in it, but that does not mean
that what we do has no meaning." Glass fell silent and for the longest minute Nona thought she would not speak again. When she did it was weak,
faltering. "The Ancestor's tree is something humanity planted and that we
have watered with our deeds, our cares, with each act of love, even with our
cruelty. Cling to it, Nona. Cling . . ." And then she did stop, as Nona remembered, and the gleam had gone from her eyes.

Nona stood, an old sob shuddering through her. Sister Rose had been
sleeping in the chair by the window when the abbess died, the sleep that
crept in behind too many nights without rest. She had woken at Nona's sob
and sucked in a huge breath of her own. Now, though, the chair sat empty
and at the door it was Sister Pan who stood, her eyes bright and wet.

The old nun spoke, her voice strangely distant. "You're getting farther
from the door, Nona."

"What?"

Sister Pan turned towards the window. Out beyond the rooftops of the refectory Path Tower rose like the line of darkness offered by a door beginning to open, or almost closed.

Nona frowned, torn between confusion and grief. She knew this for a memory of that awful day but it seemed more real than all those days that had queued between her and it. Glass had been taken by a foe Nona couldn't stand against and the heart of Sweet Mercy had broken. She had thought when the shipheart was stolen and the convent left cold, its magic gone, that no greater blow could be struck against it. But the abbess had always been the true heart of Sweet Mercy and the emptiness she left behind was more profound than any Nona had known.

"You're getting farther from the door." Sister Pan stood in the doorway but her single hand pointed at Path Tower. And in an instant the tower raced into the distance, becoming tiny, almost lost to sight. The room had gone, Abbess Glass and Sister Pan with it, and instead Nona stood in sunshine gazing out across a formal garden. She staggered, seized by vertigo, but prevented herself from falling.

She took a step forward, focused on a ficus tree in full bloom. The sound of a heavy blow hitting flesh arrested her. A second blow and an agonized cry turned her around.

Standing before the grand colonnade of his mansion, High Priest Jacob swung his staff again. The wood thunked into Four-Foot's side, a dull sound like a hammer hitting meat, and the mule grunted his pain.

"No!" The horror of the moment pinned Nona to the spot. Another blow descended and her flaw-blades shimmered into being around both hands. "No!"

Nona tensed as the high priest raised his staff, Four-Foot snorting bloody foam about his muzzle. She knew it was memory or dream but it seemed more real than her life, more solid, more important. Losses like Hessa and Abbess Glass, horrors like Four-Foot's death, were nails struck into her life, pinning those moments to her forever, the punctuation of sorrow. She could no more tear herself from the scene before her than rip the skin from her body.

Markus, impossibly young, struggled at the limit of his strength to escape the grip of the high priest's guard, wild in his passion. Giljohn stood at the cart, held by bonds of the sort that no child can see, the kind made of debt and of a bitter understanding of the world's truths, the kind that tear at a life as you struggle against them and leave wounds that won't heal.

Nona thanked the Ancestor that here in this strange dream the chains of duty and service had no purchase on her. Every muscle gathered itself as she prepared to leap at High Priest Jacob, ready to rend him into pieces.

It was raining that day. The heavens wept to see such cruelty.

At the back of Nona's mind a small voice asked why it wasn't raining.

Her leap never happened. Unbalanced, she fell to her knees, hands upon the dry stones of the path. It had been raining. It had. The water had run from Giljohn's empty socket like the tears he should have shed. Nona looked up. She knew it to be memory. She knew there was nothing she could do for the mule straining against his rope, or Markus twisting in the grasp of Jacob's guard. Even so her mind clamoured for revenge, for the joy of bloody retribution. She stood, blades ready, intent on attack.

Some distant glint caught her eye. Over the wall of the garden. Over the roofs of nearby mansions, out across the five miles of farmland to the Rock of Faith. Her gaze drawn to the tiny bumps that at this distance were all the Convent of Sweet Mercy had to offer. Again the glint. The sun reflecting on a window, perhaps. A stained-glass window high in Path Tower? Something told her she needed to be there. A path seemed to stretch out before her in that direction.

You're getting farther from the door.

Gritting her jaw against the sound of blows raining down on Four-Foot, Nona ran. She refused to look away from the Rock and from the convent's faint outline. She climbed the wall with a great leap and a lunge.

As Nona dropped into the next garden the convent vanished behind the chimneys of the neighbouring mansion. She made to rise but the wall's shadow deepened into night, miring her like the thickest mud. "No!" She struggled, desperate to return to the convent, but the darkness took her into some other place and a night filled with screaming and with fire.

Nona stood between two dark buildings. She looked slowly around, less worried by any danger than by what new tragedy might unfold, by what black milestone of her life this nightmare had brought her to.

Across an open space in front of her another building burned, the flames so bright that even the dying focus of the moon seemed pale. And although the night gave her nothing but angles and the ferocity of fire, Nona knew exactly where she stood. To her right, the home of James and Martha Baker. To her left, the stone walls of Grey Stephen's house, he who had fought the Pelarthi in his youth. Rellam Village burned around her. The shapes moving across the background of blazing huts were those of children she had grown up with, of their parents, and of the soldiers the emperor's sister had sent to cut them down.

Nona knew it for illusion or forgery or memory or all three woven together. Somehow she had fallen into a trap. Perhaps it had happened when she touched the Path. Sister Pan had endless stories of the dire ends to which it could lead the unwary, and used them regularly to scare any quantal novice in her care. Nona had to get back to Path Tower but the chance was gone and every shift of scene took her farther from the convent, putting mile upon mile in her way and allowing no time to cross them. Whatever had gone wrong, it must have happened when she had tried to walk through the wall to the Third Room. She had wandered into some realm of nightmare manufactured out of her past.

Nona ran through the darkness and smoke and confusion, ready to meet any challenge. Though she told herself that a lie surrounded her, the truth of it seduced her senses. There was nothing counterfeit here. Beneath the stink of burning, this place smelled of home, of a childhood now wrapped about her bones. This was hers, like it or not, her foundation though it stood in mud and ignorance.

Somehow no soldier came near her. Within moments she stood at the door to her mother's cottage. The two rooms where she had spent so many years, growing from mewling infant to the girl who had taken half a dozen lives in the forest upon her doorstep. It was the price of one of those lives in particular that the whole village was now paying for her.

The thatch above had begun to smoulder, sparks from the Bluestones' house starting to land among the straw. The interior lay dark. "It's not real." Nona approached the entrance. Something would be different. Something would be wrong. Every scene so far had someone out of place, some detail changed. It was a clue, a riddle. Somehow. She stepped in, steeling herself, pulling her serenity around her like a shawl. "It's not real."

It took a moment for Nona's eyes to adjust to the gloom. A single candle burned, spilling wax where it had fallen at the doorway to her mother's workroom, the place where she wove the reeds. Nona's mother lay sprawled, one arm reaching for the exit, her fingers nearly touching the toes of Nona's shoes. A ruinous wound had opened her back, the blood pooling around her, the candle's flame dancing across it in reflection. And despite all her protestations a hurt noise broke from Nona's chest, a wet splutter, a numbness in her cheeks as she fell to her knees, hot tears jolted from her eyes by the impact with the hard-packed earth. Nona's serenity shattered. She stayed on all fours, heaving in broken breaths. Her mother lay dead. Her mother. No matter what had passed between them there had always been a bond of love buried beneath the denials. Gentle times remembered, shared smiles, laughter, hugs. The bonds that formed a branch of the great tree of the Ancestor, a chain of humanity reaching back through eons to the singular taproot of the arborat.

Nona panted away the hurt and rose to her knees. This was the test. This was the trap. She wiped her eyes, sought her centre.

"Somewhere, it must be somewhere." She stood and cast around her.

Something must be wrong. Something out of place? The serenity trance insulated her against grief but her eyes kept returning to her mother's body, small and broken. "There's nothing . . ." Nona fell back to her knees, drawn down despite her trance by a weight she couldn't understand. Tears returned to fill her eyes, blurring her vision as she gathered the woman who had been her everything into her lap.

". . . tired . . ."

"Mother?" Nona blinked away the tears. But the brown eyes she found herself looking down into were not her mother's; the hand that enfolded hers was huge.

"Darla?" Nona choked out her friend's name.

Darla's brown eyes clouded with confusion, a kind of wonder, staring at some distant place above Nona's head. The smoke and fire around them wasn't that of Rellam Village. It was Sherzal's stables starting to burn. The eighty miles to Path Tower had become hundreds.

"She's gone, Nona." Kettle put her hand on Nona's shoulder.

"Darla . . ." Another raw wound. Nona ground her teeth. Darla's hand still held hers, warm, solid, real. Maybe she could still be saved . . . Maybe *this* time it would be different.

To drag her eyes from Darla's almost broke Nona. To turn her face from a friend who needed her, a *dying* friend. "It's not real." Nona swung her head around, trying to call the clarity trance though her heart ached and pounded. "None of it's real."

"Nona . . ." Kettle shook her head slowly as if the sorrow had made it too heavy. "We have to go."

"There!" Amid the swirls of smoke and the red tongues of fire a door that had not been present when all this happened, a door with no place in Sherzal's stables and no place to lead.

"Nona!" Cries from the great carriage before the main exit. "We need you."

Letting Darla's head fall felt like the ultimate betrayal. Every part of her wanted to stay. Every part of her wanted to face the danger with her friends. To save them. To do it better this time.

But she sprang to her feet and threw herself across the burning hall even as the door upon which her eyes were fixed started to fade from view.

"No!" She reached it just as the last lines melted away. "No!" Flaw-blades dug deep and in a frenzy of hacking and a storm of splinters . . . Nona staggered through.

Curved, sigil-crowded walls surrounded her, the inlaid silver gleaming in a light that seemed to be dying swiftly. Nona turned in time to see a doorway fading, and beyond it the spiral steps of Path Tower. A person's shadow, Ruli's or Ara's, lay across stone steps lit by the coloured whispers of the day that shone in the classroom above, streaming in through stained-glass windows.

A moment later the doorway had gone and Nona stood blind and alone.

"It wasn't true. Any of it." Whispered to the darkness.

Some of it was true, though. Abbess Glass had died and Sweet Mercy would never be the same again.

7

THE ESCAPE

Three Years Earlier

"THEY'RE CATCHING UP again." Nona hunched against the hard-packed snow, too cold to shiver now. The wind stole her words and ran away with them, howling. Sherzal's soldiers knew the mountains and had found better routes to gain the heights. Nona could see black figures to the south, little more than dots, almost at the shoulder between two peaks where she and Zole would have to cross if they were to make further progress towards the ice sheet.

"We have to go down." Zole pointed to an icy defile where the east side of the ridge had fractured along some hidden fault line.

"Down?" Nona tried to imagine any way she could achieve that other than falling. "That's Scithrowl." She stared at the foothills, hazy in the distance and partly obscured by wisps of cloud around the waist of the mountains.

"They will be unlikely to follow us there." Zole shrugged and continued along the ridge. Their path proved to be a serrated blade of stone coated with two feet of icy snow on the southern face and with black ice on the northern side.

THE DESCENT PROVED as hard as the ascent, though in different ways. It found a whole new set of muscles to stress. Nona's legs began to feel as if they belonged to someone else, paying scant regard to her instructions but letting her have full share of the hurting. Several times she started to fall and saved herself only by digging her flaw-blades through ice into rock. They climbed down for an hour and the world below seemed to grow no closer, though the expanse of black rock towering behind them assured her that they were making progress.

The wind blew less fiercely on the slopes that faced Queen Adoma's lands but it was far from calm. The clouds surged below them, lapping the slopes like a grey sea. Nona heard shouts before they reached the swirling layer of mist, and looking back she saw that those leading the pursuit were less than a hundred yards away. A spear rattled past her.

"We will lose them in the clouds," Zole said. She hopped down from rock to rock, making it seem that her legs were as fresh as if she'd just got out of bed. Coming to the spear, jammed against an outcrop, she picked it up.

Nona followed, frowning at the clouds. "We'll lose ourselves in there too." But she supposed "down" to be an easy direction to follow whatever the visibility.

The mist rose to meet their descent, a cold white sea wrapping them, beading Zole's hair with jewels of dew that froze into tiny pearls. Nona stumbled on in exhaustion, the shipheart's fire filling her mind with unfocused energy but doing nothing for the muscles in her thighs.

"Have you been into Scithrowl before?" Nona asked, sliding down onto a ledge as Zole led off.

"No."

"Their armies are at the border . . ."

"If we need to kill soldiers to get to the ice, would it not be better that they were Scithrowl?"

"I suppose so . . ." Nona had a fear of the Scithrowl, a heritage of endless stories told across the Grey. She expected that every part of the empire had its tales of Scithrowl horrors. Told no doubt by old ladies like Nana Even who hadn't ever been sufficiently far east to glimpse the Grampain peaks, let alone an actual heretic. Did they burn prisoners, eat babies, and practise peculiar tortures? Best not to get captured and find out.

The wind began to shred the cloud layer around them, tearing the whiteness across the flanks of the mountain and affording glimpses of Scithrowl stretching east. It looked remarkably like the empire had from the other side. In the north the ice was a glimmering white line; to the south it lay less than five miles away, a vaulting wall, all in shadow now.

"The ice." Nona stopped. She had seen the Corridor's great wall before, shorn off by the focus moon, but for the first time ever she had the elevation to look down upon what lay beyond. Zole stopped too. Even a life on the shelf itself didn't offer an overview. Mile upon mile of merciless ice, bloody with the touch of the morning sun. Here and there internal pressures rucked the sheet up into ridges or split it with chasms that looked like wrinkles at this distance but must be large enough to swallow any tower built by man. The roots of the Grampains cut across the ice every few miles, grey ribs of stone stretching from the main ridge, becoming frost-wrapped and at last drowned beneath the glacial flow.

"It is . . . a sight to behold." Zole stood statue-still, the wind tugging at her cloak.

"The black ice!" Nona pointed at a wound in the ice sheet; you could almost imagine it a hole, its sides shadowed. A black teardrop, impossible not to see now that her eyes had found it, haloed in grey, shading through the surrounding ice and drawn away to the north with the ice's flow in a broad path, dark grey at the centre. Where the grey streak across the surface reached the Corridor the ice wall also shaded grey and the land all around lay barren, a dead zone reaching out into the farmlands of the Sci-throwl levels. The margins of this dead zone were edged in brown where the Corridor's flora fought to endure. In the narrow gap between the tainted area and foothills of the Grampains to the west a chain of four fortresses stepped from one ridge to the next towards the clear ice.

Zole allowed a moment to rest. Nona collapsed into the lee of an out-crop. She huddled there, shivering, and stared at Scithrowl, stretching end-lessly to the east. The land lay green and grey, shadowed by scudding cloud, and further coloured by the rumoured cruelties of its people. If the stories were to be believed their queen was a monster, darker by far than Sherzal.

Sister Kettle had told Nona the story of her mission years earlier to learn Queen Adoma's secrets, passing images of that time along the thread-bond that bound them. Memories shared in such a manner strike hard and often burn as bright as the recipient's own until it becomes hard to tell them from genuine recollection.

Kettle was not the first or the last Grey Sister to be sent to Adoma's capital, but she had come closer to the queen than any other of the order had managed in a long time. Close enough to stand within her court in the guise of a Noi-Guin and listen to the queen hold forth to her nobles.

Among the glittering crowds beneath the palace's gilt roof Kettle had seen half a dozen of the Scithrowls' most feared Path-mages standing shoul-der to shoulder with the nobility. Each of these full-blood quantals wore a golden medallion marking them as members of Adoma's Fist, a band of quantal and marjal mages whose reputation was known far beyond the bor-ders of both Scithrowl and the empire. It was said that when Adoma's Fist struck even the ice shook.

Their leader, Yom Rala, had stood before the throne on the first step of the dais, a place of high honour. Kettle described him as a chewed stick of a man with a predilection for scarlet finery.

"He may look weak and foolish," Kettle had said, "but when he turns his gaze your way it's as if he's uncoiling every secret you own, and where he steps the ground is left smoking. Pray the Scithrowls' wars in the east keep the Fist on Ald's borders rather than our own!"

Adoma had spoken on the subject of the west and of Scithrowl's destiny to claim the coast of Marn.

Nona had seen the queen through Kettle's eyes. A tall woman, blunt-faced, solid, conveying a sense of physical power, of barely suppressed energies. Black-haired, a frothing mass of curls contained by hoops of gold, her pale skin stained and streaked as if rubbed with fresh ink. This, the Scithrowl said, was Adoma's sacrifice. In order to secure the strength to lead her people to victory she had dared the black ice and been marked by it.

Adoma's enemies called her mad, blood-drunk, cruel beyond measure, ready to inflict any torture that imagination could frame. Her people called her ruthless, relentless, born to deliver the full length of the Corridor into their keeping.

When she spoke, though, addressing her court in the fluid Scithrowl tongue, Kettle found her articulate and entirely reasonable.

"If I were a Scithrowl I would follow her," Kettle had said. "She's right. The ice is closing on us and how else are we to live but to forge east or west? The world is cruel, our choices harsh, and every alternative leads to someone's death. The only objection I have is that it's *us* that she plans to forge a path through."

However inspiring her speeches might be, the truth of the battle-queen lay in the black ice, that place of horror where even Kettle had lost her way, and from where Adoma was said to gain her power. Kettle would share no memories of that darkness, only the conviction that nothing save evil could come from it.

ZOLE GLANCED AT the cloud base billowing just a hundred feet above them and made to move on. "Come."

"I saw it. The devil." Nona hadn't meant to speak. Maybe the sight of the black ice put it in her mind. "I saw it at your wrist when you climbed onto the road."

Zole hesitated, just missing a beat, then continued her descent. "I did not think that I had any more left in me."

"Any more?" Nona hurried after her, gritting her teeth against the shipheart's pressure.

"It seems that it might take a shipheart from each of the bloods to wholly purify us. Or perhaps it is just me who needs that."

"Purify? What are you talking—" Nona slipped, one tired foot tangled the other, and she was falling. She clung to the moment but although she fell through treacle she still fell, her hands too far from any surface to save her.

"Careful." Zole closed the gap with hunska speed and caught her wrist.

Nona shook free and wordlessly scrambled away from the shipheart, its fire burning in her blood.

"Do you think that in all the vastness of the ice there are no more of these?" Zole jerked her head back towards her pack. "None of your 'shiphearts'? You think they exist only in this narrow strip of Abeth where green things still grow?"

"Well . . ." Nona hadn't really thought about it. "But the ice covers . . ."

"There are ways down. And the ice-tribes are the descendants of those who refused to run before its advance, peoples who walked the green face of Abeth thousands of years ago. They took their treasures up onto the ice with them."

Zole moved on and for what seemed an age it was all Nona could do to keep up with her. The ice-triber stopped where a trickle of freezing water spilled from a crack in the rocks. "Drink." She began to fill her waterskin.

Nona found a still smaller trickle spilling from an overhang and stood with her mouth open to receive it. After a few gulps she stepped away. "You have a devil in you, one of those . . . did you call them *klaulathu*?"

"You had a *klaulathu* under your skin, Nona Grey, an echo of the Missing. This"—she opened her hand and the palm lay scarlet—"is a *raulathu*, it is not of the Missing. It is an echo of me."

"I don't understand."

Zole narrowed her eyes; she looked past Nona, up at the slopes above her. "The clouds did not slow them as much as I had hoped. They have found us again." She turned and dropped away, landing on a huge boulder twenty feet below the ledge that Nona's stream trickled over.

Nona peered over the drop. "Damn." She glanced up at the dark spots moving on the higher slopes. With a shrug she gathered her aching body into a focused knot, stepped out into space, and let the fall have her.

THEY LEFT THE clouds behind them, clinging to the mountains' shoulders, and early sunshine welcomed the two novices into the eastern foothills. Nothing dared the rugged terrain save a few varieties of wire-grass and the goats that pursued them up from the plains. Zole led the way although she had no better idea of the geography than Nona, both of them relying on memories of Sister Rule's endless maps. They moved quickly, following streams down into the valleys, alert for any herders checking on their flocks.

"It could be the empire," Zole said. "It looks no different from the other side."

"A couple of centuries ago it was the empire."

"Perhaps the people will not be so different either, for all that Sister Wheel calls them eaters of children and deviants." Zole veered up towards the crest of the valley.

"Maybe." Nona felt it hard to shake off the expectations built by a hundred fireside tales so easily. She fixed her eyes on Zole's back and forced unwilling legs to match the girl's pace down the slope. Sherzal's soldiers appeared to have given up the chase, not prepared to venture onto Scithrowl territory. Of the Noi-Guin there was no sign, but Nona doubted that they would relent so easily. Even if their shipheart weren't at stake.

"This devil of yours . . ." Nona returned to the conversation abandoned on the rock-faces far above them.

"A *raulathu*."

"It's some part of you that the shipheart has . . . broken off?"

"An impurity of the spirit. In this state it can be purged, leaving a person closer to the divine."

"And." Nona paused to clamber over a shoulder of rock. "And you've touched a shipheart before? On the ice?"

"My tribe calls them *klauklar affac*, 'the footsteps of the Missing.' Most on the ice know them more simply as 'Old Stones.' And yes, I have touched such a thing before. Two such things, in fact. When the ice-speakers find a child that can approach the Old Stones they test them. Each new *raulathu* takes longer to split from a person than the one before and is more difficult to purge. I gave twelve to the fire. It was hard to do. Neither of the tribe's stones could find more."

"How old were you?" Nona knew that when Zole described a thing as "hard" it meant that anyone else would have been killed by it.

"Nine. The ice-speaker banished me to the Corridor. He did not say why. My uncle took me to the empire margins. I was sold to Sherzal's agent in a village called Shard."

"Do you . . . do you think that's why you have no threads?"

Zole made no answer. She had reached the ridge from where she could look down into the next valley and away towards the fortress to the north, the closest in the chain. "It seems that the battle-queen has ears in Sherzal's palace, and swift access to them."

Nona scrambled up to join Zole on the ridge. She straightened, wiping the grit from her palms. "Oh."

A column of riders was spilling down the far side of the valley, a skirmish band on the shaggy ponies that dwelt wild in the region and could run all day over such terrain.

"Sixty." Zole turned and dropped back below the ridge.

"We can't outrun them." Nona wasn't sure she could outrun a three-legged mule right then.

Zole narrowed her eyes. A momentary frown and she was moving, back down into the valley again, angling towards their original path tracking the stream. On this side of the Grampains the rivers ran their course a while before vanishing beneath the ice sheets. On Sister Rule's globe you could reverse the glaciers' advance and set your fingers to ancient oceans picked out in blue enamel. Nona imagined they still lay there under miles of ice and that the sun-warmed waters of the Corridor must eventually reach those hidden seas.

"If we're going to fight we should do it here," Nona called after Zole.

"Sixty is too many," Zole called back. "And more will come. I would rather rest."

Nona shrugged and followed. Sixty *was* too many, and rest sounded good.

8

HOLY CLASS

Present Day

TOTAL DARKNESS. AN enduring silence wrapped Path Tower's Third Room.

"Dead dog's bollocks!" Nona broke the silence, banging her shin into something hard. The curse was one of Regol's favourites, though he only used it when he thought she wasn't there. One day Nona hoped to delight Clera with it.

She bent to rub her leg, then reached out to examine the obstacle. A barrel-lidded casket. She wasn't sure if she'd seen it in the moment before the light died or imagined it after. Her fingers explored the metal banding and found a heavy lock. Would there be more troublesome protections? Thread-traps? Sigil marks? Or did Sister Pan consider the fact that it rested in the third chamber of Path Tower sufficient defence?

Nona sat on the cold stone floor. She could put a foot to the Path and summon light but how that might end, so soon after the strange paths she had just pursued, Nona didn't know and didn't want to find out.

The lock was a big piece of cold iron. Nona defocused her sight to bring the thread-scape into view. The lock blazed with them. Threads for the metal itself, leading back through the journey from the locksmith's, through the workshop, splitting through the smithies where various parts were beaten into shape, rejoining in the white heat of the forge, tracking back along rivers to the distant quarry that the ore had been dug from. All of them tangled with the lives of those who laboured to make the lock, and tangled with the old song of the earth where the iron's constituents had lain for years uncounted.

A sudden light lanced through it all, washing out the detail and causing Nona to shield her eyes.

"Thought you might appreciate a lantern," Ara said in a shaky voice. She held it up and glanced back at the wall she had come through. "Well, that was . . . unnerving." She drew a deep, centring breath and gazed around at the sigil-covered walls in appreciation. "These are more complex than in the other rooms. There are sentences written here . . ."

"How did you get in?" Nona demanded as she stood.

"The same way you did, I expect." Ara blinked.

Nona doubted that very much. "Tell me, exactly."

"Well. I went up and down a few times, and I noticed you had vanished. I found a spot where I thought there might be a door and tried everything I knew to open it. It didn't seem to work but when I got back down to the portrait room it was different . . . there was a new picture there that . . . Well, anyway, I didn't stop to examine it. I just turned straight round and ran back up the stairs. And all along the stairwell were doorways into scenes from my life, as if I could just step back into them. Passing them by was hard. I mean really hard. And I think if I had hesitated they might have just sucked me through. But I didn't stop. And halfway up was an archway showing you in front of that box. I stepped through and here I am." She smiled. "Same for you?"

"My way was a bit more complicated." Nona shrugged. "The book's in here if it's anywhere." She nudged the casket with her foot.

"And we really want to steal? From Sister Pan?" Ara asked.

"None of us wants to. I can't see another way." Nona knelt before the casket again and checked it over. No sigil marks. She brought the lock's threads back into view, hunting for traps or alarms.

"Won't she notice it's gone?" Ara asked.

"What's she going to say? 'Which one of you took the forbidden book I wasn't allowed to have on pain of banishment?'" Nona identified the threads that would undo the mechanism's riddle. Three of them. The key must be a complex piece of ironwork. "Besides, how often do you think she looks at it? It might be a year before she notices it's gone. It might be ten years!"

"So we steal a book to help us steal a different book, which also might not exist." Ara sat down, her eyes taking on that "witchy" look as she joined the hunt for any protective thread-work on the casket.

"It exists," Nona said. "Abbess Glass wouldn't have lied to me."

"That woman lied whenever it suited her, Nona. There was nothing personal in it." Ara's fingers twitched as she sorted threads, plucking one, examining it, setting it aside for the next. "Besides, she was very ill; she could have been confused. She kept calling me Darla the last time I was allowed to visit her."

"Jula knew about the book already. She tried to tell me about it years before," Nona said.

"It still doesn't make sense to me. Sherzal was going to take the Ark and use four shiphearts to control the moon. She didn't need a book."

"The four ingredients of yellow cake are butter, flour, eggs, and sugar. If I gave you those four necessary things you still couldn't make a cake that Sister Spoon wouldn't laugh at."

"Neither could you." Ara took on the nasal tones of Sister Spoon. Ruli was the better mimic but Spoon was easy to do. "Novice Nona, that is an excellent cake, perhaps the best yellow cake I have ever seen . . ."

". . . if the goal in making such a cake were to produce something suitable for hand-to-hand combat," Nona continued, holding her nose. "However, if I were to wish to eat a cake rather than bludgeon someone to death with it—"

"Then I would do better to scrape something together from the convent pigsties," Ara finished.

"Not the point." Nona tried to look serious. "Sherzal wanted the Ark, the palace, the throne. The rest she was just hoping would sort itself out. The Ark was something she needed to get Adoma as an ally. The shiphearts are the necessary ingredients. What we're after is the cookbook."

"It looks clean to me." Ara ran her hands over the casket. "Try the lock."

Nona took hold of the three key threads. She didn't need her hands but it helped her focus. Any lock is a riddle. The threads made that riddle simple, or at least less difficult, and allowed the answer to become clear through suitable manipulation. It took Nona seven tries. Ara had just opened her mouth, her lips shaping the "l" of "let me try" when the required click sounded.

It wasn't until she opened the lid and gazed upon the contents that Nona first felt guilty. Seeing the bundled letters, a carefully folded scarf of Hrenamon silk covered with a child's embroidery, the small figures of a horse and a baby carved from dark pearwood, a dozen other personal effects, Nona knew herself for an intruder of the worst kind, trampling a garden of memories.

"It must be at the bottom . . ." Nona could see no sign of a book.

"We should go." Everything Nona had just felt resonated in Ara's voice. "We have to do this."

"It's nonsense anyway." Ara stood up to go. "If the moon's secrets were written down in a book they would have been used at the time it was written. Or at least a hundred years later Emperor Charlc wouldn't have been forbidding the subject and hiding all the books in a vault! He would have used the secret himself. He wouldn't have left it to two novices in his grandson's reign!"

Nona looked up at her friend. She wished they could go. She wished they could just shut the box and walk away. "If I swore to you that the Ancestor had told me the true alchemy was written in a book . . . that all we had to do was follow the recipe and base metals would transmute to gold before us . . . would we be rich?"

"Well, yes. We'd take the book and—"

"Which book?"

"You just said the secret was written in a book. Wait, doesn't the Ancestor tell you the title?"

"Just that it's in a book on alchemy."

"Well, no then, we'd be poor because there are a thousand books and scrolls promising the true alchemy."

"And there are a thousand books promising all the secrets of the moon. But Abbess Glass, who forgot more things than you or I will ever know, and Jula, who would rather read the dustiest book than eat, and who is sharper than any Mistress Academia I've met, both said that this book was different. Jula said it might have something real to say. Abbess Glass *promised* that it did." Nona reached in with infinite care and began to remove items from the casket, committing their positions to memory. "And if Abbess Glass said it, sick or not, that's good enough for me."

Ara frowned as she had frowned so often over these past weeks. "So, if the book in the forbidden library is really what the abbess said it was, how do we use it? How do we prove it? We don't have four shiphearts. Nobody does! We don't have access to the Ark. We don't have anyone to tell who would believe us, Wheel least of all. It seemed like a bad plan when we were just talking about it. Now that we're actually doing it . . ."

Nona reached for the bundled letters with a sigh. Abbess Glass had taught her many things. She had taught Nona that you can often find an angle where any right looks like a wrong, and any wrong a right. She taught her the song of the Ancestor, the power of the long game, and the need for determination. Above all Abbess Glass had taught Nona the value of lies. The one thing she had never managed to teach her was not to feel bad for telling them.

"It's the right thing to do. The key to everything. I need you to have faith in this, Ara. I need you to make the others believe too. We're going to be taking holy orders soon so we should be good at believing, no?"

"In the Ancestor, surely, not in any old—"

"This comes from the highest authority I know."

Ara looked up suddenly, incredulous, eyes bright. "You've had a vision? From the Ancestor?" Awe and need mingled in her voice.

Nona bowed her head. "I have."

NONA FOUND THREE books at the very bottom of the casket, wrapped together in a length of black velvet. Aquinas's *Book of Lost Cities* was the smallest of the three, looking less old and less impressive than *The Mystic's Path* or *The Lives of Lestal Crow*. It looked more like a travel journal than some weighty tome worthy of forbidding. Nona took the leather-bound volume and hid it in an inner pocket of her habit before returning the other two to their wrapping and starting to replace Sister Pan's other treasures.

A moment of panic came as she reached for the figurine of the baby and discovered on the floor behind it an ancient daisy, dried and pressed, that must have fallen from between the pages of one of the books. She carefully extracted everything, unwrapped the books, and placed the flower behind the cover of *The Lives of Lestal Crow*, hoping she had guessed correctly.

At last, sweating lightly, Nona closed the lid. "Done."

"Lock it." Ara nodded towards the keyhole.

"Right." Nona found and manipulated the necessary threads. An easier task this time.

Ara went to the wall and set her hands on it. "Now we find that getting in was the easy part." Her smile was a nervous one.

"I'll follow you," Nona said. "You're better at it than me."

"But you got in first!" Ara pushed her lips into a pout.

"You wouldn't want to go back my way. Trust me."

NONA STUMBLED OUT onto the Path Tower stairway, catching hold of Ara's shoulders to keep from falling.

"At last!" Jula hurried down towards them. "I thought you'd died in there! Got stuck in the wall or something!"

"Relax." Ara smiled, holding up the lantern. "We got it."

"We have to go!" Jula pushed past them. "Bray's about to sound fourth bell. There'll be little Red Classers lining up outside any minute."

"Fourth bell?" Nona shook her head. "I didn't think we were *that* long!"

"Well, you were!" Jula all but stamped her foot. "Come on." And she set off.

"I'm surprised Pan's not here already if it's so close to fourth," Ara said, grinning her disbelief.

"She is." Jula didn't stop, just hissed back up at them around the stairs' twist.

That got both novices moving. They caught Jula as she hurried out into the portrait chamber.

"She's here?"

"I was on the stairs when she started up them! I had to go up into the classroom, hide behind the trapdoor lid, and slip out while she was arranging the chairs. It's a miracle she didn't see me!" Jula looked pale.

Ara slapped her on the back. "The Poisoner will make a Grey Sister of you yet!"

"Then I hung around on the stairs again, expecting her next class any minute and wondering how long to leave it before declaring you both lost and confessing everything." Jula led them to the north door, opened it with caution, then threw it wide. The three of them spilled out into the day.

After the unreality of the past hour, strange and emotional treks through memory, walking through walls, stealing from Sister Pan in a cause that was larger than any of them . . . it came as a surprise to find themselves in the cold light of the same day and subject to the same old timetable that had ruled their lives for so many years.

The friends stood a moment, shivering and blinking in the lee of the tower.

"Shade!" Nona remembered where she should be next. "Damnation!" And she veered off with Ara in hot pursuit, scattering half a dozen approaching Red Class novices.

9

───── ✦ ─────

HOLY CLASS

Present Day

NONA AND ARA ran for Shade class, leaving Jula to make her way to advanced Spirit class under the Ancestor's Dome with Abbess Wheel.

Sometime soon all of Holy Class would take their orders or return to their homes. If they still had homes. Under normal circumstances the newer members of the class like Nona might have expected to wait as long as two more years before being allowed to take the nun's headdress. With the world closing in on every side, sharp in tooth and claw, the time of choosing would be hard upon them. Jula had her sights set on the black habit of the Holy Sister, a Bride of the Ancestor, hers the life of prayer and contemplation resting on the foundations of her faith. Beyond her devotions the simple tasks of the convent would occupy her time. She might even aspire to teach the novices. The Black was open to any girl graduating the convent without stain upon her character. To take the Red, Grey, or Blue of the Martial Sister, Sister of Discretion, or Mystic Sister, tests must be passed to demonstrate sufficient aptitude. Ara had said she would return to her family if she wasn't offered the Red or the Grey. She needed the excitement and the challenge, not days of humility measured out by the tolling of bells.

Although Nona's free choice would always be the Red, she knew that both the Grey and the Blue offered sufficient danger and variety to fulfil her too. In the end, though, she would serve in whatever capacity the Church demanded. All the sisters would have to fight before this was over. Fight or die. Probably both, judging by the streams of incoming refugees clogging the roads both east and west.

LESS THAN A minute after fleeing Path Tower, Nona and Ara clattered down the steps to the cave where Sister Apple had just taken her customary place behind her preparation table. Alata, Leeni, Ketti, Ruli, and Sharlot all looked around to witness Nona's entrance, Ara at her shoulder. Late arrivals were always a good spectator sport, and the fact that Nona had once saved someone very dear to the Poisoner from certain death never seemed to soften any punishments handed out for misdemeanours in class.

Nona stood, pinned by Sister Apple's glance, and awaited her sentence. A seven-day spent cleaning the main cauldron had been a favourite lately. A trickle of sweat ran across Nona's ribs beneath her habit, parallel to the spine of Aquinas's *Book of Lost Cities*. If the book were to be discovered, then all the punishments ever handed out in Shade class would pale by comparison to the retribution that would rain upon her.

The Poisoner set down her notes. "Sister Mantle has been called away on other duties so further instruction in Shade-fist will have to await her return." The nun gestured for Nona and Ara to take their seats. "Thus we are at leisure to decide on today's topic of study. A session on rending would be a wise choice given the parlous state of this class's shadow-work."

Nona hung her head. Without her shadow even the simplest manipulation of the dark lay beyond her. When the lights went out she was as blind and helpless as someone without a drop of marjal blood in their veins.

Knowing where her shadow lay softened the loss, but not by much. A minor compensation was that because her shadow was still bound to the Sweet Mercy shipheart she received a small but steady contact with the heart's power. Even now she could feel it pulsing along the shadow-thread that bound them. The shipheart remained in Sherzal's keeping, part of the terms of the uneasy truce with her brother. But Nona kept to the hope that the years ahead held an opportunity both to recover her shadow and to exact justice for Sherzal's crimes. Hessa and Darla had both died because of the woman's machinations, and Nona would see Sherzal bleed for it.

"Or," Sister Apple continued, "we could practise your wire skills, which are equally in need of attention."

Nona looked up. Wire-work included garrotting, which was always a messy business, and the setting of various unpleasant traps, but at least it was something she could do.

"Any preferences?"

Nona and Ara knew better than to speak. Apple had an instinct for the truth even without her little pills, and she would choose the option neither of them wanted. Nona considered bluffing and asking for the option she least liked, but kept quiet, sure Apple would see through it.

"Wire-work?" Leeni held up a hand.

"Wire-work it is." Sister Apple allowed herself a narrow smile and bent to unlock the drawer where she kept the equipment. She rummaged for a while, then removed seven kits, each a small box of polished wood containing a set of wires cut to various standard lengths. Holding the stack of cases against her body, the nun moved around the class, distributing them.

"Thank you, Mistress Shade." Nona didn't reach for hers, instead letting Sister Apple set it down in front of her.

Before opening the box Nona slipped her hands inside her sleeves. Contact poison was a favourite punishment for tardy novices. Inside, the wires rested tight-coiled in small compartments. A set of iron thimbles and finger-sleeves fashioned from very fine chain mail were included to help avoid lacerations. Beside the finger-guards a wide variety of hooks, wedges, and blocks were set into a narrow line of depressions shaped to accommodate them. Grey Sisters might be entrusted with sigil-locks to secure wire-work at speed, but only the best were trusted with such expensive tools and every Sister of Discretion needed to be able to fall back on more basic methods.

"Work in pairs. I want the windows wired. Sharlot, you're to do the door. Lock it first, dear." Sister Apple waved them to their tasks and returned to her desk.

Ara and Nona hurried to claim the centre window. Each of the windows was a rectangular tunnel about three yards long cut through the limestone. They exited the Rock of Faith via the cliffs that towered over Verity's garden land. The windows were wide enough to move along crouched or on all fours, so wires could be set at intervals from one end to the other.

"I'll prepare, you set. Then we'll swap." Nona waved Ara into the tunnel. Nona would select the required wedges and lengths while Ara went about the fiddly business of fixing wire to block and winding away unwanted length.

Nona reached for a claw hook. Ara would want a claw hook. She would probably want six. The hooks worked pretty well on the edges and fissures you found in limestone. Her fingers paused an inch from the device she needed. She leaned in, squinting and sniffing. With a sigh she took a cloth from her pocket. "Poison on the kits, Ara." Sister Apple had worked fast, probably with boneless resin, touching a few of the key components. Up ahead Ara grunted her acknowledgement.

"You have a count of five hundred!" Sister Apple called out from her desk.

Nona put on an iron thimble and took a length of wire, running it carefully through the cloth. There were no smithies that could make wire of useful quality or length. Only Ark-steel had the strength to be dangerous at a thinness that might render it invisible to the unsuspecting or hurried. Nona had felt a certain pride on discovering that the wire in the kits had been recovered from ice-tunnels by scavengers like her father, an elite breed who would dare the inky depths of the ice hunting for treasures buried beneath its advance. There were things of great worth to be found in the cities men had abandoned centuries before. Follow any tunnel out from the margins and you journeyed back in time. Find the right tunnel, put enough miles between you and the Corridor, and the ground you trod had last been green millennia before. In rare spots traces survived, sheltered from the flow of the ice behind granite ridges, or buried in caves. The true prizes, though, were not the ancient remnants of man's work but the cities of the Missing. In such places a scavenger might find Ark-steel already formed into wire, fragments of rose crystal, quicksilver gathered in hollows, beads of nightblack, and a hundred other wonders.

Nona fixed the tiny claw hook to the wire's end, taking great care not to slice her finger. Given only slight pressure the wire could cut her to the bone. She wondered, as she always did, what the Missing had used such stuff for and what they would think of the ends to which the Sisters of Discretion turned it in the Ancestor's name.

Struck by a sudden thought, Nona defocused her gaze, wanting to follow the threads of the Ark-steel back as she had followed those of Sister Pan's lock. There was the remote possibility that somewhere along the steel's thread her father might be waiting for her. Perhaps he stood there amid visions of the exploration on which he had recovered it. But to unravel such secrets lay beyond her thread-work. Instead she saw the wire as if it were its own thread, gleaming with mystery, woven around the lives of anonymous Grey Sisters and leading back towards the darkness beneath the ice. The details of its discovery and the distant wonder of its forging were shrouded in an unsettling mist . . .

"Nona?" Ara's voice, tinged with exasperation. "Corner bridge!"

Nona started. She blinked away her thread-sight and returned guiltily to her work. "Coming. Sorry."

"Four hundred counts left," Sister Apple called. Someone in the next window-tunnel let out an oath. A moment's distraction could see you cut.

Ara set four wires, two crossing diagonally from opposite corners, one slicing off a corner where a hand might reach, another horizontal at a height level with her eyes. She retreated two feet between each placement and dusted the metal with soot to hide its gleam. A staggered placement minimized the chances of detection and meant that the victim might fall onto a second and third wire with greater force, leaving yet more, potentially both ahead and behind, to catch others.

Once Ara had crawled back out Nona went in to begin setting her own wires. The first wedge she set was a rectangular block rather like those employed by mountaineers, though far smaller.

"One hundred!" Sister Apple called.

Nona found it hard to believe so little time remained. She could hear Leeni cursing in the next tunnel. She called on her serenity and bade her fingers work faster, setting wedge and hook, stretching wires between them.

"Out!" Sister Apple had no tolerance for any who tried to finish off their work after the allotted time.

Nona retreated from her fourth wire.

"At home my little sister is learning how to arrange flowers," Ara said as Nona brushed off her knees.

"Wires, flowers, it's all good." Nona had to force the levity into her reply. She'd seen what wire-work did to people. It wasn't pretty.

Sister Apple inspected and dismantled Sharlot's work at the door first.

"Passable. You should set the low ones forward, though." After completing her inspections she turned to view the novices. "Join me in the corridor if you would."

Sister Apple led the way and the novices clustered around her in the tunnel outside.

"Every Sister of Discretion is expected to know how to traverse any wire-work she has laid, leaving it intact. It's often a necessity to pass through at speed in order to encourage others to pursue with a suitable lack of caution."

Nona felt a sinking sensation in the pit of her stomach. She tried to recall the pattern Ara had employed. Two crossing, one horizontal, one chord. Was it the left-to-right diagonal closest to the exit?

"Sometimes." The Poisoner lifted her hand towards the class chamber. "In the dark." Shadow rose in a black tide, boiling around the doorway, reaching the roof.

"Who should I pick to show us how speedy they are?" Sister Apple turned her head until her gaze rested on Nona and Ara. "Perhaps two novices who were late?"

"But, Mistress Shade. Nona won't be able to see in there!" Ara looked worried on Nona's behalf though she herself had only a touch of marjal blood and shadow-work was her only talent, both late developing and weak.

"It's not compulsory," Sister Apple said. "Unless you want the Grey."

"But Nona—"

"Will not fulfil all the requirements of the Grey if she can't complete this task. You may enter first, Ara, and after a count of twenty Nona may enter. Your classmates and I will then climb the stairs at a modest pace. If you are not waiting for us at the top, and if Nona is not there within a count of twenty of our arrival, you or she or both of you will have failed and need no longer attend my classes."

Ara shook her head. "Nona—"

"Go!" A barked command, all Poisoner and no Apple. "One!"

Nona stepped forward and shoved Ara into the darkness. "Don't be in my way when I get to the window."

"Two!"

Nona heard footsteps as Ara hurried to the central shaft.

"Three!"

She allowed herself to be shocked. Even a small error could lead to a wound that might see Ara bleed to death. The loss of a finger, or an ear, or some other important bit of a face was also a distinct possibility. When moving at speed it was a dangerous game to play, even if you could see the wires. This wasn't a simple poisoning with retchweed or similar. Being late for class had never carried a potentially fatal punishment before.

"Ten."

Lessons were over. The closed world of the convent was about to be broken open. The endgame had arrived.

"Fifteen."

Nona reached for her clarity trance, picturing a dead candle and the memory of a flame flickering above it. Her clarity couldn't pierce the shadows but it made other things clear. Clarity brought her to the realisation that Apple didn't expect her to try the challenge. This was a goodbye. She should take the Red.

"Nineteen. Twenty."

Nona ran into the night-dark room.

"Nona! What in the Ancestor's name are you doing?" Sister Apple's cry rang with genuine distress. "This is madness!"

Cold stone greeted Nona's outstretched palms, her clarity enough to bring her to the gap between the left window and the centre one that she and Ara had trapped. Knowing that Apple hadn't intended her to attempt the task brought both relief and dismay. It meant the nun had wished her no harm but it also meant that Apple didn't believe anyone without basic shadow-work fit for the Grey.

Nona felt for the edge of the window shaft. On occasion she missed Keot's acidic commentary but she'd never really missed his violation of her body until she needed to see in the dark. As unpleasant as having an ancient devil invade your eyeballs was . . . it could be very handy.

Despite the daylight outside, Sister Apple's darkness filled the window shaft. Nona knew where the wires lay but to trust to memories made with no particular urgency could prove suicidal. A moment of inspiration settled on her. She defocused her sight. With proper illumination the threadscape overlaid whatever she would normally see, and those visual clues helped make sense of the confusion of threads, a near infinite complexity of them springing from every surface, passing through each other and solid objects, leaving the world at strange angles. In darkness the mass of threads was normally far more bewildering. However, Nona already knew how the chamber looked. She had spent a good portion of her life in it. She knew the shape of the window, the nature of the stone, even the weave of the magic that had stolen the daylight. And, more by chance than judgment, she had examined the threads of the Ark-steel wires. This prior acquaintance, combined with a rough knowledge of their position, allowed her to pick out from a chaotic background the taut sections placed in her path.

Even so Nona moved far more slowly than she would have done had she been able to see. With daylight she could spot the telltale wedges and move her head for a glimmer along the wires' length. She advanced on all fours, having to negotiate a second, third, and fourth wire before being able to wholly discount the first from her considerations. Novices had been badly cut before when manoeuvring to pass a new wire and forgetting the one now level with their knee or foot.

Passing the seventh wire, Nona felt a tickle along the side of her left calf. No pain, though, not until the sharp sting as she adjusted her position and moved on.

At the cliff face Sister Apple's shadows boiled away into the day. Nona stuck her head beneath the last wire and looked up. Ara was twenty yards above her with ten more to go. She was climbing barefoot, presumably having abandoned her shoes in the cavern in anticipation.

Nona had to force herself to patience. Not until every part of her was past the last wire would she be safe. If clinging to the outside of the Rock of Faith in a Corridor wind could be considered safe.

She drew herself clear as swiftly as she could while still remaining sure that she knew where each limb was relative to each wire. A few moments later she hung above the drop to the plains some three hundred yards below.

The delay in the window shaft had left Nona lagging Ara by a considerable distance. More than Sister Apple's count of twenty could account for. Unless she closed the gap there would be no way she could make it in time. In moments Ara would disappear over the edge to the left of the treacherous section between Blade and Heart Hall. Seconds later she would be running around the back of Heart Hall. Finally a sprint along the length of the winery and across some open space would bring her to the gate that sealed the Shade steps.

Nona launched herself upwards, disdaining any attempt at finding handholds and footholds. She drove her flaw-blades into the Rock itself and hauled herself up by the strength of her arms. Each lunge risked a chunk of the limestone fracturing away and taking her with it, but the blood was boiling in her veins, a sense of being wronged drove her, and she fought her way towards the heights, screaming with effort at first, then grunting as she saved her breath.

She climbed much faster than Ara, who had to rely on fingers and toes, but would it be enough to close the gap? Rather than crab across the cliff aiming for the edge where Ara had pulled herself over at the back of Heart Hall, Nona made a direct ascent. This brought her to the sheer southern wall of Blade Hall at a point where it stood flush with the edge of the Rock. Farther to her left a ledge started that would allow her to track around the building, ducking and climbing a series of buttresses. This obstacle course was what had forced Ara across the rock-face towards Heart Hall. Nona just kept going up, plunging her blades into the stone blocks as she climbed Blade Hall. She hoped Sister Tallow never saw the damage.

On reaching the roof, Nona flipped herself up onto the sloping tiles using her core strength and ran. She vaulted the roof ridge, then slid down the far side. A leap from a height of twenty feet brought her to the ground amid a small barrage of dislodged tiles. She tucked into a roll to share the force of impact on feet and legs with shoulder, hip, and back. The roll brought her to her toes and she was sprinting as only a hunska can, straight across the plaza to where Sister Apple would emerge.

Nona could see the steps, the iron gate set farther back, but no sign of Sister Apple or of Ara. Then she saw the nun, one hand reaching for the bars, the other thrusting a key at the lock. Ara came tearing around the corner, bare feet slipping from under her on flagstones still wet from the last rain. She rolled rather than try to right herself, and as Sister Apple pulled open the gate to ascend the last half-dozen steps, Ara reached the uppermost one on all fours.

The Poisoner reached the top step a few moments later, novices behind her, all heads turned the way that Ara had come, looking for Nona's arrival in her wake. "One," the nun called out.

Nona rushed in from the other side, nearly knocking Ara down as she got to her feet.

"Two . . ." Nona heaved in a lungful of air. "Two novices . . . reporting as ordered."

"She must have cut the wire," Leenie said. Ketti and Alata, just behind Sister Apple, stared openmouthed. The nun herself, though, fell to her knees, her hands reaching for Nona's leg with a roll of bandage. "You're bleeding, girl."

Nona looked down at her crimson leg and the red footprints leading back behind her. A sudden vertigo, wholly absent when she clung above a drop of hundreds of yards, seized her and without a cry she fell into a darkness all her own.

10

---◆---

HOLY CLASS

Present Day

TWO DAYS IN the sanatorium proved sufficient for the patience trance to justify all the effort Nona had put into mastering it over so many years. The wire had sliced her shallowly but managed to open some large veins in her calf. Sister Rose sewed the wound closed and said that Nona would need a week of bed rest to recover from the loss of so much blood. After two days of staring from the depths of her trance out at the small garden cloistered beyond the sanatorium windows Nona felt herself ready to leave.

"I should try walking." Nona sat up.

"You're a patient. The clue's in the name." Ruli pushed her back down.

"I'm an impatient patient." Nona wriggled up again.

Ruli tried to distract her with gossip. She had come to visit on her own and now looked as if she wished she had Ara to back her up should restraint prove necessary to keep Nona in bed. "Kettle's home! They say she assassinated three Durn war-chiefs."

"They?" Nona had already sensed Kettle's approach through their thread-bond.

"You know." Ruli waved the question away. Nona had never got to the bottom of who exactly the mysterious "they" were. "I heard she went aboard a battle-barge to get the last one. Killed him out at sea. I hope it hurt." Ruli put her head down for a moment, the long, fair veil of her hair closing around her face. The Durns had killed two of Ruli's uncles and sunk a good number of her father's fishing boats. She'd had no news of her family for months.

"I'm sure she made the Durns regret crossing the sea." Kettle had been on the Marn coast weeks ago and some of her experience had haunted Nona's dreams along their thread-bond. Nona doubted that the Durn commanders had suffered. Kettle was clinical in her kills. But it seemed that Ruli needed to hear something more satisfying.

Ruli nodded and sniffed.

"Anyway, if Kettle is back that makes it the perfect time to get what I need from Apple's stores." Nona kicked off her covers.

Ruli's eyes widened on discovering the patient fully dressed. "Perfect? The Poisoner has eyes in the back of her head as it is. If Kettle's there it will just be harder still. You don't—" Ruli stood as Nona swung both booted feet over the edge of the bed. "Get back in there!"

"Yes, the perfect time. I've been wanting Kettle back!" Abbess Wheel had been sending Kettle away at every opportunity, and war on two fronts provided plenty of opportunities. The fact was, though, that she would have sent her on nearly as many missions during peacetime. The old woman had never approved of Apple and Kettle's relationship but even as abbess she couldn't forbid it. The Church rules on celibacy within the sisterhood concerned only relations that might add branches to the tree of the Ancestor. Denial of such opportunity was considered a sufficient marriage sacrifice for the Brides of the Ancestor to make. "It's been ages since Kettle was here. And who better to keep Sister Apple occupied?"

"Well." Ruli hid a grin behind her hand. "You do have a point. They are very loud." She blushed. "At least that's what they say. From what I've heard, if you pick your time you could batter down the stores' door with a sledge-hammer and neither of them would hear you. In fact, they'd drown you out."

"Ruli!" Nona shook her head. "It's settled then. We've got Sister Pan's book to return to the vault. Jula's made the order, complete with the ab-bess's seal—"

"Which you need to get back without Wheel noticing."

"Markus is ready to help compel any officials or guards who doubt us. And all I need now are Apple's magic drops so that if there's an investiga-tion the only thing the guards have to say isn't: 'Well, I can't remember much about them but I do recall the girl had completely black eyes . . .'"

"They're not magic drops."

"Everything's magic, Ruli. If you'd seen the thread-scape you'd know that. Everything's magic, or nothing is." Nona slipped from the bed, slid-ing beneath her friend's reaching arms to rise between them, smiling. "I'm fine. And I should do this while everyone thinks I'm still in bed."

Ruli stepped back, exasperated. "How will you even get in? The main gate and the stores' door both have sigil-locks now."

"I'll find a way." Nona went to the window. "See if you can't put a few me-shaped lumps in that bed in case anyone looks in to check." With that she slipped into the sheltered garden and clambered up Sister Rose's prize cherry tree to reach the roof.

Despite her brave words Nona was shocked by how weak her arms were once called on to do any real work. Her calf muscle burned where the wire had cut it. She gritted her teeth and edged towards the roof ridge to survey her path.

Sigil-locks were a problem. Abbess Glass had approved the expense after Hessa's death in the undercaves and the Poisoner's discovery of theft from her stores. Nona had branded herself as the thief by darkening her eyes with a self-brewed dose of the black cure, but the fact that a day before taking the cure Nona had saved Kettle's life had meant that a better lock was the only action taken.

As tempting as it was to cross the convent Noi-Guin style from rooftop to rooftop, the best practice, taught by Sister Apple herself, was far less flamboyant. Nona left the sanatorium by the door once an opportunity arose to do so unobserved. Under her habit she carried a lantern from the sanatorium, now lit and trimmed to its lowest. Already it was uncomfortably hot.

She walked to the edge of the Rock, head down, staring at a section of parchment as if memorizing it for an exam. She came to Blade Hall and waited for a cluster of Grey Class novices to pass inside before she slid quickly over the cliff edge. With her toes on a ledge she extracted the lantern, turned it up, and tied it to her belt.

Bray's next toll was near. Old Sister Grass would already be creaking up the wooden stair to sound it. Nona reached the windows to the Shade chamber and hung by her flaw-blades, wishing her arms weren't already trembling with the effort. If there had been a lesson ongoing, then the bell would have ushered the class out and offered an opportunity to enter. But no sounds emerged, and the quickest of peeps confirmed that the room wasn't filled with shadow-work or novices pressed to the walls practising the watchful patience that Nona herself should be exercising.

Nona made to swing through. At the last moment she caught herself awkwardly and hung, muscles aching, as she confirmed that the window shaft hadn't been left with a criss-crossing of wire-work. Relaxing, she dropped in and crawled through. She rose amid the familiar benches and chairs, all stained and seared with a score of chemical spills. How many punishments had been handed out to the unfortunate authors of those accidents? she wondered. How many novices saved from making the same mistakes at some later point in their lives with consequences more dire than any of Apple's punishments?

Nona reached for the door to the corridor. Even through the thick planking she could hear distant sounds from the cave where Sister Apple kept a bed. Officially the subterranean quarters were for when she was brewing mixtures that required regular supervision over a long period. Unofficially it served for times when the bed in her nun's cell off the Ancestor's Dome was too narrow and too public.

Nona and Kettle had learned to manage their thread-bond so that in general neither could sense anything of the other beyond a vague idea of direction and proximity when they checked. To gain more intimate levels of connection now required agreement on both sides. Even so, this close, and with the cries reaching down the empty tunnels, Nona started to feel distracting echoes of the nuns' happy reunion. Thoughts of Regol flooded her and if she let the influence continue she knew she might find herself running the five miles to Verity to find him, bad leg or not. Nona bit her lip, leaning against the wall as another wave of the lovers' passion threatened to swamp her. Any more of this and Verity would be too far. She might not even make it past Ara's study.

In the end Nona called on her serenity trance to insulate her from such intrusion and set about her business. The stores cave lay closer to Sister Apple's living quarters. Nona hurried there, having no worries that she might be overheard. She needed her lantern now, but if Apple or Kettle should emerge the light would give her away immediately.

Despite Ruli's suggestion Nona doubted that the sturdy door to the stores chamber would yield to a sledgehammer particularly quickly. It had that obdurate look about it that oak gets after a century or two of seasoning. Besides, the aim here was not merely to steal, but to steal without later discovery. Based on historical evidence, Nona would be the prime suspect in any new theft so she planned to leave no signs that anyone had been there.

The sigil had been set above the lock in silver, inlaid into the wood. Nona studied the thread-scape. Like all sigils this one was a knot, drawing in and binding scores of threads. The shape of the sigil etched into the visible world echoed its more complex structure and function in the deeper world that lies beyond vision. Each sigil might be thought of as the shadow of an intricate structure cast upon a flat surface.

"Tricky." Nona put her hand to the wall and focused her will.

Slowly the bedrock began to flow. Within a minute a groove had formed, allowing the door catch space to move as Nona opened the door. The lock remained locked.

Nona stepped through, alert for any further alarms, and drew the door closed behind her. The chamber beyond remained just as she remembered it from her previous theft more than five years earlier. Dried ingredients lay in neat bunches on row after row of shelves. One set of shelves was given over to a hundred or more earthenware jars, each crammed with seed pods from a different plant. Elsewhere stood glass jars filled with distillations, tinctures, and brews; a dozen kinds of snake scales in leather pouches; bones, tiny and large, whole and ground; minerals in all shades of the rainbow, some powdered, some in single crystals longer than fingers.

The cave had been chosen for its lack of leaks and the walls rendered with pitch to seal it. Even so, pots of deliquescent rock-salt stood at regular intervals sucking moisture from the air to prevent mould. The place had an aromatic smell to it, scores of herb scents mixing. A sharp edge to the mingled aromas served as a reminder that sampling what lay on display would likely kill you.

In cabinets around the cavern pots and jars lined further shelves, scores of them in tidy rows. Unlike the herb bunches, which Apple presumably thought impossible to misidentify, the containers were labelled, some with the ingredients written in the glaze, others with the identifier seared onto a leather tag tied around the neck. Cloves, green peppercorns, red peppercorns, illwort hearts, dried cow dung, elmbark scrapings . . . On and on, the ordering sufficiently abstract that Nona could see only a hint of it.

Nona's salvation in all this confusion was that the finished preparations were kept on one great set of shelves with an alphabetical ordering within various subgroups such as "contact poisons," "ingested poisons," "antidotes," and "miscellaneous."

The drops that Sister Apple had prepared were stored in a distinctive ceramic flask, wide at the base, narrow at the neck, and about two inches high. Nona found the flask quite rapidly in the miscellaneous section, sporting the label "Optorical greyjak, recipe fourteen, unreliable."

The tiny flask released its hold on its cork stopper with a small pop. Nona poured half the contents into a glass tube and sealed the end with wax. She pushed the stopper back and was about to return the drops to the shelf when a key rattled into the door's lock.

A great number of thoughts attempted to pass through Nona's mind at the same time. Everything from the excuse she would offer first to which weapon she should use. A rant about the unfairness of it all struggled to be heard among the babble. Nona refused all of them admission. Instead her hand fell to the lantern. Sister Apple's training was so ingrained that Nona had unconsciously been assessing the room for hiding places ever since she entered. The most obvious was in the gap behind the mixtures' shelf. The curvature of the rock walls meant that none of the shelves could stand anywhere near flush with the stone. Instead Nona moved with hunska swiftness towards a sack bulging with fresh pickings from the woods and fields, still unsorted. Beside it lay two empty sacks and an over-habit soiled from some recent work.

The key turned, the lock clicked, the door began to open. Nona threw herself down, arraying the over-habit and sacks across the length of her, pressing her body into the angle between wall and floor. She hid her feet behind the full sack, wishing that she were as small and flexible as Ghena, who might have concealed herself entirely in such a bag. As the gap at the door grew still wider Nona blew out her lantern and pushed it down between her legs beneath the over-habit, wincing at its heat. At the last moment she pulled her hood up to hide her face. Only then did she allow despair in. Perhaps Apple and Kettle wouldn't report her to Wheel, but the loss of trust, and the disappointment in their eyes, would hurt worse than a whipping.

As concealment went it was a pretty poor job, but people see what they expect to see and a shapeless heap of sacking and soiled clothes rarely merits close inspection. In any event neither Sister Apple nor Kettle would miss her wherever she hid. Even if they didn't notice the groove in the stone that meant unlocking the door had been unnecessary, and neither of them *would* miss that, then the smell of her lantern would be enough to set them searching. If it were Apple rather than Kettle, then at least Nona's current position held the possibility of a mad scramble for the door while her back was turned.

Nona lay as she had been taught, not rigid but boneless despite every instinct to tense. A lantern's glow pressed through the material of her hood. Why would either nun have a lantern with her? Nobody at the convent worked shadows as well as Kettle or Apple.

The person entered. A single person, their footsteps uncertain. Nona called on her clarity, letting her mind sink into the web of its senses. She could still hear distant echoes of passion, Kettle by the sound of it. Who else would have a key? And how had they got into the caves? A second key to the gate above?

The intruder moved hurriedly around the room, picking up something here, something there, a rustle, a sniff, moving on. It reminded Nona of her first raid on the stores, collecting ingredients. Clearly she hadn't been alone in thinking to make use of the opportunity provided by Kettle's return. Nona lay like a dead thing. Despite her boredom in the sanatorium she had to admit that Sister Rose might have had a point. The climb down to the Shade windows had exhausted her and all she really wanted to do was lie down, regardless of her racing heart.

Listening to the intruder's to-ing and fro-ing, Nona tried to picture where they went in the room. At least the fact that the person carried a lantern themselves left them unable to detect the lingering smoke of her own.

Even so, something spooked them. The hurried activity ceased. A long moment's silence, then a high pop as if a small bottle were being unstoppered.

The eye-drops. Nona hadn't had time to put them away.

"I can see you." A female voice. Young. Familiar. "Come out."

Nona took care not to tense. The fractional movements could give her away.

Silence. Then slow footsteps, coming closer, not a direct path but gradually drawing closer nonetheless.

"I won't hurt you . . ."

Nona reached into the rock around her. It wasn't hard to do; her face had been pressed to the cold stone floor long enough to go numb. She reached in with her mind and followed the surfaces, her perception tingling over the interior of the cave. Her marjal stone-work would never move mountains, but watching and sensing Zole at work had been enough of a lesson to help her focus what talent she had. Gritting her teeth, Nona pushed. On the opposite side of the cave a flake of stone broke free of the wall and fell. The faint sound brought the intruder round in a sharp turn. Something hit the far side of the chamber. A throwing star by the sound of it rolling for a moment before fetching up against some other surface.

"Pits!" The girl hurried over to where she'd thrown her missile.

Nona tilted her head a fraction. Enough to offer a slit of vision from beneath the folds of her habit's hood. Her view was partial, a kneeling figure silhouetted against the lantern held high before her. Even so, with the glow setting the golden edges of her hair aflame it was enough. Joeli Namsis had favoured "pits" as a curse of late.

Nona returned her head to its original position, losing sight of her enemy. They said Joeli was the best poisoner among the novices. And not Ruli's elusive "they" but everyone. Nona had, in moments of particular paranoia when Abbess Glass fell sick, wondered if Joeli was poisoning her. She'd discounted the idea on the basis that Joeli couldn't possibly be so good at the craft that she fooled both Sister Rose and Sister Apple. Additionally, continuing to dose the ailing Glass despite Kettle watching over her with single-minded devotion would have been beyond the girl. Of course . . . Nona hadn't considered that Joeli might have access to the stores cavern and the rows of preparations waiting there. Could she have been tainting the very cures that Apple applied? The thought sent a cold shiver up Nona's spine, rage burning in its wake.

Could Joeli have done it, though? Sister Apple herself was always full of praise for the girl's efforts. And that assessment stood in the face of the suspicion that her truth pill might have been circumvented in the matter of Joeli's role in Darla's death. Joeli could certainly brew with rare skill. As to the delivery Nona was less impressed. Joeli had never managed to poison her. In fact Nona wasn't certain Joeli had ever tried, which spoke of a lack of confidence in her skills as she certainly wasn't shy with her threadwork. But if all she had to do was to come to the stores chamber during a Shade class and add a drop to the abbess's medicines . . .

Joeli poked around on the far side of the room while Nona seethed with the darkest of thoughts. After what felt like an age but was probably no more than a couple of minutes Joeli finished her stealing. Seemingly satisfied, she gathered up her takings. The sound of footsteps making for the door followed.

Nona lay motionless as Joeli rummaged for her key. Apart from Mistress Shade surely only the abbess would have a key to two convent sigil-locks. Possibilities raced through Nona's mind. Would Wheel have just given Joeli the key? She had always liked the girl . . . but to risk Sister Apple's wrath like this?

The door opened on oiled hinges and a particularly loud squeal reached through from down the tunnel. Nona pressed her lips against the smile that wanted to show there. A momentary pang of jealousy ran through her. She and Regol were never so loud. Were they doing it wrong? Perhaps it was just the nuns' misplaced faith in the caves' privacy. Certainly Alata and Leeni didn't keep the whole dorm awake at night.

At last the rattle of the key being set in the lock broke Nona's chain of thought. A pause. The door closing. Another pause. Nona's heart began to pound. Had Joeli noticed the groove she'd made in the stone? Would she raise the alarm? Joeli knew the abbess would come down lightly on her, and like the Rock of Faith on Nona. Did she have the stomach to take a whipping in order to see Nona banished again . . . or worse?

Click. Finally Joeli turned the key and locked the door. Nona allowed herself a sigh of relief.

A moment later the door opened again without any unlocking. "I hope you like your mustard grey?"

Something hit the ceiling with a soft popping noise. The door shut quickly and rapid footsteps faded into the distance.

NONA DREW A deep breath, initiated by shock but prolonged by the knowledge that if Joeli really had thrown grey mustard spores at the ceiling they would not yet have had time to reach her.

She turned her face towards the rocky wall, thinking furiously. Her hands were already inside her sleeves and now she gathered the slack ends into her fists, sealing the ends. Joeli had trapped her in a dark cave that was rapidly filling with grey mustard spores. The door stood about four yards from Nona's position, with two sets of freestanding shelves to be navigated around. There was no way she could make it out in time.

Grey mustard? Would Joeli do that? Even for her it was extreme. Nona's corpse would be an ugly thing, skin blistered and burned, eyes clawed to ruin by her own hands. The agonizing death could take the best part of an hour, so Sister Apple would doubtless find her as she wrecked the stores chamber with her convulsions. There would be nothing that even the Poisoner could do, though, other than watch her die.

Nona couldn't believe it. How would Joeli even get her hands on . . . Nona remembered where she was. Joeli could have stolen some there and then. What to do? The time to run had gone, and in truth there had never been time to run, not after that first soft impact of the package hitting the ceiling.

Keep calm. Sister Apple's first piece of advice. Easily said, hard to do. Panic would burn up the air in Nona's lungs more quickly. Grey mustard spores had to be kept completely dry. They lost their effectiveness rapidly in damp conditions. In a fog they wouldn't spread and would lose potency within seconds. In the moist air of the undercaves they might stay danger- ous for five or ten minutes. But Sister Apple had taken great care to keep the stores chamber arid. It might be an hour before it was completely safe to walk around.

The mustard spores wouldn't penetrate cloth in a hurry and Nona was well covered, but if she got up and started to run they would swirl up under her habit and likely find a way into her hood and down her sleeves. Nona had seen the scars on Sister Rock's leg where she was exposed to the margins of a mustard cloud. The wounds were angry, red, and ugly. Sister Apple said the pain could last a lifetime. Which went a long way towards explaining Rock's temper.

Nona's lungs began to tingle with the first hint of the burn that would grow and grow, demanding that she draw breath. Her rock-work offered no solutions; she had no flame even if she had the skills to do more than make shapes in the fire. Her marjal dominance over water and air was less dominance and more being able to ask the occasional small favour. Speed wouldn't save her. Possibly she could walk the Path, but she felt too weak and the energies she would gain might wreck the room but they would be unlikely to destroy all the spores.

Frustration warred with raw terror. After all this time Joeli was going to win and Nona would die the worst of deaths alone in the dark.

Without hope she began to roll, keeping her legs tight together, depend- ing on the sacks, the over-habit, and the skirts of her own habit wrapping tight around her ankles. She raised her arms to pin the hood around her face as best she could. The total darkness stopped her from knowing whether there were gaps through which the spores could reach her eyes. She would soon find out if there were.

Five or six rotations were sufficient to start Nona's internal map of the cave spinning. She tried to roll slowly enough so that the sacks and her habit wouldn't flap around her, but the air in her lungs couldn't last forever. Already she wanted to take that breath.

Surprise at the sudden impact of her ankles against something unyielding almost made Nona inhale. A series of crashing sounds followed, Sister Apple's precious ingredients taking the plunge. Nona buried any guilt under the certainty that an agonizing death waited in her immediate future. Already her ankles were burning. She pushed away images of a survival that left her scorched, her face a ruin, scalp pink and scarred, the shock and revulsion as her friends first saw her . . . Regol's features stiffening, the smile falling from his lips.

An adjustment and another set of rolls brought a second collision. Another series of crashes followed. Panic wrapped itself around Nona's lungs, squeezing tight. She didn't know where she was; she couldn't roll to the door. She would have to stand, exposing herself to the spores. And even as she began to rise she knew with cold certainty that before she found the door in the darkness, flailing around as the skin bubbled from her hands, she would have to draw breath, and then her lungs would start to perish. Nona had seen men die from grey mustard; she'd watched it through Kettle's eyes deep within the Tetragode. She couldn't end like that. Fear only consumed her air more swiftly but serenity had escaped her.

Gathering her courage, Nona rose and launched herself in the direction she hoped the door lay. With arms folded over her face she crashed into something that was not a door. A whole rack of shelves toppled to the ground with Nona tangled in the structure. Pots and packages rained down and each shelf seemed to break free of the frame as the thing fell.

Nona hit the ground hard and lay face down amid the sharp edges of the clutter. She had to draw breath. The whole of her body clamoured for it.

Traitor muscles lifted her chest demanding air. She clamped her jaw, hammering the ground with her fists, refusing defeat. Spots of red light flashed in her vision, the beat of her heart became a drum, a thunder in her ears, the pressure built, beyond pain, beyond resistance. With a sob of despair she released the stale breath she had clung to so long, and hauled in a new one.

The burn hit immediately. Within moments Nona was rolling helplessly, coughing, choking, her eyes beginning to sting. Spluttering, the drool running from her chin, Nona gained all fours and crawled, direction abandoned to panic now. She banged her head against stone and sobbing she followed the wall around with blind hands. At last she found the wood of the door. It gave beneath her push and she tumbled out into the corridor.

Nona sat, wiping snot and slobber from her face. *ATISHOO!* An almighty sneeze shook her, ringing down the tunnel.

It took another moment to realise that it hadn't been grey mustard. "Pepper!" *ATISHOO!*

Apart from the echoes of Nona's sneeze there was no noise.

"Shit!"

Somewhere along the tunnel a door opened.

Nona leapt up. A whisper of light from the Shade classroom windows gave her direction and the edges of the corridor. She slapped a hand to the wall where she had carved a channel for the lock catch. A pulse of marjal enchantment and rock started to rain from the area in fragments. She hadn't time to repair her work so she hoped to hide it instead. The damage could look like the work of hammer and chisel now.

She was running before Kettle's shout rang out. She tore along the tunnel, bashed through the door into Shade class and dived the length of the window tunnel, escape now her only thought.

As her body flew towards daylight Nona clung to the moment, so fiercely that she seemed to inch through the air. She couldn't climb. Kettle was too fast. She would reach the window and look up. But down was so much farther . . .

Nona touched her hands to the wall to slow her at the exit . . . and dropped.

The cliff below the windows was near vertical. The fall was more than two hundred yards to wooded slopes that rose in the shadow of the Rock of Faith. Nona twisted as she fell. When the rock-face threatened to scrape against her she nudged herself out by fractions with hunska-speed kicks. She dropped a hundred yards, now travelling so fast that it seemed rapid even in the midst of her own swiftness.

Nona couldn't use her flaw-blades, not in sight of the window. Her descent would be too slow and the marks left behind would make it obvious who had been there. Another fifty yards of wall sped by. The treetops approached at frightening velocity.

At the last moment Nona drove her flaw-blades into the rock with one hand, at first just the tips, letting her arm take the strain of deceleration. She used the other arm to angle her blades against the stone and keep her body clear. Without that precaution she would have left half her flesh in a thirty-yard smear reaching to the ground. The force on her arm grew and grew with each passing yard, threatening to pull her shoulder from its socket. She slowed from a hurtle to a rush. The thump with which she hit the mossy boulders piled around the tree trunks at the Rock's base was the kind you hobbled away from cursing, rather than the kind that was both wet and crunchy.

Nona hugged the trunk of a screw pine and squinted up through the dense needles. Kettle's upper half appeared through the Shade chamber's middle window, tiny in the distance and pink in its nudity.

Nona slunk farther into the undergrowth, stifling another sneeze. *Pepper.* Joeli hadn't meant to kill her, just panic her and leave her to be found amid the inevitable mess. The lord's daughter couldn't have known for certain it was Nona in there, or whether she had been identified or not, but she'd been willing to take the risk on both. Clearly she felt that even if she was named as having been in there she would be protected, whereas whoever had broken in would be thrown to the wolves. Or more likely thrown into the Glasswater, or at least metaphorically from the Rock of Faith.

With the pepper still tickling her nose, Nona made her way down the slope. She needed to be somewhere else by the time Kettle thought to check for her along their thread-bond. In the meantime she did all she could to deaden the connection.

At the foot of the Seren Way a sudden panic gripped Nona and she patted her habit pockets. The damp patch and the crunching within told her all she needed to know. The vial into which she had poured those precious eye-drops had broken as she rolled across the cave floor. The others had been right. The drops weren't essential to penetrating the high priest's vault. It was vanity that had drawn her to that cave. A desire to be normal, to meet another person's gaze without seeing that momentary widening of their eyes.

Sister Apple said she had locked the drops away because of risk that they might take Nona's sight. But Nona knew now that she had been blind all along.

11

———— ✦ ————

THE ESCAPE

Three Years Earlier

THE HERDER'S HUT wasn't more than a low circle of drystone wall topped with a cone of sticks and bracken. The goat shelter proved even more rudimentary—a slanting roof on four poles, sides of woven sticks, a simple door at each end with space to look over the top.

Zole lay down on the soiled bracken bedding and motioned for Nona to join her.

"This is the worst hiding place ever."

Zole patted the withered foliage beside her.

"This is stupid." Nona crouched down. Old droppings speckled the bracken, which must be bitter stuff if the goats left it. "It's the first place they'll look." The hut and shelter stood alone, the only structures in a wide, desolate valley. The famed Scithrowl crowding seemed to be something of a myth, or at least not to carry up into the high places of the Grampain foothills.

"It is the first place they will look," Zole agreed. "Which is strange when it is, as you say, a stupid place to hide . . ."

"So what are we doing here?"

"There is no place they will not find us, but in this place it is likely that only one of them will find us."

"Oh." Nona lowered herself to lie beside the ice-triber, steeling herself against the shipheart's closeness.

They passed a minute with no sound but the moan of the wind and the creaking of the walls. The scarlet stain at Zole's wrist drew Nona's gaze.

"So the shipheart breaks pieces off you . . . off who you are . . . and you throw them away?"

"It's a ridding of impurities," Zole said, her voice low.

"But a person's flaws are part of them." Nona couldn't keep the horror from her words. "My temper is a bad thing, but it's part of who I am, like Ruli's gossiping or Leeni bedding other girls even though she loves Alata. Jula's obsession with learning, Ghena's sharp tongue . . . if you got rid of all those parts of you and approached this ideal . . . isn't that everyone becoming the same?"

Zole offered the smallest of smiles. "We have to let go of that pride, that ego. It will never bring happiness. Consider the Ancestor, who walks the length of the Path towards a perfect future, rather than the breadth of it from life to death. Is not the Ancestor a melding, a commonality in which the good is intensified and the bad fades? This is why the Ancestor's statues are smooth-faced, features poorly defined. The Ancestor is not an individual."

"But that's when we die . . ."

"What happens to Ghena's sharp tongue, to Clera's selfish ambition when they join the Ancestor? In that wholeness the good is stacked on the good, and the undesirable, the individual, the ego, is all washed away. With the Old Stones we of the ice pare ourselves towards that perfect core before we die rather than after. The wise say that if anyone ever rid themselves of their last *raulathu* they would no longer need to die. They would be the divine."

"You really do think you're the Chosen One," Nona gasped.

Zole shook her head. "Approaching divinity makes us all the same. If I am the Chosen One then at the heart of us, we all are."

Nona looked away. She was lying amid goat droppings in a tiny shed in the wilds of Scithrowl discussing divinity . . . with a mad girl.

"I—"

"Horses!" Zole motioned Nona lower.

The hoofbeats were faint but drawing nearer. A single rider. As the sound came closer a faint background could be heard, more riders following.

The novices waited. Nona felt the shipheart's aura dim as Zole somehow reined in its power.

Horses drew up nearby. Lots of them, filling the air with their snorting and the jingle of harnesses.

"Search it." The words thickly accented. Farther east the Scithrowl spoke a different tongue but in the shadow of the mountains the language of the empire clung on.

The thump of riders dismounting, their grumbles coming closer.

A moment later the upper half of a man obscured the patch of sky above the door at the far end of the goat shelter.

"You do not see us." Zole muttered the words, a certain strain behind them.

"Nothing here!" the man called out.

"Get in there and check, you lazy whoreson."

Nona tensed, ready to attack as the Scithrowl irregular kicked open the door, grumbling curses.

"You do not see us. This place is empty." Zole spoke in a quiet but conversational voice, her hands in fists, fingers white.

The man stamped in, bent almost double to avoid the low roof. He smelled of old sweat, stale beer, and some overripe meaty scent Nona couldn't place. He moved forward, kicking at the bracken, his gaze passing over both novices several times. Zole rolled slowly to one side as he approached. She gave Nona a push to indicate she should roll to the other side. The man stepped between them, frowning. He wore a skirt of leather strips panelled with iron plates. He kicked the bedding everywhere but in the places the novices lay.

"Nothing." He left by the far door, vindicated.

Outside it sounded as if a dozen or more riders had dismounted and stood in debate.

"... there's no sign they left again!" A raised voice.

"Well, they're not here." A woman's voice, deep and belligerent.

"We should burn it to be sure."

Zole began to mutter to herself. Tiny veins in her eyes surrendered under mounting pressure, lacing the whites with crimson.

"Burn it? It's a hut and a stall."

"There's nowhere to hide."

"... plenty to burn on the other side of the mountains ..."

A rumble of agreement. "Split up, comb the valley."

The riders climbed back into their saddles and within moments the company had thundered off.

Nona started to rise.

"No." Zole kept her voice low. "They could have left someone to watch."

"So what do we do?"

"Rest."

Nona set her head on her arms and tried to relax. She wondered if there really was a Scithrowl sitting on the slopes watching the hut. She supposed there might be.

Zole's demon had moved to circle her neck, a scarlet scald as if she'd escaped a hanging halfway through.

"So, when you force your latest devil out, what parts are you cutting away?" Nona asked. "Is the Zole who came across half of the empire to rescue me from the Tetragode in here?" She put her hand to Zole's throat, then tapped her forehead. "Or here?"

Zole said nothing but narrowed her gaze in concentration and the scald slid away from her neck.

"Is the Zole who once every three years makes a joke the one to be cut out or left behind?"

"Once they are separate the *raulathu* must be purged. Their voices grow louder, their ills more extreme."

"But what you cut away . . . that's life. Keot, my devil, for all his ills, was alive, with hopes of his own. You're telling me he was cut away, abandoned? And the perfect beings that remained when all that was excised . . . what became of them, shriven of their flaws?"

Zole rolled onto her back. "They say the Missing left. But some believe they are all around us, unseen, unknowable, existing in their own harmony. Others think the Missing went beneath the sea and live there in golden cities, burning the very water itself for heat, enough to last them until long after the last star has gone dark.

"In the far north there are peoples that believe it is the Missing whose heat bubbles up to melt the domes beneath the ice, and sometimes to give us the open water that sustains the deep tribes."

"Sister Rule said it was volcanoes at the bottom of the sea that did that." Nona tried to imagine golden cities beneath miles of ice and dark water.

"Mistress Academia has her own wisdom." Zole shrugged. "How can we know the truth?"

Nona fell silent. She didn't know what death held, what would become of her if the Ancestor gathered her in. She didn't know if the ice-speakers were right or what Zole would become as she shed every last one of her flaws, her jealousies, every shred of malice . . . But it didn't feel right. Not to her. Perhaps it was her pride talking, her own multitude of sins, each with their own small voice, but imperfect as she was, Nona wanted to stay here, whole, untouched, while her heart beat and her lungs drew breath.

"Where do you think the Noi-Guin are?" Nona found it hard to believe the assassins had given up. They had hounded her for nearly half her life simply for having the temerity not to die. Zole had stolen their shipheart.

"Waiting," Zole said.

"Waiting?" Nona would have accepted "coming." "Where? Why?"

"They are waiting because they know now that we are dangerous. They want the Scithrowl to weaken us. To deplete our reserves. The bulk of the Noi-Guin will be waiting at the ice, because they know it is the way I would choose to get past Sherzal's soldiers and back into the empire. They will want to keep us on the move. To exhaust us. They are at their most dangerous when waiting."

"So we'll have to get through them to get to the ice sheet?" Taking on Noi-Guin with the advantage of surprise had been difficult enough. Walking into an ambush would be suicidal. Especially with the Scithrowl in pursuit.

"It would be best not to have to," Zole said. "That's why we're going to the black ice."

"The black—" Nona broke off to sniff. "Something's burning!" She turned to see white feelers of smoke rising through the woven sticks of the wall.

Zole moved into a crouch. "Our rest is over."

12

THE ESCAPE

Three Years Earlier

THE FIRE DROVE the novices out but whoever had thrown the incendiary had not waited for them to emerge. As Zole had suggested, the Noi-Guin were playing a longer game. The column of smoke would bring back the Scithrowl riders and more besides. The two girls made directly for the barrens, favouring speed over stealth. In the distance green turned to brown. And behind miles of dead, unwholesome land the grey ice rose in towering cliffs stepping up nearly two miles to the great southern ice sheet.

The foothills descended into rolling fields in the shelter of the Grampains. With the Corridor wind in the west, hardly a breeze stirred the hedgerows. Jump-corn stood amid a riot of crops that had launched themselves from the fertile darkness of soil such as Nona had never seen. Villages lay almost every mile, the roads well maintained and set with inns, staging posts, and tiny watch-forts. Zole led the way past such places so swiftly that the locals had time only to raise their heads and wonder. Twice groups of children followed, throwing stones. Nona let them bounce off her back. And once a young man in a patched uniform three sizes too big for him chased after them, waving his arms and shouting at them in such thickly accented empire tongue that Nona could understand little past "stop." He grew breathless, angry, and finally laid a hand upon Zole's shoulder, which saw him hoisted over a wall into a haystack.

"Here." She tossed Nona the leaf-bladed dagger she'd plucked from the youth's belt—Scithrowl army issue.

With the barrens just a mile ahead and a dark crowd of horsemen thundering through the village on the ridge behind them, the novices found their way blocked by six Scithrowl knights. Nona's childhood had been peppered with stories of the heretic knights beyond the mountains. In Nana Even's tales they were always giants in iron armour, their faces hidden behind visors cast in the likeness of snarling beasts, and with the heads of empire children hanging from their belts by the hair.

The truth was six dour men in weathered steel, all looking to be in their thirties or forties, their scars and bleak-eyed contemplation of the novices marking them as veterans. Likely they had served in the endless eastern wars against the kings of Ald.

"Stop!" Their leader nudged his stallion out into the road from beneath the copse that had hidden them.

Zole didn't break her stride. She ran straight at the knight with a remarkable turn of acceleration. To his credit the man cleared his scabbard before she got there but Zole had vaulted his horse and ducked beneath the belly of the next before any blow could be struck. Nona wove after the ice-triber, swaying out of the path of the swinging sword.

They got fifty yards before the knights turned their horses and began to give chase.

"Trees?" Nona hissed the suggestion between breaths. Ahead the fields gave way to bramble and thorn bush studded with the occasional stunted copse. Nothing that looked sufficient to slow the horses more than it slowed the novices.

Zole spun, bracing on her heel as she continued to slide in the direction she'd been running. She raised her hands, fingers extended. As one the horses stopped, just as if they'd seen a wall appear before them. The knights went over their mounts' heads, crashing to the beaten earth in their plate armour. Nona winced.

"Animals are easier than people." Zole wiped a trickle of blood from the corner of her mouth. It didn't look as if it had been easy. "Come."

Nona followed as Zole led off again. Behind them riders boiled from the last village down into the road. Scores of them. She wondered if the Noi-Guin had misplayed their hand, letting the Scithrowl wear her and Zole down. Perhaps the battle-queen's people would kill them and take the Noi-Guin's shipheart for their own.

The vegetation died within the space of a quarter mile. Trees stood lifeless and brittle, branches vacant of leaves. The thorn bushes petered out. Brambles became black, twisted things, bloated with ugly growths, then gave up their purchase on the cracked ground altogether. The novices ran through an acre of dead grey grass, fraying where the wind worried at it, and beyond that the soil lay bare.

Nona turned at the drumming of hooves, not ready to risk a spear in the back. Zole stopped a few yards ahead of her. The riders slowed and spread out, seeming unwilling to advance, the animals nervous. Perhaps a hundred Scithrowl had joined the chase. Nona wondered if the knights had managed to get out of the way or if they had been trampled where they lay.

"How many horses can you scare off?"

"Perhaps we will find out." Zole came to stand at Nona's shoulder. "They are herd animals . . . but I do not know their minds well."

The Scithrowl stopped a hundred yards off, among the last scraps of bramble and thorn. Many unslung short bows.

"They look scared. Perhaps they think this place is haunted," Nona said.

"Do you doubt it?" Zole began to walk backwards, at a slow and even pace.

The first few arrows winged around them as the archers sought their range. One came close and Zole snatched it from the air. She reversed it, took two paces forward, and flung the missile back, her arm cracking through the air. A second later an archer among the riders toppled from his saddle.

"I didn't . . . know we could do that . . ." Nona said in a small voice.

A dozen archers loosed at once, more following, and for the next few moments Nona was occupied with the business of knocking their arrows aside. It brought a memory of the ordeal of the Shield all those years ago. Nona had never imagined when Zole arrived that it would be her whom she would be shielding—not that Zole needed her help.

They backed away and the business of defence became easier with a slight slowing of the arrows and decreasing accuracy, but harder as their stamina for such speed eroded. Nona slapped away an arrow zipping towards her chest, and moved her foot to avoid another that might have skewered her knee. The shafts were angling out of the sky now as the range lengthened. Nona had to squint to see the black dots against the sun. She hoped the archers' quivers would empty before her own reserves ran dry. She twisted back from the hips to avoid another shaft and swore as it tore a hot line across her shoulder.

"Run now." Zole turned and started to zigzag through the brittle remains of dead bramble to the road's side. Nona peeled off in the other direction, a dust cloud rising where she sprinted. Sister Tallow had explained that beyond a certain distance an archer could only aim at where they hoped their target would be by the time their arrow arrived.

They both ran in the stuttering shifting pattern Mistress Blade had drilled into them. More arrows scattered around both novices but their luck held and before long they stood beyond the range of a short bow.

"It's good they're so scared of this place." Nona slapped the dust from her coat.

"Perhaps." Zole seemed unconvinced.

"What are they afraid of? Ghosts? Poison?" Nona gazed across the barren earth stretching out before them, tumbled-down farmhouses and abandoned villages dotting the area. "It's hardly going to be worse than what we'll find in there." She pointed to the distant ice, sullen grey except for where the ridges gleamed bloody in the sunlight.

"This bane has been advancing across their lands for centuries. The Scithrowl are not a timid people. They were taught to fear it." Zole adjusted her pack and glanced once more towards the watching soldiers. "Let us hope we do not meet that which taught them." She set her jaw and led off deeper into the dead zone.

AT FIRST IT was only a sensation of being watched that pulled Nona's gaze towards the dark windows of abandoned houses. Here and there the corpses of trees still stood, their limbs all but gone. Even so, Nona glanced at the stark branches that remained, convinced some horror waited there, watching for its chance.

They passed a lonely way-stone, its corners weathered away, bearing only the legend "7 miles." Given the stone's age the place it spoke of might lie five miles behind the ice, lost to man generations back. The next rise revealed a graveyard and a ruined church of Hope. The markers leaned at drunken angles and every grave mounded like a pregnant belly above its occupant.

The wind picked up closer to the ice, lifting the sour dust and swirling it into momentary shapes somehow more filled with horror than any clear image could ever be. The air had a bitterness to it that made Nona press her lips together in a hard line. Her hands felt parched and the wound the arrow had scored across her shoulder burned more fiercely by the minute.

Ahead the ice walls loomed, the grey taint giving them a strange metallic look. The ice darkened towards the base, becoming jet black right at the bottom to give the impression of a yawning cave mouth. Judging size was difficult but Nona thought the black region could be no more than a hundred yards wide and perhaps thirty yards high, the corruption leaching up through fathoms of ice so that even the tops of the cliffs a thousand yards and more above were grey with it, as if rotten.

In the margins great blocks as yet unmelted by the intensity of the focus moon or the duration of the day lay scattered for a mile before the actual cliffs. The ice boulders ranged in size from lumps no larger than a fist to chunks that would conceal a house. All around them streams of meltwater cut through dead earth to expose bedrock beneath. The whole place gurgled with running water, in places swallowed away through rocky fissures, in others trapped within stinking bogs, swamps of black mud that might suck a person down and not return them before the Corridor closed.

The blocks themselves radiated not only cold but something like malice. Nona found herself staring at them, trying to fathom their translucent greyness. Zole took care to stick to the ridges and the firm ground. Where they had to descend to cross a rill or stream she took trouble not to get her feet wet.

Before long they stood amid ice boulders so thickly clustered that the only open space to be found was in twisting ravines that snaked between them. The black ice yawned ahead, the darkest part proving to cover a significantly larger area than Nona had imagined. The shape was still that of a cave mouth but several hundred yards wide and a hundred tall.

"What do the ice-tribes say the black ice is?" Nona asked. She realised it to be a question she should have asked earlier.

"They do not say," Zole replied. "They know, but these are not truths to be shared."

"Well, perhaps you could make an exception this once? I am your Shield, after all. And we'll be in there very soon . . ." Nona moved her head from side to side, trying to make the black wall yield some definition. ". . . if there's any way in." It looked like a yawning mouth filled with midnight but behind the illusion was a solid wall of black ice. Nona's conviction that there was some kind of tunnel running through it all was based purely on

Zole's assurance and Kettle's reluctant admission that she had ventured into chambers within the black. Kettle had been following the Scithrowl queen, and faced with the malice radiating from the darkness before her Nona had to agree that anyone who claimed their power from such a place should be feared.

Zole answered Nona's question after a pause so long that Nona had given up waiting on a reply. "The Missing purged their *klaulathu* . . . their sins if you like, in temples built for the purpose. The *klaulathu* are parts of an individual, not properly alive nor properly dead, and they dwell around the margins of the Path. But places such as the temples, in which so many were purged, remain weak spots where *klaulathu* can leak back into the world."

"And the black ice?" Nona had an uneasy feeling that she knew the answer.

"Is where the *klaulathu* have polluted the ice as it moves across the place where such a temple was sited. The corruption, the evil of an entire race tainting this world again."

"And this is the best way to get up onto the backs of the glaciers?" Nona couldn't imagine that it was.

"It is the best way to avoid the Noi-Guin. They lack purity of heart and are susceptible to the *klaulathu*. They will not dare to guard this path."

Nona eyed the sucking blackness ahead of them. "I'm not sure I dare to walk it. I'm susceptible too, remember?"

13

HOLY CLASS

Present Day

"WE'VE GOT TO steal the book today?" Ara looked shocked. "We need at least until the seven-day to plan."

"Today! Now!" Nona ducked out of Ara's study room. "I'm going to grab Jula."

"Wait! Aren't you supposed to be in bed?" Ara's protest followed her down the stairs.

Images of Sister Apple's face filled Nona's mind, just as she must have looked when she discovered the ruin of her stores chamber. Nona was sure she'd left the eye-drop flask out. That must have been what told Joeli she was in there. Hopefully it was lost in the mess now rather than standing incriminatingly on the worktop before the shelves of preparations.

Even without such immediately damning evidence, though, Nona didn't think it would take long for Mistress Shade to establish her guilt. What Abbess Wheel would do in response didn't bear thinking of, but Nona doubted a raid on the high priest's vault would still be an option afterwards.

"Nona!" Ara now hung from the dormitory window on the third floor, shutters flung wide. "Are you sure? This is madness . . ."

Nona looked up at the friend she was asking to risk so much. Abbess Glass had told her to obtain the book by whatever means necessary. She had given Nona the instruction when her illness first bit, and she had repeated it on her deathbed, knowing that the empire's armies were failing. Nona had promised the dying woman and she would hold to the promise with or without help, even if it meant defying the high priest and all his archons. She would do it even if she had to reduce the place to ruin and dig the book out of a pile of corpses.

"Trust me." It was all the pleading she would do. And with a nod Ara withdrew.

AT THE SCRIPTORIUM Nona sped to a rear window and jumped up, propelling herself with the window ledge to gain height so that she could check the library's occupants. As was so often the case Jula sat alone at a desk, a number of yellowed scrolls around her. Nona dropped back to the ground and hurried in through the front entrance. Sister Scar was at her desk in the scriptorium's main hall, illuminating a copy of the Book of the Ancestor. She favoured Nona with a narrow stare but said nothing.

"Jula!" Nona closed the library door behind her. "You—" She swallowed her words at the sight of a tiny novice carrying a book from the shelves. The girl's habit pooled around her feet. "We were never that small, were we?"

"You were smaller than me when you arrived." Jula looked up from her work. "There was room for two Nonas in the habit they issued you." She turned her head towards the younger novice. "Yes, that's the one. Thank you, Marta. Put it on the chair, if you will."

"We need to talk." Nona took Marta's shoulders as she straightened from setting down the heavy book. "Alone." And steered the child towards the door.

Jula sighed. "Off you run, Marta. We'll do some more on the seven-day."

They both waited for the door to close.

"What?"

"I need the order," Nona said.

"You need to get the abbess's seal back to her somehow. I know it's not used often but I'm amazed she hasn't noticed it's gone."

"That will have to wait." Nona held her hand out. "We're doing this today."

Jula reached into her habit and retrieved a leather tube, a parchment scroll inside. "Good."

"Good?" Nona took the tube and checked the document. "I thought you'd be horrified."

"Come with me." Jula got up and walked towards the rear of the library. "I've something important to show you."

Nona's shoulders slumped as they always did when Jula tried to get her excited about some aging book. She followed, frowning. Some of the writing was so old it almost seemed they used a different language, all "thees" and "thous" and words that had to be explained. Others still contained no single word known to her.

Jula squeezed past the rows of shelves stacked with scroll upon scroll and pushed right to the back. She shifted a board aside, sneezing at the dust. In the gloom and after the brightness of the reading room Nona could make out very little. Jula fiddled with a key. Nona hadn't imagined there was space in the scriptorium for another chamber, some secret vault no doubt . . . The door cracked open and to Nona's surprise daylight streamed in. Jula stepped through, beckoning her out, locking the door behind them. They stood behind the building with the barrel store and Sister Candle's workshop before them. Nona must have passed the door they'd exited by a thousand times without ever noticing it.

Jula led on, out towards the end of the spur on which the convent sat. The cliffs to either side marched ever closer as the Rock of Faith's plateaued top narrowed towards a point. Jula's shadow leapt before them, as if it were eager to reach the edge first and leap off. Nona could imagine herself alone and that the shadow belonged to her. Shadows might seem simple things but somehow they pinned you to the day. Since she'd lost hers Nona had never quite felt part of the world.

"Where are we—"

Jula ignored Nona's attempt at a question and marched on. She passed the Glasswater sinkhole and continued across pitted stone until they stood just yards from the jagged edge where the Rock dropped away. She pointed east. In the distance smoke smudged the sky.

"You've been very busy the last few days, Nona, and nobody wanted to trouble you in the sanatorium . . . but that smoke? That's Queen Adoma's front line. Sherzal has returned to the Ark. They say the battle in the field is all but lost. Heretics will be at Verity's walls in a week. Maybe sooner."

"But . . ." Nona hadn't known it was this bad. "What about the Ninth and the Seventh?" The emperor's personal divisions were an elite force with a fearsome reputation, forged through centuries. "Everyone says Crucical will deploy them."

"The Ninth went west last seven-day. A Durn army showed up at the walls of Arnton. The convent of Silent Patience and the monastery at Red Rill are both in ruins. The Seventh are lining up before the Ark but their numbers are badly depleted."

"Where do you get this all from?" Nona demanded, not wanting to believe. "You sit in that library all day when you're not in class!"

Jula pointed again and Nona followed her line back to the many-windowed spire of the convent rookery. "The armies have lost so many message birds they're using church rooks now. And Darla taught me to read the standard military codes." Jula's face fell. "General Rathon died at the coast last week . . ."

"I . . ." Nona had wanted to tell Darla's father that she had brought Joeli

Namsis to justice for her death. The general would never hear it now. Perhaps it wouldn't have given him any comfort, but Nona thought Darla would be happier. Darla had never been the forgiving sort. "Well . . . it makes what we're doing all the more important."

"Be careful." Jula managed a weak smile.

"Me?" Nona returned a brighter one. "You're coming too! There's no time for you to teach me how filing systems work now. I need you to find the book once we're in!"

THE FOUR FRIENDS met by the laundry well, Nona and Jula arriving to find Ara already waiting with Ruli.

"Joeli did this to us," Nona said by way of greeting.

"She made us steal forbidden books?" Ruli asked.

Nona repressed a snarl. Ruli hadn't seen Darla die, hadn't seen Joeli cause it. "She knows too much about us. She's a Tacsis spy, right here in the convent. We should—"

"Kill her?" Jula asked. "The Book of the Ancestor is against that sort of thing." She favoured Nona with a level stare.

"All right, all right, Holy Sister." Nona shook her head. Jula's calmness, her goodness, was something Nona valued in these situations, though usually in hindsight rather than at the time. "I wasn't going to suggest murdering her . . . not exactly."

"What then?" Ara asked.

Nona let her breath escape in a long sigh. "We'll deal with her when we get back." She stepped into the well, taking hold of the rope. "Come on, then."

The four of them descended to the chamber beneath the novice cloister, then began to thread the undercaves. They passed through the cavern where the strange freestanding ring stood taller than a man, crossed the spot where they had once faced down a holothour, and went on down the cliff beyond. Ten minutes later they passed the sad, calcified skeletons in their niche, and finally emerged back into the light through the hidden crack onto the slopes towards the base of the Seren Way.

Despite their covert escape, Nona felt watched. Joeli had driven her to this. Joeli had spurred her to sudden action. And, although she saw no sign of the girl, somehow Nona felt that the eyes on her back belonged to that same despicable puller of threads. Joeli was a spider in a web, but one bigger than she could ever have built herself.

THE SENSE OF being under observation waned as they approached the city gates after an hour's brisk walk from the foot of the Rock. Although the streets of Verity had lost none of their colour they had gained enough streaks of grey and brown to paint a very different picture from the usual scene. Groups of refugees huddled on every corner. The city guard moved them on but there were always more to replace them. Peasants muddy from their journey with tattered bundles on their backs. Townsmen leading carts heaped with their household treasures, bewilderment in their eyes. Injured soldiers, lost children, a tide of displaced humanity seeking the sanctuary of the Ark.

Nona let Ara lead them through the city's finer quarters where the press of humanity eased and allowed them to make progress. Even Verity's great mansions had a haunted air: windows boarded up, newly conscripted guards at the doors uneasy in ill-fitting uniforms.

Few among the aristocracy or wealthy walked the broad streets around the emperor's palace. Ara took them close enough to see the spires of Crucical's home. Somewhere deep within lay the Ark around which the emperors had built their power. Nona could sense its heartbeat even at this distance, a faint pulsing in the fabric of the world. Perhaps they had a shipheart in there. Perhaps something more.

Behind Nona came the grating of the gates opening at the mansion they had just passed, people emerging, the clank of armour. She ignored it.

"Novices, and so very far from home in dangerous times." A man's voice, dripping with the accents of nobility.

The girls turned to see a ring of armoured soldiers forming around four figures, three dark clad, and one in the finery of a lordling. This last one, lean, tall, his small smile full of mockery and malice, was known to Ara and Nona.

"Lano Tacsis." Ara used none of the honorifics that convention demanded.

Nona opened her mouth but her words ran dry. She had last seen the man as he stood and watched her writhe and soil herself in screaming agony on the floor of a Noi-Guin cell. Flaw-blades sprang unbidden from each of her fingers. At their last meeting Lano had watched her suffer the touch of the Tacsis family toy, the Harm, a sigil-worked torture device. Before leaving he had slit her nostril, a scar she still bore, and promised to return to inflict all manner of horrific mutilations upon her. She remembered the pleasure in his voice. The eagerness.

"Nona . . ." Ara's fingers knotted in the shoulder of Nona's habit and she found herself anchored, having unknowingly taken a pace towards Lano.

The soldiers, in Tacsis blues, set hands to sword hilts. The two dark men at Lano's side adjusted their stances. The third of his close guard was a black-haired woman, Safira, who long ago had stabbed Kettle before fleeing the convent and selling her services to Sherzal. Her presence here spoke of renewed associations between the emperor's sister and his most fractious vassal.

"Arabella Jotsis." Lano ignored Nona's advance. "I hear that the Scithrowl dance in the charred ruins of your uncle's halls. These are dangerous times. Especially for little girls."

Nona found her tongue. "You—"

"And Nona . . ." Lano turned his dark eyes her way. He glanced at his right hand and the two crooked fingers, injured when he had first tried to take hold of her years before. "I had them dig up your little friend, you know? What was her name? Saya? Saylar? . . . Saida, that was it! I had a cup made from her skull and gave her bones to my dogs."

Safira moved in beside Lano, frowning, hissing something.

"Nona!" Ara held her back with increasing effort. "It's obvious what he's doing! Don't give him what he wants!"

Nona understood. They were here for the book, that was what was important. But she physically couldn't move away, any more than she could fly. Images of Saida flooded her mind. Saida in the cage, offering comfort. Saida screaming in Raymel Tacsis's grip. Saida's body beneath the sheet before the gallows. She gathered herself to leap among the first of Lano's guards.

Lano's grin broadened and he mimed taking a drink. "I said—"

It was Jula who stepped forward. "Honoured Lano of the House Tacsis. I understand that your soldiers are skilled and that those you have beside you likely share Safira's training. I am sure that you have about your person sigil amulets that you have been assured can absorb and deflect hostile magics. But I must caution you. Nona Grey could tear this street open to the bedrock to see you dead, and level the houses all around us. She could blast you with such force that the amulets your gold has purchased would burn and fall to dust. And before I could take a single step to stop her you would all be smoking offal amid the ruin." Jula shot Nona a look. "You should know that I would do everything with my power to bring her to the emperor's justice after such an outburst. But it would be scant consolation to your corpses."

Safira must have been saying something very similar because, with a snarl, Lano allowed himself to be steered away, across the street towards another road.

Nona watched them go, attempting to regain control of her breathing. The soldiers at the rear of the Tacsis cordon glanced back at her as if even now she might give chase. Nona still wanted to. Jula had been right that she would have killed Lano, but she wouldn't have used the Path to do it. She would have cut his heart out with her bare hands.

✦ ✦ ✦

THE NOVICES RESUMED their journey in a strained silence that lasted for several blocks. Eventually Nona stopped walking and stared at Jula. "You'd do everything in your power to bring me before the emperor's justice?"

Jula turned. She folded her arms. "Yes, I would! We're being invaded. We need every citizen, every soldier. The rule of law is vital to civilization at all times, and when else more so than at times when we're under such strain? You know I'm right, Nona."

Nona fought to keep the smile from her face. "You'd take me in?"

Jula nodded. "I would."

Nona shrugged and grinned. "And when we've stolen this book you're going to confess and throw yourself on the court's mercy?"

Jula harrumphed and started walking again. "That, Nona Grey, is a very different thing!"

THE FRIARY OF St. Castor stood in one of Verity's least desirable quarters, an area given over to industry and warehouses, edged by slums. The stink of tanners curing hides hung over the streets so thickly that Nona felt she should be able to see the fog of it in the air. The shadows had joined hands to usher in evening's gloom and behind closed shutters the first candles were being lit. Ara, Jula, and Ruli walked almost arm in arm, trailing Nona by a few yards. They covered their noses and cast nervous glances at the alleyways. Not that any of them had anything to worry about. Even Jula would be able to knock down a common criminal or two. Nona supposed it to be a sort of anticipatory guilt setting their nerves on edge.

"Try to look natural . . ." Nona glanced over her shoulder at the trio.

"Yes, Mistress Blackeyes." Ruli stuck her tongue out and ringed both her eyes with finger and thumb. "Normal." The more scared Ruli got the more jokes she made.

Nona shook her head and led on. With her stolen wimple she probably looked like a mistress leading novices out. She'd kept growing when the others stopped and stood a head taller than Jula, half a head taller than Ara, with Ruli in the middle.

"Stop touching it!" Ara hissed.

Nona found her fingers at the headdress again. After the disaster at the Shade stores, wearing a wimple was likely to be as close as she ever got to being a nun.

Ahead the friary loured over its neighbours, an ugly brick-shaped building, built of huge sandstone blocks cut from the Rock of Faith. Travelling brothers from all of the empire's monasteries were afforded accommodation within the friary walls when their duties brought them to the capital. Generally those duties would be delivering illuminated manuscripts to patrons, or educating the children of the Sis, but at such troubled times Red Brothers, along with their Grey and Mystic counterparts, might well outnumber their Holy cousins on the friary guest list.

"Wait here," Nona told them.

"Yes, mistress." Next to Ruli, Jula stifled a giggle. The enormity of the crime she was about to take part in seemed to have left her slightly hysterical. Nona would make sure they were all deep in their serenity trances before they approached the records hall.

THE STREET DOOR stood a good ten feet tall, oak weathered to a pale grey and studded with rusty diamond-headed bolts. The monk who opened it looked older and more weathered.

"Yes . . . sister?" The frown beneath white eyebrows suggested that in a long life of thinking that nuns seemed to get younger every year he'd yet to see one *this* young.

"I need to speak with Brother Markus."

A pause while he looked her up and down. Even from the height of the street step he had to crane his neck to meet her eyes. On finding them wholly black his brows lifted. "Hmmm." He turned away and closed the door. His "wait here" reached her through the thickness of the wood.

Nona huddled in the doorway eyeing the street. If Jula's reports were to be taken seriously the Scithrowl hordes could be pouring past this door within days. Nona found it hard to believe. The emperor had legions at his disposal, the brothers and sisters of the Red, all the might of the Academy. Fortresses and castles dominated the Corridor from the Grampains to the Marn. The empire had endured for close on a thousand years and withstood half a hundred wars.

"I thought you were supposed to be hard to sneak up on." Markus's voice startled Nona from her pondering. Already the ancient was closing the door behind him lest the mere scent of a nun corrupt the brothers within. For an instant Nona pictured the old brother in an embrace with Abbess Wheel. They would probably get on. "Something funny?" Markus asked.

"Ah, no. Actually rather the opposite." Nona led out into the street, stepping over a fetid puddle. "We need to do it today."

"Today?"

"Today." She glanced back.

A moment of worry crossed Markus's face but he pushed it aside and made a smile so warm it brought colour to Nona's cheeks. "Today it is, then. It's not as if I need to prepare anything."

A few more strides brought them to Ara, Ruli, and Jula, the latter two staring at Markus with wide-eyed fascination while his gaze lingered on Ara's golden beauty, not for long but for rather longer than it took Nona to grow irritated.

"Novices." A large smile and a small bow.

Nona felt a pulse of the marjal empathy that Markus worked so well, at a low enough level to be an unconscious thing. She remembered how he had been in the cage before his talent flowered. A rather awkward, argumentative boy. She supposed that they had both changed beyond recognition.

"Won't you be missed?" Markus asked. The sun had set and in the broad streets of the merchants' quarter stray leaves spiralled here and there in the wind's swirl.

"No." Nona was less confident than she sounded. Ghena and Ketti had been primed with cover stories about the four of them going to bed early. They had also been encouraged to exercise all the skills Sister Apple had tried to impart to them in creating the illusion that the missing novices' beds were occupied. Ruli and Nona had long ago fabricated fake heads from dried gourds onto which they had glued their own hair, saved from past punishment shavings. But there remained the distinct possibility that Sister Rose might come up to check on Nona after her unauthorized departure from the sanatorium, or that Kettle might drop by seeking clues to the day's theft, or that Rock might burst in on one of the not infrequent chastity patrols ordered by Abbess Wheel. Nona hoped that the looming crisis would distract the nuns from the doings of novices and focus them on matters of more existential importance.

The houses grew larger, older, and somewhat more shabby as they approached the old cathedral. The building had lost its status over a hundred years before at the time the Church constructed the spectacular Sacred Blood whose spires threatened to overtop even the Ark. The old cathedral had been given over to various purposes, including housing former priests too decrepit to care for themselves, the management and payment of Church staff across the empire, and, crucially, the storage of documents deemed too important to destroy but for which regular access was not necessary.

Even this close to the city's geographic heart, and so far from the walls that not even the towers could be seen, soldiers stood on many corners. Patrols hurried past in full armour and the colours of the Seventh. The citizens watched and worried. Verity was the only city Nona had spent time in so she didn't know if other cities had moods, but Verity did, and it was scared.

"Tree of Gold." Jula pointed to the elaborate cathedral tower peering over the roof of the mansion ahead.

"It doesn't look like a tree," Ruli said.

"That would be architecturally challenging," Ara said.

Markus's deep voice sounded behind them. "At one time, the central tower bore golden branches similar to the arborat. I believe they were wooden and covered with beaten gold. The taproot runs down through the great hall and is said to burrow beneath the catacombs."

Nona glanced at the cuffs of her habit. The arborat was stitched there, a dozen of the tree symbols embroidered to encircle her wrists. Their tap-roots strained towards the first ancestor, though they thinned and vanished before reaching her elbows. She tried to imagine the arborat a hundred feet tall, the Ancestor's tree gleaming in the sun. "Serenity," she instructed, and reached for her own.

THE FORMER CATHEDRAL stood at the centre of a broad plaza where a handful of stallholders still lingered, dismantling their awnings and counters. Guards stood at attention on the main steps, six of them. Their presence was probably dictated by the fact that the clergy's wages were held somewhere within, rather than the need to watch over dusty books, but they would guard the high priest's vault just the same.

"Ruli, I want you high and watching. There might be thread-works on the vault. We could trigger an alarm. If anyone comes running do what you can to slow them up with mist and shadows."

Ruli nodded. "I'll try."

"Ara, you're on diversion. If we have trouble it could bring soldiers. If that happens they're going to need a better reason to head somewhere else. Perhaps a light-and-thunder show would do it."

Ara nodded. "I'll be up there." She pointed to the roof of a mansion facing onto the plaza.

"Markus, you're with me. All we need is for everyone we meet to be agreeable."

He nodded. "That rather depends on who we meet, but I can be pretty persuasive."

"And Jula, you're the brains."

"I am?" A moment of panic threatened from the far side of Jula's serenity. "I am." The repetition bore more confidence.

"Let's do it, then." Nona led towards the cathedral doors wondering where it was that Jula renewed her confidence and whether there was any more left there. This was dangerous. The killing kind. Stealing Sister Pan's book could see them thrown out of the convent and possibly into a cell. Being caught stealing from the high priest's vault would see them executed, no doubt in some unpleasant manner prescribed by an antiquated church law.

Nona tried to steady the tremor in her hands. So much at stake and all for a promise to an old woman. Staked on a promise and on the faith that even at the end of her life Abbess Glass could still outplay all comers in the long game.

As she mounted the broad steps Nona reached for the order imprinted with the abbess's seal of office. Jula had Sister Pan's book in a leather satchel beneath her arm.

"Sister?" One of the guards stepped down to intercept her. "It's too late in the day to go inside. All the clerks have gone home."

"I'm delivering a forbidden text to the high priest's vault." Nona nodded towards Jula, who held out the order blazoned with the abbess's seal.

"I'm sorry, sister." The man frowned at Jula's paperwork. "You should have sent ahead to make an appointment. You'll have to return in the morning." He blocked her path. He lacked an inch or two on her in height but stood far broader in the shoulders, a steel breastplate protecting the space between them.

Markus stepped up, an easy smile in place. "Guardsman, this blue-eyed nun can't wait in a war-torn city with a forbidden book. It could fall into the wrong hands. It needs to be placed safely in the vaults."

A moment's silence hung between them. Markus started to nod and the guardsman hesitantly took to nodding too. "Blue eyes . . ." A frown and then with more confidence he said, "Yes. It would be better stored away, brother."

The guardsman led them up the steps. The other guards opened the doors, two men to each, then closed them at their heels. And although Markus had won their entrance with a power that should see the three of them safely in and safely out again, Nona couldn't help but feel that those great doors closing behind them were the jaws of a trap that they had willingly stuck their heads into.

"We'll roust Brother Edran from his chambers and get that book where it belongs."

"Brother Edran?" Nona asked.

"He oversees the high priest's vault. Spends more time locked up with those books that he does with people." The guardsman shuddered.

The cathedral's great hall had been divided up long ago, timber frames set to support new levels and partition walls. The guardsman led them into a maze of corridors, smoke-stained and sparsely lit with lanterns. They passed a few elderly clerks, one busy locking doors and extinguishing lights. Here and there guardsmen slouched along on patrol, old men and boys now that the wars had claimed those fit for battle.

Their guardsman stopped at a door deep within the structure and hammered on it.

"Edran? Edran! Customers for you!"

A long pause followed. "He's a bit deaf." The guardsman shrugged apologetically. "EDRAN!"

This time a series of clatterings mixed with complaints grew louder until the door jerked open and an old man in a bed-robe stared up at them, his bald head surrounded by a fringe of white hair, with more of the stuff erupting from both ears.

"These folk have a book for the vault," the guard said.

"Has ale finally turned your brain to mud, Mika?" Edran squinted at Nona, Jula, then finally Markus. "Tell them to come back in the morning."

Mika frowned and eyed Nona with a measure of suspicion. "It *is* irregular . . ."

Markus spoke, his voice vibrant, each word sinking into the mind. "It is important. The book must go in the vault now."

"Nonsense! The day some monk, too young to shave, comes to order me about in my own archive . . ." Outrage overtook the old man's tongue. "Get out!"

Markus blinked and shot Nona a worried look. "It. Is. Important."

"It will be important in the morning. Right now it's just irritating." Edran advanced, pushing Markus before him. "Get out! Mika, drag this boy out of here or so help me . . ."

Jula backed away, looking mortified.

Nona couldn't believe how easily the old man was shrugging off Markus's best efforts. Despite herself she believed his words, more deeply than she believed her own name. She stared at the librarian, hunting for some clue to his resilience.

"Yes, Edran. Apologies." Mika interposed himself between the two men and took hold of Markus.

Nona moved quickly. She moved in front of Edran, meeting his outraged stare with her wholly black eyes, and pressed one hand firmly to his chest.

"What?" His eyes widened at the sight of hers. "How dare you!"

At the same time Nona reached around with her other arm to pinch the silver chain she had seen at the back of his neck above the bed-robe's collar. With the links between her fingertips she applied enough sharpness to part them and let the chain fall. In that instant she gave the old man a shove hard enough to rock him back on his heels. "It's important!"

Somewhere between Edran's bare ankles and slippered feet an amulet tinkled unnoticed to the floor trailing a silver chain.

"Guards!" Edran's shout was hoarse with rage.

"Explain again, Markus!" Nona called out.

Markus, halfway down the hall and being manhandled away at speed, spoke over the guardsman's shoulder. "You want to help us."

Edran's anger clouded with confusion. "Wait . . ."

Mika released the monk, brushing at his habit apologetically. "Let me help . . ."

"We need to get this book stored safely in the vault before nightfall," Markus said.

The old man threw up his hands. "If you must, you must!" He frowned at Nona as if remembering the shove. A guardsman rounded the corner, puffing, but Edran waved him away impatiently. He turned to Markus. "Wait here. I'll get my keys." And with that he retreated to his room, closing the door.

"You should go now." Markus sent the guardsman back to his post.

Nona bent to scoop up the amulet, and as Markus turned back to her she opened her hand to display it, a sigil wrought in silver.

"It's the mendant sigil." Markus squinted at it as if the thing were too bright to look upon. "To negate manipulation of thoughts and emotions. Abbot Jacob and the senior monks at St. Croyus have similar protection. The novices would be in charge otherwise."

Nona closed her fist around it. Part of her wanted to take the thing as her own. Security against Joeli's manipulations and whatever else might come her way in the future. But such a valuable object would be missed and in the resultant hue and cry her visit to the archives would undoubtedly be discovered. With reluctance she set the amulet down by the doorway. "Let him find it later."

+ + +

EDRAN KEPT THEM waiting ten minutes, finally emerging in his ink-stained work-robes, jingling a heavy bunch of keys.

"This really is most irregular. Let me see your order."

"It's here, archivist." Jula produced the document and held out Aquinas's *Book of Lost Cities*.

Edran studied both, raising a white eyebrow as he leafed through the pages of the latter. "Hmm. Amazing that such works keep cropping up." He snapped his fingers. "Let's be about it, then!"

He led them through more corridors, unlocking two sets of doors and descending a flight of steps. "I've told them a thousand times that it's madness to store books in the catacombs, but do they listen?" With his lantern raised, Edran hurried along a tunnel lined with empty niches, coming to a halt before a heavy door on which he rapped: four knocks, a pause, three knocks.

After a long pause someone unbolted the door and Edran pushed through. The antechamber beyond lay bare save for candles arrayed around the walls and a chair on which a single guardsman had been sitting. Opposite the door they entered by stood the iron portal to the high priest's vault.

"Hernas, I'm making a deposit." Edran held out an impatient hand towards Jula. "The book, girl."

The guardsman adjusted his iron helm and stepped in close, frowning. Unlike the hirelings at the entrance this was a church-guard, perhaps forty, weathered by the Corridor wind, the lines of old cuts recorded in white seams across his hands and face, his tabard displaying the Ancestor's tree, a sword at his hip. He stood in contrast to the soft boys and geriatrics they'd passed on the way in. "The vault stays shut after hours, archivist. You know that."

"I . . ." Edran hesitated.

"He's making an exception," Markus said. "It will be all right."

The last words buzzed with power, each pulling at a multitude of threads. Nona found herself nodding—it would be all right.

The church-guard's hand slid towards the hilt of his sword. Nona moved fast. Like Edran, the man before her seemed immune to Markus's influence: like Edran he was likely wearing the mendant sigil. If she could get the thing off him, and quickly, the possibility remained that Markus could smooth things over. The helm! It had to be the helm. It looked too well made, out of place on a church-guard with no other armour save a chain-mail vest beneath his tabard. She crashed into the man, contriving to cut his chinstrap and tear the helm free before they both hit the door behind him.

"Tell him, Markus!" Nona seized the man's wrist, trapping his sword in its scabbard.

Markus blinked in surprise at finding both of them on the ground. "You should help us." Spoken through teeth gritted against the strain of command.

"To arms!" the church-guard yelled. "To a—" Nona banged his head against the door hard enough to silence him.

"Well." Nona slipped a vial of boneless syrup from her habit and administered it to the dazed guard. "Perhaps we should have come back tomorrow."

"I don't understand . . ." Edran started to back towards the door.

"Sorry." Jula caught the archivist's arm and twisted it behind him. "Do you file the books using the Occadavian system? Or is this place still on Dooey ordering?"

"How dare you!" The old man bristled, craning his neck to glare at the novice behind him.

"Sorry . . ." Jula gave an apologetic smile and twisted his arm higher until he yelped. "But I really do have to know."

"Dooey! Dooey!"

Jula eased the pressure. "And is that with chronological ordering and the aleph categories for research?"

"I don't . . . yes!" Another twist replaced truculence with a squeaked affirmation.

"Got what you need?" Nona asked.

"If he's not lying," Jula said.

"I don't think he is." Markus approached, staring the old man in the face. "No."

Nona shrugged and, knocking aside Edran's hand, smeared the last drops of her boneless across his lips.

They laid him beside the guardsman, both face down.

"We should have asked him which key," Jula said as Nona pulled the bunch from Edran's limp fingers.

"It'll be the biggest one." Nona brought up the best candidate, black iron and nearly six inches in length.

The guess proved right and Nona pushed the door open on hinges that squealed louder than Edran had. Fortunately the vault's secure location put it out of earshot of all but a handful of clerics, and Markus had made Edran send those on their way.

"Ready?" Nona looked pointedly at Markus, still crouched over the paralysed men.

The monk nodded, lifting his hands from the backs of their necks, still muttering something. A sigil amulet, twin to Edran's, glimmered on a chain hanging from his fingers. He replaced it around the church-guard's neck before standing and stepping away. Nona followed Jula into the vault, Markus close behind her.

"What did you do to them?"

"I was trying to make sure that the only thing they remembered about you was your dazzling blue eyes." His gaze flickered to her face and he forced a quick grin.

"Will it work?"

He shrugged. "I hope so."

Nona turned back. "Let's give them a different story to tell." She took from beneath her habit a Scithrowl carver, the leaf-bladed dagger issued to Adoma's shock troops. Years ago Zole had given her the blade after taking it from a boy who probably got it from his father. She set it by the guard's feet before retreating into the vault and pulling the door closed. Just inside the chamber beyond she dropped a copper groat, worn and stamped with the head of Adoma's father. It bounced and rolled against the wall. She didn't see which way it landed, but heads or tails it would still point eastward.

"What are you doing?"

"A little misdirection. Let them think it was Scithrowl agents in disguise."

"Very careless Scithrowl agents!"

"The horde is on our doorstep, everyone's jumping at shadows, it won't take much to send them running the wrong way. Let them think spies were here and that soon Adoma's Fist will blow open the city gates for their queen," Nona said. It probably wasn't far from the truth in any case. She turned towards the towering shelves.

In the space before the shelves a thick and slightly narrowing length of ironwood wandered down from the ceiling and continued into the stone floor. The deepest root of the tree of the Ancestor, part of the golden arborat that once spread above the cathedral. The taproot leading back to the source. Nona wondered what she might find if she dug down after it. She shook away the thought. "We need the book, Jula!"

Jula, who had been gazing in hungry amazement at the stacks of tightly bound tomes, jolted back into the moment and began to move between the rows. The shelves bore labels relating to the books they held, each tome carefully wrapped in skeilskin to fend off the damp. The air hung heavy with mildew, mould, and the stink of foxed paper. Markus began to sneeze and Nona, feeling her own nose begin to tingle, moved to the vault door and fresher air, opening it a crack.

"I'll listen out for any trouble."

She waited, calling back the tatters of her serenity trance so that she wouldn't be tempted to urge Jula to hurry up. Outside Ara and Ruli would be imagining all manner of disasters that might have befallen them.

Time crept by, seeming slower than the deepest Nona's hunska blood could bury her between the seconds. She discovered her foot tapping without instruction. Outside the door either Edran or the church-guard made a soft grunt, probably an angry shout muted by the boneless.

More moments crawled by, mounting slowly into minutes. "How's it going?"

"I'm getting there. I've found the right section, I think. I'm having to unwrap everything, though, and then wrap it back up so they don't know what we were after."

A distant shout rang out and at the same time Ara pulsed along their thread-bond an image of soldiers crowding in through the cathedral doors above.

"Hurry! Someone's coming!" Nona hissed.

The distant sound of booted feet approaching at a run. Lots of booted feet.

"Dung on it!" Nona stepped back and pulled the door to, locking it. "We've been found out . . ." It didn't seem possible.

"Found out?" Markus hurried over. "Ancestor! They'll hang us all! How can we be found out?"

"We've been betrayed." Nona stared around the shadowed corners of the vault. There must have been a lot of them coming or Ara and Ruli would have delayed them more effectively.

"We're done for. We can't get past them!"

Nona started to walk the perimeter of the vault, trailing her fingers across the wall. "Jula! Hurry up with that book!"

Markus followed, panic in his voice. "Leave the damn book. If we don't touch it we can say this was all about turning in the other book. Just that we were rather too zealous about it . . ." He trailed off, hearing how weak the excuse sounded once said out loud.

Someone outside shouted into the pause. "Open up!" A fist pounding on iron panels.

"Barricade the door, Markus." Nona took hold of his shoulders and pointed him back at it. "They'll get another key soon enough."

"How will that help?" But he went, taking hold of a ladder used to reach the top shelves.

Nona's mind raced, shredding her serenity. She might battle a way through the soldiers who crowded the antechamber and corridors beyond, but it would hardly be an escape. Murder would be added to the charge of theft. Her own sisters would be set to hunt her down. All she had worked for lost.

She continued pacing, stepping away from the wall where the shelves demanded it, returning to set her fingers to the stone once more. Marjal rock-work allowed for more than the manipulation of stone. Nona sank her senses through the blocks lining the vault and into the ground beyond, a mixture of subsoil and rubble used for the cathedral's foundations. She moved on, her perception continuing to quest through the walls.

"Found it!" Jula had to shout over the hammering at the door. She lifted her lantern in one hand, in the other a fat book bound with black leather.

"Wrap the others. Put them back," Nona shouted.

"I don't know how long this door will hold!" Markus had the ladder wedged against it and was struggling to move one of the smaller freestanding shelves, books spilling to the ground as it lurched and wobbled.

The door looked undamaged to Nona. She hoped they'd take hammers to it and that by the time another key was found the lock would be jammed or the door panel too warped to open.

On the wall opposite the entrance Nona found what she was looking for. A void beyond the stone blocks. The space beneath the cathedral would have housed store chambers, vaults, sewers, drainage channels, and catacombs where the rich and the holy were interred. Nona wished she had the talent to tell how far off the void was, whether it led anywhere, and what lay between her and it. All she could say was that it was a reasonably large space and probably not more than a yard from where her fingertips pressed the wall.

Nona didn't want to follow through with her plan but their options had narrowed to almost none. Joeli had done this. Nona felt sure of it. She had thought that if the Namsis girl discovered their actions she would wait longer, eager to unravel more of their plan and unmask them before the abbess. But even if Joeli missed out on seeing her enemies come to grief this way, she would undoubtedly relish the idea of having them caught like rats in a trap, bottled up in the very room they had tried so hard to enter.

Something hit the door with considerably greater force than any previous blow. Nona glanced back at Jula's and Markus's shocked faces and the great dent in the door behind them. The ladder clattered to the ground and the shelf shed more books.

"You should stand back and cover your ears," Nona said.

She had only to picture Joeli's face to summon the anger she needed. Nona shut her eyes and against the red mist she saw the bright line she sought, burning through her vision. The door shuddered again, another mighty blow reverberating around the vault, and without hesitation Nona leapt at the Path.

As always the Path's touch lit her whole being, as if the Ancestor had reached out and plucked her like a harp string. The power that thrilled through her brought with it such unalloyed joy that it threatened to wash away all trace of the necessary fear that would allow her to fall from it again. Fear that even as the Path's energies burned through her they consumed from within, fraying the fabric of her being. Fear that on returning to the world she would neither be able to hold or shape what she had taken. Fear that with insufficient care she might never again find Abeth but fall into the dark places Sister Pan warned of, places from which there was no return.

Jula's scream brought Nona tumbling from the Path, building up an awful velocity as she fell back into her flesh. For an instant Nona stood, shuddering with power, light bleeding from her skin to fill the vault with crimson and shadow. In the next moment the Path's momentum caught her up and flung her at the wall like a stone from a sling.

Nona lay sprawled and smoking. With a groan she stood up, still armoured in the Path's strength, half-deafened, shaking off rock and dirt, chunks of both still falling behind her. Back through the dust-filled tunnel she had made she could see the glow of Jula's lantern.

"Come on . . ." Her voice escaped as a hoarse whisper. "Hurry!" Louder this time.

Jula came running through, head down, Markus behind her bent low, stumbling across the rubble. Another blow rang out from the vault, followed by the sound of an iron door crashing to the ground.

Nona glanced around as Jula's light started to reveal the space about her. They were in a brick-lined tunnel with a low arched ceiling. Rectangular recesses punctuated the walls, places where coffins might have been slid for eternal rest, prior to their relocation when the cathedral closed.

"Quickly." Jula moved past Nona.

"Come on!" Markus too, galvanizing her into action.

Shaking off the last of her disorientation, Nona gave chase. Shouts echoed back in the vault as the soldiers began to pour in, ready for battle.

The tunnel met a second and they turned left. That tunnel met another and another. Left, right, their choices mounted as they hurried into what proved to be something of a labyrinth.

"We'll never find our way out!" Markus turned, white-faced. Ahead of him Jula splashed on through ankle-deep water.

"We will," Nona said. "And this is good. We can lose them in here."

"I can't stay down here." Markus seemed more terrified than when they'd been moments from capture. Nona could feel the fear bleeding from him, infecting her as only a marjal empath can, filling her mind with images of being trapped, held tight in unbroken darkness far below the ground.

She shook him. "You're a monk. Have a little faith."

"I'm a monk stealing from the Church. I'm not sure the Ancestor would want to help me," Markus whispered, but a shadow of a smile came with it.

"There's a grating here," Jula called back. "It's too high to reach . . . but I can see the stars."

"There you go." Nona tried to hide her own relief. "The Ancestor approves."

14

---◆---

THE ESCAPE

Three Years Earlier

THE TUNNEL INTO the black ice was hard to see. They found it easily, though, announced by the great fan of ink-dark debris strewn before the mouth of it.

"They dug this?" Nona gazed with horror at the opening, little more than six foot high. The malice pricking at her made her want to scratch the skin from her arms. Even without Zole's story she would have known that the black depths of the ice were filled with devils. She felt them, countless, hungry, far worse than Keot, and eager for flesh to occupy. "People actually dug this?"

Zole only nodded and walked on in. Nona followed, trying to imagine the effect on those that had laboured here with picks, the black frost melting all across them.

"I can't see . . ." After twenty yards Nona felt as if her eyes had simply stopped working. Turning, she could see the circle of daylight behind her, just a patch of brightness, illuminating nothing, holding no meaning.

Zole grunted and a moment later the Noi-Guin's shipheart spilled its violet light between them. Nona could see herself now, and Zole, but nothing else. Their surroundings swallowed the glow, returning nothing. Zole led on, her footsteps cautious on the broken ice.

The passage took them perhaps four hundred yards before joining a natural tunnel carved by the passage of meltwater that had long since found a better course. They tramped down from the breach on a ramp formed from the passage debris, now frozen into an irregular, solid mass. The water-cut tunnel crossed theirs at right angles, making their choice of direction unclear. Zole crouched, considering.

"Up?" Nona suggested.

Zole scrutinized the ice for a silent minute, then another. Nona hugged herself. Her toes had grown numb in her ill-fitting boots and the cold had started to seep into her bones.

"Or down." Nona just wanted to move. A thousand eyes watched them, the freezing air sharp with their hatred.

"Up." Zole stood and started along the barely perceptible incline. She moved more slowly here, the ice slick underfoot.

Nona paused for a moment. Where Zole had crouched and waited the ice had paled to a translucent grey. In the depths beneath them the ancient flaws glimmered with the shipheart's violet light.

"It pushes them away!" Nona caught up with Zole, nearly losing her balance in the process. "The shipheart."

"It does." Zole nodded. "It breaks them free of our minds and then, if we are strong, it drives them from our flesh."

Nona kept close to Zole after that. The shipheart's radiance was hard to tolerate but it shielded her from the devils' malice and of two unbearable choices it proved the lesser evil.

The tunnel led them for an untold distance. It might have been miles, snaking through the thickness of the sheet, the vanished stream turning one way and another where pressure hardened the ice into something closer to the consistency of iron. In places where one ancient glacier swallowed another or pushed it from its path, their burden of rock and stone lay bedded through the ice in bands many yards deep.

Several times the gradient steepened and neither novice could continue without falling to her knees and using knives to find purchase. Nona tried her flaw-blades first but they would hardly scratch the black ice, just as they had proved impotent against Raymel Tacsis's devil-haunted skin.

Gaining height, they found the ice riddled with meltwater channels where surface water had drained away after the passage of the focus moon. The sound of running water penetrated the ice, a constant behind which deep-throated gurgling reverberated as chambers filled and emptied around natural airlocks.

In several places vents in the tunnel walls would erupt without warning, blasting out spray-laden air at tremendous velocity. Nona had been dimly aware of such phenomena from her father's tales but it was Zole who dived and took her to the floor when she walked unknowingly in front of one fissure just as it started to blast.

The spray of black mist hurt where it found skin, neither scalding nor freezing nor acid but somehow worse than all three, as if wrongness had been made into liquid.

"How did you know it was coming?" Nona wiped her hands on the range-coat Kettle had given her.

"Working air and water is not so different from working rock." Zole helped Nona to her feet. "There are chambers in the ice that fill with meltwater until they reach a certain level, then empty rapidly. The sudden changes in air pressure can be extreme."

Zole called several halts as they went on, waiting for vents to blow. Each time they paused, the ice's blackness faded to grey around the shipheart. In one long gallery they passed a gauntlet of a dozen vents, each blowing to their own rhythm. Zole explained that the previous night's surge of meltwater must be passing around them on its way to the hidden seas. The most powerful of the vents was fringed with icicles and blasted with regular ferocity. Nona learned the tempo of it before she crossed and was still almost driven from her feet by the tail end of the previous gust.

Nona marvelled at the volume of water that must have flowed through the gallery but it opened onto a chamber that dwarfed it. Nona could see no farther than the shipheart's glow but Zole described the space beyond as if a vast bubble had been trapped beneath the ice.

"There are several exits we—" Zole fell silent.

"We what?"

"Yisht is there."

Nona heard a tremor in Zole's voice for the first time and found it mirrored in her own. "Yisht? You said the Noi-Guin wouldn't come near the black ice!" She strained to see farther into the darkness ahead. "You can't get much more susceptible to devils than Yisht, right?"

"Maybe, maybe not. Her mind is far from weak." Zole lifted the shipheart. "But Yisht no longer has need to fear the *klaulathu*."

"She doesn't?" Nona drew her sword.

"No." Zole sat at the lip of the tunnel, setting her empty hand to the ice, ready to slide into the great chamber. "She is full."

Yisht stood waiting for them close to the great drain at the lowest point of the bubble chamber, a yawning mouth into which thin cataracts of black water cascaded on all sides. Nona knew that nobody who fell down there would be coming out again. The hole seemed to exert a pull all its own, above and beyond that of gravity on a slope of slick, wet ice.

"Why here?" Nona hissed. She released a dagger, slid a foot down the ice, anchored the dagger, pulled the other clear. "Why wasn't she waiting at the entrance?"

"We might have run away," Zole replied, sliding lower. "Here she believes she has us trapped."

Yisht had found or cut a niche where she could stand. Zole and Nona remained on their sides, Nona anchored by her knife hand, Zole somehow finding purchase with her fingers.

Their enemy stood impassive, watching, her stocky figure statue-still. The shipheart's violet light picked out edges, coaxing a detail here and there, the dark glimmer of an eye, the angular planes of her face, the razored length of her tular. Nona had already felt the kiss of a tular in Yisht's hands. Her thigh still bore the scar. Her thighbone too had been notched by the jagged end of the ice-triber's broken sword. The leg ached now as if the cold had entered her through the old wound.

It seemed somehow that through all Nona's dreams of vengeance Yisht might have been waiting for her here within the cathedral vastness of this lightless cavern, black waters rushing past her, the meltwater rain falling endlessly around her.

Yisht saw the short game with unequalled clarity just as Abbess Glass saw the long game. Nona had difficulty seeing either, but somehow she knew this would end here. One way or the other.

Nona hung soaked and freezing, enveloped in the wrongness of devil-laden water, strange urges and alien thoughts trying to ease beneath her skin. The voices competed with those from within her skull as the shipheart gripped her mind, trying to squeeze out devils of her own. She shivered uncontrollably, though whether more from terror or the cold she couldn't tell.

Above all these multiple sources of distress she felt stupid. She didn't dare stand up or see how they could possibly make progress other than on hands and knees. Would they have to crawl to Yisht?

"It would be a sorry place for you to die, child." Yisht watched Zole with blood-filled eyes. "Give me the shipheart and I will let you pass. The other"—she turned her gaze on Nona—"I mean to hurt. The best that she can hope for is that she can throw herself into the depths before I get to her."

Under Yisht's stare Nona found her old anger rising. She'd almost forgotten it in the freezing night of the under-ice but now, with the ice-triber's attention upon her, the old images that had haunted so many dreams rose again, filling her mind with Hessa's death. She sheathed her sword and fumbled a throwing star numb-fingered from the bandolier around her chest. "The Ancestor cautions us against becoming a slave to revenge, Yisht. And although I want to hurt you I will be satisfied just to see you die." She lifted her arm to throw. "How well can you dodge down here?"

Yisht opened her mouth wide, her expression savage, the snarl of a fever-sick beast. The teeth she bared at Nona were as black as the ice.

"She's been drinking the water!" Nona shuddered at the thought, then drew back her arm.

"Wait." Zole held out a hand to forestall her, then curled the fingers into a fist. "Hang on." All around them the ice began to fracture, black plates carving away and sliding towards the gullet. Ice began to explode upwards and outwards as if some creature were burrowing beneath it. The air filled with fragments.

When the frost cleared from the air a different topology lay revealed in the shipheart's glow.

"How?" Nona gasped.

"Water-work is not so different from rock-work," Zole said. "Especially when it is ice."

Zole had carved them a stepped path to Yisht two yards wide with a broader ledge immediately in front of her. She reached out and sunk the shipheart into the ice before them, so deep that only the top half remained in view.

"Why didn't you just tip her down the hole?" Nona asked.

Zole glanced her way. "She is a warrior of the ice." She stood and drew her sword. "Besides, the *klaulathu* would not let her fall. Violence is sweet to them."

Nona got to her feet, still wary of her balance, her borrowed coat hanging wet around her, dripping. She returned the throwing star to its place among the others and drew her sword.

"Together?" Nona gritted her teeth against their chattering.

"She would use us against each other," Zole said. "There is too little room."

Nona sighed and stepped forward.

"No." Zole put a hand out to stop her. "I will go."

"I'm your Shield." Nona's anger faltered under a sudden wave of relief. She wanted to end Yisht but no part of her truly believed herself capable of the feat. She saw Hessa's face again, felt her last moments, and the anger surged back. "She's mine."

"No." Zole spoke the word with that buzzing resonance that had stopped a Scithrowl rider from seeing what lay right before him. And while Nona struggled with the compulsion the ice-triber advanced on Yisht along the ledge she had fashioned.

Yisht stepped forward, tular in hand, ready to meet her former pupil. The first clash of steel broke Nona free of Zole's command and immediately she started to follow her friend.

The two ice-tribers fought within the level circle that Zole had formed, their footwork precise, hardly slipping despite the black slickness beneath them. Zole attacked with all of the swiftness and precision that Nona found so hard to counter, a relentless assault, free of flamboyance, efficient and focused on the kill. Yisht defended with unnerving skill, countering hunska speed with the ability to anticipate every attack.

The ringing of blades echoed around the vast, hidden chamber, returning in fractured peals. Once Yisht slipped and fell, but immediately Nona saw that she had allowed it to happen, dropping beneath Zole's thrust to kick her shin, taking her down too. Both combatants found their feet together and rose with swords swinging.

Whilst Yisht could mount an impenetrable defence she could find no way to pierce Zole's guard: her attacks were too slow and she hardly tried, knowing such moves left her open. Instead she relied on her greater strength, knowing that Zole's speed would fade, leaving her with the advantage.

Somehow, even with Zole, Yisht was able to see all action and consequence with several seconds' warning. Keot had told Nona that Yisht saw only what people would do. She read the future actions of her opponents. She would know if Nona was going to flip a coin, but not whether it would land heads or tails. In such a fight, though, knowing what her opponent would do seemed to be enough.

The din of sword on sword continued. Razored steel turned away from flesh again and again, sometimes with fractions of an inch to spare.

"Draw back!" Nona could see Zole beginning to slow. "I can take her!" She felt ashamed, standing there while Zole fought her battle for her, ashamed of the relief she'd experienced when Zole stepped forward. "Retreat!"

Zole showed no signs of drawing back. She attacked, her swiftness almost that of her initial assault. For a moment Yisht was forced to retreat to the very edge of the platform. At that instant Zole stamped and the ice erupted beneath her opponent, a detonation every bit as violent as those that had created the platform in the first place.

Somehow Yisht contrived to have the force of it drive her at Zole. She deflected the novice's sword thrust and grappled her. Zole slid back before the impact and drove her knife into Yisht's side, but despite the wound the woman kept her feet. A moment later Yisht held Zole's knife hand at the wrist, placed her other hand behind the girl's elbow, and spun her straight-armed out over the slope. The force and timing of the move were sufficient to loft Zole above the ice and she fell into the gullet below them without touching the sides. Her scream hung in the air far longer than she did.

"No!" Nona stared in disbelief, first at the void into which Zole had fallen, then at the space where she had been standing.

"Yes." Yisht pulled Zole's knife from her side, then reached around to remove a shard of black ice embedded in her back. Her blood should have run in rivers but somehow the devils inside her refused to let more than a trickle escape, the air around it steaming.

Terror and fury waged their old war through Nona. Yisht had killed another of her friends and now she would come for her.

Nona tried to see the Path but it was a distant thread even with the ship-heart just a couple of yards away. She had walked the Path twice in Sherzal's palace. The second time had nearly killed her. A third surely would, even if she could manage it. Half of her demanded that she run, half that she launch herself at Yisht and attack with every ounce of her passion.

Yisht picked up her tular and began to advance on her. The shipheart lay between them, the cleared ice all around it violet-lit. "I will enjoy kill-ing you, little girl."

Yisht barely seemed to notice her wounds. She walked with a hunter's confidence. Nona sheathed her sword and drew a second knife from her belt. Clutching only the corner of a plan and a faint hope, she followed her fear and ran. Pursued by Yisht's laughter she began to retreat towards the mouth of the tunnel she had entered by. She climbed the slope using the strength of her arms, stabbing her knives into the ice to advance, her goal lost in the darkness above her.

As the curve of the chamber steepened to near vertical, Nona paused to look back. She could see nothing of her surroundings, only Yisht below her approaching the island of greying, violet-lit ice around the shipheart. And just behind Yisht, defying all illumination, the black throat that had consumed Zole. The air still echoed with the memory of her despairing scream.

Yisht reached the shipheart and broke it from the ice, snarling as if it burned her hands. She stood, clutching the orb, then came after Nona, apparently unconcerned by the slickness of the chamber floor that curved steeply up to become the chamber wall. To Nona, hanging by her knives, the ice-triber's advance seemed impossible. Maybe the shipheart was en-hancing Yisht's marjal talent, or the devils inside her were powering her on in their eagerness to see violence unfold.

Nona redoubled her efforts, reaching up to anchor a dagger, heaving herself up behind it, repeating the action with the other hand. She hauled herself over the tunnel's lip, sobbing with exhaustion. All around her the shipheart's light grew stronger as Yisht steadily narrowed the gap between them.

Nona got to her feet, slipping back to her knees immediately. No feeling remained in her extremities and she shuddered with the cold, her teeth chattering uncontrollably. She stood again, almost falling again, and staggered on, tearing off the bandolier of throwing stars. She could lie in wait for Yisht, try to behead her as she crested the tunnel mouth. But Yisht could see Nona's actions in the near future. She could examine how each of her own actions and each of Nona's actions would unfold and could choose the one that suited her. Whatever Nona chose to do, she would end up dead, or worse . . . captured. With only the thinnest sliver of hope, and pursued by fear, Nona fled into the dark.

Moving with reckless speed, Nona opened up a gap while Yisht was still climbing. She could hear blasts from the air vents in the gallery ahead, the irregular tattoo of their eruptions reverberating down the icy tunnel. Soon she could feel the edge of the explosions, the pulses of freezing mist and the wrongness as the black frost settled and melted on her skin.

Nona came blind into the gallery, relying on memory, reaching for her clarity to separate and time the blasts. Numb-fingered and trembling, she pulled her throwing stars from the bandolier. If she cut herself she didn't feel it. A blast roared out close at hand and as it died away Nona found the vent. She lifted her double handful of spiked steel to the icy maw and hurriedly jabbed as many of the stars as she could into the interior. Most of them spilled from her grasp and rattled away. In the distance the tunnel along which she had retreated lit with a violet light.

Nona drew her sword and stood her ground. She thought of Hessa and of Zole and let her anger warm her as the black figure approached.

"Come on, then." Nona spoke into the lull between a series of blasts farther back along the gallery. Her sword hand trembled but her voice held steady.

Yisht dropped the shipheart at the entrance, her hands white to the wrists. By the time she had pulled her tular clear of its scabbard the stains of competing devils were already advancing from beneath the sleeves of her tunic. A scald spread across the back of her sword hand and Nona wondered if it might be Keot, eager to play his part in her demise.

Nona threw her knife with her off hand as Yisht closed on her. The ice-triber stepped aside, letting the blade cut her hair as it passed.

"I can see what you will do before you do it. You must know this by now."

Yisht thrust as soon as she came in range. Nona turned the blade from her body, almost losing hold of her own. The sword felt dead in her hand, her frozen fingers barely able to tell they gripped a hilt. She tried a swing, a clumsy effort that Yisht knocked aside with contempt.

"Hunskas . . . so proud of their quickness, so simple to undo."

Nona attacked again with little hope other than to stop Yisht from launching attacks of her own. With the cold in her fingers Nona felt as if someone else were wielding her sword. Once, twice, three times Yisht blocked swings so clumsy that Sister Tallow would weep to see them.

"Time to end this nonsense." Yisht pressed forward.

Nona took a step back. Her footing was so unsure she hardly dared move, a fact that by itself removed any advantage of her speed.

Yisht feinted left then cut in towards Nona's sword arm. Nona blocked the blow just barely but lost her grip on her weapon. As the sword tumbled from her fingers an icy gale howled in from the right, building swiftly past hurricane towards something altogether worse. The vent blast lifted both of them from their feet, and it came edged with more than ice. Glittering amid the blast in the shipheart's light came a dozen and more of the throwing stars, some torn from the ice that Nona had jammed them into, others vomited up from the depths to which they had fallen.

Nona slowed the world to a crawl. Keot had told her that Yisht knew every move she made against her ahead of time, but Nona had dumped the throwing stars too far ahead of this moment for Yisht's precognition to reach. The act that now propelled them was not of Nona's making. Yisht might be able to explore the next few seconds of any human's future but when it came to the dropping of an apple from a tree, or the roll of dice, she had no more warning than any other person.

As the throwing stars hurtled forward Nona twisted her body to avoid them, ducking her head beneath the flight of one star, pulling her hand from the path of another. She couldn't avoid them all. One of the projectiles sliced her side as she lacked the traction to move away. Yisht, however, hung as if frozen, held in the jaws of fate. One star hammered into her chest, another into her left wrist, and a third hit her forehead, just above her right eyebrow.

The blast slammed both of them against the far wall of the gallery. Yisht slid to the floor. Nona dropped too.

A wheezing laugh echoed behind Nona as she lay stretched out across the ice, all of her hurting.

"You cannot kill me."

Nona glanced back at Yisht, sitting propped against the gallery wall, almost lost in the darkness. A knife in one hand. The ice-triber, seemingly dazed by the impact, tugged at the star embedded in her forehead. The steel point came clear of the bone with a squeaking noise and blood trickled into Yisht's eye. "I cannot die." She tossed the weapon aside. She sounded like Raymel had at the last. Nona had run him through, stabbed him a dozen times, and yet the devils inside him refused to let him fall. It had been Yisht's own sigil of negation that had finally broken their hold . . . and been destroyed in the process.

"Yes." Nona's fingers found the hilt of Yisht's tular, lying where the wind had dropped it, a yard to her right. She drew her remaining knife and stabbed it into the ice, gaining purchase to spin around. "Yes, you can."

Blood had blinded Yisht on the side the blow came in from. She raised her hand even so, but the knife slipped from her fingers. Nona didn't know if Yisht was too dazed to properly mine the future, or if the circumstances simply gave no chance to evade the blow. All she knew was the rush of relief as the tular sheared first through Yisht's hand and then her neck. Her severed head followed the sword's arc and bounced away into the darkness.

15

---◆---

HOLY CLASS

Present Day

ARA AND RULI were waiting at the agreed spot by the statue of General Isen in Grampain Square.

"Thank the Ancestor!" Ara threw herself at Nona. For a long moment Nona held her, breathing the gold of her hair, grateful for the security of her arms.

Ruli hugged Jula wordlessly, leaving Markus standing somewhat bemused, surrounded by embracing novices.

"There were a hundred soldiers at least!" Ara broke away, glancing at the streets joining the square. "We couldn't stop them. They ran straight at the cathedral doors."

"Well, they didn't get us," Nona said.

"And we got the book!" Jula stepped back from Ruli and dug in her habit. Her face fell. "I had it! I know I had it."

"Jula!" Nona's stomach made a cold fist.

"Kidding." Jula produced the book with a flourish.

"Jula!" Ruli shoved her.

"We'd better get back." Ara's face grew suddenly serious. "Whoever got those soldiers to raid the archives isn't going to stop there . . ."

"They'll be waiting for us at the convent! We're all going to be banished!" Ruli grabbed hold of Jula again, as if she might somehow save her. Her mood had oscillated between carefree and hysterical ever since leaving the convent that evening, as if the gravity of their situation kept returning despite her best efforts to drive all thoughts of it away.

"We've done nothing." Nona frowned, concentrating. "At worst we've been out after hours. If we get back up top unseen we've just been out by the sinkhole moon-bathing."

"Until they find the abbess's seal on you!" Jula said. "I can't believe that she hasn't missed it yet. Just wait until she has to confirm a new nun and finds it missing . . ."

"Confirmations happen on high holy days. We've got weeks." Nona managed a confidence she didn't feel. The opportunities to get close to Abbess Wheel were few and far between.

"Fine. Well, what about this?" Jula waved Aquinas's *Book of the Moon* at her. "One look at it and we're all done for."

"So we make sure they don't get a look. We hide it before we get back. Perhaps you can find what we need and memorize it."

"I liked the whole Argatha prophecy better when it was supposed to be a four-blood who saved us." Jula frowned at the tome in her hand. "Not four shiphearts, the Ark, and some poor idiot who has to memorize a whole damn book. Just one four-blood. Nice and simple."

"I miss Zole." Ruli let go of Jula's habit and stared at the ground. "Even if she wasn't the Chosen One . . ."

Nobody had anything to say to that and for a moment only the wind spoke.

"I have to get back," Markus said. "Lovely to meet you all, novices." He brushed some of the mud from his robe.

"Brother Markus." Ara inclined her head.

Markus bowed his head in return, then looked at Nona. "I did you a great injustice at the Academy. I hope that account is now settled."

"It is," Nona said.

"I'm not sure any of us will survive the next month." Markus raised a hand to forestall any patriotic objection, though none appeared to be forthcoming. "But if we do survive, then whether it's under Durnish overlords, the battle-queen's dominion, or our own glorious emperor, long may he reign, I would like to meet you again, Nona Grey."

Nona felt the heat rise in her cheeks. Ruli and Jula stared from her to Markus and back, openmouthed. Nona opened her own, calling on the Ancestor, or the Hope, or any small god who might be listening to put some words there, any words at all as long as they were cool, witty, and sophisticated. A moment's silence stretched to the point at which any coherent sound would be acceptable as long as it vaguely resembled a response . . .

"ANCESTOR'S BLESSINGS, BROTHER?" Ruli asked, probably for the tenth time. "Ancestor's blessings?" Eleven.

"It was all I could think to say." Nona picked up the pace again. Verity's lights lay three miles behind them, the twinkling of the convent two miles ahead.

"But Ancestor's blessings?" Jula panted.

"I was stressed, all right?" Nona saw Markus's eyebrow go up again. She couldn't stop seeing it.

"Leave Nona alone." Ara came up alongside her, running tirelessly. "Brother Markus is clearly a very holy man. It's only natural that Nona should want to share blessings with him. Rather than, you know, respond to what he said."

Ruli and Jula snorted and fell back, gasping for breath.

Nona ran on towards the Rock of Faith. A kind of hysteria had infected her friends. The type that demanded you cry or you laugh. In the east distant fires peppered the countryside, too many and too bright. And on the road, despite the hour, they had already passed a dozen ragged bands limping towards the city, many with everything they owned heaped upon handcarts.

The fears that surrounded the novices were the kind that were too big to hold inside all the time. War in the east. War in the west. Both converging on the capital with horrifying speed. And now the distinct possibility that the full authority of the Church itself would be turned upon them, the novices branded as thieves of a forbidden book, a crime for which Nona had no doubt that some antique law would demand a gruesome and almost certainly fatal punishment. She vowed it wouldn't come to that, but even if the others agreed to fight their way free . . . any future that awaited them looked very bleak.

Close to the plateau's base Nona called a halt. She and Ara waited while Ruli and Jula caught them up. Ara patrolled the area, her shadow-work unravelling the night for inspection while Jula got her breath back.

"I'll go up first," Nona said. "Ara will check the Seren Way, shadow-wrapped, and get you two into the undercaves." The cave entrance lay close to the start of the track. "Ruli will lead Jula through to the novice cloisters, and somewhere on the way you can find a place to hide the book. Somewhere Jula will be able to visit alone when she needs to study it."

"What if they're guarding the track?" Jula asked. "We could all go around to the Styx Valley and come up from the west . . ."

"Too far." Nona shook her head. Gaining the plateau from the west was easy and the Styx Valley was generally unwatched but it would take a detour of several miles. "Ara will have to make a distraction so you can get into the caves, then find her own way up so she can scout the cloister exit for you." Nona stared up at the cliffs. Here and there the moonlight caught a hint of the Seren Way zigzagging its path towards the heights. "Ara can take the Vinery Stair. I'll climb."

"By myself?" Ara threw up her hands in mock horror.

"We all know the story if we're caught. I'll reach the convent first and check that nobody is waiting for the rest of you at the dorms."

"You'll check the coast is clear using . . . your legendary shadow-weaving skill?" Ruli said. "Ara should be the first in!"

"Ara will wait for you at the laundry well." Nona didn't care that Ruli had a point. If anyone was waiting for their return it would be Nona that they caught, not Ara, not Ruli or Jula.

"I have to go through the caves blind?" Jula asked. "And rely on Ruli to find the way?"

"Yes. And don't drop the book," Nona said.

"I said we should have brought a lantern!" Jula pouted.

"You did not."

"Well . . . I thought it!"

Ruli rolled her eyes and set off towards the base of the cliffs. "See you in the dormitory, Nona. Or trying to swim in the Glasswater with iron yokes on. One or the other."

Nona had no answer to that. It was an end she had come perilously close to before, and with Wheel now in charge it seemed that the oldest and cruellest of the Church's punishments were more likely to be applied than they had been for many years.

"Get Jula back safe. Don't tell anyone where you put the book. Not even me or Ara!" Nona called after her. She turned to Ara. "Make sure you get them in safe, and watch out for Joeli."

Ara gave a curt nod and set off after Ruli, pulling Jula with her, all of them grave-faced. The good humour that had sustained them after Nona's parting words to Markus had died somewhere along the road home. Perhaps as they passed the first of the refugees, or when they first caught the smell of smoke on the wind, or maybe at the point when they saw the convent lights blazing, every window in the abbess's house aglow, the comfort of routine cast aside on a night where sleep would be a stranger.

✦   ✦   ✦

NONA SCALED THE cliffs, choosing a spot that steered well clear of the windows to the Shade classroom. She came up behind the convent where the peninsula narrowed, and hung with just her head above the edge, waiting for the moon's focus to blind any watchers.

The moonlight had been building as Nona climbed, the warmth rising with her. The convent buildings began to shine, crimson in the focused light of the dying sun. And Nona marvelled, as she had so many times before, that the moon reflecting that light had been put there by men and women like her, people who now stood within the Ancestor and whose blood ran in her veins.

Nona hauled herself over the clifftop with sufficient strength to land on her feet. Keeping low amid the fierce dazzle of the focus, she ran towards the convent, hiding in the mists vomiting from the Glasswater sinkhole. Like the mist she allowed herself to be drawn away on the uncertain wind, angling towards her target.

Nona made a quick circuit of the convent, watching for any sign of trouble that might be waiting for the others. Although too many lights burned in the windows, the spaces between the buildings seemed quiet. Unusually so. She spotted Sister Rock on patrol and a subtle bump on the conical roof of the rookery tower that was likely one of the Grey Sisters keeping watch for troubles of a different order than errant novices.

Nona watched until Ara came slinking in from the Vinery Stair, betrayed only by the shadow trailing thickly in her wake. They watched together from the cloister roof, wrapped in those same shadows, as Jula and Ruli emerged hesitantly from the laundry wing and hurried to the dormitories.

Before the girls made it to the door a band of mounted soldiers clattered in among the convent buildings, their lanterns held high as if seeking something.

"Hells, they'll be spotted!" Ara hissed.

Already Sister Rock was hurrying towards the sound of hooves and the bump on the rookery roof had detached itself, now no doubt flowing invisibly to join the riders. If Jula and Ruli were hauled before the abbess's desk their whole night's work could unravel. Wheel wasn't shy of using harsh methods to get to a truth that satisfied her, and if she had discovered the theft of her seal there was no telling what anger might drive her to.

"Go after them. Get them inside," Nona hissed back. She grabbed a rooftile and with a crack of her arm sent it scything through the night to explode against the side of the bathhouse. The detonation drew all eyes. Ara was already gone.

Nona launched a second tile, this one aimed at the flagstones past the bathhouse, farther from the soldiers. Before it hit, Nona had slithered on her belly and dropped from the roof.

Kettle would be out there on the rooftops or prowling between the buildings. After the disaster in Sister Apple's stores Nona was far from sure what sort of reception she would get from either of the nuns. She wasn't keen to find out.

Nona had never been able to spot Sister Kettle. Her friend was one of the few who could put fear into her. There's nothing like running in the dark and knowing that you are exposed, vulnerable to attack from any angle. Nona relied on her foot speed. She ran towards the rear of the dormitory, the flesh of her back crawling with the knowledge that at any moment a venomed dart might come speeding from the shadows to bring her down.

Nona reached the rear wall of the dormitory and released a sigh of relief. To avoid the activity towards the front of the building, along with any of Joeli's thread-traps, she climbed the wall and slipped the shutter catch to Ara's study room, creeping from there to her bed. Part of her wanted to cross the room, haul Joeli from her bed, and pin her to the wall, with flaw-blades if she put up a fight. The truth would come out swiftly enough.

Nona bit back on her instincts and went to her bed instead. Ara already lay in the neighbouring bed feigning sleep and faintly illuminated by the hooded lantern on the wall. Nona slid beneath her covers, straining her ears for sounds of heavy feet on the staircase. Those soldiers had come for a reason. It couldn't be long before they brought the abbess to the dormitory doors and began to ask questions about the theft from the high priest's vault.

She lay staring at the dark with the need for violence twitching in her fingers, still wanting to haul Joeli from her bed before the soldiers arrived. Kettle had once advised that she count to ten in such circumstances, or perhaps a thousand. Nona found that Abbess Glass was more of a help than counting. Not something the abbess had said, just how she had lived. The abbess had taken on more powerful enemies than Nona had, and bested them by playing the long game, a game her opponents had thought they were winning right until the moment of their defeat. The abbess had never raised her hand in anger, but the blows she struck were more powerful than any taught by Sister Tallow.

Nobody came. No tramp of boots on the dormitory stairs. Perhaps the soldiers had arrived on other business . . . As sleep took hold Nona saw again the abbess lying pale on her deathbed, the flesh wasted from her, eyes fever-bright. On that last night she had summoned Nona to her side and found the strength that often comes before that final goodbye. She had spoken to Nona, rediscovering the lucidity that had been a stranger to her for many days.

"A million words won't push the ice back, not even the breadth of a finger. But one word will break a heart, two will mend it, and three will lay the highest low."

Abbess Glass had spoken and Nona had made promises. Promises to a friend. Promises she meant to keep.

THE BELL THAT drew Nona from her dreams spoke with a steel tongue. Bitel! All around her fellow novices were jumping from their beds, shedding nightgowns, grabbing habits, shouting questions. All except Joeli, who sat on her bed, fully dressed, her hair already brushed to its usual golden magnificence. She watched with a private smile as Nona struggled first into her smalls and skirts, and then the latest in a series of habits, this one already too short for her.

"This is bad." Ara hopped across to Nona's bed, trying to get her foot into her shoe.

"You should be ready to run," Nona said.

Ara stood, frowning, her foot half in the shoe. "Where's Jula going to run to? My father lives in a castle . . . Jula's has rooms above an ink shop in Verity. And Ruli would have to cross fifty miles under Durnish occupation."

Nona didn't have an answer. She could have pointed out that Ara would have to cross more than twice that distance under Scithrowl occupation to reach her father's holdings. And would likely find it smoking ruins, or home to one of Adoma's royal cousins. If Lano Tacsis had spoken the truth, the main Jotsis stronghold had already fallen.

Ruli joined Ara, white-faced at Nona's bedside, and all the while Joeli smiled. Nona laced her shoes and wondered yet again if Joeli, with her key to Sister Apple's stores, could really have been poisoning the abbess's medicines. Or had Glass's death, like so many evils in the world, been a simple matter of blind chance? Certainly the abbess had thought so. *I'll meet my son again in the Ancestor, so don't cry, Nona Grey.* She had taken Nona's hand in the withered claw of her own, still scarred by the flame of that candle long ago. *The fight matters. But in the end it is never truly won or lost, and victory lies in discovering that we are bigger than it is.*

"Where's Jula?" Nona could see no sign of her, and her bed lay empty.

"An hour after we got back last night she took a lantern and went off to read that book." As Ara answered, Jula appeared at the doorway, dark circles around her eyes, hair in disarray, and a look of mild panic on her face.

The opening of the door sparked a mass exodus, with Alata first out, pushing past a confused Jula. Within moments Nona and the rest of them were hurrying down the stairs, joining the stream of younger novices and the crush at the main door as everyone spilled out into the day.

Bitel's harsh chimes ceased almost as soon as Nona left the dormitories. In the east the sun still occupied the notch that the Corridor put in the horizon and every shadow pointed to the abbess's house.

Nuns and novices had begun to line up, organised by class, as Nona arrived. Bitel had rung out only a handful of times in her decade at the convent and on no occasion had the bell heralded anything good. Nona watched for church-guards or the soldiers from last night. Finding none, she studied the disposition of the Red Sisters. If Abbess Wheel meant to detain them, then given her low opinion of Nona's piety she wouldn't expect mere obedience to hold her in place while the yokes were brought out. Her heart sank as she saw that the Red Sisters were arrayed around the novices in a loose circle. Sister Tallow stood close at hand.

"It looks like a trap," Ruli hissed.

"Ruli, the abbess doesn't need to trap us if she thinks we've done wrong." Jula sounded bone-tired, as if she had been reading the whole night. "Abbess Wheel speaks for the Church, and we obey."

Nona understood then that breaking the rules once to get the book was as far down the road to damnation as Jula was prepared to go. If Abbess Wheel ordered her surrender, she would not be running. It spoke volumes that Jula had been prepared to come with her when she said she couldn't find the book alone. Of all of Nona's friends perhaps Jula was the only one with true faith, not only in the Ancestor but in the Church as an institution. Something she intended to devote her life to in the black habit of a Holy Sister.

"All the Reds are here. Even the ones who should be on patrol." Ara kept her voice low, shuffling into the line beside Nona. "The Greys are positioned too, from what I can see." She motioned upwards with her eyes towards the big house. "Bhenta's on the roof."

"Sister Cauldron," Nona corrected. "Don't underestimate her."

Abbess Wheel did not emerge until all the novices were gathered and in order. Sisters Superior Rose and Rule stood one step below the abbess's doorway, Sister Apple a step below them and with her, Sister Iron. It hurt Nona to see the woman in Sister Tallow's place and she looked again for the older woman in the crowd, finding her still close, beside Sister Rock.

As Wheel's assistant, Sister Ice, opened the door Sister Pan came up the steps to join Apple and Iron. She cast a grim eye over the assembled novices.

"Ancestor . . ." Jula muttered a prayer.

"She doesn't look happy," Ruli hissed. "Is she there to own up to the forbidden book?"

If she was it would be the last nail in their coffin. Who else could have stolen Pan's book but Ara or Nona? And Sister Pan never joined the abbess on the steps, not even when it had been Glass, someone she liked, rather than Wheel, someone she did not.

Wheel emerged and scanned the crowd with her customary glower. Nona's fingers closed about the abbess's seal in the depths of her habit pocket. It was hard to tell from the old woman's face whether she had discovered it missing. She looked close to fury most of the time anyway.

The abbess thumped her crozier for attention. It put Nona in mind of High Priest Jacob stamping his staff at Abbess Glass's trial.

"Novice Nona, approach." Wheel glared in her direction.

Nona's heart sank. She didn't know if she would try to fight her way past nuns she had known for years, or surrender to injustice. She couldn't take her friends with her. Certainly Jula wouldn't come. The knowledge paralysed her.

Her cheeks prickled with shame or shock. Nona wasn't sure which. Half-dazed, she walked towards the abbess's steps. After Zole the old woman had abandoned all talk of the Argatha prophecy. There had never been a moment following Nona's return when Wheel had indicated that *she* might be the

Chosen One. The abbess had shown no interest in the interpretation that said four shiphearts rather than four bloods were the key to the Ark. With Zole gone the whole matter was over as far as Sweet Mercy was concerned.

Abbess Wheel scanned the assembly with a sour eye. "These proceedings are highly irregular but we live in pressing times and haste is required." She gestured imperiously with her crozier to a spot before the lowest step. "Stand there."

Nona stood, summoned by the steel bell, the focus of the whole convent upon her, head bowed.

"Well, Sister Pan?" Wheel said. "Get on with it."

Pan frowned and hunched her shoulders. She raised her voice. "Novice Nona has entered the Third Room of Path Tower. She is judged . . ."

Nona readied herself to run.

". . . to have passed the Path-test. And I offer her the Blue of a Mystic Sister."

Sister Iron coughed. "The novice has passed the Blade-test and is acceptable to wear the Red. I offer her a place as a Martial Sister."

Nona looked up. Bewildered.

Sister Apple fixed her with a narrow stare. "Novice Nona has passed the Wire-test and I can find no legitimate reason for her not to be offered the Grey of a Sister of Discretion."

"There you have it," Abbess Wheel snapped. "Choose. And hurry up. You're not the last to take her orders today. There's war on our doorstep."

Nona glanced past Wheel, past the roof of the abbess's house. Smoke streaked the sky as if Verity's chimneys had crept to the foot of the plateau overnight. She opened her mouth, then closed it. How close must Adoma's troops be now?

"Well, girl?" Abbess Wheel stamped her crozier again. "You have what you wanted. Take it."

Nona returned her gaze to the steps, to Sister Pan, bowed beneath her years, dark eyes watching from a dark face, to Sister Iron's level stare, to

Apple, pale in the morning light, her headdress as ever unequal to the task, a red coil escaping.

Abbess Glass had said this day would come. She had said it on her deathbed and Nona had nodded and said that she believed it and felt guilty because she did not.

"I . . ." Nona looked from one sister to the next. Unexpectedly she thought of Zole, the girl from the ice-tribes with her quest to achieve perfection in this life rather than in the embrace of the Ancestor in the time beyond.

"Well?"

"A Holy Sister," Nona said. "I want to be a Holy Sister."

A burst of exclamation rose behind her, a swell of muttered questions, quickly silenced as the abbess came down from her steps, pushing past the sisters superior.

"A Holy Sister? You wish to be a Bride of the Ancestor?" The old woman raised her hand and Nona resisted the urge to block the blow.

"I do, abbess."

Wheel clasped her bony fingers to Nona's cheek. "A Holy Sister!" She raised her voice. "A Holy Sister! For faith is what is needed in the darkest hours. Faith!" She stared past Nona at the ranks of novices behind, daring any to disagree. Her gaze returned to Nona. She drew back her hand. "Perhaps I was wrong about you . . ." A shake of her head. "Perhaps."

The old woman embraced her as every abbess must embrace each soul called to the Ancestor's service.

"May I serve, abbess?" Nona went to her knees as all novices do to receive their orders, rising again as nuns.

Wheel stood above her. She patted the front of her habit, then frowned as if remembering some annoyance. Her fingers paused over a lump beneath the cloth. The frown deepened. She reached to her neck and drew from beneath her collar a necklace of prayer beads, the Ancestor's tree in gold on a silver chain, the keys to her front door, and . . . on a knotted leather thong, her seal of office. Nona had tied it around Wheel's neck during their embrace just a moment before. She hoped that she had hidden the act in the moment as Mistress Shade had taught her. Times when all eyes are upon you are often those when such sleight of hand is most easily accomplished.

"A day of miracles!" A rare smile twisted the abbess's lips. She took the seal and pressed it to Nona's lips. "Stand, Sister Cage, stand!"

And Nona stood. Sister Cage of Sweet Mercy Convent, Bride of the Ancestor. Holy Sister.

"Novice Arabella!" Abbess Wheel called. "Approach the steps."

16

THE ESCAPE

Three Years Earlier

NONA CROUCHED IN the margins of the shipheart's glow and watched the devils slowly leach from Yisht's corpse into the ice, a sliding patchwork of grey moving across the woman's hands. Rats abandoning a ship that had sunk.

One patch of colour lingered on the back of Yisht's hand even as others flowed over, under, and around it. In the end it remained, sinking by fractions towards the two fingertips that touched the ice and through which the rest had drained into the greater blackness.

For a moment the blasting of vents and the gurgling of meltwater in hidden channels fell almost silent.

"Keot?" A whisper. In this frozen place of horrors, so deeply buried, anything familiar could be counted a comfort. Even a devil carved from the mind of one of the Missing eons ago. "Is that you?"

Nona sensed no reply. Whatever fault line had let the devil into her when she killed Raymel Tacsis no longer seemed wide enough to admit Keot.

Killing Yisht had been an empty thing. Even now, with the woman's torso cooling in front of her and her severed head lying somewhere in the dark, Nona felt no satisfaction in the deed, just the echoing loss of her friends.

Nona watched while Keot finally drained away, and she wondered whether it had been him who had made the knife slip from Yisht's fingers as she tried to block that final blow. Some things were beyond knowing. Nona left Yisht's body untouched. The woman might be carrying things of use, but the Noi-Guin often set traps for the unwary in an unused pocket with venomed needles, and Nona had no wish to find out if it was a habit Yisht had acquired too. She stood and waited, timing the blasts from the vents, and crossed to the shipheart.

Even moving the shipheart awkwardly before her with the tip of her sword brought Nona far deeper into the thing's radiance than she felt she could endure for long. The light dazzled rather than illuminated, seeming unaffected by niceties such as whether her eyes were open or closed. The shipheart drove from her mind the insidious whispers haunting the dark all around her, but replaced them with a louder muttering that bubbled many-voiced from her own interior darkness.

"I don't know where I'm going. I've forgotten why I'm going there." Nona spoke so that her own voice would sound louder than any of the competition. She nudged the shipheart ahead. It rolled a few feet and stopped. On the blade of her sword Yisht's blood looked black in the strange light.

As she approached the bubble-shaped chamber where they had first encountered Yisht, Nona took care that the shipheart not run away from her. If it went over the lip where the tunnel met the chamber it would roll down to the bottom and vanish down the throat that had claimed Zole.

Nona sheathed her sword and took a knife in her left hand. "I have to do this." She gathered around her all that could be found of her serenity and bent to pick up the ball of light. It seemed to weigh nothing and to burn her bones. With a snarl she stepped over the edge into the void beyond.

She slid nearly to the maw at the chamber's base before her knife found sufficient purchase to bring her to a halt. All around her narrow streams of meltwater divided the ice, cutting deeply into it before spraying out into the shaft. A dozen voices filled Nona's head and she could hardly tell which of them, if any, was hers.

". . . ooona!"

"What?" Nona tried to concentrate. She needed to edge around the hole and somehow climb the far side of the chamber one-handed in search of another exit. She wondered if her father's explorations had ever left him this terrified, this lost . . .

"Noooo!" A distant echoing cry amid the cacophony inside her skull. "Na!"

"What?" Nona lifted the shipheart for greater illumination but the shaft dropping away just beyond her heels devoured its light and gave nothing in return. "Who's there?" She bit down on further questions. Even she knew better than to talk to the voices. It made them real. Helped them break free.

". . . ole!"

"I know you're a hole." Nona lay cold against the wet ice, anchored by the point of her knife, the shipheart burning in her hand and in her mind. "I'm talking to the hole . . ."

"Zoooole!"

"Zole?" Nona sat up.

". . . heart!"

"What?" she shouted.

"Need the . . ."

Nona felt suddenly terrified. "You're in my head, aren't you? One of my devils . . ."

". . . eeeeed . . ."

Nona stared into the inky nothing before her. "You want me to drop the shipheart into that hole? After all I've been through to keep it?" A laugh spluttered past teeth beginning to chatter with the cold once more. All around her the ice had paled to a translucent grey. Of course the devils wanted her to throw the shipheart away. It was all that was keeping them from sliding beneath her skin and turning her into something worse than Yisht.

"Noooonaaa?"

The voice seemed to echo up from the depths where Zole had fallen, but so many other voices clamoured for attention. How could she accept any of them as real?

"Zole?" She leaned forward, yelling into the hole.

". . . ooow it to meeee . . ."

"Throw it to you?" Nona's laugh came edged with hysteria. "You're dead!" The shipheart burned her and splintered her thoughts, but it was also precious beyond measure and the only source of light in this place of endless darkness.

The voice in the hole fell silent while those in Nona's skull grew louder.

"Zole?"

Nothing.

"Zole?"

Only the clamour behind her forehead as her mind began to break into the fragments that would drive her mad. It was the silence that convinced her. Zole would never plead. The ice-triber had said her piece and there was nothing more to say.

Nona looked into the glare. Zole had called it an Old Stone. No part of Nona wanted to let it go, even as it hurt her. She tilted her palm and felt the voices falter. The greatest treasure she had ever held rolled across her fingers. The shipheart fell from her hand, rolled to the edge, and dropped suddenly from view. A rapidly descending band of violet light lit the black gullet, finding the occasional gleam from faults and fractures. A moment later it was gone and Nona sat alone, blind in the dark.

＊ ＊ ＊

TIME NEEDS SOMETHING to be counted against. Nona had nothing except for the slowly building pressure as the devils made their return to the ice beneath her. The shipheart's presence had driven them from it and now they reclaimed what was theirs. She felt their malice like tiny claws, trying to slice a way under her skin.

"I won't die here." Numb fingers fumbled a second dagger from her belt and turned to begin the climb back to the tunnel. She would rather stagger back into the Corridor half-dead and fight the Noi-Guin than face insanity alone in the freezing dark.

She reached, stabbed, and hauled herself up. With no light she might miss the entrance entirely but trying would at least warm her a little.

What followed was a long, blind nightmare of stabbing, straining, and slipping. Nona had no idea how many minutes or hours she laboured at it, how many times she slid back, how many times she cursed the Ancestor. She even called upon her father's ghost for help.

"I can't . . ." She hung on the ice wall, so steep it was near vertical. The strength had left her arms and although she could no longer feel her grip on either knife she knew that it was weakening. Her hands looked shockingly pale. "I can't." No hope remained to her. Not even the hope of an easy death.

She looked again at her hands, hardly feeling she still owned them. Both were tinged with violet. "How?" How could she see them?

Nona turned her head and there, far below her, Zole stood at the edge of the shaft into which she had fallen, the shipheart in her hands.

AT THE SIGHT of Zole, Nona lost her grip on first one knife, then the other, and plummeted down the side of the chamber. Somehow Zole managed to intercept her and arrest her considerable momentum with just one hand while keeping both her balance and her grip on the shipheart.

The ice-triber seemed unhurt, untroubled by the cold. Nona wondered if she was a ghost, the product of her own fractured mind. But the grip on her wrist was warm and real. "How . . . How are you here?" Nona gasped.

"You threw me the Old Stone," Zole said. "It gave me the control over the ice that I needed in order to climb out." She managed the smallest smile. "Thank you."

"It was nothing." Nona coughed an amazed laugh over chattering teeth. "Damn thing was killing me anyway."

Zole lifted her gaze and scanned the darkness as if considering her options.

"You'll have to leave me here," Nona said. "I can't go any farther."

Zole didn't appear to have heard. She was staring at a particular spot, high up. "Come."

"I said I can't."

"You can."

Nona tried to stand but her legs went out from under her and she fell. Zole caught her wrist again, her grip iron. Without further words she hauled Nona to her feet again, bent, and took her over one wet shoulder as she collapsed.

"Don't be silly . . . you can't carry me out."

"Can." Zole straightened with a grunt. "And will."

Zole began to walk towards her goal. With each step the ice splintered beneath her feet, reshaping itself to form footholds.

Nona fell into her own darkness and missed most of their escape from the bubble chamber. She had glimpses of the steep ascent, Zole hugging the wall, sinking the shipheart into the ice and somehow using it to steady herself as she moved from one ledge and created the next. Nona missed much of what followed too, and while conscious put most of her effort into fighting the shipheart's effort to break her apart, but slowly the warmth of Zole's body began to penetrate her own chilled flesh.

"I can walk." The weakness in Nona's voice made her doubt her own claim but Zole set her down without debate.

The ice around them had shaded from black to a dark grey, and not just where they stood but ahead and behind.

"We are getting closer to the surface." Zole sounded weary. "If your clothes are wet when we come up into the wind you will not survive."

Nona coughed. "How do you propose I dry them?"

"Body heat," Zole said. "We run now." And she began to jog ahead.

Nona groaned and staggered in pursuit.

THEY NOTICED THE sound first. The distant howl of the wind, blowing across the mouth of the tunnel an unknown distance ahead of them and reverberating with a low tone. Next they noticed the light. Just a whisper at first. A hint reaching down through the ice, a suggestion that even this long night would come to an end.

Zole called a halt. "Take off your coat."

"Really? Because I'm cold enough with it on." Nona shed Kettle's range-coat despite her protest. Meltwater had gone right through it and had frozen on the outside, leaving the garment too stiff to fold.

"And the shirts."

"No!" Nona folded her arms across her chest. Both layers were warmer following their run but still damp. Sister Tallow had told them many times before their ice trek that something as simple as working up a sweat could get you killed on the ice once you cooled down and the wind got to work.

Zole shrugged her backpack off and set the shipheart down. The contents of her pack were wrapped tightly within a sealskin. The knots put up considerable resistance and finally had to be cut. At last Zole pulled out a thick woollen vest and unrolled what looked to be leather leggings. "Dry." She started to draw out strips of velvet that looked to have been cut from a lord's cloak. "To wrap around your hands. Fur would be better but this should make sure you keep your fingers."

"You could have told me earlier!" Nona took the vest and began to strip off her layers.

"And if you had got wet again your death would have been assured."

"Fair point . . ." Nona struggled into the dry clothes and hugged herself. She felt warmer already, though a vest and leggings would be scant protection out in the open.

She cast a suspicious glance at Zole, who had stooped to pick up the discarded garments. "Why aren't you wet? You climbed up through half a dozen waterfalls!"

Zole stood, holding one of Nona's shirts, frowning. A stream of grey water started to run from the lowest points of the dangling sleeves. "I find ice harder to work than stone, and water more difficult than ice. But I can do it." The stream became a dripping, and then the dripping stopped. She handed the dry shirt back to Nona.

Nona put on each item as Zole dried it. The range-coat came last, ice flaking away from the outer surface as Nona slung it around her shoulders. Being dry after so long made her feel human again, the tainted water gone from her skin. With daylight in the distance she felt almost good. "Let's go!"

A few hundred yards on and the end of the tunnel blazed ahead of them, a circle of hope.

"Follow me." Zole raised her voice above the wind's howl. "Step where I step. It is dangerous on the ice."

"It's dangerous under the ice!" Nona hurried towards the light.

Zole put an arm out to stop her. "More of those who leave the Corridor die on the ice than below it. Walk with respect here, Nona Grey. The white death waits."

17

HOLY CLASS

Present Day

"How could you not tell me you'd taken the Blade-test?" Nona asked. Ara held up her hands. "To begin with I didn't want to put pressure on myself. If I failed I wanted to tell people in my own time, not have them lined up to ask me. And then afterwards I didn't want to put pressure on you. Tallow said you'd be called up next."

Nona shook her head. "I can't believe you beat me to it."

"I'm almost two years older than you!"

"You know what I mean. We joined the same day." Nona looked up at Path Tower. They had gone with the rest of the class to the lesson only to have Sister Pan gently point out that neither of them were in Holy Class anymore and as such had no business in her classroom.

"Explain it again," Ara said. "Nona Grey, a Holy Sister?"

"I told you."

"You did, but I'm hoping it will make sense second time around."

"What's wrong with being a Holy Sister?" Nona asked. "It's good enough for Jula but not for me? Don't you love the Ancestor, Sister Thorn?"

"I love the Ancestor fine, Sister Cage, but I know you love this." Ara patted the sword at her hip. "How are you going to live without all of . . . that?"

"Abbess Glass didn't need all of *that* and she made a difference. She was more dangerous than a dozen Red Sisters, or Grey, more deadly even than Holy Witches."

"But to never swing a sword again? And you're so good at it! Isn't it a sin not to use a gift the Ancestor gave to you?"

Nona said nothing for a long moment, her eyes on Ara's sword. "Any sister can be drafted into the Red during an emergency. Jula says that the convents east of the Grampains armed even the youngest novices when the enemy came for them." Nona quoted: " 'Every child of the Ancestor wore red on that day when the Scithrowl arrayed their number before the Convent of Wise Contemplation. They ran short of habits for Red Sisters and instead painted the newest novices with the blood of captured heretics.' "

Ara opened her mouth. Then closed it.

Nona looked up at the smoke-stained sky and shook her head. "I don't think many days will pass before I'm handed a sword again, Sister Thorn."

"I should go and report to Sister Tallow—I mean Sister Iron," Ara said. "I take instruction from her now. And she from the abbess."

"And the abbess from the emperor . . ." Nona frowned. "You don't think the emperor actually talks to Wheel, do you?"

Ara shook her head. "Father told me that the new Lord Glosis is the emperor's military advisor. Glosis instructs the generals, and General Wensis oversees the deployment of martial brothers and sisters in times of crisis." She glanced across to Blade Hall. "I'd better go . . . I guess I'll see you tonight at the dormitory—"

"We'll be given cells. We're big girls now."

"Oh yes. Well, at least we won't have to see Joeli every morning." Ara frowned. "Why do you think she didn't report us? I was sure the abbess had us rung out of bed to face charges."

"I guess whoever she tells her tales to wants what we were after. Once we escaped they couldn't be sure to recover it. If it were just up to Joeli she would have seen us humiliated and punished."

"Who does she pass her stories to?"

"Lord Namsis pulled a lot of golden strings to get her back here, didn't he?" Nona asked. "Do you think he's really that keen for his oldest daughter to be a nun? My guess is that the tales Joeli tells reach Sherzal in at most three steps. You can't think that the emperor's sister has forgiven any of us? We ruined her alliance with Adoma. For Ancestor's sake, we set her palace on fire!"

Ara made the sign of the tree over her heart. "I've been telling you what she's like for years. I wanted us to be a lot more careful over this book business, more secret . . . but you wouldn't listen. Getting that monk involved was madness. You hardly know him!" She held up her hand to stop Nona's reply. "I have to run. I don't think Sister Iron is any more easygoing than Tallow! You'd better hurry too. I'm sure there's some important praying that needs doing . . ."

With a shake of her head Ara sped off, sword bouncing against her leg. Nona watched with a certain degree of envy as her friend crossed the square. Ara's pity had been poorly hidden and it stung, though Nona understood it. She had turned her back on the sword, on the shadow arts, and on the mysteries of the Path. It would take time for her friends to understand the choice. With a sigh Nona looked towards the Dome of the Ancestor. She could smell the char on the wind now. If ever there were a time for praying, this was it.

KETTLE INTERCEPTED NONA outside the doors to the Dome.

"You made a hell of a mess in Apple's storeroom. What on Abeth was that about?"

The lie starting to form on Nona's lips evaporated under the intensity of Kettle's scrutiny.

"It was a stupid mistake. I'm sorry."

"Well, you should be!" Kettle shoved Nona's shoulder, still angry. "Appy's furious!"

"So why did she offer me the Grey?"

"The real question is why didn't you take it?" Kettle shook her head as if trying to shake off the foolishness of Nona's decision.

"I asked first, sister."

"She—well, she would have offered you the Grey anyway . . . at least she would have if there had been time to calm down. But . . ." Kettle paused and her eyes grew bright with tears.

"But what?" The backs of Nona's arms prickled. She knew what Kettle was going to say.

"But . . . but she promised Abbess Glass that she would offer you the Grey, come what may."

Nona's eyes misted, her mouth too dry to speak. *Come what may.*

"Why didn't you take it?" Kettle asked. "Apple thought nobody could be a Sister of Discretion without being able to work shadow. She was always going to offer you the Grey because of the promise, but she didn't actually want you to take it until the day you passed the Wire-test. Then she did. You were born to this, Nona."

"I didn't take it because I made a promise of my own. On her deathbed Abbess Glass asked me to become a Holy Sister, and I swore that I would."

They stared at each other for a moment.

"She's still doing it, isn't she, sister?" Kettle said. "Even dead, she's still playing a long game that none of us understand." She stepped in, gave Nona a fierce hug, and left at a run.

Nona went into the Dome of the Ancestor, deep in her thoughts. She hadn't known of the promise Abbess Glass had asked of Sister Apple, but she knew, or thought she knew, the game that was being played, and she would play it to the end.

IN THE VASTNESS of the Ancestor's Dome, kneeling before the statue of the Ancestor and deep in her serenity, Nona hardly noticed the other Holy Sisters come and go. Hours slipped by and the bells spoke them, Bray and Ferra competing for her attention, though now the iron voice of Ferra spelled out the day for her as it did for all the nuns.

On her first night as a Holy Sister Nona had slept in her nun's cell, by chance the same one that she had slept in nearly a decade earlier on the night she arrived at the convent. Lying wakeful in her narrow bed she had thought of Ara in her own narrow bed three cells down. Ara who had taken the Red. Ara who she could not allow to come to harm. Not because of some cryptic request from Abbess Glass but by the order of her own heart. And when at last her dreams had come they had been troubled ones, filled with screaming, with blood, and with the light of shiphearts.

With her fast broken Nona had been following Ferra's call to the Dome for second prayers when she noticed novices streaming from their cloister towards Blade Hall. Not just one class but all of them mixed together. Holy Class novices with Red Class girls half their height running between them. Nona allowed herself to be drawn along with the flow. Blade Hall was not the destination. Instead the novices, and half a dozen nuns, joined others at the edge of the Rock. Nona's height allowed her a clear view.

"Ancestor watch over them." At Nona's elbow Sister Rose wrung her hands, staring out at the smoke-dark sky.

The fires in the east had advanced overnight and seemed to burn against the very walls of the capital itself. Even from Sweet Mercy Nona could see that the road stretching the five miles to Verity lay choked with traffic, all headed one way, to the sanctuary of the emperor's walls.

The sharp tolling of Bitel brought the convent to the abbess's steps. The gathered nuns and novices learned that the enemy were indeed within ten

miles of Verity, their skirmishers moving through the surrounding countryside in bands of tens and hundreds.

"None of you are to leave the convent except by my authorization,"
Wheel declared from the doorway of the big house. "We will await orders
from the Church. Sisters Iron and Apple will organise our perimeter."

Unexpectedly, the abbess descended the stone steps in front of her
house and came to stand among the novices of Red Class. She ran her bony
fingers through the blond curls of the smallest girl. "If the heretics come
to our door we will fight them. Fight them to the very last drop of our
blood." The fierceness left her voice. "Until then . . . pray, sisters, pray."

NONA RETURNED TO the Dome of the Ancestor and followed orders. While
Ara joined the patrols of Red and Grey Sisters defending the convent Nona
bent her knees before the Ancestor's golden statue, one figure among many
offering their devotions.

Abbess Wheel joined them for a while to read aloud from the Book of
the Ancestor. She read that they were blessed, that eternity awaited them
in the glory and goodness of the tree to which all born of a woman are
connected and in which all are joined. Later she took to her knees beside
Nona and prayed in silence.

When she left, the old woman set a hand to Nona's shoulder to help her
rise. "Pray, child." She stood and looked across the rows of bowed heads.
"Your faith is a gift that keeps them strong."

NONA REMAINED ON her knees and though many thoughts battled for her
attention she ran through her head the litany of St. Affid, whose day it was.
Nuns in black prayed to either side of her, each with an incense stick
smouldering before them. And towering over their heads the Ancestor
stood, silent as ever, promising nothing but to watch their lives and wait
for their arrival.

Though none of them had talked about it, it seemed that they might all be called to the Ancestor over the course of the next few days or weeks. The Scithrowl were no more merciful to the perceived heresies of the Church than the Inquisition was to theirs. They might let the Dome of the Ancestor remain standing, but none of the sisters who tended it would outlive the fall of Verity.

"A penny for your thoughts, Sister Cage." Sister Rose got to her knees beside Nona with some difficulty.

"I was praying." Nona looked across at the shorter woman. It was odd to see Rosie out of the sanatorium.

"We all say that." Sister Rose made the sign of the tree, a single finger tracing up from the taproot, all of them spreading for the branches. "But we're always thinking of something."

Nona sighed and nodded. "I was thinking of Zole." She had been thinking of what it would be like to be one with the Ancestor. The perfection that Zole and the ice-tribes sought in life both fascinated and repulsed her. It seemed like a kind of death, and life was for living. But the faults she clung to brought her pain as often as pleasure. She had been thinking of Regol too. Forbidden by her own oath now that she was a sister, a bride to the Ancestor. Regol, Markus, all men were her brothers now. Had Zole cut that particular weakness out of herself first? she wondered.

Bitel's harsh chiming cut through Nona's thoughts.

"Twice in one day?"

"I've been at this convent thirty-eight years," Sister Rose said. "I've never heard that bell sounded twice in a day."

Nona helped the nun to her feet, then took off running for the abbess's steps.

A DOZEN CHURCH-GUARDS and a tall man in armour waited in front of the big house, the armoured man still mounted, his cloak of gold and green streaming in the wind.

"The emperor's colours!" Ruli came up beside Nona. Nobody was trying to group novices into their classes. The chaos felt more unsettling even than the sight of church-guards and the emperor's man. The convent had always been a place of order.

Abbess Wheel came from the direction of Blade Hall, flanked by all the Red Sisters still residing at the convent. She climbed a few steps to get the elevation needed to see over her gathering flock.

"We're in for it this time!" Jula came up, panting. "Joeli must have told."

Ara joined them. "I think there are bigger fish than us to fry today."

Abbess Wheel stamped her crozier for attention, unnecessarily since every eye was turned her way.

"Today is a glorious day!" Wheel shouted above the freshening wind, her voice thick with the passion she usually reserved for reading the most dramatic passages of the Book of the Ancestor. "Today, sisters and novices, we get to stand before the Ark and defend our faith with blood and bone."

"Oh hells," Jula said weakly.

"All senior novices and all nuns of a fighting age will accompany me to the Ark where we will join with our sisters in the Red under the direction of General Wensis." Wheel's eyes gleamed and she gripped her crozier like a weapon, as if all her long years had been leading up to this moment and her life's ambition had been to march her fellow nuns and the children in their care onto the battlefield. "Sister Iron will oversee the immediate equipping of our force from the convent stores." The old woman raised her arm. "Follow me!" And she stalked off towards Blade Hall, followed by Sister Iron. She at least had the decency to look worried.

"Oh joy." Sister Apple somewhere behind Nona, in a dry tone. "A lifetime dedicated to the arts of discretion . . . and now I get to stand up in broad daylight and stop arrows for the emperor."

"I won't let any arrow near you." Kettle, fierce and upset.

Any more of their conversation was lost beneath the general outbreak of worry and complaint as three quarters of the nuns and half the novices surged after their abbess.

+   +   +

NONA EMERGED FROM Blade Hall wearing the oldest Red Sister habit she had ever seen. It must have been defying moths at the back of the storeroom for decades. Tatters trailed both sleeves, perhaps sliced free by the blows that cut the last occupant from their mortal remains and sent her to join the glory of the Ancestor.

At her hip hung Sister Tallow's sword. The nun had pressed it on her, ignoring all protest. "The best artist needs the best brush."

Sister Pail took Nona's arm as she stepped through the crowd of novices comparing weapons outside the doors.

"The abbess wants to see you." She gave a tug, then started to jog away. "Hurry!"

Nona glanced back to see Ruli emerging, a Barrons-steel sword in her hand. Jula had a group of Mystic Class novices around her, admiring the long-hafted battle-axe that she'd been issued. Ara had yet to come out.

"Come on!" A distant shout.

Nona set hand to hilt and ran. It had been a long time since she had worn a sword outside Blade Hall.

THE CORRIDORS OF the abbess's house were crowded with nuns and church-guards. Abbess Wheel was waiting for Nona in her office under the painted gaze of a score of previous occupants. Abbess Glass's portrait hung over the door where Wheel's gaze would rest each time she looked up from her papers. Nona looked up at it as she came through—a good likeness that removed a decade or more but caught with perfection the stare that seemed to be fixed on something distant only she could ever see.

"I've been told to leave you behind," Wheel said without preamble. She held up a roll of parchment. *"In the event that the sisterhood is called to the emperor's aid it is fitting that the Shield be left to guard the younger novices."* One bony finger moved to indicate the high priest's seal. "He means 'to guard the shipheart,' of course."

Nona felt as if she'd been punched in the stomach. "No! Abbess! I can't stay here while all my sisters are facing the enemy on the battlefield. I won't!"

Wheel raised her hand. "I must admit it seemed a strange instruction. To single out a particular novice, and even if High Priest Nevis had somehow anticipated your elevation to the sisterhood, to give such a significant duty to such a young nun." She rested her gaze on Nona. "I haven't held a high opinion of you, Sister Cage, but you showed a wisdom beyond your years when you chose the Black. Truly, faith may reside in the most unlikely of receptacles . . ." She looked at the parchment in her hand. "I sense politics at play here. Favours bought and sold. And if there's one thing I despise almost as much as heresy it's politics. Unfortunately, there seems to be no choice but to obey."

Nona's mind raced. To be left on the Rock of Faith watching over children while her friends fought and died together before the emperor's walls was not an option. "It's the shipheart the high priest wants guarded. And it's the shipheart that puts the novices most at risk . . ." Nona glanced at the window and the Dome of the Ancestor beyond. "We should take it with us!"

"What?"

"Take it with us. The shipheart. You know I can bring it up from the vault and put it somewhere safe at the palace. We need it on the front line: all the quantals will fight more effectively, and if we lose there the enemy will get the shipheart whether it's with us or hidden here."

Abbess Wheel tilted her head, considering. "Do it."

Nona stood in shock for a moment. Wheel had actually agreed with her! For once she had done what Nona needed her to do. It struck her then that this was at least part of what Abbess Glass had wanted, what she had purchased with the promises she had extracted. How else could Nona Grey have obtained the goodwill and cooperation of Abbess Wheel?

The abbess frowned and tapped a finger to a ledger on the desk before her, the record of novices. "The young ones will still need guarding, though. Someone capable. Maybe—"

"Ara could do it! Sister Thorn, I mean!" The idea struck Nona from nowhere. They didn't all have to face the Scithrowl. She could save Ara. If the Ark fell Ara would lead the novices away to the west. Even the Durns would be better than the Scithrowl: they had their own gods and weren't given to burning people over the finer points of Ancestral doctrine. Ara could do it. A weight lifted from Nona's heart.

Again the abbess tilted her head. "She should have followed your example when called to her name, sister. Today of all days it's faith that's needed." More tapping of fingers on the ledger. "I suppose you're right. Once upon a time I thought she was the Chosen One come to save us all. Let her save the children at least."

"Thank you, abbess!" Nona could have wept. She made for the door as Wheel waved her dismissal.

Nona ran down the steps, weaving past startled sisters. She felt ready to endure the shipheart's awful power, ready to stand with her sisters against the Scithrowl shock troops, ready for anything. All that scared her now, the only thing she felt unready for, was telling Ara that she had saved her.

18

———— ✦ ————

THE ESCAPE

Three Years Earlier

THE GREAT WHITE sheet, in which every part of Abeth save the green thread of the Corridor was wrapped, seemed to Nona as terrible a place in its own way as had the chambers and tunnels within the black ice. The very personal malice of the multitude of devils was replaced by the impersonal malice of an endless freezing wind beneath a bone-pale sky that stretched to forever in all directions. The openness of it staggered her, even though she had stood in places within the Corridor where the walls could not be seen. This was something different. A relentless exposure that made her feel like a single tiny dot of ink upon a vast unwritten page.

"We're going the wrong way." Nona spoke through the cloth that Zole had given her to bind around her face.

"We are going the right way."

"We're heading away from the Corridor," Nona said.

"We need to make a fire," Zole said.

"How in the name of the Ancestor will we do that? I mean it would be nice . . ." Just the thought of it made Nona pause to visualise crackling flames. "Should we find two icicles and rub them together?"

"This close to the Corridor the tribes cache timber and coal. Out on the far ice there are far fewer caches and they will hold whale oil and dried blubber."

"And how are we going to find one of these caches?" The idea seemed ridiculous. With the exception of the Grampains thrusting through the ice some miles to the west the sheet seemed entirely featureless.

"They often lie along pressure ridges."

"But . . . we're not following a pressure ridge. I can't even see any."

Zole said nothing, just carried on tramping across the snow. Nona, lacking any alternative, bowed her head against the wind and followed.

A mile farther on Zole halted. "Look." Ahead of them the wind had eroded the snow across several acres, exposing the ice beneath. White striations lay in parallel lines, running through the translucence all around them. "Pressure lines. The thickest of them often turn into pressure ridges."

They carried on. The wind was beginning to get the cold into Nona's bones in a way that even the freezing wetness of the tunnels had not. Her fingers became strangers to her again. She knew from Sister Tallow's lectures that frostbite could set in in less than an hour. First the flesh turned a dead white, later black, and finally it would rot, poisoning your blood if the affected area were not amputated or cut away.

"You were right." A pressure ridge had begun to make itself known. Ahead of them great plates of ice lifted like broken teeth, a fractured line following a roughly straight path off into the distance.

Zole walked as close to the ridge as the surface allowed, affording them a degree of relief from the wind. They walked another mile, then another.

Nona glanced left then right, across the endless white relief. Here and there the wind tore plumes of snow crystals from low drifts and set them racing across the ice in rivulets.

"You really lived here? Whole tribes live here?" Just crossing an expanse of the sheet felt like a foolish gamble. To spend a whole life in the vast unchanging whiteness, always freezing, always torn by the wind, didn't seem remotely possible.

They followed the ridge for another mile.

The sun grew low in the west, skimming the ridge's shadow across the ice for dozens of yards. Soon it would throw the shadow of the Grampains across them and night would descend.

At a point no different from any other Zole stopped. She stalked around, head down, kicking snow aside here and there.

"You should dig in this place." Zole stamped.

"Me?"

"We do not have the correct tools. It would be foolish to risk our swords when you have blades that are sharper and more durable."

Nona sighed and knelt at the spot. She extended her flaw-blades and began to cut the ice. Zole used her knife to prise free the blocks that Nona incised. Within a few minutes they could see a dark mass below them. It turned out to be a sack of charcoal packed with a small amount of kindling.

"Now a shelter."

Zole employed Nona and her blades to cut slabs of ice from the ridge where the untold pressures beneath had broken them clear of the sheet. By the time it grew dark they had, through Nona's labour and Zole's expertise, constructed a small shelter with three walls and a half-roof. Zole produced an iron fire-bowl with three legs and made a tiny charcoal fire. They placed it in the middle of the shelter and squeezed into either side of it. The change was marvellous. Nona felt as if she might almost survive the night.

"WAKE UP."

Nona groaned. All of her hurt. Even groaning hurt. Even in the turmoil of her nightmares, waking up was not something she wanted to do.

"Wake up!"

"No."

Nona found herself being dragged from the cold to somewhere much colder. She opened her eyes, trying to remember where she was.

"The focus is coming." Zole pulled her to her feet.

The moon, already bright, was growing brighter by the moment.

"I was sleeping," Nona complained, her voice weak and wavering.

"We need the warmth," Zole said. "And to keep dry." She tugged Nona higher up the slope formed by the pressure ridge. The ice splintered around them as Zole used her water-work to make a flat platform. "Do not fall."

The moon's heat built around them. Nona sighed with pleasure, spreading her arms. Zole hung a damp shawl over both the outstretched limbs, clothing she had not taxed herself to dry earlier. "Let them dry but put them under your coat when the mist rises."

The heat built from a luxurious warmth towards something fierce. All around them the sound of dripping water started up. The ice began to melt beneath their feet, meltwater sheeting down the slope. A short while later the water stood an inch deep in places and started to steam.

"Ancestor! I thought I'd never feel warm again!" Nona screwed her eyes shut and opened her coat. The simple pleasure of not being cold made her want to cry. She gave silent thanks to whichever of her long-distant forebears had set their moon in her sky.

A mist rose above the steaming waters and Nona rolled Zole's shawls beneath her tunic then closed her coat around them. She stood, first knee-deep, then chest-deep in the milky ocean rising about her. She met Zole's gaze briefly and the white tide drowned them both.

From the inside the mists took on a bloody tinge. Nona stood, enjoying the heat though knowing that when the wind found its strength again and stripped the ice clear, her hair would freeze solid.

Eventually the focus began to pass and the brilliance paled. The steam flowed on a strengthening wind, a white sheet that began to tear, then tatter, then shred. For miles all around the ice stood like a dark mirror showing the firmament of crimson stars anew, a second moon fading in the reflected depths.

"It's like we're standing on a lake." Even as Nona spoke she saw the first white threads of ice spreading out across the surface, frost-fingered. She doubted that the water stood much deeper than an inch anywhere. A distant gurgling reached her.

"It will soon be as it was. We should get back into shelter." Zole brushed the frost from her hair, then ducked back into the ice house they had made. Its walls were thinner now, but still good against the wind.

Nona stood watching a while longer as the tracery of frost spread across the water's surface, growing from multiple sites now, with the farthest-reaching tendrils joining hands. Soon the moon's work would be undone.

"Doesn't it drain away?" It seemed wrong somehow. So much heat wasted. So little impact. If the passage of the moon really did melt an inch from the ice sheet every night, who knew what might be accomplished?

"Some does. Most refreezes. We are nearly ten miles from the Corridor."

Nona joined Zole in the shelter and pressed against her. They huddled around the embers in the fire-bowl. Even before sleep took Nona back, no patch of open water remained. The ice had frozen again and the wind swept a thin dusting of snow back across its smoothness.

NONA WOKE TO a deafening cracking and splintering.

"What?"

"The ridge is growing. We should move." Zole had almost completed her packing. In the east the sun was struggling to break free of the horizon. "Now." Shards of ice peppered the walls of their shelter, shattering away where new blocks lifted from the main sheet.

"Do not look back." Zole left the shelter and strode away.

Nona followed. Chunks of ice hit the back of her coat with considerable force as she came into the open, others flying past and skittering on for hundreds of yards.

Once clear Nona and Zole halted, turning to face the way they had come. Beyond the line of the pressure ridge, and a second and third beyond that, the Grampains rose, implacable stone teeth shearing through the ice.

"I don't want to climb those." Nona felt cold just looking at the peaks. Her fingers and toes were numb already.

"We will wait here." Zole folded her arms.

Nona sighed. "Come on, then." She started to move off. Zole stayed where she was. "Good joke." She beckoned the novice on.

"Joke?"

Nona trudged back. "Why would we wait here?"

"I am meeting someone."

Nona scanned the white expanse around them. "A snowman?"

Zole frowned. "I do not—"

"It was a joke, Zole!"

Zole's frown deepened. "Are jokes not supposed to make people—"

"Just tell me who we're meeting!"

Zole pursed her lips and squinted into the middle distance. "Tarkax Ice-Spear."

"Tarkax?" Nona blinked.

"Yes."

"Tarkax as in Tarkax who worked at the Caltess? Tarkax who was supposed to be protecting us when Raymel Tacsis came to kill me on the ranging?" Nona supposed that the man was an ice-triber at least, but the idea of meeting anyone in this wilderness was hard to believe in, let alone someone she knew.

"Yes."

"It doesn't look as if he's coming." Nona made a slow circle, calling on her clarity. "How would he find us in all this anyway?"

"We have a shadow-link. He can locate us more easily if we remain in one place."

"Ah." Nona hadn't seen Tarkax since the day she killed Raymel Tacsis. Clera had stuck Tarkax with a pin coated in lock-up venom. Nona guessed that the incident had been somewhat of a blot on the warrior's reputation.

For a while only the wind spoke.

"How long are we going to wait?" Nona had grown steadily colder and she had been cold to start with. At least walking generated some heat.

"Not long now."

"You can sense him?"

"I can see them."

"Them?" Nona followed the direction of Zole's gaze. She saw nothing but white. Her clarity had introduced a few more shades into the icescape but it was still just a palette of ice and snow.

"Wait."

Nona waited, staring until her eyes began to swim. She still saw nothing. "I don't—"

"Hello, novices!" A man's voice calling from somewhere to her left.

Nona spun around. Tarkax was about fifty yards from her, approaching at the head of a group of six other tribesmen, all in white furs, near invisible even if Nona had been looking in the right direction. "You tricked me into looking the wrong way!" Nona shot a scowl at Zole.

The girl shrugged. "I thought you should know what a joke was."

"Nona! The Caltess ring-fighter!" Tarkax's cry forestalled any reply to Zole.

Nona nodded a greeting. The tribesmen gathered around as Tarkax drew Zole into a hug, which the girl tolerated with a long-suffering look. He released her and slapped her on the back before turning to Nona. "How are you enjoying the ice?"

"I'm not dead yet."

"Ha!" Tarkax punched her shoulder, then returned his attention to

Zole, unleashing a torrent of tribe-tongue. It sounded like a dozen questions all asked at once.

While Zole replied in the same guttural language Nona glanced around at the others. They stood impassive under her scrutiny, all with the same reddish skin tone and flat features that Tarkax and Zole displayed. In the Corridor a hundred shades mixed, remnants pressed together from all the lands and kingdoms that had once covered a whole world. On the ice, though, it seemed that the tribes had sprung from more singular sources, or that the harsh conditions whittled away at any not perfectly suited to survival. Nona noted that each carried a heavy pack and an array of tools hanging from their belts, fashioned from the black iron that the ice-tribes favoured for its reluctance to shatter when chilled. They returned her scrutiny with dark eyes, and Nona wondered how in the immensity of all this wilderness someone she and Zole both knew happened to be so very close . . .

Eventually Tarkax's string of long questions and Zole's series of short replies came to an end. Tarkax stamped his feet and frowned at Nona. "Well. We had better go, then."

"Where?" Nona asked. "Can you guide us across the mountains?"

Tarkax snorted. "I wouldn't wish that on a Pelarthi!" He stamped again. "My brother's daughter has convinced me to show you a quicker way home."

"Quicker than crossing the mountains? We have to cross them . . . they're in the way!" Nona pointed west in case the miles of raw bedrock had somehow escaped the Ice-Spear's attention. "Wait . . . Zole is your niece?"

"Am I not blessed?" Tarkax didn't sound as if he felt blessed. Several of his companions snorted, their breath plumes streaming on the wind.

"But . . . why didn't you look after her when she was orphaned?" New confusion mounted on the old.

"I could think of a thousand good reasons!" Tarkax said, to more snorts. "But the best answer is to note that my brother is still alive. Though with a wife like that I have no idea why he didn't make his snow-bed long ago!"

"But . . ." Nona turned to stare at Zole. "You're not an orphan?"

"Have I ever said that I was?"

"Well . . . no . . . but Sherzal . . ."

"You believe the emperor's sister in this matter?" Zole raised an eyebrow.

"Fine!" Nona threw up her hands. "Why on Abeth were you with her, then?"

"Is that not obvious, Nona Grey?" Zole asked. "I have been spying on you."

19

---◆---

HOLY CLASS

Present Day

I N THE END Nona left it to Sister Kettle to inform Ara of her new appointment to guardian of the convent. Looking east from the cliffs of the Rock of Faith it seemed that all the width of the empire was aflame. Nona doubted that any of them would be returning from the defence of the Ark. She didn't want her last words from Ara to be angry ones. And in truth she didn't know how to say a last goodbye to her. Not without breaking.

Abbess Wheel gathered her war-party before the forest of pillars. Nona joined them to find the old woman shouting at someone.

"You are most certainly not coming! This is an open battle we're walking into."

"Hold my bag, Ruli, dear." Sister Pan affected not to have heard the abbess.

"You are one hundred and two years old, Mali Glosis! I will not have you dying at the end of a Scithrowl arrow!" Wheel sounded as angry as

Nona had ever heard her, but there was more to it than anger. An edge of fright . . . of distress perhaps.

"You don't think I will be of use?" Sister Pan turned towards the abbess, rubbing her hand over her wrist stump.

"I don't think you'll make it the down from the Rock! You are over *one hundred* years old!"

"Heh!" Sister Pan waved the idea away. "I've a few tricks left in me yet."

Nona agreed with Wheel. Sister Pan walked at a shuffle. Her eyesight was poor. There was no doubt that Pan knew everything there was to know about the Path. In the past few years she had taught Nona to do more than she ever thought was possible. But not once in all her time at Sweet Mercy had Nona ever seen her so much as touch the Path. Certainly she could walk to the hidden rooms and see the thread-scape . . . even pull a few when the need arose. But when it came to enduring the Path long enough to gather its power, that was a young person's game. The fierce energies that coursed through a body on the Path would tear a frail old woman apart.

Abbess Wheel stamped her crozier. "Sister Pan—"

"Are we all here?" Pan peered around at the nuns. "Sister Oak, are you sure? Perhaps you should stay, dear?"

"Sister Pan!" Wheel roared. "I am giving you a direct order as your abbess. You will remain here at the convent!"

Sister Pan shook her head, smiling. "I'm Mistress Path, child. I go where I please." And with that she began to shuffle towards the pillars.

THE WIND BLUSTERED around the departing war-party, the Corridor wind contemplating a reversal of direction and an ice-wind seeking to insert itself into the confusion. The stink of smoke gusted from the east and no doubt the Durns' fires were drawing closer on the western front.

Their band held precious little of the strength that Sweet Mercy had been training for so many years. The bulk of the Red Sisters and the Grey had been sent ahead to war, some in the weeks and months before, some dispatched only hours earlier. Of the Grey only Sisters Apple, Kettle, and the newly appointed Sister Cauldron remained. Wheel's force of Red Sisters was limited to Sisters Tallow, Iron, and Rock. Sister Pan was their only Mystic Sister and where the others might be no one could say. Thread-bonds were an invaluable means of communication and as Sister Tallow taught it, good communications were more help on the battlefield than a spare army. If Abbess Wheel had her way every Mystic Sister would be bound to every other, and Nona to every marjal too. However, without a significant degree of affection between the two parties such bonds were extraordinarily difficult to form, and impossible to sustain or endure. Much to the abbess's annoyance.

Abbess Wheel led them down the Vinery Stair belting out the battle hymn of the Ancestor, the convent's ancient banner snapping above her on a pole gripped by Sister Pail. The nuns formed the vanguard, novices behind. The shipheart sat in an iron casket on one of the carts used to transport wine barrels. Six novices pulled it using a long pole. Nona still burned with its aura. She had brought it up from the vaults using two laundry paddles but that was closer than she ever wanted to get to the thing again. The memory of its violet light tingled along her bones. The others couldn't feel it the same way she did, but a sense of unease set in at around ten yards, becoming terror at three, and madness much closer than that.

Nona could feel Ara's anger vibrating along their thread-bond but she kept a tight hold on the channel and refused to open a discussion. Ruli had said they gave Ara black-skin armour and an Ark-steel sword. Abbess's orders. Ara was a Jotsis, after all, even if a nun was supposed to have no family. Nona took comfort in that. Ara would survive. There would be time for recrimination and apology if Nona also lived to see the week out. And if not, perhaps the thread-bond might offer a moment for goodbye if whatever blow took her life was not instantly fatal. There might also be a moment for honesty. To let Ara know truths that Nona barely admitted to herself. With Regol it had been easy for there had been no friendship at stake that might have been ruined with the wrong words. With Ara that friendship had always been too precious to risk with the admission that Nona wanted more.

They marched on singing the hymn into the wind.

"I've never even seen a Scithrowl," Sister Oak muttered into a pause between verses. She was marching between Nona and Kettle and looked as if she would much rather be watching over Red Class. Nona doubted Oak had held a sword since she had taken holy orders over twenty years before.

"Don't worry, Sister Oak, Sister Cage has seen hundreds and lived to tell the tale." Kettle grinned across at Nona.

"I have." Nona didn't mention that she'd had Zole with her all the while and that they'd spent the whole time running away or hiding.

At the top of the Vinery Stair Nona turned to see if Sister Pan had given up or fallen behind yet.

"Holy Ancestor!" Nona stopped dead.

"What?" Ruli and Alata turned with her.

Sister Pan was sitting on the barrel cart with one arm resting on the shipheart's casket, apparently untroubled.

"Keep it moving!" Sister Rock scowled back at them. Beside her Sister Mop managed a small smile. Ruli and Alata turned, pushing an amazed Nona onwards.

The plateau's arms formed an alcove where the convent vineyard was able to catch the sun while sheltering from the wind. The Vinery Stair wound a gentle gradient high above rows of grapevines offering a limited view to the south. Having lost three quarters of its elevation, the track rounded the northern arm of the alcove and suddenly the destruction at their doorstep was revealed. Farmhouses, upon which Nona had rested her eyes countless times across the years, now vomited flame towards the sky. Others were now nothing more than charred patches of ground, trailing smoke. She hurried to join Ketti near the front of the nuns, astonished at how quickly the destruction had been wrought, and within sight of both the convent and the city walls.

Abbess Wheel's song halted abruptly at the scene and silence reigned while they rounded the last turn that brought them to the turnpike gate near the end of the track. Ahead of Nona the abbess turned the corner and stopped in her tracks. Nona found herself pressed against Wheel's back and struggling to prevent the nuns behind from knocking them both flat. A Scithrowl war-band was advancing in the opposite direction, a dozen foot soldiers in chain-mail vests, padded armour on their arms and legs, stained with soot and blood. They came in three ranks of four, the first row shouldering long spears, the next with greatswords at their backs and shorter blades on both hips. Behind them four archers. A skirmish band out to kill and burn. No doubt Adoma sought to goad the emperor's forces to leave the city and protect his peasants. Crucial would of course allow no such thing. On open ground the Scithrowl numbers would make a slaughter of his soldiers.

Where every other sister paused, Sisters Tallow and Iron, who had been flanking the abbess, kept walking. They drew steel from their scabbards, fast enough to make it sing. Two of the Scithrowl first rank, startled by the unexpected encounter, were too slow to lower their spears. The nuns wove past the thrusts of the other two spearmen. A heartbeat later they were among the foe, three Scithrowl collapsing behind them while a fourth tumbled from the outer edge of the track. The soldiers with greatswords reached for shorter blades and died before taking a swing. Two of the archers managed to run. Tallow and Iron both took up spears from the fallen. Tallow hefted her weapon, taking a moment to appreciate its balance and weight, and launched it before either archer had made it fifty yards. Iron's spear gave chase and both struck their targets between the shoulder blades. The soldiers' mail prevented them from being transfixed, but both fell, badly hurt.

Iron reached the two fallen archers first. One of the Scithrowl raised her hand for quarter. She received a quick death, the sweetest mercy on offer.

Abbess Wheel led her flock through the carnage, pausing only to recite St. Hedgemon's *Cursed Is the Heretic* over the corpses. Many of the Holy Sisters paled as they passed the fallen. Ugly wounds gaping, the stink of death too ripe and real to ignore. The novices, closer to their training, seemed more composed, though Jula did retch once. Nona glanced across at Joeli, stepping over a man whose head lay at an odd angle, neck half-severed. At least her smug little smile had vanished.

Looking back, Nona saw that Apple had stopped among the dead with Kettle and Cauldron, all three of them tugging armour and clothes from corpses.

"You were up all night reading that book, Jula?" Nona asked, dropping back a few steps to walk beside her.

"Ssssh!" Jula motioned for Nona to keep her voice down, eye-pointing towards Joeli.

"Did you find anything good?" Nona moved closer.

"I found out that I would have spent the time better practising with an axe." Jula swapped the weapon in question from her left shoulder to her right.

"Wasn't there anything useful in there?"

Jula made a sigh that turned into a yawn. "There's a lot in there. Aquinas seemed pretty confident about it all. But without seeing the parts of the Ark he claims to be describing I've no way of knowing if it's all a fever dream. And even if it makes any sense at all to someone inside the Ark sanctum, it still doesn't mean that any of it would actually work."

"You didn't bring the book with you, did you?" Nona asked.

"Of course not. You told me to hide it. I memorized what I thought was most important . . . Though I should have stuffed it under my habit. It's good and thick. Could probably stop an arrow!"

Nona glanced at Joeli once more, now closer to them and feigning indifference, then returned to her place behind Wheel.

ON THE RUTLAND Road leading into Verity they joined an almost continuous line of wagons, carts, ragged soldiers, worn travellers, whole villages afoot, driving the flocks before them. Despite the crowding a sizable space opened up around the convent cart and its iron casket. People moved out of the way whether there was room or not, and lingered behind with troubled expressions.

A battalion from the Seventh Army under General Jalsis was stationed in and around a large commandeered farmhouse close to the road. Possibly the plan had been to oversee the safety of incoming refugees, though the place looked more like a field hospital now, treating casualties from ongoing skirmishes out across the nearby fields.

Abbess Wheel began the battle hymn again and the sisters joined in. Many of those on the road took up the song and it seemed to lift them. For a moment Nona felt a pang of sadness at the thought that Clera would have liked this part. She was always proud of her voice. Their friendship had fallen into pieces and now the world seemed to be doing the same thing. Nona only hoped that, as with Clera, some element of what had been precious would survive.

Things grew more chaotic the closer they got to Verity. The officer that General Wensis had appointed to direct their efforts was called away by a senior officer to join a small group of cavalry. They galloped off towards the north gates, trampling crops and leaping hedges. A vast wave of smoke rose from the east of the city, subsuming the smoke of all the lesser fires. Nona knew a great battle must be raging but even though the nuns had dropped their song she could hear nothing save the wind, the creak and rattle of carts, and the worried complaints of peasants. It amazed her that things had come to this so swiftly, but Sister Tallow had often said when teaching the lessons of war that a defence could hold and hold and suddenly, like a dam collapsing, be swept away with little warning.

They passed bodies by the roadside, peasants, farm labourers, travellers, some hewn down by sword or axe, some studded with arrow shafts, some blackened and burned. Not all were dead but any that weren't at least crawling towards the city were surely dying.

Abbess Wheel raised her crozier and led the sisters into a field, the cattle absent long enough for the dung they had left behind to have crusted over. She clambered onto a stile to address the nuns and novices before her.

"We won't go through the city to join the defence. The North Gates will be jammed and the streets behind them choked. I aim to take us around the walls and enter closer to the palace."

The collective intake of breath was audible. Nona had reconciled herself to standing before the Ark but she had imagined that they would at least have the city walls between themselves and the foe. Surely Crucical wouldn't have his troops out in the open. If he could stop Adoma's forces in the field he would have done it two hundred miles east of his front door.

The abbess continued, unmoved by the shocked faces before her. "Mistress Shade will select three Sisters of Discretion to scout ahead of us. We will act on their reports. If need be the defenders on the wall will bring us over with ropes."

"How many Grey Sisters do we even have with us?" Ruli hissed.

"Two," Nona said. "If you don't count Sister Apple."

A hand fell on her shoulder. "Sister Cage." Apple turned Nona to face her. "I'm appointing you to the Grey temporarily. Get out there with Kettle and Cauldron and try not to die. Also, anything you can do to keep Wheel from marching us into ten thousand Scithrowl while singing at the tops of our voices will be much appreciated."

Nona gave a curt nod. She let Ruli and Jula hug her, bracing herself against their combined impact. Over her friends' heads she met the eyes of Ketti, Ghena, Alata, Leeni, and others of her former classmates. They all looked frightened. A weight of responsibility settled on her as her friends released their hold.

Kettle went by grim-faced but as she passed Apple her fingers trailed across the other woman's hand, and Apple, turning bright-eyed to watch her go, whispered something after her.

Kettle joined Cauldron, who was already changing into clothing taken from the dead Scithrowl on the Vinery Stair. It was more convincing than what they'd brought with them from the Shade stores, less than a uniform but more than random garb: the soldiers had worn similar tabards that had once sported bright designs, and their garments had elements of design that set them apart from what was common in the empire.

"Take the bloodiest stuff, Nona. You'll be the injured one if we're challenged." Kettle tossed a rough shirt her way, stained with crimson at the breast. "No mail for you. We'll be bringing you back to be bandaged up. It'll also hide the fact you can't speak Scithrowl."

"And you can?" Ghena asked from the ranks of watching novices.

"*Yar, irh ken hem gutya.*" Kettle didn't look up from fastening the buckles of her chain-mail shirt.

WITHIN A FEW minutes they were ready to leave.

"Watch. Take your chances. We left Sweet Mercy behind us, show none to the enemy." Apple handed Nona the standard Grey Sister field kit: a bandolier holding all the poisons, antidotes, wires, picks, and tricks of the order.

"I will, Mistress Shade." Nona fixed the belt beneath the heavy shirt. Kettle and Cauldron were already moving off.

Nona glanced once more at Jula and Ruli, then back at the convent, almost invisible in the distance on the edge of the Rock. A deep breath and she took off running, hard on Kettle's heels.

Kettle led the way into the next field where the corn grew to chest height, the husks withering. Bhenta veered across to join Nona, cornstalks whispering their complaints behind her. *Cauldron!* Nona hadn't grown used to Bhenta's bride name. She made a mental note to get it right when they spoke, then settled into her running and her clarity trance, letting the countryside ahead open itself to her and shout out its secrets.

To their right the walls of Verity curved away. Here and there the ancient blocks of the original wall were replaced by sandstone quarried from the plateau and the wall dipped to as low as fifty feet in height, but in the main the structure was the one that had stood for centuries, an even seventy-foot barrier broad enough to support a walkway along the top with a guard wall to protect those who patrolled it.

The defenders weren't exactly thickly clustered. Nona imagined that most had been called upon to join the battle to the east where the city wall came closest to the emperor's palace and the Ark within. Even so, the helmed heads of guards studded the wall top at regular intervals and no doubt reserves waited to rush in reinforcements where called for. Sister Rule had taught them that Verity had never suffered the attack of another nation but had held against sieges during several insurrections. The most recent of those had been over a hundred and twenty years ago, however. Plenty of time for the lessons taught in blood to have been forgotten.

NONA HAD TRAINED under Apple's supervision in fields not far from the ones they now moved through, but watching Kettle's advance taught her that she still had much to learn. Kettle had been the length of the empire, to both fronts of the war, and had gambled her life against her stealth more times than she could remember. She took them around small bands of Scithrowl scouting for weaknesses along the walls, and past watchers concealed deep within crop, copse, or cottage. Some of these were skilled out-runners for the Scithrowl force, marjal shadow-workers among them, but none had been pushed into shadow like Kettle had and their weaving of the darkness sent out ripples that she could read as no other save the Noi-Guin. Nona knew she would be reporting their positions to Sister Apple along their shadow-link.

"We could get a clear view from Malden's Mount," Bhenta said.

Kettle shook her head. "It'll be covered with Scithrowl. There's a lone pine by Eld Stables. We'll take a look from there."

She brought them the quarter of a mile to the pine, crossing fields, ducking along lanes, skirting burning farmsteads. Nona had never seen a taller tree.

"You're up, Sister Cage." Kettle lifted her chain mail to show she had no intention of climbing in armour. "The shadow-worker hiding in the branches is all yours. We'll take the ground troop."

Nona had seen the Scithrowl irregulars concealed around the empty stables block. The shadow-worker had escaped her notice. "How far up?"

"Right at the top. Must be a little one to climb so high. Give us a minute, then go."

Kettle lifted both hands and the shadows rose around her like a mist. Cauldron reached out to snare some of the shadows, wrapping them around herself. The pair wove themselves in, not simply clothed in darkness but robbed of colour and distinction so that the eye wanted to slide across them without pause. Moments later they were both on the move, a smooth advance towards the stables.

Nona made a silent count. She didn't expect any screams. When she reached her target number she ran for the tree. A flat sprint without any attempt at concealment. The watcher hadn't chosen so high a position to then stare at the ground around the trunk.

A leap brought the lowest bough into reach and Nona swung herself up, climbing rapidly through the branches. As she rose the branches became narrower and closer together and she had to force a passage through thickly packed needles. Smaller branches snapped around her, scratching at exposed skin and leaving her sticky with their sap. The only chance she had at remaining undetected was if the general sway of the pine and the seething of its limbs in the strengthening wind was hiding the racket she was making.

Higher still and the density of branch and needle thinned a little, though now she needed to think about where she chose to step as many of the tree's limbs would be unequal to her weight. Nona paused some twenty feet shy of the top.

Have the Scithrowl put a child up here?

Very little space remained where the watcher could be concealed and if she got much higher she would be open to any missile they might throw her way. Nona strained her senses, her clarity biting so hard it made her whole body tingle. She felt every tiny cut on her skin, the light sliced across her eyes, the clamour of wind and creak of wood assaulted her ears. She knew each ridge of the bark beneath her fingers. And she saw the slow upwards flow of shadow all around her.

Nona grabbed the trunk, now so narrow that she could encircle it in a double-handed grip. Sister Apple had said that they had left mercy behind them when Wheel led them from the convent. Whoever lurked above her doubtless had an array of knives and needles coated in the very worst venoms, and climbing vertically to attack a well-prepared enemy was never a healthy strategy.

She locked her legs around the trunk, drew back an arm, summoned her blades, and swung. The entire top section of the tree fell. The watcher made a brief wail, quickly lost in the tearing of branches and ended by a dull thud. Nona was left at the pine's new vertex with a clear view across the hordes arrayed to the east.

Nona hadn't imagined that Scithrowl held so many people, let alone that their queen could march them over the Grampains and across hundreds of miles to the emperor's doorstep. True fear gripped her for the first time that day. Skill couldn't prevail against such numbers. A Red Sister might cut down fifty of the foe only to find five hundred more throwing themselves at her. Gazing at the ocean of humanity stretching out to the east, Nona at last understood the enormity of the threat. This tide would wash across Verity and not stop until it reached the Marn Sea. Her friends, every novice, every nun, would die. They stood no chance. None.

The line of attack lay to the east. Rows of war machines hurled their missiles, siege towers rumbled forward, and ground forces surged towards the walls, carrying long ladders and grapple chains, borne by gerants huge enough to throw them over the ramparts.

The great majority of Adoma's force held back, though, marshalled in ordered ranks before acres given over to their accommodation and enclosed within rough stockade walls. A second city had sprung up, this one of tents, an endless patchwork of canvas and hide, speckled with flags of many colours. Nona saw the signs of industry, smoke from iron chimneys where weapons and armour were being repaired, horses reshod, swords sharpened. Siege machines not yet committed to the battle hulked like giant beasts recumbent amid the ant swarm of foot soldiers. Elsewhere horses in greater numbers than she had ever seen before milled in their pens, herds of them even though the main strength of the Scithrowl came to battle on their own legs.

The wind carried their stench to her, more ripe even than Verity's, the sewage of men and animals in their tens of thousands, perhaps a hundred thousand and more, the stink of a thousand cook fires and a thousand latrines.

Here and there grand pavilions stood among the massed troops, the brilliant colours of their fabric an assault on the senses. Above them pennants cracked in the wind.

Most of the pavilions were too far away for a good view but one stood just a mile off and barely beyond the range of Verity's bolt-lobbers, close enough for Nona to note its exceptional quality and remarkable size. A line of six large catapults stood fifty yards ahead of it, their missiles earthenware jars of highly flammable liquid. With low and throaty twangs they lobbed their burning cargo over Verity's walls into the city beyond, where the destruction could only be guessed at and smoke spewed skywards.

Nona looked back towards Wheel and her band, now lost in the distance. The small gate through which Abbess Glass had once led her from the city stood free of attack thus far and as close to the battlefront as you could get without finding yourself part of it. Around fifty of the city guard held the ground before the gate and defenders clustered on the wall high above. It was the last eastward entry point where the city could be entered without enduring an arrow storm and it would reduce by a considerable margin the distance that had to be traversed inside the walls to reach the palace. Nona took one more glance around at the unreal panorama, a landscape she knew well made alien by war, and began her rapid descent.

"THAT'S THE LAST way in for them. Otherwise they're just going to get swarmed and cut down at the foot of the walls." Nona pointed at the spot.

Kettle nodded. "What's that gate called?"

Nona shrugged. "I don't know . . ."

"It's called 'the Small Gate,'" Bhenta said.

"There you go." Nona scanned the fields for any sign of approaching enemy, then looked at Kettle. "Can you make Apple understand?"

Kettle nodded again, her brow furrowed in concentration. Her shadow-bond with Apple was an exceptionally strong one and this close to her it allowed for basic information to be communicated. "Done."

"We should join them." Bhenta met Nona's gaze with those alarming blue eyes of hers. Apple had once taught them to brew a particularly unpleasant poison that was exactly that colour, a "fake blue" Nona called it.

"Or . . ." Nona raised an open hand towards the east.

"It's too dangerous," Kettle said.

"This is a day for dangerous. We're going to face the Scithrowl one way or the other. Do we want it to be when they've breached the city wall? Us waiting at the emperor's gates and a rank of pikemen advancing while the arrows rain in . . . ? Or do we want it to be as Sisters of Discretion, behind their lines, hitting at what they would rather keep safe? You don't put up a pavilion like that for a minor general or some princeling. I saw you do it less than a month ago!" Nona had watched through her thread-bond with

Kettle as the Grey Sister killed the commander of five hundred Scithrowl within the luxury of his tent, slitting his throat while he slept beneath the furs of a hoola. "They're not afraid of us! They're arrogant and stupid. We could do some real damage here. It might be Adoma herself! Even if we die we will have sold our lives for something of worth, more than we could achieve cutting down foot soldiers as they climb the walls."

"It's still too—"

"You didn't see them, Kettle. Words can't paint it. Numbers that big don't have meaning. They're an ocean, a wave. They will roll over the walls and grind us down and nothing we have will stop them. We need to cut off the head. Come at their leaders where they're most vulnerable. This is what Apple trained us for!"

Kettle shook her head and turned to go. Nona grabbed her arm. "Go up the tree, then tell me."

Kettle rolled her eyes. "Sister Cauldron, don't let her do anything stupid while I'm up there." And with that she was gone, fairly sprinting up the pine despite the weight of her chain mail.

"You should learn to follow orders, sister." Bhenta watched Nona through narrow eyes. "Sister Kettle has seen more war than any of us."

Kettle dropped back to the ground before it seemed that there had been time to reach the top. She joined them, white-faced.

"Let's do it."

20

---◆---

HOLY CLASS

Present Day

NONA COULDN'T UNDERSTAND any of what was said at the four layers of the Scithrowl perimeter but Kettle proved sufficiently convincing to get through. Kettle even managed to earn a slap on the back and a few laughs at the last checkpoint. Bhenta remained largely taciturn during these encounters but interjected a few comments unasked since silence provokes questions. Bhenta adopted the heavily accented empire tongue that predominated in the shadow of the Grampains on the Scithrowl side . . . though Nona supposed that both sides of the range were now the Scithrowl side.

For her part Nona spoke the international language of pain—groaning and holding her side with bloody hands. She had been hurt enough times to know how to play it. Whatever she was asked she planned to stick to moaning. Her written Scithrowl was rudimental, her spoken Scithrowl worse.

On receiving directions from some minor officer Kettle began to lead them briskly through the outskirts of the main Scithrowl force. Nona hobbled after her with one arm over Bhenta's shoulders for support, her head down so that the blackness of her eyes would not draw comment or attention.

The smell of the place was overpowering. Smoke from the battle at the walls drifted back to mix with that of countless cook fires and communal blazes, along with the pervading stink of latrines, the aroma of unfamiliar stews bubbling in cauldrons, the odour of close-packed humanity, of draught horses, cavalry, penned cattle and pigs, stray dogs, and a shanty town of camp followers to the rear. It was as if a vast city had been turned out into the fields, given weapons, and dressed in armour.

Although Kettle was discreet about it Nona could see that she was noting every detail, and the telltale furrow between her eyebrows meant that she was sending to Apple all the information their shadow-bond would allow. Nona could only imagine what Apple might be sending back. Demands for her return. Pleading? Threats, even? Or did Mistress Shade have the discipline not to distract a Grey Sister with her personal fears even when that Grey Sister was Kettle and the mission could very well be one that allowed no return?

Turning sharply behind a latrine trench sheltered by a wall of woven sticks, Kettle snatched up an empty water barrel and thrust it at Nona. "You're all better now. Hold this over your 'wounds' and walk with purpose. We need to get into that fancy tent and, if it seems worth the risk, kill whoever we find."

They came around the back of the latrine, still under the casual gaze of countless eyes, and Kettle turned their path a few degrees towards the distant pavilion. As they progressed both Kettle and Bhenta acquired burdens, a pile of blankets for Kettle, a heavy coil of rope for Bhenta. Apple always stressed the authority that a simple burden conveys upon the person carrying it.

At each point at which their path was blocked and they had to move aside or go around, Kettle ensured that they emerged on a heading more closely aimed towards their goal. Nona noticed that both of the nuns also managed to dump their entire supply of deadwort into two separate communal water barrels. If the slightly acrid taste went unnoticed the first victims wouldn't start to die for hours yet, giving plenty of time for more to join them on the casualty list.

"This isn't going to be easy. If there's anyone of real note in there, then they will have guards every bit as well trained as we are." Kettle breathed the words as they walked, pitched just for their ears.

"Distraction?" Bhenta muttered.

"Has to be." Kettle nodded.

A LINE OF hard-eyed soldiers in brighter and less ragged uniform than the regulars stood a perimeter around the pavilion. Kettle didn't approach close enough to be warned off. Another of Apple's maxims: *make one sure move, nothing tentative.*

"The catapults?" Kettle spoke directly to Nona across their thread-bond. "Can you do it?"

"Yes." Nona had never mastered the ability to work fire beyond the snuffing of candles and making figures dance in the hearth flames. But the great clay pots in which the flaming oil was being lobbed . . . those were something she could reach out and touch with her rock-work. Especially this close to the Ark with her bloods singing to its tune.

"Not too close. We don't want the pavilion catching. It could scatter our targets."

The pavilion's exit ran beneath multiple awnings hung between poles carved from a dark wood that Nona didn't recognise. Anyone emerging from the tent would find themselves looking out over the row of catapults some fifty yards away. Kettle led them on a circuitous route, approaching the pavilion from the side. As they closed the distance she and Bhenta drew shadows to them, a subtle gathering that kept the darkness to a mist barely rising above the trampled grass while it flowed behind them.

Nona paused and stared at the catapults, frowning in concentration. A series of defensive ranks were arrayed before the great camp against the remote possibility that Emperor Crucical's armies should sally forth. Beyond those ranks lay several hundred yards of churned earth. Then came the sea of armed humanity surging around the base of Verity's walls, weathering rocks and arrows as they waited their turn at ladder or scaling chain. To the left, annoyingly just out of the catapults' line of fire, the first of half a dozen vast siege towers had just met the wall.

Nona reached out with her rock sense for the feel of fired clay, hunting the roundness and fullness of the containers. The catapults launched without rhythm, each firing when ready, the faster crews slowly overhauling the slower.

The sensation of finding her goal was like that of suddenly remembering a name that had eluded her. How could she ever not have known it? She selected a pot that had already been hefted into a catapult's throwing cup by the rope netting sewn around the clay. The top of the pot was shielded from the wind by a perforated copper housing, and the wick within had just been lit. As Nona watched, the man who worked the lever took position. A moment later the throwing arm snapped up, the twisted hides releasing their tension with a throaty twang. The arm slammed into the arresting bar, jerking the whole back end of the wheeled framework from the ground. The pot sailed on, still rising.

Nona slowed the world, ground her teeth together, clenched her fist, and the pot shattered. Flaming oil spread, slowed, and fell upon the heads of a division of Scithrowl archers all busy lofting their own missiles towards the walls of Verity.

The shadows that had been gathered now wound up Nona's legs, wrapping her with a cold dark thrill. While all eyes turned towards the flames and screams ahead of the catapult line the three nuns sped forward, swift and indistinct. They kept low and passed between two soldiers guarding the tent. Nona pushed at the man facing them with whatever marjal empathy she had: *you don't see us.*

Kettle slit the pavilion's billowing side, low down, and all three of them slid through in a trice on knees and elbows.

Nona understood their mistake the moment she came through. The interior was a single space lit by shifting colours as the sunlight penetrated the walls. The ground was uncovered grass. Five figures in the mottled white tunics of softmen stood around a man seated in a plain wooden chair at the centre. Softmen were dangerous enough on their own, assassins as deadly as the Noi-Guin, versed in their own martial arts and peculiar variants of shadow-work. It was the man at the centre who caught Nona's attention, though, even before she was off her knees. Sigils sewn in threads of silver and of gold overwrote the black velvet of his robe. Dozens of them. Such expense might be lavished on a king or queen, but here in this empty tent it meant only one thing. The whole thing was a trap designed to draw in the best assassins the enemy had. The man was clearly a mage, waiting here to ensure that none of those lured in would escape again. Either the Scithrowl had learned from their long haul across the Corridor not to signal where their battle commanders slept, or they had been deliberately stupid, sacrificing leaders, or perhaps even simply using actors, in a game of bait-and-switch. They must have known that the best of the empire's assassins would strike in the last days and hours before they reached the emperor's walls.

To their credit, Kettle and Bhenta rolled smoothly away on either side, coming to their feet while unleashing a barrage of throwing stars. Sadly the distraction that had allowed them to enter unobserved from the outside had simply let the softmen know that something was coming. Each of them held a pair of pain-sticks, thin iron rods about two feet in length. The sigil at the end, activated by shadow-work, caused such agony that even a light brush against exposed flesh would leave the victim screaming on the floor. The artefact that Thuran Tacsis called the Harm had been fashioned along the same principles.

With hunska speed the softmen deflected the hail of missiles, taking particular care to protect the man in their midst. The mage rose to his feet. He looked to be in his fifties, grey hair cropped short, a hard dark stare. A tattoo dominated his face, blue lines radiating from between his eyes. It had something of a flower about it. Also something of a spider spreading its legs. Nona knew him for a quantal. She couldn't say how, except perhaps that he lacked any of the deformities common to many marjals who draw too deeply on the elemental arts or those rarer and more strange talents sometimes brought to bear.

"Three! Three is a prize worthy of my efforts."

Nona felt the man set foot on the Path. The weight of his footfall shuddered through the fabric of everything. He smiled. A Scithrowl Path-mage with decades of experience preparing to snuff out a trio of Grey Sisters who would likely have fallen to his softmen, though not without cost. Even if he knew Nona for a quantal he had nothing to fear, armoured as he was in sigils of the highest order. To her eye the robes were surely capable of draining thirty steps' worth of Path-energy to the void. More likely they would withstand fifty or even more. Nona had never come close to thirty steps. She had nearly died trying to own what she had taken from fewer than twenty steps outside the cave where Raymel Tacsis had come for her.

The anger that had been waiting its moment ever since she had first realised that she had led her sisters into a trap now burst loose inside Nona, an explosion against which the oil bomb's flare seemed pale. An instant later, driven by that same fury, Nona hit the Path running.

This close to the Ark, Nona saw the Path with new clarity, finding it wide beneath her feet, though in truth it was no more beneath her than it was above. The Path was a mountain river, an avalanche, a lightning bolt all in one, all that and more, pouring through her. She forced her mind to impose the simplest interpretation on what lay before her and ran the Path as she had run so many times. At each stride boundless energy swelled inside her. She felt the fierceness of its gift start to fray her mind, start to unravel every fibre of her being.

Nona knew she needed to find her enemy before he took his power, shaped it, and blasted her to ash. She had no protection and even if she could take enough steps and own enough energy to overload his robes, which she knew she couldn't—she hadn't the time. The mage would leave the Path and destroy her before that could happen.

Sister Pan had taught Nona that when a quantal runs the Path they are in no one place along its length. When something has no end and no beginning it has no middle either, and soon your mind begins to realise that if there is no way in which to specify where you are along its length then in many ways you are *everywhere* along its length.

That, Sister Pan had said, *is the key to finding your enemy. It merely requires the understanding that there is no place they could ever be other than before you.*

Nona had never been sure of the logic and she couldn't claim to understand the Path, but she believed the ancient woman who had taught her with such patience, and somehow, there on the Path itself, she knew every word to be true.

Belief proved sufficient. She saw the Scithrowl mage ahead, walking towards her on a beam of twisting light now grown as narrow as the pipe the novices trod in blade-path. She saw the idea of him rather than the person, etched by streamers of the Path's energy.

Sister Pan had spoken at length of contesting the Path but never allowed the novices to practise as such contests were almost invariably fatal to the loser. Falling from the Path and owning what you took from it was hard enough, but being pushed from it made the task far more difficult. Most quantal Path-walkers avoided such duels because they were often fatal not only to the loser but to both contestants. Sister Pan likened it to wrestling on a tightrope. It wasn't so hard to make the opponent fall, but to not fall after them was almost impossible.

Nona's vision of the approaching Path-mage told her that he stood deep in whatever meditation mages used to find their serenity, advancing in cautious steps. He walked the Path as Sister Pan taught, as all quantals Nona knew walked it. Sister Pan in all her years had never met another who threw herself at the Path and raced its length with such disregard. Now Nona hoped that speed might somehow save her.

Nona charged on with the reckless haste that she always brought to the Path, clutching her growing power around herself like a cloak. The mage saw her only at the last fraction, lifting his gaze from the study of the way before him, shock and horror in his eyes.

There was an impact, at once both as vast as worlds colliding and as slight as the momentary chill of a passing cloud. Nona knew herself to be both on the Path and at the same time scattered from it in all directions, her bones tumbling as they burned. Falling and not falling. A choice. Her flat sprint had thrown the mage from the Path, dumping half her energy into his lap, slowing her but deflecting her only by degrees. Still, her balance escaped her one fraction at a time and just as on the convent blade-path she knew that the error would grow with each step until she fell. She took two more steps and dropped from the Path by choice.

Her race along the Path had taken almost no time. Kettle and Bhenta had closed half the distance to the first of the softmen. Throwing stars hung in the air between them, their rotations lazy. Nona saw that the Path-mage had begun to fall. Bright crackles of blue-white energy had broken from his skin, and his face was starting to twist with horror.

Even as Nona struggled to own the Path energies raging through her, the out-of-kilter resonances that throbbed between her and the mage confirmed that he was failing to do the same. Being thrown from the Path with such violence had left him off-balance, unable to contain what he had taken. And although he wore the value of half a city in the sigils upon his robes, capable of deflecting the strongest blast Nona might throw his way, his protections couldn't save him from himself.

Nona sucked into her flesh all that the Path had given her. Her skin wanted to blister and bubble away, her bones wanted to ignite. She screamed her denial and launched herself at Kettle's back. She brought the nun to the floor a yard before the first of the softmen. The legendary impassivity of the softmen cracked at the sight of one enemy tackling another. Shaved brows rose in momentary surprise. Nona shook with barely contained power, pale violet flame licked across her skin, and versions of herself kept trying to escape along their own courses. She hauled them all back in. The pain made her want to faint but it was too cruel to allow any such relief.

With a sob Nona used her Path-born strength to throw Kettle one-armed, aiming her like a skittle to take out Bhenta even as she slashed at the first softman to intercept her. Both Grey sisters went tumbling towards the pavilion wall. Already the Path-mage shone brighter than the day, shuddering with power he couldn't contain. Nona followed her friends, her feet tearing deep gouges in the ground as she hunted for acceleration. A pain-stick lashed out at her but the Path's invisible armour turned it away.

The detonation behind Nona came at the same moment she landed on top of her sisters, still tangled together on the grass. She spread her arms as the shock wave rippled overhead. A light, whiter and more intense than that of the sun, lit the material of the tent walls as the shock wave shredded them in strange geometric patterns. They hung there for an instant and in the next they were gone. The explosion that scattered the Path-mage reduced the perimeter of guards outside the tent to a red mist and then shot that mist at the surrounding army, who fell like corn before the scythe for fifty yards on all sides. A moment later the oil stores went up with a *woof* and a firestorm swirled skywards around the catapults.

All about them the ground lay scorched and smoking, the only green where Nona, armoured in her own Path-energies, had lain. She mourned the loss of the Path-mage's robe. If he had worn it inside out the garment might have survived. With a groan she rolled off Kettle, who in turn rolled off Bhenta. The Path's energy still burned in her, demanding release.

They lay near the centre of a circle of destruction. Nona had never seen someone walk the Path and fail to own what they took. She never wanted to see it again.

She found her voice. "Get back to the others." The confusion would hide their escape.

Without giving either woman a chance to respond Nona jumped to her feet and took off at flat sprint towards the Scithrowl assault massed at the base of Verity's great wall. In the past three years of intensive training under Sister Pan's direction Nona had grown into her heritage and learned all manner of ways to shape and master the power with which the Path filled her. She still couldn't walk the Path twice in two days without enormous risk, though, and so she aimed to put what she had now to good use.

The speed the Path gave her was like the swiftness a steep slope lends running legs. At first it was just that the running was effortless and far faster than anything you were capable of. And then it would almost be like flying and your feet would beat as rapid a tempo against the ground as your fingers could drum on a table. And almost immediately after that you would know that you had no control and that very soon you would fall and it was going to hurt. A lot.

Nona broke free of the waiting horde before any of them could tear their attention away from the carnage centred on the pavilion. She crossed half the open ground ahead of the walls before the first arrow zipped past her ear.

She crashed into the backs of the soldiers massed at the base of the closest siege tower and broke several of them before their bodies arrested her fearsome momentum. A dozen arrows hammered around her, taking down several more soldiers. She began to weave then, still clinging to the Path's power, refusing its demands to be spent in one glorious act of ruination.

The troops before her had no idea an enemy was among them. Without exception their sole focus was to get into the siege tower before being found by an arrow or a rock from the great wall looming above them. Nona shouldered armoured men and women aside as if they were small children. The siege tower stank of the pine sap bleeding from its raw timbers, of the uncured hides nailed across its walls, and of the fear of those climbing it. The great wheels lay to either side now that the structure stood tight-pressed to Verity's wall.

Nona barged inside and began to run up the ridged wooden ramp that formed a square spiral within the tower. Everywhere she stepped a glowing footprint remained to record her passage, scorched into the timber. Rather than fading, each footprint grew brighter and then more bright until on her sixth stride from the print it detonated, a blast powerful enough to blow out the sides of the tower in a cloud of splintered planking and torn hides. The chain of explosions chased Nona up the tower, tearing apart the soldiers she left tumbled behind her, and setting fire to the main beams.

The tower had begun to collapse by the time Nona burst through the curtain of chains screening the doorway just below its roof. She ran across the platform that bridged to the battlements and, with hunska speed, threw herself between the legs of the defending line. At the far edge she snagged the stonework and slid down the interior wall in a shower of sparks as she tamed her descent with her flaw-blades.

She found herself amid a crowd of startled defenders who a moment before had been racing around on various errands to fight fires, reinforce weak spots, or bring supplies like arrows or rocks to the wall.

"I'm a Bride of the Ancestor!" Two men levelled spears at Nona and she raised her arms. "I'm here to help."

21

THE ESCAPE

Three Years Earlier

"YOU'VE BEEN SPYING on me?"

"I have been spying on all of you. On the sister of the emperor, on the Red Sisters and the Grey, on the Church of the Ancestor." Zole looked as unapologetic as it was possible for a person to be.

"Why?" Nona could think of no other question.

Tarkax stepped forward. "The Corridor holds millions of people. What will happen when the moon falls?"

"The Corridor will close and we'll all die," Nona said.

"Most will." Tarkax nodded. "But even if just one in every ten makes it to the ice, and if just one in every hundred of those makes it to the hot seas that are all that will be left to sustain us . . . they will outnumber the tribes."

Nona blinked and discovered that frost had begun to form on her eyelashes. She had known the ice-tribes were few in number, especially those that spent their time in the deep ice rather than hunting the Corridor seas and the beasts that lived in the margins. It had never occurred to her quite *how* few they might be. "So what is it you plan to do?"

Tarkax shrugged. "Being prepared and forewarned is a plan in itself. But there are those among us who think that the Corridor can be saved, at least for a while longer. A few centuries perhaps. Zole has been gathering information. There's no treachery intended. We want to help you and, by doing so, to help ourselves."

"How?" Nona narrowed her eyes at the warrior. For years she'd imagined him to be some wandering mercenary. It took an effort of imagination to refashion him as Zole's uncle, watching over his niece and hoping to save all the nations of Abeth.

"Ah, well that is the tricky part." He twisted a smile. "We didn't send Zole just to watch you."

"You sent me because I needed to learn more than the ice-speakers could teach," Zole said.

"We did." Tarkax nodded. "You may have noticed, Nona, that my brother's daughter is an exceptional child. Our tribe has access to two Old Stones and no member of our people has ever held both and been fully purged. Not before Zole. And still she has not ascended. The ice-speakers now say that it will take four Old Stones, one attuned to each of the bloods, to forge her fully." He glanced at the hand Zole had just unwrapped. In the wind's bite her flesh looked paler than Nona had ever seen it, but across her palm a scarlet stain spread like oil on water. "And now she has exposed herself to a third."

Nona shuddered, and not just from the cold. "And if Zole does 'ascend,' so what? Will it stop the ice from closing on us?"

"We are also interested in your emperor's Ark, Nona."

"Because it can control the moon?" Nona shook her head. "You thought Zole could open it? But surely the Argatha prophecy was just nonsense, made up for local politics, to entertain the people."

"The Ark *can* guide the moon." Tarkax glanced around at his fellows as if they too might need convincing.

"If that were really true, why would the emperor, and his father, and his father's mother before him, all have banned the books that say it, and made criminals of anyone trying to find a way? If shiphearts were the key to the Ark, why would they still lie scattered? Wouldn't generations of emperors have been trying to bring them to Verity? I know Sherzal and Adoma seem to think it's true, but that doesn't mean it is. Or even that they really believe it."

"Your emperors tried many ways to open their Ark, Nona, for hundreds of years. But do you know the most important thing that they discovered?"

Nona kept silent and waited for Tarkax to answer his own question.

"They discovered that when you hold a treasure of incalculable value and potential, having it closed to you and beyond use is not the worst thing that can happen. The most dangerous thing that can happen is for someone else to discover, or even just believe that they have discovered, the means to open and use it. Such individuals will gather strength to themselves and seek to take your treasure from you."

Nona frowned. Zole had wrapped her hand once more and stood silent. "So . . . what are you going to do now?"

"We're going to send you home, Nona." Tarkax grinned, then raised his sealskin mask as the wind strengthened. "There are two marvels that will allow it. The first marvel is a work of the Missing. The second marvel is that it is close enough to reach in a day."

NONA TRUDGED AT the back of the group, her mind racing. Zole walked beside her.

"You were spying on us? Sweet Mercy took you in! The abbess gave you her protection!"

"Has Tarkax not taken you in and given you his protection?" Zole asked. "Are you not gathering all the information you can and preparing to share it with Abbess Glass on your return? Does the convent not exist in part to train spies?"

Nona opened then closed her mouth. They walked without speaking for several hours after that. Nona watched the other ice-tribers, trudging with bowed heads to either side of them, three men, two women, and Tarkax, all so swaddled in skins and furs that they resembled great forest bears. Two of them dragged a long, heavily laden sled behind them, sliding along on wooden runners. Nona wondered what the tribes of the deep ice, thousands of miles from the Corridor, built their sleds from. The bones of leviathans hauled from the sea perhaps.

"Where are we going?" Nona had really wanted to ask whether they were nearly there yet. Her feet were strangers to her and she wondered whether her toes would have to be cut away when they thawed.

"To the place from where the black ice flows," Zole said.

"Why?" Nona had really wanted to say that she didn't want to go there and that she would rather scale the Grampains naked in an ice-wind.

"Because there is a wonder buried in that place."

Nona could have asked what the wonder was, but without that mystery to draw her further she felt her legs would just abandon their duty and leave the task of getting her there to her arms.

It took them until nightfall to reach the long dark streak in the ice and follow it to where it grew darker still and finally turned black before abruptly giving way to white once more. Nona knew from her view while crossing the mountains that the stain looked like a great teardrop from above, the long tail of it running to the Corridor wall miles north of them.

Zole took over the lead as the light failed, the darkness being nothing to her eyes. She halted them in a place where the malice from below was still only a whisper.

"You and I will go alone, Nona. We should be swift."

Tarkax and the others huddled as close as they could come to the shipheart and formed a barrier against the wind. Tarkax lowered his frosty mask, revealing a grin. "Be strong, niece. And you too, Nona Grey. Be fierce and true, like I am." He struck his chest with his gloved fist. "Zole is the hope of our people, but there is a hero in you too, girl. I have seen her."

Nona couldn't help but grin back, though her face ached with the cold. She liked Tarkax despite his boasting. She nodded and made a short bow to the ice-tribers. "May the wind be at your backs." Sister Rule taught that this was a common blessing on the ice.

"Hah!" Tarkax showed all his teeth in a broad smile. "War is coming, little Nona. Wars are always coming. You give them hell! Remember that anger. You'll need it!" And with that he covered his face and walked away, the others following.

Zole and Nona watched them go, standing in silence while the wind moaned around them. When the swirl of ice at last swallowed Tarkax and his people from view, the ice felt a very lonely place indeed.

Nona turned to gaze out across the wasteland where their path would take them. Here and there a crimson star stood reflected in the smoothness of the ice. Before her, though, there were no stars, only a consuming black void. "If the focus comes while we're down there we'll both drown!"

"There is no focus here, Nona. We are in my home now." Zole walked out into the darkness. A moment later she took the shipheart from her pack and Nona followed its alien light.

"Walk where I walk," Zole said. "The ice is rotten in places."

Nona moved closer, gritting her teeth against the invisible, cold fire of the shipheart. She had always imagined the things to be blazing sources of heat and right now she would love for that to be true. In reality the convent pipes bore sigils where they had passed through the shipheart's vault and it had been those specially crafted sigils that had converted the radiance into something as commonplace as warmth. If she had the skill Nona would have drawn such sigils on both her boots there and then.

The malice radiating from below grew as the ice darkened around them. It reached her even through the shipheart's radiance and Nona knew it to be far fiercer than she had experienced before. This was the source, the place where the evils the Missing had purged to obtain their so-called divinity now leaked back into the world.

"Here." Zole halted in front of a fissure disturbingly similar to the one into which she had fallen during her fight with Yisht. "We go down here."

"Shouldn't we fix a rope or something?" Nona had seen that Tarkax's companions carried iron spikes, hammers, and long thin ropes of woven sinew. "We should have asked—"

"Their ropes were not long enough." Zole pulled a coil of the stuff from beneath her coat. "Neither is mine."

"If we tied them together we'd have hundreds of—"

"We are going to the bottom. It is more than two miles."

"Oh." Nona felt for her knives, then remembered that she had left them under the ice. "What's the rope for, then?"

"To tie you to my back. It will be a difficult climb."

As usual, when Zole said "difficult" she meant "impossible." And as usual she managed anyway. Nona clung to Zole's back, seeing nothing but Zole's arms and glimmers where occasional flaws in the ice returned a fraction of the shipheart's light. Zole had secured her pack across her front, with the shipheart inside and the flap left open to let the glow escape for Nona's benefit. Despite being tied to Zole, Nona clung on grimly. She became thankful for the rope later after hundreds of yards of descent. Her arms were aching and her mind too fragile this close to the shipheart to worry about whether her hands kept tight hold. Zole made steady progress. Her strength was inhuman and she compelled holds out of the ice as it suited her.

While Zole climbed Nona heard nothing but the sound of her breath and of the ice splintering to answer her needs. Each time Zole rested, a new set of sounds became apparent. A constant groaning, a creaking, sometimes bright and almost metallic, sometimes so deep that Nona felt it only in her chest. The slow river of the ice, flowing endlessly towards the Corridor.

"There's hardly any dripping here."

"No."

"Why is this hole here, then?"

"There is a source of heat below. Only a little above freezing, but just enough to keep this path open."

Zole resumed their descent. The shaft was not vertical but slanted with the flow of the ice. Half a dozen times they passed older shafts that had once served as vents but had been drawn too far by the glacier, forcing the heat to create a new escape.

Time lost meaning: repetition stole it away.

When Zole finally dropped a foot or so and landed on raw rock, Nona started with shock as if waking from a dream.

"Where are we?"

"A temple of the Missing once stood here." Zole untied the rope that bound Nona to her. Nona staggered back, almost tripping on the uneven floor, her limbs unresponsive, chest aching.

They had descended the wall of a low-roofed ice-cavern with a floor of bare stone. Where the rock lifted it lay scored all across with parallel lines, wounds gouged by the slow passage of glaciers.

Nona took several more steps back, eager to put some distance between herself and the shipheart.

"Stay close." Zole reached out to restrain her. "The *klaulathu* here are many and they are strong."

"So, where is this marvel?" Nona looked around and saw nothing but the dark. The *klaulathu*'s hatred needled out at her, ancient and hungry.

"Here," Zole said. "Where else would it be but beneath the passage its heat has wrought?"

Nona turned and saw what Zole was pointing at. A huge ring lying where the rock dipped. It was three yards across, its perimeter a foot thick and two feet wide. The flat surface had been marked with sigils unlike any Nona had ever seen. Their fierce potential screamed into her eyes, twisting the world around them.

The ring wasn't bedded in the ground. In places Nona could have slipped an arm between the peculiar crystalline metal and the bedrock beneath.

"I think . . ." Nona stepped closer to the artefact, unable to look away, her gaze anchored by the sigils. "Have I seen this before?"

"I do not know. Have you been to the emperor's palace?"

"No." Of course she hadn't been to the palace. She was Nona Grey. A peasant child.

"That is unfortunate. If you had seen that one, then it would have marked you and helped draw you to it. It is unlikely that you have seen another. Although the ice-speakers say that the Missing fashioned one thousand and twenty-four of them and set each within an Ark."

Nona stood beside the ring now, her hand extended towards it, fingers tingling with the desire to touch the water-beaded metal. "What does it do?"

"It will take you to another such ring. As if you had simply stepped between them." Zole joined her and the shipheart's pressure started the voices chattering again, down in the depths of Nona's own darkness. "Sherzal showed me a drawing of another such ring that stands in her brother's palace. It lies within the Ark but not within the inner sanctum."

"You want us to go to Crucical's palace?" Nona raised her eyebrows at the thought of the reception they would get.

"No." Zole gestured for Nona to step into the circle. "I want you to go there."

"But . . . me? Alone?" Nona shook her head at the madness. "You're coming too."

"No."

"But . . . what would you do here?" Nona waved an arm at the cavern. "This is crazy."

"There are things I need to do on the ice." Zole met Nona's stare. Her face, lit from beneath with violet light, was free of emotion.

"Things?" Nona shook her head. "No! You belong at Sweet Mercy with us. With your sisters. With me."

"I would like to go with you, Nona Grey."

"Well, come on then!"

"But I cannot. I made a promise."

Nona reached for Zole's hand. "Break it." She stepped backwards into the ring, hauling on Zole's arm to bring the girl with her. Zole resisted, bracing a foot against the outside of the ring.

"I cannot."

Nona released Zole's arm and took a step back. "It doesn't matter!" A bitter laugh burst from her. "It doesn't work." She laughed again, amazed at herself for ever believing that it would. A ring that could spit a person hundreds of miles across the world!

"It requires the power of an Old Stone." Zole lifted the shipheart. "You must carry it through with you."

"And leave you in this place! At the bottom of a hole two miles deep? Now I know you're crazy. The shipheart has broken your mind."

"You must focus on the distance and direction that you wish to travel." Zole carried on as if Nona hadn't spoken. "It is that direction." She pointed. "Otherwise there is a possibility you will emerge from another more distant ring."

"Zole! Come home with me." Nona's voice caught in her throat. The hardships of the journey, and being constantly caught between the mind-tearing power of the shipheart on one side, the invading malice of the *klaulathu* on the other, had left her weak, awash with broken emotion.

"I want to," Zole said, her voice low.

"Who did you promise?" Nona took another step back. An idea blossomed within her skull repeated by voices that were hers and yet not hers. "Yisht was there to steal the shipheart . . . She was from your tribe!" Nona had seen it when she saw Zole and Tarkax together with their companions, but she hadn't understood it, not until this moment. They all had the same look. "Yisht was from your tribe . . . neither of you was working for Sherzal. Not really. You were both working for the tribe. To open the Ark whichever way you could!" Nona stopped dead and tilted her head, staring at Zole as if she could tear the truth from her with the power of her will. "Hessa? Hessa was a price worth paying?"

"I never intended for—"

An awful conviction seized Nona and in that moment she didn't care whether it sprang from reason or from the devils of the Missing. "Who *is* Yisht to you? Cousin? Older sister? Mother . . ."

"I—"

"Whose promise is it that's keeping you here?" Nona was shouting. What dark vow would have Zole remain in this unholy place and see her scale two miles of black ice to begin a trek into the terrible wilderness above? "Whose promise?"

"I cannot say—"

"Whose promise, sister?" Nona put every ounce of her marjal skill behind the question to compel an answer, an effort so fierce that it even quieted the strange voices in her mind.

"Abbess Glass. I promised Abbess Glass."

And with that Zole threw the shipheart at Nona, hard, fast, straight, and true. All around her the ring's sigils lit with an ancient light. And

Nona was falling, and though she clung to the moment she couldn't save herself.

WITHOUT THE PASSAGE of enough time for her heart to take a beat Nona stumbled through a freestanding metal ring. She stepped into a limestone cave, with the shipheart dropping from the hand she had used to ward it away. On every side the air was filled with broken flowstone, fragments tumbling lazily away, blasted from the ring that they had coated. And for the first time in an age Nona knew exactly where she was.

22

HOLY CLASS

Present Day

THE DEFENDERS BEHIND Verity's wall gave Nona free rein, which to her mind was a considerable lapse since she had come over from the Scithrowl side in the enemy's uniform and the walls of the emperor's own palace lay just two hundred yards farther on. It seemed that she was so smoke-blackened, muddy, and blood-spattered that others could no longer tell what she was wearing. In the general chaos at the base of the wall just not trying to kill anyone proved sufficient to identify her as not being Scithrowl.

She picked her way through the injured, lying haphazard in the wall's shadow among scattered equipment. Carts stood laden with all manner of things from barrels of tar and sheaves of arrows to tight-wrapped bandages and water tubs. One cart was a foot deep in scattered pieces of antique armour, as if the grand houses had turned out their spares, and another sported dozens of fresh army tabards in the emperor's green and gold, unsullied by use, as if someone expected to recruit fresh conscripts while the veterans rained down from on high, arrow-shot or run through with Scithrowl steel.

"I know you." A young soldier bumped into her as his sergeant led the way to the nearest wall ladder.

"Cage! From the Caltess!" The soldier's companion stopped to stare. "You are her! You have her eyes. You beat Denam—"

The man behind him pushed him on and the column passed Nona by, all of them staring, eager to distract themselves from the screams above and the zip of arrows sailing past.

Nona turned towards the nearest buildings. The city had long ago flowed out to press against boundaries that had once seemed foolishly overgenerous. The houses of the great and the good stood cheek by jowl, crowding to find a place beside the emperor's own. Close by, in the shadows of the city wall, nestled all the services that money likes to keep on hand. Bathhouses, stables, goldsmiths and silversmiths, jewellers, tailors, dressmakers, and establishments where a person of quality might throw their money after cards or dice, sample poisons that twist the mind in strange ways, buy the company of a young bed-partner, or satisfy less common urges proscribed by the laws of both State and Church.

And all of it was burning.

NONA GUESSED THAT the Path-mage she had killed might have been part of Adoma's Fist. She still had hope that the battle-queen's wars on her other border had kept the Fist in the east. The idea they might be here, among the horde, scared her in a way that mere numbers could not. She knew that their role was to crack open fortresses and cities that defied their queen, and the west held no bigger defiance than Verity.

If the Fist *was* here, then probably they were holding their strength in reserve and waiting to see if the walls would fall to more conventional assault. That or just waiting for enough defenders to mass in one place so that when the Fist struck it would cause maximum carnage.

In Nona's brief period of contemplation two men fell from the wall, hammering into the cobbled street close enough that she felt the warm spatter of their blood across her face. She moved quickly out of the danger zone. The corpses of other casualties that had fallen since the last clear-up lay strewn around, Scithrowl among them. Farther back the buildings not yet aflame had been opened to the most badly injured. Their screams, as overworked healers bound wounds and set bones, rose to challenge the clamour from the walls above.

Nona pushed on, past the wounded, the supplies, a skittish donkey standing in the stays of an empty wagon, past the reserves and into an alley leading between the first buildings.

The stink of charring flesh pursued Nona towards the palace. She made her way towards the emperor's spires, visible even above the roofs of mansions. In a street still a hundred yards shy of the palace walls a line of grim-faced men from Crucical's elite palace guard turned Nona aside. Seeing the suspicion in their leader's eyes as he tried to see past the mud on her tunic, she didn't stay to argue.

Nona's goal now was to reunite with her friends. The smoke-haunted streets were hauntingly empty. Spent arrows lay here and there, curious in isolation, flames licked up amid the apple trees in a nearby garden where one of the Scithrowl fire-pots had landed. All the windows were shuttered as if the grand houses had closed their eyes to the day's horrors.

Nona hunted for her serenity and sought direction. Her thread-bonds with Kettle and with Ruli had been pulling her in different directions but now they started to converge. She followed their guide, jogging along broad streets between mansions with boarded windows. She worked her way around blocked and burning roads, seeking to join up with Abbess Wheel and the convent party.

A body lay by the gates of one pillared manse, a white-haired old lady whose broken string of Marn pearls was scattered across the flagstones. An arrow protruded from her chest. Nona found it hard not to believe all this a dream. The mighty Verity, rich, powerful, untouched by war for genera-tions. Before nightfall Scithrowl warriors would prowl where the nobility promenaded the evening before. Only days ago Nona had met Lano Tacsis in these very streets. Much as she wanted the man dead she wanted his soldiers lined up in the defence of the city more. It would have been a poor time for her to have killed their leader. Even so, she hoped the Scithrowl would catch him and give him a cruel death.

Nona turned onto another wide, tree-lined avenue where but for the drifting smoke everything could have been normal. The wind gusted, clearing the air, and there out of nowhere was Abbess Wheel, crozier held aloft as a golden beacon, half of Sweet Mercy hard on her heels.

IN THE CHAOS of the defence Abbess Wheel found nobody of sufficient authority and interest to allocate Sweet Mercy's strength with any direction or goal. Rather than commit her force blind, Wheel had sent Kettle and Bhenta back out to scout for any Scithrowl forces already at work within the walls. She kept Nona close to monitor Kettle's observations through her thread-bond.

In the meantime the abbess gathered her flock in the shelter of a high-walled garden where no stray arrow would find either novice or nun, and set up her own command post. Nona hugged Ruli and Jula quickly, deflect-ing their questions as she hurriedly changed back into the old Red Sister habit that she had been issued and tossed away the filthy clothes that had come from a dead Scithrowl on the Vinery Stair. Kettle and Bhenta rejoined the group as Nona finished changing. The ease with which they had scaled the wall underlined the fact that Scithrowl assassins were almost certainly at work within the city. Apple pushed through the novices to take Kettle into her arms, careless of Wheel's disapproval. They held tight for a mo-ment, then parted. Apple kept any recriminations for their risk-taking be-hind tight and worried lips.

"Sister Kettle, Sister Cauldron, report!" Abbess Wheel's crow-screech demanded their attention.

Kettle pushed a stray strand of red hair back into Apple's headdress and hurried to the abbess. Nona followed.

To her credit Abbess Wheel listened in grim silence and had only praise for their efforts. Minutes later Kettle and Bhenta were leaving again on Wheel's orders, this time to scout for any sign of a breach where reinforcements were needed. Nona was to monitor Kettle's progress despite her protestations that Apple could do that almost as well.

Nona stood, watching through Kettle's eyes while describing what she saw with her own mouth. There were no breaches yet but in half a dozen places the battle atop the walls was slowly being lost.

"Those siege towers are the primary threat." Sister Tallow addressed the assembly as if they were standing on the sands of Blade Hall. "The emperor has doubtless massed his forces at the Amber Gate, but you will have observed that the soldiers here stand too thin to withstand the flow of Sci-throwl up those towers for long."

"A Mystic Sister could reduce one to kindling . . . We've seen what a Holy Sister can do!" Wheel cast an approving glance at Nona, having been apprised of her efforts on the way into the city. "Though we have precious little to work with here."

The Mystic Sisters ordained at Sweet Mercy were under Wheel's orders on behalf of High Priest Nevis, but they had long ago been dispatched to the eastern front or the western one. Whether any still survived was unclear. Sister Pan had been able to confirm the deaths of the three most powerful of her former pupils.

Wheel's gaze flickered across the nuns in front of her. Sister Pan was looking around with a slightly confused smile as if she thought they were on a trip for seven-day. Joeli had hunched down, perhaps worried she might catch an arrow even here. Her thread-work was remarkable but she wouldn't be exploding a siege tower with it. Nona had already walked the Path, and a second walk, even if it were tomorrow, would be a huge risk. Wheel beckoned Sheryl and Haluma, novices from Mystic Class. "Sister Pan tells me that you girls have walked the Path . . ."

A monk hastened past, his habit splashed with crimson, a longsword in hand. "Grey brothers have fired the towers!" He ran on.

Nona hurried out into the road for a view of the wall, past the novices who were risking quick looks around the corner of the street. The slanting, hide-covered roofs of the five surviving siege towers punctuated the battlements of the city wall. White smoke vomited from the chain-screened doorways, spilling out over the drawbridges anchored to the walls. It swirled around desperate Scithrowl charging out, more scared of what was behind them than the bloody steel of those waiting outside.

Nona called back her observations to Sister Apple, then returned to shelter beside her and the abbess.

"How could Greys set things like that afire? And unseen?" Nona shook her head in wonder.

"A structure like that?" Sister Tallow frowned. "To fire that with what a man could carry, and carry undetected . . ."

"I hope they got away," said Nona.

"No," replied Apple. "They did not."

"They would have had to infiltrate the Scithrowl," Apple said. "They would have naphtha oil hidden all across them in waterskins beneath their clothes. Then, Ancestor take them and love them, they must have lit themselves up inside the structure. Somewhere near the bottom, but not too close to the entrance."

It took half an hour to clear the walls of Scithrowl. By that time the siege towers were pillars of flame, starting to collapse in on themselves. Kettle reported that the besieging Scithrowl had retreated to join the greater body of the horde, abandoning their ladders and scaling chains before the walls among the heaped bodies of the fallen. Nona watched the retreat through Kettle's eyes, invited in as the Grey Sister took a place on a wall tower.

"Look!" Ruli tugged at Nona's arm, pulling her from her visions.

Approaching along the broad, paved expanse of King's Road, named in a time before the empire, came a strange band, each wearing robes of a single pale colour, no two shades the same. Their advance was slow, almost reluctant. At their head walked a white-haired man, his eyes milky, skin thick with old burns. Nona knew him. "Rexxus Degon!" The Chief Academic who had watched Nona when Sister Pan had brought her with Hessa and Ara to compete at the Academy. Beside him was a woman with long grey hair, her robe almost white. They looked to have come direct from the Academy building, huddled up against the emperor's walls on the far side of the palace. Many of their following were no older than the novices around Nona.

"Academics!" Jula said. "I thought there were more of them."

"There were," Apple replied.

"And now there are not," Sister Iron said.

"There are Mystic Sisters with them!" Nona spotted the sky-blue habits at the back. Sister Pan always wore the common black of the Holies and the sight of the blue was a rarity, even at Sweet Mercy. Two Mystic Sisters that she didn't recognise, a pair of Mystic Brothers too, twins to look at them. "What are they doing here?"

Whatever answer might have been forthcoming went unheard as an urgent tug from Kettle stole Nona away. She stood within Kettle's skin once more, alongside the ragged defenders waiting on the wall tower. The elevation afforded a view of the Scithrowl's endless horde arrayed across Verity's garden-lands, an ugly scar where fields green with jump-corn had once swayed. Something was coming. Nona couldn't see what Kettle was looking at, just that a great number of Scithrowl were on the move, swirling around, pushing.

"They're getting out of the way of something," Kettle said.

A space opened around a group of perhaps two dozen people. Flames leapt from nowhere, winding up into the air around those approaching the wall, a bright fire torn on swiftly cycling winds that seemed to centre on the newcomers.

"Adoma's Fist!" Kettle raised the bow she had acquired and lofted an arrow towards the Scithrowl mages.

Others on the wall followed her example and soon scores of arrows had taken flight. None of them seemed to reach their targets. Perhaps the winds had turned them from their path.

As the Scithrowl drew closer Nona could see individuals. A group of five, two men and three women, nearly naked, dancing at the base of the rising firestorm; three more in white cloaks, advancing with their arms raised. Workers of flame and air, weaving a protection against arrows. Three heavyset men, in bronze armour, walked at the fore, the fires overhead reflecting on the scales of their mail and the oiled thickness of muscle on huge arms. Rock-workers perhaps, come to tumble the walls. And behind them, a dozen individuals, some tall, some short, some old, some young, clad in all manner of styles, some in the loud colours favoured by their people, others in black cloaks; one in a leather dress set with silver plates; a painfully thin man in antique armour lacquered with red enamel. This last one was their leader. Nona remembered him and many of the others from the memories Kettle had shared of her time in Adoma's court. One thing only united them amid their variety. Sigils. Even at this distance they scratched at Nona's mind. All of them wore at least a couple of sigil wards. Like the Path-mage had . . .

"They're all quantals!"

Nona realised she was back with the abbess and had spoken aloud.

"Tell me!" It wasn't Wheel who was shaking Nona. Sister Pan had her arm in an iron grip. "What did you see?"

"Adoma's Fist," Nona said. "Adoma's Fist is coming."

Rexxus Degon and his allies had reached the convent party. Ahead of them, beyond the walls, the windstorm had twisted the day's smoke into strange patterns. The remnants of the siege towers collapsed before the strengthening gale, sparks and embers filling the air.

"Kettle showed me. Adoma's Fist is coming," Nona repeated. She hadn't thought there would be so many quantals. If the marjals were full-bloods specializing in fire, air, and stone-work they alone could threaten the walls, but with two dozen Path-mages at their backs there was no chance of resisting them. On Scithrowl's distant border with King Ald's lands it was said that Adoma's Fist had struck down great castles and laid waste to armies. They had never been seen within the empire, though. Not by any that lived to tell of it. The hope that they would remain in the east, occupied with the war against Ald, had always been a vain one, but now as it shattered Nona realised how hard she and many others had clung to it.

"Well, it's too late to save the wall now." Sister Pan released Nona's arm and shuffled out to intercept the Academics.

Nona followed to ensure that no stray arrows found the old woman since she seemed wholly oblivious to the threat.

"Mistress Path." Rexxus Degon favoured Sister Pan with a low bow. "If you will excuse us. Duty calls. I'm sure you will have sensed the presence of our enemy beyond the walls." Even as he spoke Nona sensed it too. Vibrations rippling out through the thread-scape. Trembling in the spider-web. Footsteps were being taken along the Path. Many footsteps, as if an army were marching along it.

Sister Pan made no move to get out of the old man's way.

"We really must hurry." He looked far from enthusiastic about the prospect. Nona wasn't sure how much the man saw with those blind eyes of his, but it was clearly enough to know that he would much rather be somewhere else. "Duty calls . . ."

"Duty . . ." Sister Pan held her hand out, palm up, and a charred flake settled into it from the air. Others were descending all around like a black rain, some still glowing. "It's too late to save the wall." The black flake became lost against the darkness of her palm.

"We'll save it!" Rexxus leaned on his staff, his voice lowering. "Or die trying."

"I remember you as a little boy, Rexxus." Pan shook her head. "You had the bluest eyes. And your nose was always running. You should stay here with your friends."

Rexxus bowed his head. "I wish I could, Mistress Path. Even so, the strength of the empire is not wholly spent. My fellow mages and I may not have reputations for murder and carnage, but Adoma's creatures will find that we know a few tricks of our own. If we must sell our lives the price will be a dear one, and far fewer of our enemy than they expect will live to see what they have purchased. Now, if you will excuse me, dear lady." He raised his staff and turned to those gathered behind him. "Onwards!"

"Wait here. I'll deal with this." Sister Pan began to walk towards the city wall. Above it black clouds swirled, shot through with streaks of fire. The defenders cowered now, crouched behind their battlements.

"Nonsense!" Rexxus hurried to overtake Sister Pan. The Academics followed him, the Mystic Brothers too. Only the pair of Holy Witches kept their place.

"Wait here."

Sister Pan never moved her fingers when thread-working. She said it was a habit you grew out of. Like moving your lips when reading. Even so, Nona saw the moment when she pulled the Chief Academic's thread.

"Yes!" Rexxus turned to his followers with new conviction. "We should wait here!" He announced it as if it had been his plan all along. On his neck the mendant sigil that should have kept him from such manipulation, even if his mind did not, glittered impotently.

Sister Pan carried on towards the wall, her stride longer and more sure than Nona had seen it in her ten years at the convent. The sinking sun threw the ancient woman's shadow before her and in the dying crimson of its light she seemed no longer old.

"Sister!" Nona caught up with Pan, keeping her gaze on the wall, alert for arrows. "I have to take you back. It's not safe." She reached for the ancient's arm, prepared to carry her if need be.

"Stay. It will be all right, child." Pan walked on.

"Yes, it will." Nona suddenly understood that Pan going to the wall alone was a fine idea. She wondered why she hadn't seen it before. She stood there, puzzling. A moment later Nona decided that the plan had a small flaw. She would go with Pan, even though she had been told to stay. Then it would be all right.

Pan registered Nona's return with a raised eyebrow, then a shrug. She gestured towards the stonework rising before them. "Can you see where the blocks will fall?"

"What?"

"It's written right before us. If you look at how the threads run through the granite you can see where it will break. Seeing where the parts will fall is a little harder, Nina, but threads run into the future as well as the past. You can see the trajectories they will . . . Ah! Here. No, a little to the left." She pulled Nona to a particular spot.

"It's Nona. And—" The rest of what Nona had to say was lost in a cracking that split the world, a rumble as deep as the black ice, and the screaming as the great wall of Verity began to tumble inwards. The section of wall that exploded was a hundred yards wide and centred right in front of them.

Nona slowed time's steady march to a crawl. Huge blocks descended on gravity's arcs, their languid rotation spraying smaller stones and broken fragments, plates of ancient plaster scything through the air, others bursting, dust trails spiralling in their wake.

True to Sister Pan's reading, although blocks the size of carts hammered down all around her and Nona, nothing save a few pebbles and two fist-sized fragments came directly at them. These Nona managed to deflect.

Even before the impacts had stopped vibrating through the soles of Nona's feet, a thick cloud of dust began to rise. For a minute or so they stood blind, surrounded by dust so dense that even the howling winds couldn't strip it away. The world returned in snatches and then, in one fierce, hot blast, the air was clear. Nona and Pan stood alone, both of them coated grey.

Adoma's Fist emerged from the smoke, picking their way over and around the rubble. First a lone woman in her leather battle-dress, then two men, one in courtly attire, the other in a robe so overblown that he might be mistaken for a street magician were it not for the sigils marked in gold thread. Over a dozen others followed with the thin man in the red armour leading them. The quantals were to the fore now, the marjals working their magics to the rear. A fire-laced hurricane rose around them, a shell to protect from arrows, with Nona and Pan inside its perimeter. All eyes were on them, the Fist variously amused, surprised, or dismissive.

The "street magician" seemed outraged. "Is this all the emperor sends to stand before us? A child and a crone?" He spoke the empire tongue with harsh angles but clear enough.

"Wait!" The thin man in red raised his gauntleted hand as several around him made to summon their power. "Can it be? The Path-mage of Sweet Mercy? I had heard you were dead!"

"Not quite, Yom Rala, not quite." Pan smiled but there was sadness in it.

Yom Rala. Nona remembered his name now and the fear that had coloured Kettle's voice when she spoke of him. The man had a deadly reputation.

Yom Rala addressed his colleagues. "You will have heard of Sister Pan. In the Antral Wars they whispered her name. She brought Darlamar low before most of us were born, and the Mage of Elon too. When enough time has passed for her to be counted as history they will set her name among the most famed Path-walkers of this empire and speak it with that of Sister Cloud and Sister Owl."

"She looks as if walking to her grave would be beyond her!" cried a young woman in a sigil robe of fiery yellows and oranges.

Several of the younger Path-mages laughed.

"We will show Sister Pan respect!" Yom Rala barked. He repeated himself in Scithrowl, then addressed the nun in softer tones, his accent almost unnoticeable. "I would offer to duel but it is said you haven't walked the Path in twenty years."

Sister Pan bowed to the Scithrowl mage. "This is untrue, but I cannot duel you."

Yom Rala tilted his head. "You can still manage a few steps? Remarkable at your age, sister. But I should have expected no less." He glanced at Nona. "Have you brought a champion to stand in your stead?"

"Nina? She's a little girl. She really ought to start running now." Pan motioned for Nona to go and suddenly it seemed like a really good idea. Even so, Nona stayed. The suggestion's power blew her will away like clockseeds in a Corridor Wind, but something stronger anchored Nona to the spot. She hadn't realised that she loved the old woman before. But she did. And Nona Grey could no more walk away from that than from her own skin.

Through the wide hole torn in the city wall Nona could see Adoma's horde surging forward. Tens of thousands armed for war, running full tilt towards the breach.

"She's a crazed old nun." One of the senior mages came to stand at Yom's shoulder. "The softmen say she hasn't reached the Path in a decade and more."

"It is true," Pan said. "I haven't reached the Path since before this girl beside me was a twinkle in her father's eye."

Yom bowed his head with regret and waved one of his flame-weavers forward. "Kill her and be done."

"I haven't reached the Path in twenty years because in all that time I have never left it." Sister Pan glanced again at Nona. "Run, child. Please."

And Nona was running, even as she knew it was wrong and that she should stay with her teacher, even as her eyes clouded with tears . . . she ran. That "please" had made her go. She ran faster than she had ever thought she might without the Path to speed her way.

She felt the step that took Sister Pan from the Path. The Path where she had walked every day and every hour of Nona's life. What that might be like lay beyond Nona's imagining. She only knew that not even the Ancestor could own that much power. Sister Pan had walked in glory all this time, knowing that to leave would be the end of her. That single step from the Path sent shock waves through the world. Waves that would ride the thread-scape around the entirety of Abeth's globe. There would be no quantal, not even an ice-triber at the edge of some distant hot sea near the planet's pole, who would not know that some great thing had fallen.

What saved Nona, more than the distance she was able to put between herself and Sister Pan, was that even though Pan could not hope to own what the Path had given her, she somehow managed to give it direction.

The blast lifted Nona from her feet and threw her the length of the street, almost to the feet of the abbess and the Chief Academic. All of them were felled. Nona struggled for her breath and, despite the pain all along the side where she hit the ground, was among the first to rise. She gazed back the way she had come, towards the yawning breach and the fires fringing it. Nothing lay beyond save a great wide trench torn yards deep in the black earth of the empire and smoking all along its length.

23

HOLY CLASS

IN THE AFTERMATH of Sister Pan's spectacular demise Nona became aware of three things. First that although Adoma's Fist had been so broken that not even a tatter of sigil robe fluttered to the ground where they had stood, and although the many thousands charging for the breach had been reduced to fragments of charred bone, the Scithrowl horde remained tens of thousands strong and against all sense, rather than running for their homeland in panic, they were once again advancing. The second thing was that Sister Pan's death had struck her like a knife between the ribs. Nona thought of the dried flower that had fallen from the nun's hidden book and found she had tears running from her eyes. The third thing she realised was that neither Jula nor Ruli were among the novices regrouping before Abbess Wheel.

"Where's Jula?" Nona tried to shake an answer from Alata. Discarding the disoriented Alata, she caught hold of Ketti, who was bleeding from a gashed forehead. "Where's Ruli?"

"I . . ."

"Concentrate!" Nona's own senses were ringing, and not just from the physical force of the explosion. Her blood still resonated with the energies released. Perhaps the Path itself had quivered like a plucked string. Nona had been shaken to her core and felt in no condition to exercise any of the gifts her quantal or marjal heritage had bestowed upon her. "Ketti!"

"I . . . thought they were helping them . . ."

"Who?"

"That woman and the guardsmen." Ketti touched her forehead and looked at her crimson fingers in astonishment.

"What woman? What did she do?"

"She was helping Ruli up." Ketti gestured down the street. "Over there. By the gateposts with the carved lions." Between Nona and the gate stood the cart in which Sister Pan had ridden with the shipheart. It sat listing on a broken wheel, the iron casket nearby, lying on its side on the flagstones.

"Where did they go?"

"I . . ." Confusion clouded Ketti's eyes. "I thought they came this way. The men were carrying Jula."

Over by the garden wall Abbess Wheel called Nona's name. The foremost of the Scithrowl horde were now charging through the charnel-filled trench where their brothers and sisters had perished just minutes before. Sister Iron and Sister Tallow were leading the way towards the breach, with soldiers emerging from the side streets to support them. The setting sun threw their shadows towards the enemy and stained all their steel with blood. On the nearest stairs from the city wall defenders queued to descend and join the stand.

Mally came running back from the main group. "The abbess wants you to bring the shipheart, Nona . . . I mean Sister Cage."

Nona ignored her, taking Ketti's face in her hands and steering it towards her own. Once Ketti had been much taller than her. Now she had to look up. "Concentrate! The men, what were they wearing?"

"Scarlet. Guards' uniform."

Nona released her. Ketti wiped the blood from her hand and started back towards the other novices around the abbess. "And silver!" she called over her shoulder before drawing her sword from its scabbard.

"The shipheart, Nona!" Mally pointed, unwilling to go near the fallen casket.

Scarlet and silver. Sherzal's colours. The men who had caught Nona in Rellam Forest just outside her village, the men who had set her on the long path to the place where she now stood: beneath the dirt and blood those men had worn Sherzal's colours too.

"Sherzal's guards have taken Jula!" Nona tried to open the thread-bond she had forged with Ruli using the commonality of their marjal blood. Immediately deafening echoes of Sister Pan's final act filled her skull and she doubled up, both hands pressed to the sides of her head.

"Are you . . . all right, Nona?" Mally, at her side now.

Nona looked towards the breach where the Scithrowl charge was already within the long shadow of the walls. Abbess Wheel was leading Nona's classmates and teachers towards that gap. The people who had been Nona's life since she was a small girl. Before them lay only torn earth, broken stone, and certain death. The Scithrowl were numberless, unstoppable. She saw Ketti at the back. Alata and Leeni side by side, ready to die as they had lived; together. Ghena looking short beside Sister Oak. A fresh pang of sorrow stabbed through Nona. She saw Sister Pan's sad smile. None of them wanted to die. Not even Pan with a hundred years behind her. But at least they would die together, and fighting.

With an oath Nona turned her back on them all and ran from Mally towards the emperor's spires. On the way past the broken cart she scooped up the shipheart in its casket.

THE SHIPHEART'S AURA beat at Nona, tearing at the roots of her personality as she ran, eager to reshape her. She endured it for two streets, then threw the casket over a high garden wall. A mansion lay behind the garden, and behind that an open plaza that stretched to Crucical's gates. The ring of imperial guards that had turned her away before would be waiting for her. She scaled the wall and dropped beside the casket before moving away to crouch by the trunk of an elm tree. Dusk filled the garden and for a moment the battle seemed far away, already half a dream.

Nona muttered her serenity poem, "She's falling down, she's falling down, the moon, the moon . . ." and wrapped herself in the cool distance of the trance. "Ruli . . ." She opened the thread-bond to her friend.

"OH, THANK THE Ancestor!" Ruli lifted her head from a one-eyed contemplation of the patterned floor.

"What?" Jula hissed. "What?"

Close by, in front of a pair of tall bronze doors, half a dozen of Sherzal's guards stood tense and ready as their captain engaged in heated conversation with three men in the emperor's green and gold who barred his way.

It's nothing. Nona spoke the words inside Ruli's skull.

"It's . . . nothing," Ruli said. "I just remembered that we have a friend looking out for us." She tried to open her other eye but it stayed swollen shut.

"A friend?" Jula glanced up at the nearest guard. "What do you . . . oh!" She closed her mouth and pressed her lips firmly together.

I'm coming to get you both. Just make sure to show me everything. Nona could have deepened the bond and steered Ruli's gaze where she wanted it but she could feel her friend's apprehension. Any deeper and she would lose control over how much they shared through the bond, and sharing fear would do neither of them any good. They both had plenty of their own.

The guard captain appeared to have won his argument because the emperor's men stepped back and pulled open the doors. Ruli found herself being hauled roughly to her feet, and Nona realised for the first time that her wrists had been bound together behind her back.

Before being led through the doors Ruli took a long look back the way they had come. A wide corridor lined with paintings and statuary stretched off towards a distant chamber lit by a curious blue light.

"Move it!" A guardsman shoved her and Ruli staggered into another chamber, this one with a domed ceiling offering the darkening sky through a round window high above. Streaks of black crossed the patch of midnight blue, and the smell of smoke, absent in the corridor, could be smelled again.

Crucical's palace appeared to be even more of a warren than Sherzal's. It seemed that the idea was to impress the emperor's grandeur on the world by covering as much of it as possible with endless chambers, halls, galleries, shrines, and corridors. Ruli's good eye flickered left and right, picking out detail. The place seemed almost deserted; no doubt the guards were protecting the exterior. The other occupants were probably huddled together in some inner sanctum since misery loves company and since the empire had run out of places for people of quality to flee to.

Eventually, after descending three flights of stairs they came to an iron door manned by two guards in scarlet and silver. Behind the door lay a library. Not the grand, showy kind that Nona had glimpsed on her rare ventures into rich men's homes but something more akin to the high priest's vault or the small collection within Sweet Mercy's scriptorium.

Among the dusty browns and blacks of leather-bound tomes, Sherzal's diamonds and gown of silver-white seemed wholly out of place.

"Novices!" She greeted them with a wide, gleaming smile. The Scithrowl might be cutting a path towards the palace but Sherzal had taken the time to have her rouge applied, her lips painted scarlet, the dark red curls of her mane brushed to a high shine. "Ruli . . . and . . . Jula." She pointed at them in turn with a long, sharp-nailed finger. "I'm glad you could join us."

"We need to be with our abbess!" Ruli's voice came out as a squeak. She deepened it and tried to inject some outrage. "The Scithrowl are through the city wall."

"Yes, yes. Adoma and her tedious horde." Sherzal turned and walked to the back of the room. "You girls will do a lot more good here, I can assure you of that. It's no coincidence that I chose to meet you in a library . . ."

She pushed aside two piles of books, letting them topple to the floor. Behind her the iron door opened again and a young woman clad in a grey tunic with a black chain-mail shirt of very fine gauge entered. She took the novices in with dark eyes above high cheekbones.

"Safira . . ." The recognition leaked from Nona's mind to Ruli's lips. The memory of the woman carrying Jula from the aftermath of the explosion rose in both their minds. A day before she had been in the company of Lano Tacsis.

Safira raised a brow at Ruli, then turned to Sherzal. "I have the code. I had to kill the knight-protector."

"No matter." Sherzal returned her attention to the area of wall that had been obscured by the piled books. She unsheathed a knife and started to pry at the stone blocks. "Now, where are you hiding?" She tutted and tried the point of her blade a little farther along. Without warning the block opened, the whole thing just a stone front attached to a wooden door a foot long and six inches tall. Behind it lay a set of three gleaming steel wheels set into a steel plate marked with numbers.

"Ten, twenty, four," Safira said.

Sherzal rotated each of the wheels to the numbers she had named.

A grinding noise started up behind Ruli and she turned with a start. A rectangular section of what had seemed to be tiled floor was now drawing back under the rest to reveal a set of stairs.

"The wonders of our forefathers!" Sherzal clapped her hands with enthusiasm. "But of course you two girls know all about that." She picked up one of the lanterns from the reading table and began her descent even before the floor had fully retracted. "Come along! Quickly now. It will slide back on you if you dawdle."

The guards followed, Jula and Ruli prodded along between them, Safira bringing up the rear.

The stairway led down on a square spiral and the turns kept coming. The depth of the emperor's cellars seemed remarkable, even to novices who had lived with the cave-riddled thickness of the Rock of Faith beneath them.

Eventually they emerged into a surprisingly dry chamber with no hint of cave about it. Sherzal turned to face them and raised her lantern. "You'll like this." She cleared her throat. "Lights."

Across the ceiling rectangles of white light flickered into being. Others appeared along the length of two corridors leading off in opposite directions. Nona had never seen illumination so steady or so white. It wrought strange changes in the colours it shone upon.

"Come!" Sherzal led off again, her gown billowing with each long stride.

They passed doorways left and right, opening onto square white rooms, echoingly empty, or sometimes dark rooms, or rooms lit by flickers. Occasionally Ruli would glimpse something within. An object covered with a sheet—a chest or cabinet perhaps—a section of black metal, perforated with circular holes, broken from part of some larger structure maybe, a toothed wheel of a metal too orangey to be gold; a mass of wires emerging from a silver-grey sphere . . . did they wriggle, or was that a fluttering of the light? While Ruli marvelled, Nona was put in mind of the inner sanctum at the Hope Church in White Lake. What had Preacher Mickel said? *The Sis build their homes over the best of what remains in the Corridor. The emperors themselves built their palace above the Ark and bind the Academy to them with its power.*

"Wait." Sherzal held up a hand and stopped in a section of corridor that seemed no different from any other. "You'll like this too, novices. My father showed it to my brother and me long ago . . . before our sister was born." She tossed her knife out in front of her. It jerked in the air, becoming a shower of bright pieces that fell to the ground in front of one of the dark doorways. A surprisingly musical tinkle accompanied the destruction. "You'll like it less if you disappoint me. It can be used with more subtlety to unpleasant effect. Well . . . unpleasant for the person being peeled. It's quite fun to watch." She went to the wall and tapped out a rapid, changing beat. A panel slid back and she pressed her finger upon a glowing disc inside. "Safe now!" Even so she motioned the guardsmen through before her.

Ruli glanced to the left as she stepped over the pieces of Sherzal's knife. A dark room, the same on the right. Just as her eyes slid away a flicker of light offered a confusion of hard lines and stark shadows. A circle? Nona made her friend's gaze linger for one more heartbeat, piercing the darkness with Ruli's shadow-work. A great ring, taller than a man and leaning against the rear wall?

Sherzal stopped again ten yards on and waited for them all to pass before tapping the same pattern on the wall. For a moment the corridor behind them filled with faint lines as if a hundred glass blades were criss-crossing it. They faded from sight in moments. "That annoying friend of yours can do something similar, no? But in the days when our people built the Ark we knew how to make mere mechanisms that would do as much! Our forebears could take a few cogs and gears, mix in some wires and lightning, and have a device that could do anything!"

An echo of Nona's hatred for the woman curled Ruli's lip. Which of them clenched her hands into fists neither could tell.

Patience, Nona said, as much to herself as to Ruli. *I will find you.*

Sherzal resumed the lead. A hundred yards on, the corridor terminated in a white door. Safira came to join the emperor's sister at the front. Sherzal stepped forward and the door slid away to reveal a large white-walled chamber. Six white doors stood spaced around the perimeter. A huge circular silver door had been set into the floor at the centre of the chamber, its single hinge thicker than a man's leg. Around it stood a trio of the emperor's guards, their breastplates enamelled in green and gold.

"If you would." Sherzal nodded towards Safira. "Oh, wait!" She raised her voice and turned towards the three men. "Unless you'd like to join my cause and pledge to my service, of course. I'm much more agreeable to work for than my brother."

The men drew their swords together.

"Oh well." Sherzal motioned Safira on. Four of her guards followed the woman out towards the centre of the chamber.

NONA BLINKED AWAY the vision as the blood began to spray. Safira was every bit as dangerous as Kettle. She settled back into her own flesh, surprised by how dark the night had grown.

Nona steeled her will and summoned her flaw-blades. Even in this tranquil garden just a stone's throw from the walls of the emperor's palace she could now hear the clash and roar of the battle in the streets. Her sisters would be crossing blades with the enemy. She felt Kettle's urgent query along their thread-bond and closed it off with a shake of her head.

The iron casket surrendered before her blades and the Noi-Guin shipheart rolled out onto the grass. No part of her wanted to touch it. Nona remembered Abbess Glass, her hand above the candle flame, flesh melting from her bones, refusing to withdraw despite the agony.

"Damnation." She reached out and picked up the glowing ball. Immediately its cold fire ran along her bones and the whispers began inside her skull. Touching the shipheart didn't hurt. It was more like being forced to remember being hurt.

Rather than climb out one-handed Nona scowled at the wall between her and the palace. With the shipheart to augment her rock-work the bricks and mortar surrendered in moments. She swirled the rising dust around her, lifting it behind her like the wings of a dragon. Theatre was her only real key to the palace if she wasn't prepared to kill her way in.

Crucical's ring of guardsmen had tightened so much that their backs were literally against the wall. High above them the light of a burning city danced across battlements. The palace, while fortified, was far from being a fortress. The city walls and the emperor's armies were his defence. When the Scithrowl came against his home it would not take them long to force an entry.

Half a dozen guards came forward from their positions, more starting to advance to either side. The officer among them, a gerant standing at least eight foot tall, levelled her spear at Nona's approach. The gleaming point trembled as the fringes of the shipheart's aura rooted out the woman's private terrors.

"You can stop where you stand or die a step in front of it!" Sweat beaded her dark brow but duty bound the officer to the spot. Her subordinates, however, took several paces back.

"I am Sister Cage, and this is a shipheart." Nona's augmented windwork let her voice carry all along the line, overwriting the sounds of the as-yet-unseen battle. "It belongs to Emperor Crucical, and the Ancestor has bidden me to bring it from the Convent of Sweet Mercy to aid him." She pressed with her marjal empathy, willing them to accept her word, and took another step forward. "Will any among you take this burden from me and deliver it to the emperor in my place?" She held it out, letting the wind carry the sound of battle to the walls, making it seem even closer.

The gerant guard ground her teeth and furrowed her brow, proving resistant to suggestion. "I don't know you, sister. I cannot admit you without someone to vouch for—"

"I know her!" A shout from the walls above. "And you know me. Let her in, Kerla!"

Nona squinted up at the walls. Regol waved at her. "You know Regol?" she asked.

"Everyone knows Regol." The woman stepped back with a relieved expression. "Meet her at the Scholars' Door!" she roared up to Regol. "She's your responsibility!" She pointed a blunt finger to the left. "Small door with stone scrolls above the lintel. About a hundred yards that way."

The word went along the line and all the guards cleared out of Nona's path. She walked rather than ran, concentrating on resisting the shipheart.

"WHAT IN ALL the hells is th—" Regol's jaw snapped shut and he backed away with the guardsmen behind the Scholars' Door. He paled as the shipheart reached out to twist his mind.

"You have to stay away," Nona said.

"Thanks for the advice." Regol pressed his back against a column and stayed where he was. After a moment he found his smile and forced it onto a white face beaded with sweat. "I don't think I have any choice in the matter. Damn near soiled myself!"

Farther back among the antechamber's columns five guardsmen huddled together, spears ready. Two of them were weeping. Nona felt like crying herself. That or screaming to drown out the voices echoing in her fracturing mind. The power that the shipheart gave her was incredible but her skin was already crawling as if a dozen devils were following their separate paths across her.

"How are you here?" The question escaped Nona despite her gritted teeth and the urgency of her mission. It shamed her to admit to herself that she hadn't once thought of Regol in the past two days. If she had, she would have expected to find him with the Caltess fighters rather than within the palace. And all Partnis Reeve's fighters had probably been conscripted to join the force at the Amber Gate. For a moment the image of Denam in full armour flickered across her mind. If anyone could give the Scithrowl pause it would be that ten-foot stack of muscle and hate. "Why aren't you with the others?"

"You know me." Regol's smile twisted. "Darling of the Sis. Everyone wanted me in their personal guard. I had to choose which invitation from which lord's lady I wanted to accept."

Even before he had finished speaking Nona knew that she would be asking no more questions. She had to get to the others. "A blue room. A room with blue light. I need to get there!"

Regol frowned. "I know it. Follow me."

Nona followed, her pace even, the shipheart held in her two hands, as far out in front of her as she could reach. Its light infected the illumination of crystal lamps hung on golden chains, turning each corridor into something otherworldly and sending straying servants back screaming into the rooms they'd looked out from. She fixed her gaze on Regol's retreating back and walked on.

He's betraying you with some Sis whore.

The voice in Nona's head was hers, but she didn't own it.

What you had together was precious, sacred, holy. A different voice. Also hers. Also not hers.

Tear out his heart!

Nona felt her flaw-blades spring into being and a liquid rage replaced her blood. Her eyes fixated on the spot between Regol's shoulder blades where Sister Tallow used to instruct her to sink the knife for best effect. She tore her gaze away and a glance at her hands confirmed her fears. Both were stained with devils of her own making, writhing in the shipheart's glow.

She choked down a horrified laugh. To pass Abbess Wheel's Spirit-test and take the black of a Holy Sister, every novice had to be able to recite the thirteen methods for purging a devil and to give a detailed account of how the victim should be put to death, and how their corpse should be disposed of. The method depended on the nature of the possession and whether the devil was driven from the victim successfully or not. She'd not worn the black a week and here she was, unholy and unclean, fit only for killing.

Nona! A fresh voice shook her from her contemplation. This was a voice she didn't own. One she knew. Urgent. Desperate even. *Nona! Where are you?*

Nona let the thread-bond take her. Anything to get away from the shipheart. She left just enough of herself behind to keep her upright, legs moving.

+   +   +

KETTLE SPRINTED ACROSS a terra-cotta expanse, pushing herself to the limit. Ahead flames leapt, roaring from a shattered roof. She raced along a blazing rafter, too swift to burn. Bursting clear of the fire, she ran on with reckless haste. Apple needed her. She leapt from the slope of one tiled roof, across a broad street, and crashed into a roof on the opposite side. Hunska speed carried her up the slope, scattering broken tiles beneath her heels. She crested the roof ridge and before her lay the wideness of the King's Road, crammed with Scithrowl warriors from one side to the other, their numbers stretching back a hundred yards to the shattered walls of Verity and the ocean of their countrymen still massed beyond. Their howls and screams shook the air, resonating in Kettle's chest, an inhuman noise, at once terrifying, desperate, exhilarating.

The emperor's lines stood ten ranks thick but the Scithrowl's surging advance had isolated pockets of defenders. One such group lay beneath her, now twenty yards within the Scithrowl horde, trapped against the wall of some lord's town house. The stranded defenders included a score of empire soldiers and all of Abbess Wheel's party. Kettle's gaze anchored itself on a glimpse of long red hair, the owner on the ground between Leeni and Alata, who fought like demons to clear the space around her.

"Apple!"

Without hesitation, Kettle threw herself down the far side of the roof and jumped from the guttering, trailing shadows. She drew her sword and dagger as she fell, dropping deeper into the moment than any but a full-blood hunska can.

Kettle's descent became a flying kick that broke a man's neck and she rode him to the ground, cutting the throat of a Scithrowl to the left and taking the head of the one to the right. Before that head bounced its way from chest to back to ground among the tight-packed enemy, Kettle had struck half a dozen more blows and six of her foe were starting to pump their life's blood from the wounds that would kill them. She caught glimpses of her sisters, a face here, spattered with blood and twisted with rage, another pale and serene. A novice bleeding so heavily from a head wound that Kettle couldn't even recognise her but swinging her sword all the same. Nona knew Ara would never forgive her for having her left at the convent, but part of her rejoiced that her friend wasn't here and that she didn't have to watch her die.

Wrapped in hunska speed, Kettle sidestepped a lazy knife thrust and leaned away from a swinging blade. A series of kicks and trips sent four more Scithrowl to the floor, clutching their spears. Kettle swirled the darkness around her, lent it teeth, and poisoned it with fear. Lacerated by unseen edges and filled with horror, the nearest of the enemy threw themselves back, clearing space.

"Apple!" Kettle was on her knees at Apple's side. The nun's habit glistened above her ribs.

Apple reached for Kettle's cheek with bloodstained fingers. "I knew you would come."

Kettle's hands were busy tearing the stubborn cloth to expose the wound. A spear thrust, a crimson hole in Apple's pale flesh. A hole that bubbled and sucked. Kettle's horror tore through Nona with such ferocity that she was nearly driven back to her body in the palace halls. The Grey Sister let none of it show on her face but worked calmly, maintaining her peripheral awareness of the battle around her.

"It got your lung." Kettle took Apple's hand from her face and set it to the wound. "Pinch it closed!"

Leeni staggered back, spraying blood, and Kettle lunged back to her feet, seizing up her weapons again. Three huge Scithrowl with large round shields and short but heavy axes pursued Leeni's retreat. Kettle dived between their legs, cutting tendons and muscle on her way through until she found herself in a forest of Scithrowl. Rage bubbled at the edges of her serenity. Apple lay dying. Apple! A gerant warrior tried to stamp on her while on all sides others changed their grips on their spears, preparing to stab down at her as she rolled and twisted.

A heavy boot kicked the sword from her hand. Kettle tried to pull venomed pins from her inner pocket but had to abandon the attempt to writhe between the first two of many spear thrusts. The Scithrowl hammered down at her in the same manner that peasants pound grain with milling poles.

In the midst of Kettle's thoughts Nona could see that the situation offered no hope for survival.

Give me your body. Nona reached out along Kettle's limbs, seeking to drop the dagger she still clenched.

Save her, Nona. And in a show of ultimate trust Kettle surrendered her will entirely.

Nona abandoned the dagger and bunched Kettle's hands into fists. In Nona's own two hands she held a power so great that it was killing her, driving every talent she had past its maximum potential, burning her up. She drove forth the flaw-blades that had been part of her life for so long, not from her own flesh but from Kettle's, and made of them not many blades but one from each hand, both as long as a great sword. As they sprang from her flesh the nun's blood painted their invisible length, giving them form.

Nona used Kettle's breathtaking speed to lift her from the ground, flinging her arms wide and spinning as she rose. The Scithrowl fell to pieces on all sides: chain mail, shields, spears, swords, all sliced apart. Kettle cut a broad path back to Apple, restraining her butchery only when Alata came into view, battling several of the foe.

For thirty long seconds under Nona's guidance Kettle spent her reserves of speed with reckless abandon, piling Scithrowl bodies in broken drifts. Behind her Sisters Tallow, Iron, and Rock organised a fighting perimeter. Even Abbess Wheel took a place, wielding her sword with savage glee and a degree of skill that reminded her flock that she had once passed the Blade-test. They fought in darkness now. The sun had gone down on a day that would be long remembered, though it seemed unlikely that any of them would see another dawn.

In the midst of her circle of carnage Kettle paused. "Where are . . ." Nona struggled to remember the names of the quantal novices from Mystic Class. "Sheryl and Haluma?" She loaned power to Kettle's voice and a marjal compulsion that demanded an answer.

"Here." Sister Oak coughed the word bloodily from where she lay with one arm around the corpse of a young girl. "There." She nodded to a wounded novice, propped against the wall.

Kettle reached Haluma in three strides. She knotted her fingers in the back of the novice's habit and hauled her to her feet. Blood spilled down the girl's leg from a deep cut but she had hold of her wits.

"I am going to throw you at the Path. You are going to take what you need and open a way back to our lines. Understand?"

"N . . . no." The girl stared at her wide-eyed. "What are . . . what are you talking about, Sister Kettle?"

Nona set the palm of her other hand to Haluma's forehead, reached out with the shipheart's power, and shoved the girl at the burning line of the Path. She felt Haluma's first step, watched as she ran on, trying to tame her speed, nudged her back when she started to fall. After eight steps Haluma missed a twist completely and jolted back into her body. Immediately she started to shake apart. Nona clasped both hands to the sides of the girl's head, pressing hard to support her weight but pressing still harder in ways that mattered more, holding her together.

"Own your power."

And Haluma did.

An instant later she released it in a blast of light and heat. The channel that Haluma cut through the Scithrowl lay littered with blackened body parts but was otherwise clear.

"Drag the wounded!" Through Kettle, Nona grabbed the nearest novices and shoved them towards the backs of the last few Scithrowl between them and the emperor's soldiers. She moved back through the convent group shoving one after the next towards the defensive line until she found herself face to face with a shocked Sister Tallow.

"Keep the passage open until they're through."

"Sister Kettle?"

"Do it!"

Nona moved on, pressing Ketti and Ghena into dragging Sister Oak. They had to pull Sheryl too as the nun refused to release the girl's body, unable to admit that she was dead. The sudden wave of emotion that seized both Nona and Kettle, seeing Oak cling to the novice's broken corpse, threatened to shake Nona back to her flesh. She held tight.

Wheel ordered other able-bodied novices to pull away more of the injured. Alata hurried past with Leeni in her arms and Scithrowl closing on her. The closest man hurled his spear. Using Kettle's hunska speed, Nona caught it and hurled it back without reversing it. The wooden haft felled its former owner, knocking the helm from his head and shattering the orbit of his eye. Kettle cast around for Apple. Had she been taken back to the defenders' main line? There was no time. Too many soldiers crowding in. Nona summoned twin flaw-swords again and threw herself into the advancing mass of enemy warriors.

"Nona!" Something hit her, bounced off, and shattered. "Nona!"

Nona had the feeling that the person had been calling her name for a while. She blinked the violet light from her eyes and looked up.

"Nona!" Regol stood at the edge of the chamber against one of a number of tapestries depicting great seascapes. He had a vase in one hand ready to throw. It looked very valuable. A stained-glass ocean decorated the dome above them. The first stars had started to show in a black sky.

Nona spun around. Her eyes fixed on two marble statues of wrestlers sizing each other up across an archway leading from the chamber. More statues, alternating with portraits, punctuated the corridor leading away from the exit.

Regol's been bedding some Sis whore. Force him to speak the truth.

Nona felt her face contort with the ugliness of her suspicion.

Cut his lying tongue out.

She turned back towards Regol with a stare that should have transfixed him.

Kill them together.

"I hate you!" The words broke from her, dripping venom.

Nona snarled, shaking her head to rid it of the voices. She tried to bite down on their anger; it was something she didn't own. With an effort she lowered her gaze from Regol's confusion to the stains rising slowly up her wrists from where her fingers made contact with the shipheart.

"Stay here! If you follow me I'll kill you." And then without looking back, she turned for the archway and began to run.

24

HOLY CLASS

NONA RAN THE length of the hallway to the bronze doors at the far end. Both of the guardsmen who had delayed Sherzal's men were still on duty. Nona slowed to a walk as she drew closer. Nothing in her appearance qualified her for entry and the two men were drawing their swords before the unease they felt at the shipheart's approach turned to fear and then terror. The slowness of her advance allowed them to retain enough of their wits to be able to unlock the doors. They ran through, leaving the doors wide open behind them. Nona followed them.

She gathered her recollection of what she'd seen through Ruli's eyes, and it proved sufficient to get her to the iron door of the library. Considering the lock, she pulled its thread without so much as a twitch of her fingers. Once in she took the last lantern, upended the reading table, and struck a leg from it. A flaw-blade jabbed into the far wall soon uncovered the hidden alcove. Nona didn't waste time on the complex tangle of threads that might or might not yield to her efforts and undo the lock for the stairs. Instead she simply set the wheels to the same numbers that Sherzal had.

She squeezed through and was already a third of the way down the square spiral of steps before the door in the library floor had finished opening.

Her devils spoke with separate voices now, their opinions tearing at her in ways Keot had seldom been able to. Ignoring them, Nona hurried down the long corridor. The Ark-lights still shone but she spared no time to marvel at them. She held the shipheart in one hand with the lantern hanging from her wrist. In the other she held the table leg, which she repeatedly threw ahead of her and retrieved. The process stopped when the leg came apart midair, reaching the ground as a scattering of neatly sliced cubes.

The far end of the corridor looked to be closer than Nona had thought it should be, and there was no door there. Rather it was as if a blank wall had risen up since the others passed this way, sealing the passage closed.

Nona went to the sidewall where Sherzal had tapped out her rhythm and did her best to reproduce it. Nothing happened. She cut the muddy hem from her tunic and tossed it forward to check if anything had changed. It fell to the floor in pieces. She snarled in frustration. One of her devils tried to turn it into a scream of primal rage while others fought to take hold of her limbs.

Nona bit down and focused her will. She sat and rolled the shipheart to the opposite wall where it would exert less pressure on her thoughts. After a moment to regroup she reached for her clarity and for her serenity. She pictured Amondo's hands moving as they would have to if the juggler were to sustain not three or four balls in the air but nine. She passed the image of the missing flame and the lines of the falling moon from one side of her mind to the other. The keys to both trance states circulated through her, drawing every worry, every demand and secret terror, into their orbit as she achieved both states simultaneously.

The memory of Sherzal striking the wall became Nona's sole focus. Her joint trance gave it a crystal clarity. Sherzal's hand hit the beat, the vision repeating, recycling until the tempo ran through Nona's veins like the erratic pounding of a second heart.

Nona stood up and struck the required pattern. The opening appeared in the wall and she pressed the glowing disc inside the recess. A second cloth test showed the trap to be disarmed and Nona hurried on.

Before she cleared the area protected by the blades something struck her, not a flaw-blade but still sharp and invisible. Ruli's agony. It reached out across their thread-bond like a spear thrust.

When Nona was new to the skill, the distress would have hauled her mind across to join Ruli without allowing her any choice. Now, she had the mastery to resist the pull, but it had never been in Nona to ignore a friend, even if not doing so meant that she had to share their pain.

In a heartbeat Nona occupied Ruli's flesh. They had her on the floor with wrists and ankles bound, hands behind her back. The guardsman who had been kicking her stepped aside to reveal Sherzal smiling broadly. Behind her Jula, similarly tied, sat at the feet of several more guards.

"Well, this is rather silly." Sherzal came closer, her smile fading into concern. "Look at you, all bloody." Nona reminded herself that the emperor's sister had all but owned the Inquisition and had watched them burn her court rivals alive on trumped-up charges over matters as slight as unkind, though likely accurate, gossip. The concern on her face was entirely manufactured. "You understand that Dillon here is just softening you up? The idea is to save us having to go through the part where I ask you about the book and you pretend that you don't know what I'm talking about."

"But—" Ruli's protest was cut off by a heavy kick to the stomach.

"We'll get to the questions in a short while. And if we don't get answers Dillon will have to take out his knife. And if that doesn't work . . ." Sherzal gestured past the guards with Jula to the door behind. Safira stood poised and ready, and at her side a sulky-looking Joeli Namsis. Nona's hatred for the girl curled Ruli's lip. Joeli must have been just ahead of her all this time.

". . . Safira has her poisons and needles. And look! She's brought your friend to play. I really want to keep young Joeli fresh for what comes later, but if we must then she can pull what we need out of your skull. Though I'm told it may leave you rather broken."

Ruli groaned and rolled her head, bringing the other half of the chamber into the view of her one good eye. The pristine floor lay spattered with blood from the killing of Crucical's guards, and long smears indicated that the trio had been dragged away through a door opposite. A kick took Ruli in the back below the ribs, and as she jerked her head up Nona saw something that pushed the rising agony back down into being a mere distraction. Glowing molten and gold at the end of a long length of chain that had presumably been used to drag it to the chamber lay the Sweet Mercy shipheart.

Another kick crunched into Ruli's ribs, doubling her up with pain. Sherzal moved around so that her feet came into Ruli's eye-line.

"A little bird has told me that you and your friends have been busy stealing books. And by your friends I mean Nona Grey and Arabella Jotsis, both of whom owe me a great debt for damaging my alliance with Adoma."

"Damaging?" Ruli spat out a bloody laugh and Nona loved her for it. "Adoma . . ." She hadn't the breath to say it but Adoma had driven her armies through the Grand Pass and taken Sherzal's palace at the very start of the invasion three years earlier. As soon as the Noi-Guin shipheart was lost to them, the alliance to secure the Ark had fallen apart. It was "damaged" in the same way a snail is damaged beneath a descending heel. Officially, of course, the treachery had never existed, but if Crucical truly believed that, then he had never really known his sister at all.

"Yes, damaging." Sherzal frowned. "But with the right incentives Adoma can be brought back into line. We have what she *really* wants right here, and all the doors are locked tight. Further, you will notice the cylinders attached to the walls." Sherzal waved an arm. Ruli fixed on one of maybe a dozen white cylinders somehow adhering to the sides of the chamber, each longer and thicker than her leg. "My brother entrusted these into my care. They date from the Second Age when our ancestors mastered the secret fire again. At the push of a particular button they will explode with as much force as a quantal Path-walker can direct." She drew from her gown a short, fat stick with a red button at the end. "They were supposed to seal the Grand Pass and make it a tomb for ten thousand Scithrowl. I told my brother they failed to function, and at the time I said it I believed it to be true, thanks to some clever thread-work. But sweet Safira, keeper of my secrets, showed me their hiding place and I brought them here.

"I doubt they can open or destroy the Ark but they can certainly bury it deeply enough that it would take Adoma many years to dig her way back to it. So she needs me, just as she needs my shipheart and I need hers. I give you this information because if you tell me what I want to know there could be a place for you in my service, little unruly Ruli."

Ruli shook her head. "If it was true, if you really thought they would still work, that they might explode, you wouldn't be here. You would be on the other side of the city, or in the west, if there are any forts still holding there."

"Sadly it requires the ignition button to be close. It won't even work through a wall. Once perhaps, but not now. All these wonders are fading . . . Besides, I know what happens to losers. It isn't pretty. If it must come to that, then my end will be swift and glorious and my grave deep."

"So . . . the shipheart you stole. The two the battle-queen owns . . ." Nona spoke using Ruli's mouth. "That only makes three."

Sherzal held out four fingers and started to count them down. "Well, there's one"—the guard marked the count with a kick to Ruli's thigh—"here that Abbess Glass kindly donated. And number two"—a kick to the ribs—"and three"—and the head—"are with Adoma. The fourth—" The guard stamped on Ruli's ankle. "The fourth shipheart I need will be delivered to me by Lano Tacsis and the Singular of the Noi-Guin from the sack of the Convent of Sweet Mercy." Sherzal leaned over and waited for Ruli's groaning to subside. "So you see, Adoma needs me. I have quite a bit to bargain with."

The convent! Even as she shared Ruli's pain Nona found it crushed to insignificance beneath the terror that Sherzal's words brought crashing down on her. Lano Tacsis at the convent. The thought of Ara standing lone guard against the Tacsis forces and the Noi-Guin had her tumbling back towards her own body. Ara! She had forced Ara to stay. She'd thought she was saving her!

Nona clung to Ruli even as her fear for the convent tried to steal her away. Sherzal was still talking.

"But it has come to my attention that even when we open the Ark, actually controlling the moon may be an annoyingly complicated business. My little bird tells me that Abbess Glass set you children on the path to finding a book that should help on that front. Quite a wonder, that woman. I'm so glad she's dead. But her annoying cleverness is the reason I can't afford not to take this book seriously. Owning that knowledge would really be the cherry on the cake. Which is why I had you two brought here. Disappointingly you don't have the book on you, but you can tell me where it is. And if young Jula really is as studious as Joeli tells me she is, then I think it's worth investing the time to torture her on the assumption she has the information we need locked behind that plain little face of hers."

Nona bit down on Ruli's pain and spoke into her mind.

I can save you. I'm going to try the doors but if I can't get through I'll need to take control of your body. You really have to trust me for that to happen.

Ruli made no attempt to hide her relief. *You can do the hurting and I'll sit back and watch you kill this bitch. But even if you take over you'll still be me . . . and I'm a bit tied up.*

That's why I want to try the doors first. Stay strong.

Hurry, Nona! He's getting his knife out . . . and that's supposed to be easy compared to what Safira is going to do to me! I'm not strong like you . . .

NONA RETURNED TO her flesh with a shuddering breath. She turned her stare towards the blank wall ending the corridor, reaching out with her rock-work. It didn't require much skill to understand the nature of the barrier. Even from fifty yards away she knew. The corridor had been sealed with a slab of iron two feet thick.

Nona paused, considering her options. From Kettle's thread-bond a pulsing mix of grief, anger, and fear nagged at her heightened senses along with the rush of combat. The pain from Ruli's beating still throbbed at the end of her thread-bond, but the rising terror of the approaching knife eclipsed it. Nona steeled herself to join her friend, but even as she gathered herself something far stronger than fear or rage hammered through her. It came from the bond she had with Ara. The bond that had registered nothing but a sullen silence since Nona left the Rock of Faith. Now suddenly it echoed with Ara's first step upon the Path, and the reverberation rang through her louder than any bell.

By the time Nona had pushed her way into Ara's mind, her friend had dropped from the Path into a fight so one-sided it made the defence outside Crucical's palace look like a meeting of equals. Ara fought alone amid the forest of pillars against not scores but *hundreds* of Pelarthi mercenaries.

Lano Tacsis was behind this. Sherzal had said so. His coin had brought the Pelarthi from the ice margins. Abbess Wheel had said that the high priest had ordered that Nona be the one to stay. Tacsis gold and Tacsis influence had steered High Priest Nevis's hand to set Nona alone before the convent and its shipheart. Only the long reach of Abbess Glass had enabled her to step clear. Nona remembered the promise she had made to a dying woman. The promise that she would choose neither Red nor Grey nor the sky blue of the Mystic Sister but instead take the black of a Holy Sister. Even on her deathbed Glass had seen who would replace her as abbess and how much favour such a gesture would win from her. Without that goodwill it would be Nona at the convent miles from the shipheart, unable to work any of the wonders she had been working along her thread-bond and those she still planned to work.

Nona crouched, pinned by indecision. She felt Abbess Glass's hand upon her shoulder but found no sense of direction in it. Even the old woman's legendary foresight had its limits. She could not have seen this end. It fell to Nona now and she felt unequal to the challenge. Ruli's terror and pain began to spike along their thread-bond. Kettle's despairing exhaustion reached out to Nona through the bond they shared. Five miles away another friend released the awesome power of the Path in her single-handed attempt to destroy an army that had been sent to kill not Sister Thorn but Sister Cage.

Nona couldn't lose Ara. Not her. With a cry of despair she threw herself across the corridor, scooped up the shipheart, and ran into the darkened room to her left. The shipheart's glow revealed what Ruli had glimpsed on her way past, what Zole had spoken of back in the black ice. A huge ring, too large to have come into the small room through the single doorway. It leaned against the rear wall, too tall to stand vertical. Its dimensions and markings were identical to those on the ring that Zole had sent Nona through against her will three years earlier. Without pausing to think, Nona leapt into the circle. She held the shipheart out before her, and every fibre of her being tensed for collision with the wall behind the ring.

The cave into which Nona stumbled was too big for the shipheart's light to find its sides. Behind her a ring of strangely crystalline metal rocked gently on its edge. The glow was already dying from the scores of symbols around its perimeter. On the floor for yards in all directions lay fragments of the flowstone that had once coated the ring. The pieces lay in the same broken chaos in which they had landed when Nona had emerged here three years earlier. That time she had travelled far more than five miles. Zole had flung her a hundred times farther from another of the ring's counterparts beneath the black ice.

Nona had discovered this ring with Ara and the others in her early exploration of the undercaves. A holothour had guarded it using nothing but terror. Those days seemed long ago and simpler. Part of Nona wished the ancient magic could send her back across the years as easily as across miles.

For a moment, as the light died from the great circle, the shipheart flared. Cavern walls appeared, described in violet and black, a roof above, hung with a downward-questing forest of stalactites. Pools patterned the undulating floor, each surface still trembling with the shock of Nona's arrival. Nona's senses flared too. The world of threads, in which humanity's paper-thin reality hung, lay stripped bare before her eyes. Her rock-sense ran wild, reaching out through the void-riddled vastness of the Rock of Faith, echoing down passages unknown to man, stealing along secret ways, lacing around the sleeping mass of the Glasswater, the weight of its countless gallons held back behind such a thinness of stone . . .

Nona shook away the sensations and wasted no time. She ran, following paths that she and her friends had explored years earlier. It took no more than a couple of minutes to reach the passage where once she had struggled to climb a fissure to reach the scene of Hessa's murder.

Nona leapt towards the opening overhead and within three heartbeats was pulling herself out of the fissure's mouth into the space before the shipheart's old vault, the place from which Yisht had once stolen it.

"Lano wants you." Nona spoke to the shipheart. "He will not have you." She pushed the sphere against the smooth wall of the passage and exerted her power over the rock. Moments later she withdrew her hand. The shipheart remained, entombed behind inches of stone with few signs of disturbance to betray its presence.

The voices of her devils called at her in the silence that remained now that the hurricane of the shipheart's power no longer blew through her. They told her to run. To take the shipheart and escape through the ring to some distant place. They whispered that Ara was false, a child of the Sis, raised on gold; they told her that Ara had always seen her as a peasant, never as a true friend. They told her that golden Ara would laugh at her secret passions and never love her in return. They told her that in her place Ara would run.

And Nona believed them.

"It doesn't matter." She stumbled on along the tunnel, away from the shipheart. With her mind splintering, her thoughts drawn one way then the other, Nona clung to the simplest of her truths. Those she first found. "It doesn't matter what she thinks of me. It doesn't matter if she hates me. She's my friend. *I* won't leave her."

She ran on blind, following her memory of the place, trailing a hand against the wall, falling, rising, crawling, wriggling, reaching Apple's caves. The gate to the Shade steps surrendered to a slash of her blades and she emerged to run through the convent where she had grown from a small child into the young woman Abbess Glass had burdened with too much trust.

Few lights burned in the windows but torches ringed the courtyard before the dormitories and on the steps sat Sister Scar. The nun looked older than Nona had ever imagined her behind her desk in the scriptorium. She clutched a cleaver from the kitchens in her lap. Above her at the Holy Class windows, where junior novices were forbidden on pain of a beating, dozens of small faces leaned out. They looked ridiculously young for the battlefield.

"Protect the convent!" Nona paused and met Sister Scar's wide eyes. "No quarter. Let the Ancestor take care of mercy."

The faint edge of a scream that reached Nona from the forest of pillars was lost in the far louder scream that threatened to shatter her skull from within. Ara! At the same time a white agony speared its way between her shoulders, an echo of Ara's injury.

Ara! Ara! I'm coming!

Nona sprinted towards the battle, her mind reaching ahead of her for her friend and finding only darkness.

✦ ✦ ✦

THE PELARTHI STOOD between the pillars, a loose halo around the place where Ara lay in a pool of her own blood. To Nona's amazement Clera stood above the fallen girl. For a bright moment Nona thought that somehow her friend was there to save Ara, but as their eyes met across the intervening yards a cold certainty took hold of her. Clera had been the one who had brought Ara down.

Clera opened her mouth to speak, and said nothing, condemned by the close company of the mercenaries all around her. Of all of them, in that moment only Clera seemed to have seen her.

Nona drew her sword as she ran towards the first of the Pelarthi. Sister Tallow had pressed the weapon's hilt back into her hand barely an hour before and as Nona spun through a group of six she took her first lives with the blade. The Pelarthi knew all about her arrival then.

Back in the convent compound Bitel rang out. It seemed fitting. The bell had never heralded anything but disaster.

Nona scanned the forces arrayed before her. She felt her devils moving beneath her habit, their voices crying out for blood, and she found herself in agreement. The Book of the Ancestor says that for everything there is a season. This was a time to reap. A time for death. A time to die.

Bows creaked among the Pelarthi ranks, spears were lifted, knuckles whitened on the hilts of sword and axe. A hawk-eyed archer caught Nona's eye, her cheek torn and bloody. She drew back her string but there was a tremble in her aim.

The Pelarthi would know stories about her. Clera was a teller of tales and they were here for her. They would know her as Nona, as the black-eyed child who slew Raymel Tacsis, the girl who broke Lord Thuran Tacsis's mind with ancient pain magics. They would have heard that to some she was known as the Argatha, the Chosen One. Given Joeli's spying they probably even knew her by her new name. Sister Cage.

Kill them all.

Make a red slaughter.

Fill the air with their screams.

Nona listened to the cries of her devils and found a dark smile on her face. The trembling archer let her arrow fall with a clatter. She turned without a word and began to push her way back, past the warriors of her clan. To her left another turned, a man thick with muscle, the names of his forefathers inked in runes along his arms. Two of those he pushed aside turned and ran with him. Sister Thorn had already shown them what a Red Sister could do.

The trickle became a flood. The Pelarthi left the scores of their dead, still scattered or heaped where Ara had killed them. They ran as if Nona had rolled the shipheart among them. Her devils howled their disappointment and it echoed through her.

NONA STRODE TOWARDS Clera and saw where Ara lay at her feet.

"Is she dead?" Her heart hurt, despair overwhelming her rage.

"How are you here?" Clera ignored the question. "You weren't supposed to be here! How did you know? . . . And even then, how did you get here?"

Nona ignored the questions. Clera was an accomplished liar but seemed incapable of seeing that another Tacsis brother had lied to her. Again. About the same damn thing. Nona had always been the target, never Ara. "Is she dead?" She rushed forward, pushing Clera away from Ara, who was still coiled around a spear. Nona knelt, reaching out to touch the spread gold of her hair. "Ara?"

"You should never have let me go." The words sputtered from Clera as if she were hurt, as if it were her wrapped around a spear. "You had me bound. Guilty. You should have let them drown me."

"I wouldn't do that to a friend." Nona had fought Zole, Darla, Ara . . . all of them, and insisted that Clera be allowed to run. What might have changed had she not? Who might still live that now walked with the

Ancestor? She shook the thoughts away and set her fingers to Ara's neck, seeking a pulse. The smallest of groans rewarded her, the smallest tremble of a hand. Nona found she could breathe once more.

A short laugh burst from Clera, sounding as much like pain as mirth. "They all think you're the big bad. The Church's hammer. Cage the Shadowless. And you're still acting like a child, Nona! You run into everything heart-first, expecting . . . what? You didn't understand how people work when the abbess brought you here as a dirty-footed peasant. You didn't understand when she sent you away. And you don't understand now. People lie, Nona: they steal, they cheat, they're unfaithful. People hurt you, they let you down. They sell you out."

"It doesn't mean I have to be like that." Nona stared up at Clera, who flinched. The devils inside her wanted Clera's blood, and Nona strove not to make that desire her own. "We have a whole church built on ancestors." She waved an arm at the Dome. "Family. Dead family." She took Ara's hand in hers. "You *choose* your friends. If you're going to worship dead people you didn't choose, then perhaps the bonds of friendship shouldn't be so easily broken. No?"

Clera shook her head. "You're a fool, Nona Grey. Are you going to kill me now, or let someone else do it?"

Nona fought to block out the voices of her devils. She had seen enough death for ten lifetimes. She had chosen the Black. Abbess Glass had made her a Holy Sister for a reason. War was not that reason.

"Ara could live. If we get her to Sister Rose. Now!" Nona glanced back towards the convent. They were coming. The old sisters and the young girls.

Clera waved her hand at the distant nuns, exasperated. "Let them take her. I don't care. I didn't come for Ara. She was just in the way."

Nona released Ara's hand with a squeeze and stood. "I've missed you, Clera. It's been too many years."

Clera glanced out across the plateau. "We were children, Nona. Children make and break friendships all the time. It's not important. This, what we're doing now, this is important. It's about sides in the great game that's being played. And you're on the wrong one. The losing one. You should change sides."

Nona shook her head. "I'm not playing. And I've always been on your side, Clera. You've just not properly understood it."

Clera looked down at Ara. "I wanted her to run."

"I know."

"She should have run. There were too many of them for her. Why did she have to be so stupid?"

Nona shrugged, a slow gesture giving the lie to a racing mind. "Where is Lano Tacsis?"

"You know the Tacsis." Clera nodded towards the plateau stretching out beyond the pillars. "They like to let you spend your power against people they consider expendable, then arrive to finish the job if anything's left to finish."

"They do."

"He's out there with his soldiers and eight Noi-Guin. His teachers from the Tetragode. Others too."

Nona looked down at her sword. "My power's not spent."

"You think you can kill me without reaching for the Path, little Nona?" Clera drew her sword, a twin to Nona's, taken from the body of a Red Sister.

Nona turned away, her back to Clera, and looked out across the plateau. If her friend struck her down then, she would be at peace with it. She didn't want to live in a world where Clera would do a thing like that. "I think I won't need to kill you. I think you'll fight them with me. Sister."

As Nona spoke she saw that some of the convent girls had followed her out among the pillars. They watched now, peering around stone columns. She waved for them to advance and four Grey Class novices came forward. At Nona's nod they lifted Ara, carrying her rapidly away, back through the pillars. "Take her to Sister Rose! Hurry!" She turned back to Clera. "Well?"

"Fight them *with* you?" Clera threw up her hands. "Even if Lano *only* had a second *better* army out there you wouldn't stand a chance. But he has eight Noi-Guin, Nona! Eight!"

As Clera protested Nona pulsed an urgent plea to Ara, begging her to wake up. Nothing. She gritted her teeth against the backwash of her friend's pain and tried again.

"Eight of them! And one of them is the Singular." Clera shook her head. "And he is flat-out the scariest bastard I have ever known. He's the spider at the middle of their web of shadow-bonds. If it was just him on his own, no army, no other Noi-Guin, you still wouldn't stand a chance—" She broke off, seeing Nona's distracted look. "I'm sorry, am I boring you?"

"I'm not going to fight them today! Not out here on their terms! That would be insane! There are *eight* of them!" Nona steeled herself against the desperation and pain now pulsing at her down three thread-bonds. Ara had found her senses and joined her distress to that of Ruli and Kettle. Nona spoke a message into Ara's mind, then raised her eyes to meet Clera's outrage. "I'm going to run, of course! I'm in a hurry. Other things to do. I need you to get out there and appear as if you're still loyal."

"That won't be hard. I like to be on the winning side."

"Tell them I'm scared. About to run. Tell them they'll lose their chance at me unless they act right now. I'm going to make for the undercaves. For the shipheart vault where Hessa died. Make sure you're in the lead. In the lead, Clera. It's important."

"In the lead. You want us to hunt you down . . ." Clera frowned. "I can do that. But when they find you, Nona, they'll kill you. I can't stop them."

"Just bring them. Bring them all. And we'll see who sinks and who swims."

Clera met her eyes for one last time, then turned and fled, out across the rock to where the lights and banners of Lano's first rank were just starting to come into view.

+ + +

"WHEN THEY COME you must be Grey Sisters, not Red." Nona addressed the young novices and old sisters, no more than two dozen of them, all watching her in the heart of pillar forest. "Nobody touches the Tacsis lord or the Noi-Guin, don't go anywhere near them. Draw the house troops out among the pillars. Use the convent buildings. Don't take risks, just take opportunities. Wound rather than kill. You want to slow them down, make them rethink, give them a reason to retreat. In the end you're to run rather than make a stand. You carry the convent with you." She waved her hand towards the convent buildings. "These are just stones piled up to keep the wind off."

Nona dispersed her sisters to hide while she took her place among the Pelarthi dead, heaped in dozens, scattered in scores. She bit down on the urgency from her thread-bonds, closed her ears to the whispering of her own devils, and called her clarity to her. The hidden world of detail opened itself to her, from the star-speckled, smoke-streaked vault of heaven above to the complaints of the Rock of Faith below. The Rock's voice came too deep for ears but rumbled faintly through her bones as the stone cooled beneath the night's wind.

The Tacsis torches and pole-lanterns would be hard to miss but if the Noi-Guin came ahead of them, insinuating themselves into the darkness between the pillars, they could murder her before she knew they were there. Nona defocused her sight to see the thread-scape. Sister Pan had said that ultimately a true quantal mage would see only the world's threads for they were the deepest truth and revealed not only every single thing as it was but also the past, the future, and the relationship of each thing to every other. Indeed, when watching the thread-scape you learned how artificial ideas of individual objects, or even people were, since each was infinitely connected and interwoven with the world around them.

Nona focused on the now. She saw the pillars and saw through them. In that moment of her clarity she saw that they might be a map, perhaps a pillar to mark each Ark. She pushed that insight aside and looked beyond.

She saw the rock, the caves beneath, the motion of the wind. The soldiers of Lano's army appeared as complex multidimensional knots sliding along a multitude of threads. And ahead of them slid a handful of knots bound more tightly than that of any soldier. Each of these was shot through with black threads and also joined by them in a web of their own making. Noi-Guin, coming for her.

To their rear all the dark threads converged on a black central node. The Singular, advancing behind his minions.

With a start Nona realised that the assassins were already much closer than she had imagined they might be. She turned and began to sprint, winding herself around the curve of the pillar at her back. The sharp retort of cross-knives hitting stone followed her, beginning at the spot where she had been standing just a heartbeat before. Without warning another of the Noi-Guin broke from the darkness beside a pillar immediately ahead of Nona and attacked with breathtaking speed and the advantage of surprise, his weapons serrated kill-spikes designed to anchor in flesh. It was all Nona could do to twist out of their path and fall to the ground. Another assassin came at her with a black-tipped spear. Nona, knowing she couldn't evade the blow, reached out hoping she might somehow deflect it.

In that instant something black hurtled into the assassin. A small novice. A hunska. Nona didn't even know her name. Two more leapt at the man with the kill-spikes, one of them screaming as she was immediately impaled.

"No! Run!" Nona was on her feet. She struck a cross-knife out of the air with her hand.

More novices came charging in, knives in hand. They would all be dead in seconds. With a scream of her own Nona started to run again. The girls wouldn't retreat if she made a stand. She couldn't have all their deaths on her hands.

Nona fled as if all the demons of the black ice were at her heels, and in truth there wasn't much to choose between that and the reality of the situation. She sprinted through the pillar forest and broke out into the open ground in front of the abbess's house. Here she was at her most vulnerable. Once the Noi-Guin emerged from the pillars they would have a clear shot at her. As she ran Nona reached for the strap across her chest. Kettle had given her the Grey Sister's full field equipment. She jagged left, right, left. Cross-knives hissed past her. She knew that even as she slowed herself, hoping to evade the missiles, others among the Noi-Guin would be sprinting towards her flat-out on straight lines. Her fingertips counted along the vials in the harness and searched for the coded markings. Sister Apple had had them hunt out specific vials in the most difficult of circumstances on many occasions. The rule was that you drank whatever was in the vial you picked, no matter whether you picked right or wrong. A cross-knife hammered into Nona's shoulder and she stumbled, almost dropping the vial she'd torn free. She flipped the top and knocked back the contents, sliding to the left as more knives hit the rock around her.

Nona reached the convent buildings with at least two Noi-Guin hard on her heels, the furious tempo of their feet still muffled as if there were no circumstances under which the assassins could ever be considered noisy. Another cross-knife hit her, a razored punch into the back of her thigh.

A sharp turn along the alley between the laundry and winery buildings allowed Nona to pull the trick that had won her many races with her friends, kicking off the wall to make the tight corner without losing speed. She shot into the dormitory building, up two flights of stairs, crashed through into the Holy dorm, and leapt through the window above her study desk, shattering the shutters. She landed on the roof of the cold store across the way, rolling over the roof ridge with a scream as the cross-knife tore free from her shoulder. Two more rolls dropped her from the gutter and she hit the ground running, heading back towards the far end of the laundry. Her thigh was a white agony but she ran on with hardly a limp. Flaw-blades sliced into stone, allowing Nona to slingshot herself around a corner into the mangle room and then on through the washing gallery, down some steps and into the well room. Here laundry bags had been piled around the wall of the well, each tied by a length of rope that dangled down into the shaft. Without pause Nona jumped down the well, grabbing the ropes as she fell. The heavy sacks came with her, sliding some five or ten yards before choking together as the shaft narrowed. Nona jolted to a halt, cursing at the agony from her shoulder. A second later she let go and fell the rest of the distance.

She caught the stonework at the very bottom of the shaft with her flaw-blades and swung out over the pool into the cavern beneath the centre oak.

"Hello?" Spoken into the darkness. Her fingers found the hilt of the knife in her leg and she gasped despite herself. If she drew it out she would likely bleed to death. If she left it in, then any venom still on the blade would continue to feed into her.

"Nona?" A weak voice, trembling.

"You tell me. You're the one who can see." A grin broke through Nona's pain. She turned towards Ara's voice.

"Help me up." The rasp underlying each word spoke of a damaged lung. Broken ribs most likely.

"You're all wet," Nona said, finding Ara in the dark. She lifted her friend, trying not to put too much weight on her wounded leg. The pain *now* made it seem as if it hadn't really hurt until she stopped running.

"The novices lowered me into the pool like I told them to." Ara leaned against her. "Like you told me to tell them to. And they set up the bags ..." She straightened and gasped. "If someone wants to find us, then a few sacks of dirty habits aren't going to keep them out for long."

"No." Nona limped a step forward, bringing Ara with her. "So let's not stay here long."

THE TWO NUNS struggled on together, Nona wholly blind and navigating only by memory, Ara able to see but less sure of the route. Nona kept one hand pressing a cloth to the wound in her shoulder. The lead she had opened and the blockage in the well meant that the Noi-Guin would have to track her. Once they reached the undercaves they would have Clera guide them. Nona let a little blood spill here and there. She wanted a trail Clera could follow rather than having to cede the lead to one of the assassins more skilled at tracking even though unfamiliar with the surroundings.

In a narrow passage a hundred yards on, nausea overwhelmed Nona. She leaned against the wall and retched, spraying the ground before her.

"Nona!"

"I'm all right . . ." She felt dizzy and sick. The black cure she had taken while running fought its battle with whatever venom had coated the Noi-Guin's little knives. She bent double, hands on her thighs. Only her gasps, the rattle of Ara's breath, and the drip, drip, drip of the caves broke the silence. And in her head Nona's devils whispered fears to her. Fears so secret she had hardly acknowledged them even to herself.

Clera will betray you.

Arabella Jotsis has hated you from the start. To her you're the same muddy peasant now as on the first day you arrived.

You'll die down here, in the dark.

Tacsis, Jotsis, Namsis . . . all of them the same.

Yisht almost throttled you to death in these tunnels. You think you can escape eight Noi-Guin?

The Singular is with them. He's worse than the other seven put together.

Leave the girl. She's slowing you down.

"Shut up!"

"What?" Ara stiffened.

"No, not—" Nona shook her head. "Never mind. Let's keep moving."

Nona limped blind through damp and narrow spaces with an untold weight of rock above her and a desperate need not to lose her way. In places both of them had to drag themselves across the floor like wounded animals. The knowledge that the most deadly assassins in all the Corridor were pursuing them proved unhelpful. Each of the killers would be wholly in their element, the ancient darkness flowing through their veins. Imagination filled the quiet between her breaths with soft sounds of stealthy approach. Several times Nona turned back along her path, determined to study the thread-scape and see how close the threat lay, only to tear herself away, unwilling to spend the time uncovering information that wouldn't change her course of action. Ara made no complaint at any of these pauses, simply hung on Nona's shoulder drawing slow painful breaths that scraped in and rattled out. Nona thought of Apple, lung-struck in the chaos of battle. With a sob she hauled Ara on.

Finally they reached Nona's goal. She felt the pulse of the shipheart from within the rock wall in which she had sunk it.

"Stand back." Nona dug her fingers into the stone as though it were clay and pulled forth the shipheart, her hands black around its alien light. Immediately the glow made familiar surroundings that had seemed so foreign when revealed only through her touch. The devils in her flesh retreated from the shipheart though it had been the one to spawn them.

"You carried *that* here?" Ara leaned back against the opposite wall, her face deathly pale, lips almost black.

"I didn't want to!" Nona screwed her face up as the whispers inside her head became shouts. "I'm not Zole . . . I can't heal us with it. I'm sorry."

"Hells," Ara muttered. "I'd rather hurt than touch that thing again."

The fissure up which Nona had climbed lay just feet away. Before approaching it she retraced her steps ten yards down the passage, her heart pounding, expecting at every moment to meet a knife winging out of the dark. She pulled a thread from the stone, just one of the multitude that glimmered in her witch sight. It told the tale of the rock from its constituents and formation to the carving of the channel by ancient waters. She drew it forth and knotted it to a thread in the opposite wall. A tremor of wrongness vibrated across the length of it, then went still.

With her heart pounding, certain that the Noi-Guin would be on her at any moment, Nona went to the fissure's edge. She exerted her rock-work skills, breaking stone from the fissure's sides and at the same time reaching her rock-sense out along the passages that threaded like veins through the plateau. She could sense the silent bulk of the Glasswater; the sinkhole lay just a few hundred yards off, but even with the shipheart's aid the water and bone of any human bodies approaching along the tunnels proved too small to register. Giving up on the search she dropped the shipheart, giving it a flick to send it rolling down the passage under her. It clattered off out of sight, far enough that no whisper of its light still reached up from the tunnel beneath. Nona allowed herself a sigh of relief at being free of the thing.

"Ara, you have to go down." Nona pointed after the shipheart.

"Down?" Ara groaned. "I can't."

"Seriously." Nona patted through the dark towards her and grabbed a handful of habit. "It's a ten-foot climb. The floor's another eight foot below the bottom of the fissure."

"I can't!"

Nona started to drag Ara towards the crack. "You have to climb."

"The drop will kill me!"

"Stay here and it will be the Noi-Guin who kill you instead of the drop."

"Noi-Guin?" Ara sounded faint.

"Eight of them." Nona hauled Ara to the edge, wincing at the girl's groan of agony. "I made footholds for you."

Ara descended painfully. Nona wriggled in after her. She hung by her blades from just beneath the lip of the fissure. Below her Ara reached the roof of the passage underneath them and cried out in pain as she tried to hang down into it. A dull thud followed, then silence. The hurt that flared along the thread-bond almost made Nona lose her own hold and suggested that Ara had fainted from the pain.

Nona waited, hanging from invisible claws, one shoulder starting to ache with the strain of her suspension, blood dripping from the other, her thigh a mass of white-hot agony, her stomach sick, her body weak with echoes of what the Noi-Guin's venom wanted to do to her. It seemed to take an eternity before anything happened, and all the while the voices of her devils grew louder in the silence, their demands harder to ignore. They made her sanity seem insane. Why wasn't she running?

"You know where the bitch is heading?"

Nona had already known they were coming. She had felt her thread return to its natural place when the first of them had passed through it. Nona had tied her knot to fail at such intrusion and, as it snapped back, the thread she had set sent ripples through something deeper than the stone. Sister Pan had tried to teach her the trick but it was from Joeli Namsis that Nona had finally learned the subtle arts of thread-traps, watch-threads, and warning threads. She'd had to fall foul of a lot of them before she mastered the technique. As Keot had once told her: your foes shape your life more than friends ever could.

Nona had known they were coming but until Lano Tacsis spoke she hadn't dared to hope that he had joined the hunting party. He must have shed a royal fortune in sigil-stamped armour at the well-head, but he would still have enough protection in the form of sigiled amulets and robes to stop a Path-blast. Not that Nona could manage one of those.

"There's an exit near the base of the plateau. It's where I'd go." Clera's voice. "She'll have set traps for us somewhere. Wires maybe."

Nona steeled herself, against her pain, against her weakness, against the voices in her head telling her, not unreasonably, that Clera had betrayed her again, that Clera would not have followed her instruction.

Nona waited. A figure began to step over the fissure. With all the speed and strength left to her Nona lunged up, ignoring the scream of her injured shoulder, and seized the person's ankle. In the same movement she retracted her flaw-blades and let the whole of her weight haul both of them into the depths.

The fissure crawled around them as if they sank in honey. Nona left her victim to fend for themselves, concentrating instead on her own landing.

When her head cleared the fissure she hunted the shipheart's glow. As the rubble-strewn floor approached, Nona extended her good leg to absorb the first impact. She knew one leg would not be sufficient. Her other foot hit the ground and she strained to keep her body from hammering into the rocks. The wicked little knife bedded in the back of her thigh cut deeper as her muscles tightened around it.

With a howl Nona sank to her haunches and immediately launched herself at the shipheart. She slapped a hand to it and with an effort that she thought might shatter her already-clenched teeth she brought the fissure walls tumbling in. Quicker than thought she rolled, hand extended towards Ara, slumped senseless beneath the opening. At the touch of Nona's rock-work several large chunks of stone became dust, sifting down through the air while smaller pieces bounced everywhere but on Ara.

A black-cloaked figure rolled to a halt beside Nona.

"What in the—" It scrambled rapidly away. "Ancestor's balls! That's a fucking shipheart!" Clera arrived against the opposite wall on her backside, straining to get farther away. "My brain feels like it's being cooked!"

Nona glanced up at the jumble of broken stone choking the fissure in the roof above them. The effort of bringing it down had left her with a headache that was bad enough to compete with her shoulder and thigh for attention.

"That's your plan?" Clera followed her gaze, her face pale and beaded with sweat. "That's not a plan!" She slapped a dirty palm to her forehead. "No! I can't believe I've been this stupid. What is it you do to me, Nona? Some marjal mind-trick? That's it isn't it, a mind-trick?"

Nona ignored her and crawled to Ara's side. Her friend's headdress had come loose and her golden hair was crimson with blood from some new head wound. Nona took a vial from her Grey Sister supplies and opened it beneath Ara's nose. The sharp smell that rose made Nona's eyes water, and with a cough and a splutter Ara came back to herself, pushing the vial away.

"You've just bought yourself half an hour, an hour tops!" Clera stamped away, then stamped back. "They'll find a way round, they'll track us, they'll kill us." She kicked a rock and limped off cursing. "You've just killed me! What were you thinking? This isn't a plan!"

"No," Nona said. "*This* is a plan." She raised the shipheart, her grip so tight that she thought her finger-bones might break. For a moment the light within the stone flickered and dimmed. Nona reached out along silent, lightless tunnels, her rock-sense questing. She found the distant wall she wanted . . . and broke it. It felt as if the effort had broken something inside her in return. She fell to the floor, hot blood welling from her mouth, and the shipheart rolled from her nerveless hand.

The Rock of Faith rumbled.

"Nona?" Ara asked, her voice trembling. "What have you done?"

Nona lay where she had fallen. "Sinkhole."

"The Glasswater?" Clera breathed. "What did you do?"

Nona got a hand under her chest and pushed herself from the ground. It seemed that she weighed as much as ten nuns should. The rock beneath her palm trembled.

"The tunnel above us is about to become a river again." She used the wall to help herself to one leg. "Then a bit later, so will this one." She reached to drag Ara from the ground. "So we have to get out of here fast."

25

HOLY CLASS

NONA KNEW THAT the darkness, and the speed with which water under pressure will travel through a tunnel, meant that all they would know at the end was that the distant rumble would suddenly become a *whoosh* and a heartbeat later they would all be dead.

Already the air was in motion, blasting them from behind no matter how fast they moved.

"We'll never make the Seren Way!" A frantic Clera paused twenty yards ahead of Nona and Ara. The shipheart's glow caught faintly on her face and hands, making her a suggestion in the dark.

Ara shuffled forward in a kind of broken jog, groaning every time she misstepped on the uneven ground and jolted herself. Nona kept pace with an awkward gait, crippled by the pain in her head and swinging her injured leg around stiffly, unwilling to bend it.

"Hurry!" It was clear that Clera was moments from speeding away to leave them to it. "Faster!"

"We're not going to the Seren Way!" They would never make it that far,

Clera was right about that. "We just need to reach the holothour chamber and the ring." Nona held the shipheart higher. "With this!"

"So you can die somewhere more familiar?" Clera shrieked. She turned to go.

"The ring's a gate. A magic gate. This is the key!" Nona tried to speed up but her body seemed unwilling to listen to her.

Clera held back, waiting for them. Too terrified to stand still, her nervous energy had her bouncing off the walls. "Hurry! Hurry!"

Nona drew close to Clera with Ara a few yards behind. The girl started to back away. It said a lot for the shipheart's aura that even knowing it was the key to her salvation, Clera didn't seem in the least bit tempted to snatch it and run off.

The distant thunder had definitely become less distant. An intensifying roar echoed their way, punctuated by a series of booms. The air rushed past them so fast now that it seemed to push them along, almost lifting them off the ground.

Ara's breath grew ragged, drawn in in great despairing gasps. Nona felt the knife in her leg every time she set her weight upon it, and hot blood trickled down her back. Clera danced ahead of them, wild with fear, screaming at both of them to hurry up. Nona retreated into her core, her world reducing to a monotony of pain and running, one agonizing step after the next. Back along the tunnels Lano Tacsis had died. A sudden death and better than he deserved, but Nona's spite had burned itself out on the father, Thuran. The cruel end she had given that old man, who lingered even now, was a stain on her soul. She knew that. One that all the rushing water aimed in her direction would not clean away. With death so hard upon her heels she wished she could have been a better person, wished she could have saved her friends.

"Which way?" Clera waited for her where the tunnel split.

"Here!" Nona forced the shipheart to burn bright and turned a corner into the holothour's cavern. The creature that they had banished long ago had been one of the few things to have scared Nona more than what was currently rushing up behind them.

As Nona turned she saw something. At the far end of the long passage they'd run down a white wall was rushing towards them. And halfway between Ara and the fury of that flood something dark and terrible raced forward, almost as fast as the water. One black figure whose lack of definition somehow suggested things far worse than any detail could.

"The Singular!" Clera tore into the chamber ahead of Nona.

Of all their pursuers somehow the dark heart of the Noi-Guin had kept ahead of the deluge and was now within moments of catching them. The shadows that surged ahead of the Singular carried a new terror with them, a threat that made the white fury behind seem a kindness.

"Ara!" Nona started to sprint, working her wounded leg, careless of what new damage the knife embedded in her thigh might wreak upon her. "Run!"

The great ring loomed ahead of them. Clera reached it first and turned, howling at them, "Run, you bitches!"

The Singular broke into the chamber, a dark fury of shadow boiling around a void, nightmare shapes reaching forward to rend flesh and slice souls. Ropes of darkness lashed out to coil around Nona, sinking midnight teeth through her habit. She staggered on as if dragging a laden wagon behind her. She found herself screaming and every devil in her screamed just as loudly. The Singular's anger beat at her like hammers.

"Run!" Clera howled from the ring.

Just yards remained between Nona and Clera. She heard the *whoosh* as the Glasswater's untold gallons hammered around the corner, jetting out into the cavern. She slapped a hand to the ring, crashed into its side, and turned. Ara was a spear's length behind her, snared and flailing, a red froth around her gasping mouth, the Singular the length of three spears behind her, the talons of his shadows closing around her legs. And behind him, the first surging wave of the flood.

"Run!" Clera screamed again, her speed breathtaking as she unleashed a barrage of throwing stars into the void where the Singular should be.

Somehow Ara tore free of the Singular's shadows and launched herself headlong at the ring. Nona leapt forward in the same moment, knocking Clera through ahead of her. The flood's roar swallowed their screams. The coldness of the water as it hit them was shocking.

SUDDENLY THERE WAS only Clera screaming. She drew another breath, cried out, and fell silent. All that remained was Ara's gasping and rattling, and Nona's own panting, barely audible over the deafening pounding of her heart. As she had stepped through the gate Nona had felt the Singular battling her for control of the shipheart, his mind reaching for it. Somehow she had torn free, though, and sealed the gate in the instant she fell out into the emperor's palace.

Relief hit Nona, not as a striking of bonds but as a constriction of her throat, a sob, the grief for Ara's and Clera's deaths escaping only now that they were saved. She forced herself to hands and knees, crawling clear of the others, taking the shipheart away before collapsing again. Clera stopped screaming and even Nona's devils were quiet in the moment of silence that followed.

All three of them lay sprawled in several inches of freezing water in the small square chamber from which Nona had departed Crucical's basement.

Clera patted weakly at the water, now running out into the corridor. "Sorry, probably my mess. I think I wet myself." She levered herself up. "What in all the hells was that? And where are we?"

Nona rolled over, groaning. "The emperor's palace." She pushed herself into a sitting position, her back to the wall, injured leg stretched out before her. Blood clouded the water around the knife hilt. "Ara?"

"Aren't I dead yet?" Ara didn't move a muscle, just lay on her front in the draining flood, her chest heaving.

"Sorry," Nona said, "no time for that. I have things for you to do." She tapped out the code that activated and deactivated the blade-wall outside. "You need to learn this." She tapped it out again. As her fear, exhaustion, and pain started to subside from the heights reached in the extremes of the escape Nona began to feel Ruli's distress again, echoing down their thread-bond.

"One question." Clera got to her feet, dripping. "Wouldn't it have been better to start your flood once we got to the ring?"

"Nearly cracked my skull trying it from the vault. I don't think I could have done it from the holothour cave. Too far." Nona drew in a breath, trying to undouble her vision. "Have you got the pattern?"

"Yes." From Clera.

"No." From Ara.

"Good enough. I have to go."

"Go?" Clera splashed towards the doorway, wanting more distance between her and the shipheart. "Go where?"

"Don't leave!" Nona added a layer of marjal coercion to the alarm in her voice. "Check the trap's not on first." She pulsed instructions to Ara along their bond. It was easier than talking.

"Got to . . . got to help Ruli . . ." Nona let out a sigh and dropped her chin to her chest. A moment later the thread-bond took her.

RULI'S SCREAMS WERE so loud that Nona couldn't imagine how they hadn't heard them in the corridor less than a hundred yards away. The agony was worse than anything Nona had endured that day and yet somehow she knew the girl hadn't said a word about what she'd seen in the book.

The pain slackened and as Ruli drew breath Nona heard Jula's sobs. The novice had been far less closemouthed than her friend. In between her tears she had been telling Sherzal everything she remembered from Aquinas's *Book of the Moon*. Which, given it was Jula, was pretty much everything that lay between the book's covers. Clearly Sherzal's guards were better educated than most because one of them was making extensive notes as Jula spilled her guts.

"Stop hurting her! You said you would!"

"I said I might. When you've told us everything."

Ruli unscrewed her eyes and brought Sherzal into hazy focus. The emperor's sister was pacing in front of Jula, who sat nearby against the wall. In addition to the note-taking guard two others flanked the girl.

"Shall we try that again?" A gentle voice close by Ruli's ear.

Ruli shivered and tried to turn away but strong fingers gripped her chin and steered her face towards Safira, crouched at her side. Behind Kettle's former lover stood Joeli Namsis, looking slightly sick.

Give me your body, Ruli.

Nona? Sweet Ancestor, I thought you'd abandoned me!

Give me your body.

I thought you'd never ask, dear. And with that Ruli fled to the sanctum Nona offered her, surrendering all control.

One of Ruli's arms had been bound to her side. The other was in Safira's grip, the hand flopping uselessly on a broken wrist. But the broken wrist wasn't the main source of Ruli's pain and it didn't stop what Safira was doing to her fingers from reaching her. Safira took another black needle and prepared to push it under one of the only two of Ruli's fingernails that didn't yet have one bedded beneath it. Nona supposed they must be coated with something like Red Asp venom. Just needles beneath the fingernails on their own surely couldn't account for the monstrous agony coursing through Ruli's hand?

"Ready?" Safira asked.

"You're right to think that Aquinas's book is the key." Nona struggled to keep her voice steady, hissing her words past Ruli's teeth.

"What?" Safira narrowed her eyes.

"The book was the key. But you never understood what it was the key to."

Safira studied Ruli's eyes, suspicious. "What are you saying?"

"Yes, child, do explain yourself." Sherzal loomed over them both, still smiling. Ruli's lack of screaming and pleading had drawn her interest. Even Jula's sobs had fallen silent.

"Wh . . . who do you think you're fighting here?" Nona forced a smile onto Ruli's lips. "The Scithrowl? Your brother? A handful of novices?"

The smallest frown rippled Sherzal's brow just above her nose. "Adoma. It's always been Adoma. At least since Shella Yammal passed to the Ancestor." Sherzal stepped closer to peer at Ruli's face. "I knew her of old, you know. Before this silliness of convents and abbesses."

Nona spat blood from Ruli's mouth and forced herself to look at her fingers. The pain was unreal but somehow with the shipheart burning through her nothing else could quite seem to feel more important. "If you had truly known Abbess Glass then you would have known death would not stop her."

Sherzal's eyes widened and she took an involuntary step back. Nona felt Ruli's surprise too, along with a sudden shock of betrayal. Nona hadn't told any of them the truth. Not all of it.

"When the abbess set us hunting for that book she wasn't after something that held the secrets of the moon . . . just something that you would want very badly. Abbess Glass always played the long game. I thought you knew that?" Nona spat again. "She wanted us to take something that would have you bring us here, past all the emperor's secrets and defences, right to the gates of the Ark. Why do you think we left it so late? There were years to take that book in. Why do you think we hid our plans so poorly? We couldn't make it *too* easy, though. Was it Joeli who found out what we were doing and told you?" Nona drew a breath and locked Ruli's eyes on Sherzal's. "Or Markus? Or both?" A pang ran through Nona at the unintended admission on Sherzal's face. The others had thought including Markus was a stupid move. That he would betray them all in a heartbeat. But they had trusted Nona's judgment in the end. And while Nona had chosen to include Markus so that there was yet another way Sherzal would know what they were after and want to take it from them . . . deep down Nona had believed Markus would be true, that the fellowship forged in the cage would endure . . .

"This is nonsense!" Sherzal pulled herself together. "The girl's just trying to buy time. Get on with it, Safira. And you!" She turned towards Jula. "Every detail, or I will cut this child's nose and ears from her face and drop them in your lap."

Safira leaned in with another needle.

"Sorry, Kettle," Nona muttered, and Safira paused, momentarily puzzled. Nona drew on the shipheart's power and as Safira came into line with the finger intended for her needle Nona drove out a single flaw-blade, twice as long as her usual ones. Safira froze, skewered. The blade entered beneath her chin and emerged from the back of her skull.

"Safira!" Sherzal stepped forward, impatient with the delay.

Safira twitched, then slumped. Nona vanished her blade and the woman fell, pinning Ruli and her injured arm to the floor.

Nona bit down on the pain and continued to address Sherzal as if nothing of consequence had happened. "You brought us here, under pressure, in haste, careless, and you showed us the way in, showed us each trick and trap and secret."

"Kill her!" Sherzal barked the words at Joeli and ran for the door by which they had entered.

"I wouldn't advise it, Joeli." Nona locked Ruli's eyes on the Namsis girl. "I'm waiting for you and there's no place I won't find you if you hurt another of my friends."

Sherzal halted by the door. "Show me the corridor."

What looked like a clear window opened in the middle of the door, but the view shifted as if the window were moving swiftly along the corridor outside.

"Stop!"

The image fixed upon three figures. Three dirty, wet, bloodstained figures advancing towards the door. Nona was in the lead and in her arms she held Ara's limp form, the girl's eyes glittering through slits. Clera walked ten paces behind Nona, nervous, glancing back along the brightly lit hall.

"You think the guards you have here will stop us?" Nona asked. It felt very strange to see herself walking towards them. Ara was controlling her flesh just as Nona was controlling Ruli's.

"What I think is that the blast doors outside can only be opened from in here," Sherzal said. "That's what I think."

"If you leave now you might still escape," Nona said. "You know ways out of this city, tunnels beneath the walls. You have money, contacts, followers. You could buy your way along the ice and come down somewhere where Scithrowl and Durn are half a dozen kingdoms away."

"There's no 'might' about it," Sherzal sneered. "I have sleds that would take me to Reemarla, so far west that Durn is just a rumour. But why should I run? I have everything I want here."

Out in the corridor Nona stopped, put Ara down awkwardly, and produced the Noi-Guin shipheart from inside her habit.

"Lano Tacsis is dead. The Noi-Guin Singular is dead. The Noi-Guin he took with him to Sweet Mercy Convent are dead. We have the shipheart." Nona said it with Ruli's mouth, but the smile was all her own.

"Those girls out there are barely able to walk. Clera is the only one of them who couldn't be knocked over by a strong breeze." Sherzal returned the smile. "And she's mine."

"Would you bet your life on it?" Nona asked. "Because I would bet mine that she isn't." With Ruli's good arm bound and the other arm trapped beneath Safira's cooling body Nona had little to use now but bluff, and she had never been a good liar. The only advantage she had was that she believed what she was saying.

"If I open the blast doors, why would you let me go? If Clera's on your side, what would stop her from killing me?"

"I swear by the Ancestor that we will make no move to stop you from leaving."

Sherzal snorted. "The Ancestor?"

"You have your button. Let Clera and the two nuns past. Show Jula how to raise the blast doors again. If any of them come anywhere near you or try to stay on your side of the doors . . . make your explosion and have your grand end," Nona said.

"And if the Scithrowl are already in the palace?" Sherzal demanded.

"Life is full of gambles," Nona said. "But my sisters are defending this place and they are not the kind to be overcome easily."

"It is important, when killing a nun, to ensure that you bring an army of sufficient size," Jula quoted, and offered a bloody grin from among Sherzal's guards.

"She's right," said Nona. "And I've seen how many Adoma brought, and frankly I don't think it's enough." Without the shipheart Nona held, Sherzal had nothing to bargain with when Adoma came. Nona and her friends could bottle her in the Ark and leave via the travel-ring as the battle-queen arrived.

The eyes Sherzal narrowed at Nona sparkled with fury. "This isn't over. You know that? It won't ever be over for any of you while I live." She took the short rod from her gown and wrapped a hand around it, thumb on the button. She folded her arms before her to shield the hand holding the rod. She raised her voice and started towards the exit. "Lower the blast doors." Turning back, she called to Joeli. "Come, girl." She waved to the guards with Jula. "Leave her."

"No." Nona said. "They all stay. Someone has to pay."

"Vindictive little novice, aren't you?" Sherzal allowed herself a smile. "At least we have that in common." She shrugged. "I've plenty of guards upstairs. And Joeli's never really had the stomach for all this, have you, girl? A pity. I thought you might have more of your father in you, but once it got to be more than a few convent games you went to pieces."

Joeli shook her head. "No! No! I can do it. Take me with you!"

Sherzal laughed and strode away. "Perhaps you can change my mind, thread-worker."

Nona saw Joeli's fingers twitching as she tried, but Sherzal had never seemed like someone who would be easily swayed . . . even if every article of her jewellery weren't worked with sigils to absorb destruction and to anchor her threads.

At the door Sherzal paused. "Abbess Glass really was a remarkable woman. I underestimated her too many times." She spoke loud enough for the room to hear but didn't look up from her hand upon the door. "But if it's the long game that impresses you, then don't start to relax. This isn't over."

She looked at the strange window to check where Nona, Ara, and Clera were, then opened the door. The thick blast door outside had retracted into the floor. Sherzal walked out, arms crossed before her, thumb on the hidden button that would detonate the explosives she'd installed in the Ark.

Nona, under Ara's control and carrying Ara, moved to one side of the corridor to allow Sherzal to pass by as far from the shipheart as she could get. Clera nodded to the emperor's sister as she went but said nothing.

As the three of them crossed over the blast door Nona returned to her own body, Ara slid back into hers, and Ruli returned to her own flesh with a series of whimpering gasps.

"Blast doors up!" Nona called, and behind her ten tons of iron slid smoothly into place.

The special window continued to show the corridor as if inserting a two-foot-thick wall of iron made no difference to the view. Nona hobbled in and watched as Sherzal turned their way. She jabbed at the button experimentally, happy to blow them all to the Ancestor now the door had risen between them.

"How frustrating for her." Nona narrowed her eyes at the woman. Even now her devils screamed for her to chase Sherzal down and hack her apart.

Beside Nona, Clera helped Ara to her feet. Ara, for her part, allowed Clera to aid her and didn't punch her in the throat, which wouldn't have been unreasonable given the fact that Clera had thrown a spear at her back less than an hour before.

"This isn't over," Ara said, joining Nona at the window.

"No," said Nona, watching as Sherzal stopped at the blade-trap.

The emperor's sister tossed a coin out to check that it hadn't been reactivated. The coin hit the floor in four silver strips. She shot a foul look back at the blast door and pushed the button uselessly.

"You should go out there and kill her." The guards had cut Jula free and she had crossed to help Ruli who was struggling to roll Safira's corpse off her.

"If we open the blast doors she can blow the explosives," Nona said, not looking away.

Sherzal tapped out the sequence to deactivate the blade-trap. Ever cautious, she tossed in a second coin. It hit the ground with a chime and rolled to a halt. Satisfied, she hurried through, picking up speed, anxious to reach her guards and flee before the Scithrowl broke in.

She was clear of the blade-trap when suddenly she jolted, slowed, then carried on at a reduced pace. The jolt would have been the first wire breaking. Invisibly thin, it would have cut to the bone before Sherzal's momentum broke it. The slowing was the result of the multiple wires behind the first biting into her. By this point the pain would have registered. The blood appeared as thin red lines first, blotting the sliced edges of her gown. As she staggered, large folds of flesh and muscle began to flay away from the bone. The top half of her face did something similar, the detail thankfully hidden behind a rising crimson mist. The emperor's sister managed five more steps before falling in a gory ruin. The sound of her screaming didn't reach into the Ark.

Beside Nona, Ara and Clera looked ready to vomit.

Nona nodded slowly. "Now it's over."

26

---✦---

HOLY CLASS

"I'LL BRING IN the wires." Ara looked as if she would rather do anything else, even if she weren't battling just to keep standing. But the first and last thing that Sister Apple had taught them about setting wires was that you cleared up afterwards.

Who had actually set the trap for Sherzal was open to debate. Nona had used her thread-bond with Ara to ask her to do it. Ara, too weak to set the wires, had used that same bond to inhabit Nona's body while Nona in turn inhabited Ruli and spoke with Sherzal behind the blast doors. The bloody lengths of Ark-steel would be returned to the wire kit that Kettle had given Nona along with the poisons and cures carried by every Grey Sister.

Even so, it was Ara's task to pull the wires from Sherzal's gory remains.

"Go with her, Clera." Nona nodded and motioned the two of them back into the corridor. Ara would need support.

When the way was clear Nona would let Sherzal's guards go. Joeli would stay here. Jula had tied the girl with Safira's cords. Joeli might be good with threads but Jula tied better knots.

"The book was a lie?" Ruli came closer, cradling her injured arm as if it were made of eggshell. Jula hovered around her, trying to help. "I went through all that for nothing?" Now that Nona had set the Noi-Guin ship-heart against the far wall with the Sweet Mercy shipheart, both novices could approach her.

"Maybe not a lie," Nona said. "Perhaps just misguided and unnecessary. What was important was that you believed its value. That's what got us in here and what kept you both alive. It was always Abbess Glass's intention that the book would be the key that got us to the door of the Ark. I don't imagine she knew it would be with the Scithrowl fighting in Verity's streets."

"So how do we control the moon, if we could even get in there? Which we can't," Jula asked. "Aquinas's instructions are very complex . . . If they're wrong, then I don't know what to do."

"Well. The first thing to do is to open the door, no?" Nona tried to shut out the voices of her devils as they raged against Jula's stupidity. If the girl came any closer Nona might just reach out in an unguarded moment and end her. She leaned back against the wall. "Before that, though . . . I need this fucking knife out of my leg!"

Jula flinched as Nona's voice rose to a shout, or perhaps at the cursing, or both. Even so she came forward, already unbinding her habit cord to use as a torniquet. Nona put her head to the wall and ground her teeth while Jula set to work.

"How can we open the Ark?" Ruli asked. She had a right to ask. She had had envenomed needles driven under her fingernails.

"I—" Nona roared as Jula drew the cross-knife from the back of her thigh and tightened her habit tie above the lacerated muscle.

"Nona!" Clera came back in, trailed by Ara, pale-faced and bloody-handed. "Are you . . ."

Jula stood up, tossing the little knife to the floor. "She'll live."

Nona turned her black-eyed stare on Sherzal's guards. "Out!" She snarled the word through gritted teeth. "Join the defence if you want to survive the night."

Clera spotted Joeli, sitting bound on the floor. "I know her. One of Sherzal's creatures."

Nona bit back the accusation that Clera was nothing more than that herself, and tried to drive the devils from her tongue.

"We should get the truth out of her," Clera said, ignoring Jula's and Ruli's staring. "Sherzal didn't have all her eggs in one basket. She was only going to share with Adoma as a last resort. She was after more shiphearts of her own. I know that much. She had an agent among the ice-tribes and she'd set her hunting down Old Stones. You really don't want to know who I heard it was . . . But rich girl here, she knows for sure."

"Nona!" A call from Ara at the doorway.

Out in the corridor a fierce light had overwhelmed the ambient illumination. It glared from the doorway of the chamber that held the travel ring. The blaze made harsh silhouettes of the guardsmen now frozen a few yards from it. A deep throbbing buzz trembled through the ground.

Nona drew her sword. Ara struggled to draw her own. Clera's blade cleared her scabbard with a hiss.

A crack rang out, like the world ending, and the light died. At first Nona could see nothing. Afterimages filled the corridor, swimming across each other. As they faded and the dark shapes of Sherzal's men reasserted themselves Nona saw that a new figure stood there ahead of them, and in her hands burned two balls of light, one a virulent green, the other the red of iron just starting to glow.

"Yisht!" A scream from Joeli behind them.

"Oh hells . . ." Clera's blade wavered, the point dropping.

Nona blinked away the remaining traces of her blindness, and there, alone in the corridor now as the guardsmen ran off in terror, stood the ice-triber, so thickly patterned in devils that no patch of unstained skin showed.

I can't die. Yisht's last words and Raymel Tacsis's too. Perhaps if the black ice taught any lesson it was that evil never truly dies . . .

"Nona?" Yisht's smile twisted. A moment later the rest of her rippled and in her place stood Zole, her face tight with strain.

"Zole?" Ara gasped. "You're dead!"

"She's playing games with our minds!" Clera backed a few paces.

"With two shiphearts in my hands I could make you see anyone I wanted to," the figure said. "But I am Zole."

"She's lying," Ara said. "Zole died."

"No," Nona said. "It's Zole."

And as she said it Tarkax Ice-Spear stepped out into the corridor, ten yards behind his niece and wincing as if he stood too close to the heat of a fire. Zole continued her advance and others of Tarkax's tribe emerged, pushing at his shoulders.

Sherzal's guards ran towards the stairs and the battle above. As Zole drew closer Ara and the novices backed into the chamber. Even Nona couldn't endure the combined pressure of both shiphearts.

"How is she here?"

"You knew? You lied to us?"

Nona shook her head. "I promised Abbess Glass. Zole did too."

When Nona had returned alone with the shipheart she had reported to Abbess Glass immediately. On the abbess's instructions she had let them all believe Zole to be dead and had made no mention of Yisht. Somehow the absence of any mourning among the novices had deepened Nona's affection for Zole. The girl walked a lonely path and she walked it without complaint or compromise.

Nona hadn't heard from Zole again for nearly two years and when she did it was to discover that they were thread-bound. Somehow during their long escape from the black ice, when Zole carried her half-senseless from that freezing hell, the ice-triber had forged the bond between them.

At Abbess Glass's suggestion Zole had set herself the task of bringing to the empire both of the shiphearts controlled by her tribe. At the same time, and seemingly at her own behest, Zole had set to convincing the emperor's sister that Yisht still lived and was attempting exactly the same thing—to bring Sherzal the two shiphearts she needed. All those years ago Abbess Glass had seen the pieces before her and set them in motion. Tarkax Ice-Spear's ambition to protect the tribes by keeping the Corridor open was just one more factor to wrap into the long game. Quite how she knew where the cascade of cause and event would lead, Nona had no idea, but the abbess had always made it her business to know things. Nona had seen the results; the application of knowledge could unlock doors that her flaw-blades couldn't so much as scratch, and it could bring down those so mighty that no feat of arms would stay their hand.

Zole had waited on the ice, ready with the Old Stones. Nona had told her that it was safe to come, and here she was, with the other half of the key to the Ark.

ZOLE STOOD WITHIN the chamber where Sherzal had tortured Ruli. She held the two shiphearts from her tribe, one like iron red from the forge, the other a poison green. The Noi-Guin shipheart and the Sweet Mercy shipheart lay against the far wall, one a black-violet that seared the eye, the other golden. She had grown from the girl who sent Nona back from the heart of the black ice. She stood before them a woman of the ice, hard, uncompromising, perfect. Zole watched Nona and the others as if from some distant place, no hint of recognition in them, no warmth, just a focused efficiency.

"Can you do it?" Nona asked. Of all of them only Nona could stand within spear's reach of Zole and meet the awful light in her eyes. "Can you take all four and open the Ark?"

"It will be hard."

Nona wondered if she stood alone in seeing the hints that remained of that younger Zole. She had been hard and seemingly without emotion even then, but Nona remembered that Zole had named her friend and come to the Tetragode to save her. She remembered the shy edge of Zole's tiny smile when she made one of her rare jokes, so dry that it might pass by entirely unnoticed.

"Hard?" As always when Zole called a thing hard it meant that it was essentially impossible . . . a suicidal act.

"Very hard." Zole's eyes held something as close to fear as Nona had ever seen.

"Try." Nona reached out for the wall and sagged against it. "The Sci-throwl are coming. I need to help . . ."

Nona didn't feel herself fall but she hammered into Kettle as if she had dropped from a great height.

27

───────◆───────

HOLY CLASS

KETTLE LAY SPRAWLED, stunned by a blow from one of the small
shields that many of the Scithrowl in this wave seemed to favour.
The man who had stuck her down now leapt over her into the space
created. Another Scithrowl followed, this one a squat woman, her skin a
peculiar purple-red that Kettle had never seen before. She carried a short
spear with a long serrated blade that looked to have been used to finish off
a fair number of wounded enemies. Without pause she thrust it down at
Kettle's chest. Kettle lacked the strength to do anything but throw up an
empty, helpless hand.

"No." Nona's word on Kettle's lips.

Lying in the same chamber as four shiphearts made Nona feel like a
candle burning not just at both ends but along the whole of its length.
Their power filled her even as it tore her apart. Quick as thought, she drove
a sheet of flaw-blade from Kettle's palm, cutting the Scithrowl woman in
half.

Get up.

Kettle struggled to her feet. Her speed had left her. Exhaustion dragged her down more than the minor wounds that stuck her habit to her in bloody patches. Several blows fell on the flaw-armour Nona moved around Kettle as she rose.

Let me in.

"They're all dead, Nona." Kettle waved her arm and Nona filled the air with a moving storm of flaw-fragments. The Scithrowl in front of her fell in pieces. Behind them the length of King's Road lay tight-packed with their kin, stretching all the way back to the breach in the walls and the ocean of Adoma's horde pressing in.

Over a hundred yards back but now within the circle of the city walls scores of Scithrowl bore a stepped platform on their shoulders, rising yards above the sea of heads. On the lowest step a dozen archers in black chain mail loosed arrow after arrow from their eagle-bows, sending them soaring over the spear tips of their army towards the palace walls or up at bowmen on Verity's rooftops. On the next step four wind-workers plied their arts to shield the archers from incoming missiles, but Nona imagined they focused their efforts primarily on the third and highest step where a figure sat in crimson armour upon a throne of gold. Adoma, the battle-queen herself, entering the city and driving her followers into a frenzy. The woman commanded the eye, her skin like a hole in the night. It was said she had melted the black ice and drank the waters to gain her powers. Even at this distance Nona could feel the malice bleeding from her.

Let me help, Kettle! Where's Apple?

"I don't know." Kettle stepped back and with an elbow to the back of the neck felled the man who had so recently struck her down. "I don't know!" Her voice broke as she retreated among the emperor's guards fighting in front of the palace walls. Images flashed before Nona's eyes. She saw Leeni fall with a spear driven through her chest. Alata had died fighting above her corpse. She saw Sister Tallow and Sister Iron fighting back to back, with the Scithrowl clambering over the circular wall of dead ringing the pair. She saw Sister Tallow with her sword deep in the body of the biggest gerant Nona had ever seen. Somehow the old woman had pierced the man's armour but where the Ark-steel blade she had given to Nona might have sliced free, her Barrons-steel remained caught. When the Scithrowl cut her down Tallow looked surprised. Not scared or proud or at peace or defeated . . . just surprised.

Kettle's memories assaulted Nona. She saw Ketti, broken by an axe. Tall, quick Ketti. Always talking about boys. Now she would never find one to hold. Nona blinked the vision away, blinked away the deaths of other novices, of nuns she had known most of her life.

"No." So much marjal empathy rang in Nona's voice that even those in the front line paused to listen, weapons stuttering midswing.

Abbess Wheel stood nearby, her right arm in a makeshift sling, bandages across her forehead. A pitifully small band of convent survivors stood tight around her.

"No!" Nona stepped back towards the battle-line. Men and women of the palace guard jerked out of her path as if seized by invisible hands. The Scithrowl howling for blood just yards ahead of her fell silent although she was only Kettle, wounded, unarmoured, unremarkable.

As Nona raised Kettle's arms, an arrow hammered out of the fire-broken night. It shattered inches from her shoulder. Another glanced away. She brought her hands together over her head, struggling against some opposing force. Stone blocks and roof slates tore free from the buildings to either side of the King's Road, flinging themselves into the army packed across its width. Walls groaned and collapsed in rolling clouds of dust.

"The moon is falling." Nona's voice shuddered through men's bodies as if Abeth itself had spoken, and terror followed. "The. Moon. Is. Falling."

She swung an arm at the backs of Scithrowl trying to retreat over those still advancing on the palace. Spinning fragments of flaw-blade sliced through armour, flesh, bone. Even the paving slabs beneath the enemy's feet were cut into pieces.

Nona led the charge, slipping and sliding in a street that had become a charnel house. The gerant captain who had sought to block her passage into the palace as night fell now joined her counterattack.

They couldn't win. Perhaps a dozen Nonas might turn the tide, but even as the Scithrowl died in heaps their dead were trampled by fresh warriors eager to bleed for their queen. And all along the road the Scithrowl were starting to spread out, clambering over rubble, seeking ways to encircle the palace, ways to come at it from all angles while Nona could defend only one.

Nona let the empire soldiers advance around her. She saw little Ghena hurry past, a bloody spear gripped in both hands, looking both fierce and exhausted at the same time.

For a moment Kettle's weakness overwhelmed her and Nona found no strength of her own to replace it. So much death and hurt lay before her. So much blood that the storm drains would soon overflow. Murder, murder, and more murder. What else could they expect when the ice kept closing? All of mankind reduced to wild animals in an ever-shrinking cage.

"The moon is coming." Nona used Kettle's mouth to speak words for Kettle's benefit. "Be ready to get out of its way."

28

HOLY CLASS

NONA JERKED HER head up. Only she and Zole remained in the chamber. Nona lay slumped against the wall. The others stayed outside, watching from the passage.

Zole could be seen only indistinctly, a dark figure orbited by four balls of light, four shiphearts, one attuned to each of the tribes that had come to Abeth in the long ago, plunging from the darkness amid a galaxy of dying stars. They had come seeking the warmth of a sun that burned hotter than those they left behind. Whether it was desperation or miscalculation that had beached them on Abeth's shores the stories could never agree upon. Perhaps they could travel no farther, but they had found a world already abandoned by those who had settled it. Scant millennia passed before the continued retreat of Abeth's star from the red fury of its expansion began to see Abeth freeze. The world started its return to the ice-bound sphere it had always been before the sun's death throes briefly thawed it.

Zole had said the Old Stones were things of the Missing, just as the Arks were. The Church taught that they were shiphearts, the vital force that had driven the vessels that brought the four tribes across the blackness of infinity to Abeth, and that the Arks were the work of Nona's ancestors too. Perhaps that story was simple pride, though, claiming some wonder for the Ancestor rather than having all of humanity's tribes be painted as savages living within the ruins of a greater race. Now as Zole advanced towards the great round door at the chamber's centre Nona could easily imagine her a creature very different from any that walked the Corridor.

Zole reached the vault door, light and shadow in constant motion around her as the shiphearts continued on their slow trajectories. Nona had thought that the door would fight her, that the earth would shake around them, that the ceiling would crack and the dust sift down. Instead the huge circular slab of silver-steel rose without noise or drama until it stood vertical, revealing a flight of stairs. Zole raised her arms and the shiphearts shot outwards to the four points of the compass, embedding themselves in the walls about halfway between floor and ceiling. Nona couldn't tell if there had already been structures to receive them or if they had made their own holes.

"How do you feel?" She limped across to Zole, who looked like a statue. Now that she could approach her Nona realised how tall her friend had grown. She lacked the thick muscle of a gerant but she had the height, making Nona feel like a child beside her and dwarfing the others. Zole's skin had turned greyish, as if the shiphearts' power had burned her to fine ash, awaiting just the lightest touch to fall apart. Nona wouldn't have been surprised to find on closer inspection that Zole's flesh was polished to a high shine or just gently smoking. "Are you . . . Are you . . . still you?"

Zole's eyes had turned a steel grey and Nona tried to see something of her friend within them. "I am shriven."

"I . . ." Nona reached along their thread-bond but found nothing. "Zole . . ." Her heart hurt. She wished in that moment she had known the woman who stood in front of her before she had ever touched an Old Stone, before the imperfection was burned from her. She would have held her friend but the devils in her own flesh refused to move any closer.

"Hurry up!" Clera arrived at Nona's shoulder, with Ara and Ruli coming along behind. Tarkax and Jula had hold of Joeli and were bringing her too. The rest of the ice-tribers remained to guard the corridor. "Quickly!"

Clera's urgency was born of the desire to get farther from the shiphearts but it re-ignited Nona's own. Outside her sisters were still dying.

"Lights on," Nona ordered, and the dark steps beneath the door were illuminated just as the corridors outside had been when Sherzal demanded light. She led the way down, cursing each time her damaged leg had to take her weight.

THE ARK PROVED completely different from anything Nona had anticipated, and her imagination had painted dozens of possible scenes. The stairs led down some fifty feet to a small circular chamber, a room, dirty and bare of anything save a single curving chair of some unfamiliar material, lying on its side near the wall.

"Aquinas said there would be levers, a machine . . . He saw them in a holy vision!" Ruli pushed in past Nona. "I kept that bastard's lies secret when that bitch was wedging needles under my fingernails!"

Jula stumbled in with Joeli. It was getting crowded. "There are supposed to be four dials, each within the other . . ."

"There's nothing here." Even Joeli sounded disappointed.

"How would you have worked such an engine, even if it hadn't been stolen centuries ago?" Clera spat on the ground and sent the chair skittering across the floor with a kick. The years had turned it brittle and it shattered against the far wall.

Nona frowned, staring furiously at the broken pieces. "Aquinas's book was the key to get us in. A lie. I never expected it to help once we were inside. Though it would have been nice if it had." She looked slowly around the chamber, hunting any clue. "The abbess told me that the goal of any design is simplicity." She spoke the words haltingly, gathering certainty as fragments of the day's events came together. "What makes our most complex devices hard to use is that we lack the understanding to make them easy to use."

All of them watched her.

"Lights off." The room plunged into darkness. "Lights on." The illumination returned, soft, pervasive, casting no shadows and having no source. "When Sherzal closed the blast door . . . she just asked for it to close. Why would you think that the builders of an Ark where that happened would require levers and dials to command the moon? Sherzal's first instinct was right. The abbess just made her doubt herself, made her think she needed a book full of secret knowledge."

"Show us the Corridor," Zole said. She spoke it to the air.

Instantly a ring of light appeared before them, hanging in the air, crowded with tiny features in shades of green and brown, fringed with white. A shadow divided it into night and day.

"Show me the moon's focus."

A wide red circle appeared, wider than the Corridor, maybe half as wide again. A much broader pinkish region extended around it within an elongated ellipsis.

"Show us where we are," Nona said.

The ring turned and grew steadily larger, the bulk of it fading from view as a closer and closer look filled the space before them.

"The Grampains," Jula whispered, "and the Marn Sea."

"Closer!" Nona said. And in moments she saw forests and rivers spread before her as if Sister Rule's precious maps had joined hands and unfolded themselves for inspection. All washed with a faint pinkish tinge.

"Closer!"

They saw Verity, the Rock of Faith, and the farmlands all around. Tiny fires twinkled. Smoke streaks followed the wind.

"Closer!"

They saw the city walls, the streets, individual rooftops, the flicker of flames, the dark mass of Adoma's army, the palace itself.

"What does the pink mean?" Jula asked.

"There is sufficient angle and resource to centre the focus at any point within the pink zone."

All of them save Zole jumped at the unexpected voice. Like the light, the voice seemed to have no source, and like the light there was nothing about it that was natural. Clera glanced around nervously. "Who are you? Show yourself!"

"I am Taproot."

Jula's eyes went wide and she made the sign of the arborat, a single finger rising to trace the taproot that began with the first ancestor, then all fingers spreading to show the branches of the Ancestor's tree. Ruli and Ara exchanged shocked glances.

"Are you—"

Nona cut across Clera's question. Outside the palace the last of their friends were dying. "How small can that focus be made?" Nona asked.

A red dot appeared at the centre of the image of the palace. It looked to be about ten yards across.

"Can you make the focus here?" Nona reached out to touch the spot in front of the palace where the King's Road opened onto the plaza. "And have it follow between my finger and thumb?"

"Yes. It would consume one third of one percent of the remaining propellant to institute and later correct the major attitude changes."

"What would that do?" asked Clera, leaning in. The image's light patterned fascination on her face.

"I think it would burn through the ground and melt the rocks themselves," Nona said.

"Adoma has a hundred thousand Scithrowl out there." Jula peered at the image. Individuals at the edge of the horde appeared like motes of dust. "Could you kill so many with a touch?"

"In a heartbeat!" Clera swept her hand along the King's Road, finger and thumb set to its width, widening the span as she reached beyond the wall to encompass the whole mass of the invaders. "Wait! Nothing happened!"

"Focus is already at authorized minimum. Narrower focus is deemed hazardous to flora and fauna."

Nona thought she understood. The focus had narrowed as the Corridor narrowed, increasing intensity as the cold intensified. But it had reached the maximum safe intensity years ago and the ice kept coming. Any narrower and the focus would scorch the crops, blind the animals.

"How can we authorize it to narrow further?" Nona asked. *Could you do it?* Jula's question repeated itself over and again in the back of her mind, though her devils all but drowned it out with their shout for blood and fire. *Could you do it?*

"Only the Purified has clearance."

"The Purified?" But Nona knew the answer before the words left her. The silent stranger in their midst, burned clean of humanity by the combined fire of four shiphearts. Had the shiphearts themselves ever been needed, or just someone stripped of all flaws by them? Was Zole more than human now, or less than human? And this voice that claimed to be Taproot, was that human? An ancestor who travelled to Abeth on the ships that sailed between the stars, or one of the Missing who had left before they even arrived?

"Will you do it, Zole?"

Zole stood statue-still, only her head turning to meet Nona's gaze. "Do you ask it of me?"

Even with her friends dying outside Nona didn't want to ask to have that power in her hands. The devils in her screamed *yes*, but somehow their voices failed to dominate her. In a battle, in a fight, to take the lives of those raising their weapons against her had always seemed her right. Though even that certainty had weakened as her skills and powers grew, making the contest more and more uneven. Now, in this place, she could take the lives of more people than she could properly imagine, even with their image floating before her. She could do it in a heartbeat, with no effort or risk. Do it without them ever seeing her face or knowing the blow was coming . . .

"Would you do it if I asked?" Nona asked.

Zole reached out to the light before she answered, letting the images of Verity flow across her grey hand. "I feel . . . different, Nona." She spoke as if the two of them were entirely alone. "As if I were falling away."

"Falling away from what?" Despite the death unfolding in miniature all across Zole's palm, it was the faint sadness in Zole's voice that made Nona's eyes prickle and fill with tears.

"From everything. I see a wider existence. As though all of Abeth were just like your Corridor, a slice through something bigger."

"Would *you* do it, Zole?" Nona spoke above the hunger of her devils even as she felt them rising, reaching up across her neck. "How many would you kill to save how few?"

"Nona!" Ara grabbed her shoulder. "The empire is *burning!*"

"There is no empire!" Nona replied. For a moment she managed to block out her devils and speak with the voice of the Nona who had been left behind when they were broken from her. "Scithrowl meets Durn now. The battles are all but over!" She shook her head. "Aren't all of us brother and sister? Should I murder them for the sake of pride, or should I accept that the ice has narrowed and that there is a new order now?"

"Look!" Clera pointed at Nona's neck. "She's like Yisht!"

Jula and Joeli stared at her in horror. Even if they hadn't known Yisht's story, a convent education breeds a terror of possession.

"It's true." Nona turned to face them. "I can't make a decision like this. Half of me wants to burn a path a mile wide right through every Scithrowl city . . . The louder half says that we should burn it all . . . I am unfit to judge. Sister Thorn should do this if Zole will allow her." She stepped aside to let Ara speak with Zole, and found her missing. "Ara?"

"Here." Ara was behind the others. She had slid down the wall to sit at its base, blood on her lips, her face almost as grey as Zole's. She looked unsurprised by news of Nona's devils, but then she had already inhabited the tainted flesh in question herself.

"I can take the *raulathu* from you." Zole stepped forward, her hand raised towards Nona's neck.

"What?" Clera demanded. She looked from Nona to Zole as if ready to fight them both or run. "What the hell is she talking about?"

"She means the devils," Nona said. "My devils."

"The Old Stones break them from us. As a sculptor chips away ice to reveal their creation." Zole reached for Nona.

Nona stepped back, pressing against Ruli. "No."

"No?" Zole cocked her head, curious.

"They're *devils*, Nona!" Jula sounded on the edge of hysteria.

"They're me," Nona said. "Pieces of who I am."

"Terrible pieces," Ruli said. "I felt them through the thread-bond but didn't understand." She fell quiet, confusion on her face.

"If you divide the ingredients of the black cure into two halves, both make a poison that will kill you. Together they are something different." Nona set her fingers to the rough skin along the side of her neck, finding it hot to the touch. "Can you put them back, Zole?"

"I can draw them out and give them to the fire."

"But can you put them back as they were?"

"It would make you less pure, further from the Ancestor." Zole watched her without judgment.

"Even so." Nona leaned her head to expose her neck to Zole. "You've burned away all your sins and weaknesses, and it's left you so distant from us you hardly care who lives and who dies. I can't make a decision like this with my head full of broken pieces, but I can't make it with those pieces gone either." She met Zole's grey eyes. "Please."

Zole set her palm to the first of Nona's devils. The feeling as it fell apart and unwound beneath her touch, beneath Nona's skin, was something both bitter and sweet. Something lost and something gained.

Zole found the second and third of Nona's devils without needing to look for them, even though they fled from sight. In moments Nona's anger, her thirst for revenge, and her capacity for hate were no longer screaming at her from separate sources but woven back into the fabric of who she was, the good with the bad.

Nona took a deep breath and addressed the air. "Won't the focus burn up the whole city as it narrows, or have to burn a path in from outside?"

"*The moon's albedo can be rapidly varied between zero and one.*"

"What?"

"*The moon will go dark until it is pointed and focused.*"

"You can turn the moon on and off at my request?"

"*Yes.*"

Nona stood for a moment in blank amazement before finding her voice again. "Zole, tell this thing to obey me." She approached the image. The counterattack had faltered and the remaining defenders were pressed against the walls. At points around the palace the Scithrowl were unopposed, deploying ladders and scaling chains against the battlements where the guards fought to throw them back.

"Why would I put such a power in the hands of one who has yet to be shriven of a single *raulathu*? You are unformed clay, Nona Grey."

"At least I care. At least it will hurt me, whatever decision I make. At least I'm terrified!" Nona defocused her eyes to see the thread-scape. She had learned to look far deeper than when she had tried that first day in Path Tower and declared that Zole had no threads. Sister Pan had been right to correct her. Everything had threads. Even now the water that comprised the bulk of Zole's body had countless threads joining it to the world. But the threads that really mattered, the brightest ones that Nona had been unable to see on her first attempt, the threads that both described Zole and

bound her to the people around her . . . those threads were more completely absent than they had ever been.

"In the end none of this will matter, Nona Grey." Zole spread her hands.
"Who will know our names in a hundred years? Who built the forest of
stone upon the doorstep of Sweet Mercy? Change runs through everything. Perfection is the only constant."

"It matters to me. *Now.*" Nona took Zole's cool grey hands in her own,
filthy with mud and blood. "You're leaving us. I know that. I don't know
where you're going. To join the Missing maybe. But you're going. And it
doesn't matter. What matters is that you're my friend, Zole. I would die for
you. The least you can do is give me the moon."

Nona wasn't sure if she imagined the brief and tiny curl of Zole's lips,
but if the smile was imagined the order was not.

"Let Nona guide the moon."

29

HOLY CLASS

THE SOUND OF a battle can be described as a roar, and sometimes it truly is. When a thousand warriors charge, a roar precedes them and swallows up all other noise. But in between charge and counter-charge there is the screaming of those too wounded to hold their peace and not yet close enough to crossing the Path that they fall silent. There is the clash of weapons, most often on shields, for tight-packed conflict is an ugly, graceless thing and there are few parries made. There are the desperate cries for aid and there is the sobbing of the lost.

Kettle heard all these things. She saw a forest of legs and bodies rising around her, and at her back the palace wall. She saw the black sky above. Here and there crimson stars shone through the wind-torn smoke. Of the Hope there was no sign.

She didn't hurt so much as ache, her pain a dull throb beneath the blanket of exhaustion that smothered her. She wouldn't think of Apple. Instead she left those raw voids in her mind untouched, her thoughts skittering around them. The Scithrowl sounded very close. She would not have to avoid thinking of Apple for too long.

+   +   +

I<small>T DID NOT</small> seem that anything short of the Ancestor in person, stepping out of thin air and clad in glory, could silence a pitched battle. But when, without warning, the focus moon lit around them, all the many thousands locked in combat paused in astonishment.

The focus, not due for hours yet, had not crept upon them, rising smoothly to its blazing climax. One moment it had been dark, the next they were plunged into the fierce heat of the moon. Every flame looked pale now—all the city's fires, the torches and battle-lanterns amid the throng, the flame-serpents coiling around Adoma's throne platform, all flickering ghosts of themselves. Those closest to death knew with certainty that they were now looking across the Path.

In that following moment, when one soldier might think to take advantage of his enemy's distraction, a second wonder happened. In the space of three heartbeats the moon dimmed to a dull crimson disc on which the eye could rest. And every eye rested there. This was a wonder past the skill of any mage.

Kettle raised her head, an action she had thought beyond her. She pushed with her legs, sliding her back against the emperor's walls, rising from the dead and wounded heaped about her, and struggled up, drawn by a communal intake of breath all around her. Across the face of the moon something was being written as if by a dark finger. Two words in black on red. Written in the Scithrowl tongue.

Go home.

A muttering spread across the length of the King's Road and out to the fields beyond. The literate among Adoma's horde sharing the meaning.

Far back among her forces Adoma rose from her throne, a distant figure gleaming crimson. The battle-queen's words reached Kettle as if she were standing at her side, reverberating across the intervening yards through the art of the wind-workers ringing her seat. Few among the

332 • MARK LAWRENCE

emperor's forces understood her words but the tone left no doubt that her message was one of defiance.

"The Scithrowl do not run from lights and tricks! This is our home now. Before me lies my palace." Power lay behind those words. Hers was a voice to stir a heart to violence, to wake pride in any chest. The army around her had claimed hundreds of Corridor miles in the battle-queen's name. They wouldn't run. Not beneath her gaze and with victory just a spear's throw ahead of them. The Scithrowl warriors began to raise their weapons and find their voice.

The rising cheer faltered as the moon went wholly dark, leaving twice a hundred thousand eyes night-blind. Kettle cursed herself for letting her training slip and allowing herself to lose an edge. Apple would scold—

The moon lit again, though not to full focus. A brilliant light fell around Adoma's throne, filling half the width of the road. The intensity rose from dazzling to blinding so swiftly that there was almost not enough time to look away. A moment later the searing circle of light had gone, replaced by a general illumination bringing the day to Verity's night.

Kettle blinked away afterimages and tried to see what had happened. She heard the screaming before she saw the source. All around the fringes of the area where the brilliance had risen, Scithrowl were burning. The screams came from farther back where warriors rolled around the pain of their scalded flesh but were not actually on fire. In the place where Adoma's platform had been borne on the shoulders of a hundred men there was nothing. Just a black circle twenty yards across. No trace of the platform, of the throne, of the people upon it or beneath it. Even their smoke seemed to have been burned from the air.

The moon dimmed and the words returned.

Go home.

And everywhere the Scithrowl started to run.

✦ ✦ ✦

IN THE ARK chamber silence reigned. Nona had controlled the moon by voicing her desires and using her fingers to place and size the focus on the image before them. She had watched the results through Kettle's eyes. It seemed wrong to see the death of a queen and so many of her subjects as a flash of light that could be covered by a fist and have the ant-sized survivors run noiselessly from the fringes of the blackened circle left behind.

"You should have killed them all," Clera said. "While they were in one place. They'll scatter now. You can't use the moon to hunt down thousands of small bands roaming the countryside."

Nona stepped back from the image and looked around at her friends. Ruli still hugging her injured hand. Jula red-eyed, forehead furrowed with concentration. Ara slumped, breath labouring but watching even so. Joeli stood amazed, as if she had forgotten where she was or that she was bound, a traitor to the emperor whose palace they stood beneath. Tarkax watched Nona, his dark eyes unreadable. And Zole . . . Zole stood tall, apart from them all though she was within arms' reach, her head cocked as if she were listening to music that no one else could hear.

"Why didn't you kill them all?" Jula asked.

Nona frowned. "I had thought Abbess Glass made me promise to take the Black and become a Holy Sister because she knew it would change Wheel's mind about me. That was part of it. But the abbess rarely did something with only one goal or said anything with just one meaning." Nona looked down at her habit, sticky with blood. "At Sweet Mercy they made a weapon of me. They honed every skill into a sharp edge. They put a sword in my hand, because there will always be foes who must be opposed, always violence that must be met with violence.

"But that was never the heart of Sweet Mercy. The shipheart wasn't the foundation of the convent. It was always the faith. Always the notion that all men and women are our brothers and our sisters. And that faith doesn't end with borders. It doesn't care about heresies used to divide us, or whether you speak your prayers to a white star, or to the fields and forests and stones.

"Abbess Glass spoke to me on the day she died. She told me that when she lost her child, at first she took every novice at Sweet Mercy as her own, to fill that hole, the emptiness only a mother can know. But the Ancestor taught her not to be so narrow. She came to understand that the children before her, those she could see, those the Church gave into her hands, were no more or less important than any other. She saw that all of us are children, no matter how many years we might have walked through.

"She taught this to us every day. Even Sister Wheel taught it to us despite herself, if you listened hard enough. It's written in the Book of the Ancestor and no matter who speaks the words or how they try to twist them . . . the truth is there.

"Abbess Glass wanted me to take the Black because she wanted the moon to be wielded by a Holy Sister. Not as a weapon but as a tool. As the healer might use the knife, sometimes to cut, but ultimately to heal."

Clera looked astonished. "But they'll just come back. The ice is closing. There's not enough room or food. Someone has to die. Lots of someones. Sister Rule taught us that in our first year at convent. The point is that it not be *us* who dies!"

Nona looked around the room once more. The others were looking at her as if she were some new creature standing in a friend's shoes.

"Maybe Sister Rule will have to learn a new lesson to teach."

THEY LEFT THE chamber at Nona's insistence. Tarkax carried Ara up the steps since she lacked the strength for the climb, and Nona hobbled up behind half-wishing that she had someone to carry her. More than half-wishing it.

In the circular chamber above, bathed equally in the auras of the four shiphearts spaced around the walls, Zole employed her marjal healing. It had always been one of her least developed skills, but with the power of four

Old Stones buzzing through her she worked swiftly and well. Ara's lung repaired itself and her flesh knitted together. Nona's thigh and shoulder wounds sealed, the muscles rejoining beneath. Ruli's wrist grew straight, the toxins beneath her nails neutralized.

"What are we going to do with Joeli?" Ruli grabbed the bound girl with her newly healed hand.

"She killed Darla," Clera said. "Doesn't she deserve to die?"

"I didn't!" Joeli protested, her pretty face ugly with fear. "I wanted her to run!"

"That's a lie!" Ara roared, suddenly furious.

"But . . . I took Sister Apple's truth pill!"

Ara shook her head violently. "Your father paid to have your memories altered." She grabbed Joeli's shoulders. "I don't know how many of our friends died out there tonight but it will be too many. I don't think I can let this . . . stain . . . walk out of here."

"I swear! I swear it on the Ancestor! I wasn't trying to kill Darla! I sw—"

"Ara!" Nona shouted. This wasn't how Ara behaved. If anything it should be Nona wanting Joeli's blood for her friend's death and a hundred smaller crimes.

With a snarl and clear effort Ara unlocked her hands from Joeli's habit and strode away. "You're the senior nun here, Sister Cage. You pass judgment."

"Senior?"

"The abbess raised you before me."

"By one minute!"

"Even so."

Nona looked Joeli in the eye and the girl tried to back away. Ruli held her tight. Jula looked on, her lips a bitter line. The desire to just reach out and press a flaw-blade through Joeli's heart rose through Nona in a hot wave. But she'd heard the voice of each devil in that mix before, separate and unbound. Somehow, even though she had accepted those parts of herself back into the whole, back into the mess of contradictions that was her, it felt easier to discount them now, as if knowing them "raw" as she had had helped her to moderate their demands.

"She killed Darla!" Clera reiterated. "She can't walk away from that."

"You never even liked Darla," Nona said. "You poisoned her and left her helpless for Raymel Tacsis and his soldiers. So perhaps you should hold your tongue, Clera." She looked at Joeli, trying to see what calculation might lie behind the terror on her face. "Abbess Glass allowed Joeli back into the convent. And that woman only made the compromises she wanted to make. It's not my judgment to pass . . . Zole? Have her memories been changed?"

Zole stepped in until she stood face to face with Joeli, who looked away, struggling to escape.

"I see no signs of it. Is it so hard to believe that in battle she made poor decisions?"

Nona slid a flaw-blade through Joeli's bonds. "I don't like you. If you cross me I will give worse than I get. I will speak the truth of your service to Sherzal and hope to see justice brought to bear. But your crimes are not mine to judge, and your punishment not mine to give."

It was Tarkax who spoke into the astonished silence that followed. "Are we done here?"

"We need to get out of the palace," Nona agreed. "The emperor is probably on his way already."

"And?" Clera asked. "He should heap gold on us until only the tops of our heads show!"

"His sister is lying in the passage, and she's not pretty," Ara said.

"She was betraying him!" Ruli sounded outraged.

"So you say," Ara replied. "Will Crucical choose to believe you, novice? The killing of a royal never goes unpunished. It sets a bad precedent."

"Are we leaving the shiphearts?" Jula asked.

"I'm returning Sweet Mercy's shipheart to the convent," Nona said. "It has something of mine that I want back. Besides, the other one was never so good at heating the water."

"Will you take the others, Zole?" Ara asked. "Or leave the Noi-Guin's shipheart for the emperor? It might allow him to overlook his recent loss ..."

ZOLE LEFT THE Noi-Guin shipheart bedded in the centre of the silver-steel door. She left the door closed. "Let Crucical take it if he can."

She activated the travel ring with greater mastery than Nona could manage and left it open while she stepped away to allow her fellow ice-tribers to return.

"How will you get out of the black ice?" Nona asked as Tarkax, the last of them, approached the ring.

"We're going to a different ring," he said. "A thousand miles from the Corridor." Then a sigh. "But we still have to climb three miles! So think of us, little Nona, when you're warming your toes by the light of your own private moon!"

"Little?" Nona grinned. She was a hand taller than the man.

Tarkax returned the grin. "Never call the Ice-Spear short!" He stepped into the light and was gone.

Zole made to follow him, the shiphearts burning in her hands.

"What will you do?" Nona called after her. She had been to the ice and yet she couldn't imagine how people endured up there, let alone lived. "What will you do, now you're so ... perfect?"

"What will you do with your imperfection, Nona Grey?" Zole asked. "We will both seek our purpose just as we have always done."

"And what's that?" Nona genuinely hoped for an answer. The Book of the Ancestor held answers aplenty but they had never seemed to fit her questions. "What are our purposes?"

"Do you assume they are not the same?" Zole asked, curious. She turned towards the ring. "I am changed. The Ark called me 'purified.' I hear a whisper and it seems important. Perhaps the Missing are calling to me. Perhaps their voice will be clearer up on the ice where the wind blows. I think that is my purpose for now, and maybe it is yours too. To listen." She made to leave.

"Thank you, Zole." Nona felt a sudden hollowness, a pain in her throat. She wanted to say more, but the words seemed too clumsy to speak. "I'll miss you."

"I will miss you too, my friend."

And Zole was gone.

30

——— ✦ ———

HOLY CLASS

IN A TIME of crisis the sisters of Sweet Mercy were expected to minister to the injured, say the rites over the dead, and pray that the Ancestor would receive all who had crossed the Path.

It turned out that the survivors of Abbess Wheel's flock were so few in number and their dead so numerous that it was all they could do to tend their own.

Nona and Ara found themselves the only two of the convent's nuns uninjured, though their wounds were newly healed and the flesh beneath was still sore. As such it fell to them to gather the survivors and to set those still able to walk to helping drag or carry from the battlefield those unable to fend for themselves.

The emperor and the Academy both opened their doors to the wounded, but Nona had the injured nuns and novices taken to St. Helliot's. The new cathedral stood a quarter of a mile from the palace and the eastern wing was still smoking from an earlier impact by a particularly far-flung incendiary. Torches lit the main steps, where High Priest Nevis himself stood organising the treatment of injured nuns, monks, and novices by over-worked church healers and volunteers from among the faithful.

"Place the dead in the mausoleum. With honour! We will hold services for them on this day for a hundred years. I will have them carve it upon the walls." Nevis looked overwhelmed but he kept working with the grim efficiency of a merchant squeezing the margins, directing his resources to maximize survival.

Nona helped carry Abbess Wheel into the mausoleum. High Priest Jacob had commissioned the building for himself as soon as he took office. Under Nevis the work had continued, though quite who would now be interred within had become less clear.

"Lay her here."

Nona hadn't needed any help. Wheel seemed to weigh nothing in her arms. Without her fierce will to animate her she seemed small, an old woman, mostly skin and bones. Ara, Sister Oak, and Ghena had insisted on lending their strength to the effort, though, despite the latter two being barely able to stand. Ghena bore a host of minor cuts and perhaps had broken ribs. Sister Oak sported a livid bruise across her forehead and the left side of her face. Being knocked senseless early on had saved her life. She seemed dizzy, unsure of herself.

The four of them laid the abbess out, straightening her limbs, arranging her habit. They stood around her corpse, careful not to step upon the dozens all around them, and said the prayers of farewell. Nona had last heard them from Wheel's own mouth when old Sister Bone had failed to rise from her bed on a cold morning three weeks before.

It took many trips back and forth from the King's Road to find the fallen. Some they couldn't locate. Nona had seen Ketti drop, the wound mortal. She remembered roughly where it had happened, but even so, despite lifting and rolling a hundred bodies, she couldn't find her friend.

"Could she have crawled away to die?" Clera asked, white-faced, wiping at her eyes, claiming that the smoke stung them.

"I don't see how she could have." Nona blinked and tried to keep the waver out of her voice. "I can't . . ." She snarled, lifted a large stone from a collapsed wall, throwing it several yards. Nothing lay beneath.

In the end they had to let it go.

In the east the sky paled to grey and dawn threatened, as if this had been a night just as any other and the sun would rise to bear witness on a new day.

They laid Apple and Iron and Tallow and Rock and Chrysanthemum close to Abbess Wheel. Kettle lay across Apple heaving with sobs yet making no sound. Ruli wept, Ara was pale, Jula ran outside to be sick. Nona called on her serenity and wore it as armour, unwilling to face her feelings. Wheel would have told her that sorrow was a luxury she could keep for later, when the work was done.

However, even the armour of Nona's serenity proved ineffective when they set to carrying the novices through to lie with their sisters. Two girls from Red Class had somehow joined the abbess's war-party, though Wheel had said only seniors were to come. How their presence had been missed Nona couldn't say. They were children, and she cried as she set them down beneath the great marble dome of the high priest's mausoleum.

THE SUN HAD risen and a cold wind had stripped away the smoke before the remaining sisters and novices of Sweet Mercy set off for the convent. Kettle was not with them for none of them had the heart to pull her from Apple's side.

Nona had retrieved the shipheart from the fire-gutted mansion she had left it in, kicking away hot ashes to uncover it. She placed it in a leather sack and had it dragged behind them. The wounded rode in carts commandeered for the purpose by the high priest. The five miles to the Rock of Faith had never seemed so long.

"Sister Rose will tend to them as well as any in the city can, and she will have more time for them." High Priest Nevis stood on the steps to see them off, looking as if he had gone without sleep for days. He had called Sister Oak over as the oldest surviving nun, but he called Nona with her and addressed his words to them both. "As sister superior it will fall to Sister Rose to occupy the abbess's house for now. She is a good woman and will be the first to say she lacks the fire necessary for the office. I will appoint a suitable replacement by and by when we have made an accounting of the dead and seen which sisters among the Red and Grey return to the Rock of Faith. Until such time Abbess Rose will need the counsel of her sisters." He waved them off. "May the Ancestor stand with you all."

A messenger in Crucical's green and gold passed their convoy of carts as they pulled away from the cathedral. By the grandeur of his uniform and bearing Nona judged him to be a personal emissary rather than a mere deliverer of scrolls sealed with the emperor's stamp. He hurried past, then retraced his steps, drawing up before Nona at the head of the group. He stood a touch taller than her and met her gaze with a narrow stare.

"The emperor has commanded me to bring the novice Nona Grey before him. She has cursed black eyes and casts no shadow. Have you seen any such?"

"Not recently." Nona seldom had use for mirrors. "I am Sister Cage."

The messenger gave a curt nod. "If you see her, tell her that her immediate presence is commanded before the throne." He hurried off towards the cathedral.

"The emperor wants you, Nona!" Ara managed a smile. "You're in demand!"

"Why didn't you go?" Jula asked.

"I will," Nona said. "But not now. We've got more important duties first." She paused. "What confuses me is how he didn't recognise me by my eyes . . ."

"You don't know yet?" Ruli blinked. "I thought I said something . . . But, no . . . Maybe we were too busy."

"Know what?" Nona raised her hands to her eyes, confused.

"They changed when Zole healed us," Ara said. "She must have repaired the damage that that novice-made black cure did to you. I thought you knew . . ."

"What confuses me," Clera said, leaning forward, "is how he didn't notice that you don't ha—Nona! You have a shadow!"

"I know." Nona allowed herself a faint smile and raised her hand to track her shadow across the street. "It was drawn into the Sweet Mercy shipheart when I sent it after Yisht." She wiggled her fingers and watched her shadow dance, anchoring her in the world. "I took it back."

By noon they arrived at the convent. Nona had feared to find it in ruins, but it seemed that after their master's death Lano Tacsis's men had had little interest in earning themselves more trouble with the Church and the Ancestor.

Sister Rose was in the sanatorium treating half a dozen injured junior novices. Three others had died. When they told her she was to be abbess, Rose shook her head and returned to changing dressings, tears rolling over her cheeks. "I haven't time for that nonsense. Not at all. Too much to do here." With infinite care she helped a novice who was struggling to turn and indicated to her assistant, a tiny child that Nona couldn't imagine old enough for the habit, to take water to another girl.

In the end Ara brought one of the spare croziers out to the sanatorium and hung it above the door since Rose wouldn't move to the big house.

Much later Nona found herself alone by the stairs down to the Shade classroom. Apple would never climb them again. It hurt Nona's heart to know it, a hurt that would stay with her, part of who she was now, like the wound Abbess Glass's death left upon her and that she would wear through all her days. *Some lessons must be written in scars*, Sister Tallow had said. Nona would miss her too.

On the last day that Abbess Glass had spent with them she had told

Nona many things. Secrets about the future and about the past. At last she had fallen quiet, half smiling, half sad. *All leaves must fall in time*, she had said. *The lives we lived fall away from us, but something remains, something that is part of the tree.*

Glass had been sick when she laid her plans months before her death. She had met in secret with Nona and Zole on their separate returns and even then she had said that she did not expect to see the seeds she was planting come to flower.

"To sow knowing that you will not reap is an old kind of love, and love has always been the best key for unlocking the future." The abbess had set her hands upon theirs. "You, my dears, are both the Chosen One, but it's only me who has chosen you. Each of you is a die cast against the odds. Zole dear, remember to hold on to what makes us love you. If you reach your journey's end without that, you will have gone nowhere. And Nona, my fierce little Nona, remember mercy. Mercy for others in victory. Mercy for yourself too. You deserve happiness, child. Never forget it."

Nona had a bar of the Shade gate in each hand and her forehead to the metal when a hand settled on her shoulder.

"Ara . . ."

Her friend joined her at the gate and for a time they stood in each other's silence. Ara's left hand holding the same bar as Nona's right, almost touching.

"It's hard to believe she's gone," Ara whispered.

"She's not gone." Each of them could be speaking of so many shes, but Nona was thinking of Apple and how these stairs, this gate, would always lead to her.

"Abbess Glass spent her thoughts on might-bes," Ara said. "I find myself thinking too often about might-have-beens." She turned her head to look at Nona. "It's strange to see your eyes. As if you've been hiding from me all these years."

Nona opened her mouth to speak but another, darker shadow fell across her, one she could only feel and not see. "Kettle is coming back." Nona took her hands from the bars. "I have to go to her."

The sun was falling as Nona reached the Seren Way and began to descend from the convent's heights. Nona felt Kettle's approach stop and the muted echoes of her grief became a tolling along their thread-bond, like the lament of a great and hollow bell. She carried on down, searching for her friend, and found her lying crumpled at the base of the Rock as if she had fallen from the windows of the Shade classroom. Kettle had dropped only from her feet, though, and rose like a broken doll when Nona pulled her into an embrace.

"She was my life, Nona."

Nona held her tight. "You have sisters. You're not alone." They wept then, the river of Kettle's sorrow washing through Nona until at last they could breathe again and Nona led her sister up the winding steepness of the Seren Way to Sweet Mercy.

EVENING FOUND NONA and the handful of seniors gathered around one of the refectory tables, a cold meal before them, rustled up from stores. Most of the nuns were in the Dome of the Ancestor, praying for the lost. Sisters Oak and Rule had helped Kettle across the convent to the Dome to join the prayer, though Abbess Rose had insisted she stay in bed.

Nona sat, chewing on a heel of bread. Sister Elm had baked it. She would never bake another. At her side Ara sipped water from a clay cup and watched the light of the setting sun finger through the shutters.

"The Durns are still coming." Clera banged the end of her knife on the table. "Are you going to light up a few of their barges and hope that they run away too? Because sooner or later you're going to be standing before the throne and the emperor himself is going to order you to burn their cities to cinders."

"Have you ever been on the ice in a focus moon, Clera?" Nona asked.

"No." Clera scowled. "I didn't last long enough at the convent to go ice-ranging. And why would I want to? It's just Church stupidity, sending children up there."

"I used to think that," Nona said. "But I've been up there and I've waited through the focus, miles from the Corridor. You know what happens? The ice melts. An inch of ice melts. Then it freezes solid again. There's nowhere for it to run. All that heat wasted. All the moon's energy spent melting the same inch of ice night after night."

Ruli looked up from contemplation of her tortured hand. "But now *you've* got the moon! You can have it do anything!"

Jula shook her head. "The Ark told you that if you narrowed the focus from what it is, it would kill plants and animals. That's why it wouldn't let you . . . until Zole said it should."

"We've seen it kill . . ." Ruli gazed into space as if imagining the black circle of char that was all the moon had left of the battle-queen.

Nona shook her head. "The focus stopped narrowing a long time ago. Anything that couldn't live with what we experience every night has died out. What has survived has toughened. We can narrow the focus and see how things go. Or we can narrow it to a torch and run it along the edge of the ice, the whole focus burning along a strip a mile wide. We could burn channels to take the meltwater to the sea . . . the possibilities are endless . . . but the point is that we have control. We can try. We can change.

"And even if we choose not to use it, the moon is a weapon beyond all others. We can institute a peace. And with peace comes progress. We lost our knowledge through the course of a thousand wars. We fail to rediscover it only because our minds are always turned to survival, the ice is always pressing, and war is the result. Constantly. The moon can deliver peace. No army will march, no fleet set sail, if they know the moon itself will sear them from the world.

"Peace, progress, hope. We can buy centuries and in those years discover new answers. The old tales tell us that the Missing learned to burn the ice itself! I think we have enough of that to keep us warm forever!"

Ara had stood and begun to pace while Nona set her ideas before them. Now she stopped. "And if the emperor won't listen? If he wants to burn the Scithrowl and the Durn from the Corridor? What if he doesn't want to stop even there?"

"It would still be a peace," Nona said. "But the moon listens to me, not him, and unless Zole comes back that is not going to change. If Crucical wants murder then I will tell him that I answer to the high priest and not to the emperor."

"The same high priest who ordered you to be left alone to guard the convent?" Ara snorted. "Nevis has sold himself to the emperor and the Sis before. His price might be higher than his predecessor's, but he still has one."

Nona shook her head. "It was Abbess Glass who set the high priest's staff in Nevis's hand. If you know anything about that woman you'll know that that was no accident. She could have engineered for Archon Anasta to take the staff, or either of the other two. But she chose Nevis. He has his price, but the abbess knew his heart and thought him worthy. Nevis is a merchant. Merchants love peace. They love prosperity. Merchants will sell themselves when they have no other bargain to make, but when I place myself and the moon in Nevis's hands he will understand that the power lies with him and the bargains he makes then will be very different ones."

Nona stood. She knew now how Darla must have felt, towering above the other novices. "Abbess Wheel was right to believe in the Chosen One. The Argatha came to the Ark and the moon is ours. Zole chose me . . . so I guess that makes me the Chosen One now.

"We're going to build a new future, sisters. So have a little faith. Because that's what the future is always built on."

EPILOGUE

——————◆——————

"Mistress Blade! Mistress Blade!"

Nona raised her hand and Red Class came to a halt. The thrown novices picked themselves up and brushed sand from their habits. Their partners, standing to attention, watched Nona.

"Come." Nona waved in the novice at the doorway, Adela from Mystic Class, she thought. Or Abela.

"Abbess Rule needs you at the big house."

Nona sighed. "Novices, repeat that throw. I want to see at least one of you get it right by the time I get back."

She followed Adela, or Abela, from Blade Hall. The Corridor wind was in the east, streaming their habits before them. Mistress Spirit rounded the curve of the Ancestor's Dome with a string of Grey Class novices at her back. There had been some consternation when Jula was appointed to the post at such a young age, but Abbess Rule had threatened to raise her to sister superior if that would make it more fitting, and the objections subsided. Abbess Rule also pointed out that the high priest couldn't find a nun across the whole of the empire who knew the Book of the Ancestor better than Sister Page . . . and nobody could dispute that.

A novice ran ahead of them lugging a crate of wine jars, a hulking girl who put Nona in mind of Darla. She beat them to the abbess's steps. Nona had always thought Ruli would end up running the convent winery, but she'd ended up running her father's fleet of trade-ships, quadrupling the tonnage and landing enough Sweet Mercy red on the Durn shores to drown the barbarians.

A novice with golden hair hurried from the door as they approached. A new recruit. Sister Rule had scouts out looking for suitable girls. She'd even contracted Giljohn to join the effort; the old man had a rare eye for early signs of the bloods. Terms and conditions of the acquisitions were rather different these days, though. The novices returned to their families twice a year.

The girl rushed by with a "sorry!" She had Ara's hair. She'd be a beauty too. Nona had heard that all the lords' boys for two hundred miles had lined up ready to woo Arabella Jotsis when she returned to the ruins of her uncle's castle. Her home might have been a charred heap of rubble, but the Jotsis lands remained and as the closest surviving heir Ara had to accept the lordship. Apparently she had rejected all her suitors so far. Perhaps someone else still had hold of her heart.

"You're in so much trouble!" Clera sat in the abbess's hall, her jacket a subtle symphony in shades of black, moleskin, and suede, the diamonds in her earlobes the only open admission of wealth. They called her the Farmer in Verity. Merchants whispered that she could plant a copper and pick gold from the tree that sprang up. Quite why she had so many business interests to discuss with the abbess Nona hadn't yet fathomed. She suspected that Clera just liked visiting.

Nona sent her escort back to her off-class duties and knocked on the abbess's door.

"Come."

Abbess Rule sat at her desk. Regol stood with his hands bound behind his back, Kettle behind him wearing a wicked grin. "I caught him trying to sneak in. Again." She flashed Nona a look. "He's fast but not very bright or good at hiding." Sister Cauldron stood at the abbess's shoulder, watching Kettle as Nona had seen her do so often, waiting for that day when Kettle might see past Apple's ghost and find her waiting there.

Abbess Rule reached for her crozier, which she employed in much the same way she had her yardstick when she had been Mistress Academia. "This is getting silly, Sister Cage. I can't have this young man climbing cliffs and creeping through the undercaves. I simply won't tolerate it! It's extremely dangerous. If Verity's most renowned ring-fighter were to be killed on convent property there would be all hell to pay!" She rose from her seat and glanced up at Abbess Glass's portrait. "She of the Moon" they called Glass these days. Rule's eyes flitted to Abbess Wheel's portrait, "She of the Battle." She sighed. When the abbess spoke again it was with the voice she had used in class laying down the law, not of the Church but of the world itself. Harsh and immutable. "Sister Cage, you must consider your options. We all have to find our own path and walk it as long as we may. You are young and the places your road may lead you are many, some beyond imagining. Take some time. Think hard. Return to me with your answer. Whatever it is, whether it leads you from this convent or not, you will have the Ancestor's blessing. And mine."

"Vows?"

Regol and Nona were sitting together on the edge of the Glasswater sinkhole. She nodded, frowning, torn. The horizon lay green and distant but her memory still crowded it with the smoke of war. When the end had come so very close it had been her sisters who filled her thoughts. *Ara.* Though they were no less capable of looking after themselves than Regol. She gazed down into the sinkhole as if the answer to the riddle of herself might lie within.

There was no lake now, just thirty yards of newly exposed wall, black with slime, and a dark tunnel leading off from the muddy bottom. It didn't smell too good but if you sat on the windward side it wasn't a problem.

"Vows?" Regol repeated.

"Vows," Nona said.

"You're sticking to your vows?"

"I am. I vowed them."

"But . . . nuns are celibate." Regol tossed a loose stone. It looped down into the mud far below their feet.

"And you wouldn't want me if you couldn't have your way with me?" Nona leaned in quizzically, one hand placed lightly between Regol's shoulder blades.

"Now . . . wait . . . I didn't say . . . I mean . . ." He gripped the edge of the sinkhole, seeming suddenly very aware of how deep it was.

"You can't keep coming here, Regol. And I can't leave."

"Can't?" A hardness found its way into his eyes.

"I need to stay. This place . . . it's more than old walls and a place to lay my head. I named myself after that cage I rode in, and I was only in it for a few weeks. I've been here more than a decade. It's in my bones."

"You want me to go?"

" 'Want' isn't the right word. But you will go, and the ladies of the Sis will thank me for it, and you will be the glorious champion of the Caltess, and this small blow to the heart will be something you walk off."

"I don't think it will, Sister Cage." Regol bowed his head. "It's more like a denam."

"A what?"

"That last kick to the groin you gave Denam. It's a recognised move now with its own name." Regol raised his face again, his old smile back in place, though somewhat crooked.

"Did he . . . I mean, is he—"

"Survive? No. He died at the Amber Gate, but you should hear how he fell. He slaughtered so many Scithrowl that—Well, there's a song about it."

"He would have liked that."

"Yes, he would."

Regol got to his feet and Nona rose to hers. He took her hands. "The Caltess taught me that on occasion everyone loses, but to do it with grace because you never know what might happen." He raised her right hand and kissed the back of it. "It still hurts, though. Goodbye, Nona Grey."

Regol let her hand go and walked away towards the convent buildings, slow at first, then more briskly. By the time he was halfway to the nearest of them he had started to whistle.

"Goodbye, Regol."

NONA SAT A long time at the sinkhole's edge after Regol had left. She stared into the depths as shadows filled them. She thought of those she had lost and those she had saved and those who had saved her. She thought of the riddle of her life and the fact that even Abbess Glass's best advice on the subject had been that people are complicated, especially from the inside.

The sun began to sink, kissing the ice to end another day. Nona sighed and made to stand again but a shadow fell across her.

Nona looked up. "Lord Jotsis . . ." Ara stood there beside her in trousers and a fine jacket embroidered with gold. The wind billowed her cloak behind her and the dying sun made a fire of her hair.

"No, just Sister Thorn. I made my little sister the lord. She always wanted it."

"You came back." Nona found that she was whispering.

"You left me to guard the convent once, then came back for me," Ara said. "You didn't think I would leave you when you needed me?"

"How did you know I did?" Nona's mouth felt dry. A trembling ran through her. She wasn't sure if she was going to cry or laugh.

"We have a bond." Ara reached down for her hand.

"A thread-bond." Nona laced her fingers with Ara's and let herself be drawn to her feet.

"That too," Ara said.

For a long moment they stood face to face, just an inch between them, the wind tugging this way and that as if it couldn't make up its mind which way to blow. And then, hand in hand, both turned and walked slowly back to Sweet Mercy.

MOONS MIGHT RISE and fall, empires wax and wane, even the stars come and go, but there are constants too, and though the story of our kind is ever-changing it is also always the same.